Praise for Carlene Thompson

"Mary Higgins Clark fans take note: loaded with more
mystery and suspense than the real thing."
Kirkus Reviews

"Thompson pulls no punches showcasing her high caliber
writing gymnastics and leaves her imprint for those iconic
writers in the suspense/thriller genre."
Examiner.com

"Thompson creates smart, interesting characters the reader
cares about within a gripping suspense story."
Judith Kelman, author of *After the Fall*

"Sure to please readers who pride themselves on sniffing
out clues. Definitely . . . for fans of Mary Higgins Clark."
Library Journal

HAVE YOU READ . . .?

TO THE GRAVE

Catherine Gray has returned to her hometown of Aurora Falls.
Her first love James has recently divorced and they can finally
build a life together. But then Catherine stumbles on the
murdered body of James's first wife Renée, missing for the past
three years. Catherine begins to ask herself how well she really
knows James, but as she looks into his past she draws ever closer
to an obsessed killer who has marked her out as his next victim.

YOU CAN RUN . . .

Peggy Conley is still recovering from the untimely death of her
husband. She and daughter Willow have become firm friends
with Peggy's boss, Simon, and his niece Diana.
Late one night Diana receives a call from a distraught Penny.
When Diana arrives at Penny's house, it explodes, leaving
Penny in a coma. Diana vows to figure out what happened, but
as new facts about Penny's dark past start to come to light,
Diana begins to wonder if she ever really knew her friend at all.

Also by Carlene Thompson

All Fall Down
Black for Remembrance
Don't Close Your Eyes
If She Should Die
If You Ever Tell
In the Event of My Death
Last Seen Alive
Last Whisper
Share No Secrets
Since You've Been Gone
The Way You Look Tonight
To the Grave
Tonight You're Mine
You Can Run . . .

CARLENE THOMPSON

Nowhere
to Hide

HODDER

First published in Great Britain in 2014 by Hodder & Stoughton
An Hachette UK company

1

Copyright © Carlene Thompson 2010

The right of Carlene Thompson to be identified as the
Author of the Work has been asserted by her in accordance
with the Copyright, Designs and Patents Act 1988.

A CIP catalogue record for this title is available from the British Library.

Book ISBN 978 1 444 77891 5
eBook ISBN 978 1 444 77892 2

Typeset by Hewer Text UK Ltd, Edinburgh
Printed and bound by Clays Ltd, St Ives plc

Hodder & Stoughton policy is to use papers that are natural, renewable
and recyclable products and made from wood grown in sustainable
forests. The logging and manufacturing processes are expected to
conform to the environmental regulations of the country of origin.

Hodder & Stoughton Ltd
338 Euston Road
London NW1 3BH

www.hodder.co.uk

To my mother

Thanks to Anne Bensson, Keith Biggs,
Hilary Rubin, and Jennifer Weis

PROLOGUE

"You think we should go back to the boat now?" Marissa Gray said as they leaned against the trunk of a large tulip poplar, its vibrant yellow-green flowers visible even in the dark.

Eric Montgomery traced a line of tiny kisses from behind her earlobe down her neck. "I don't *want* to go back to the boat. I'd rather we just set up housekeeping here on the island. After all, it's Gray's Island. Your great-grandfather bought it."

"My great-great-*great*-grandfather Lucian, the most anti-social leaf on the family tree. His business was in town, but every evening he came back to his domain."

"His big house and his own little church and—let's see—how many slaves?"

Marissa groaned. "Too many. Lucian liked using a whip on them. One died from a beating. They got their revenge by burning down his house and their quarters at the end of the Civil War. They spared the family and the church." Marissa frowned. "Why are you so curious about Gray's Island tonight? You've heard all about it before."

"Not from the horse's mouth."

Marissa's jaw dropped and her eyes widened. "Are you comparing me to a *horse*?" she spluttered. "Why, I *never* ..."

"You never what?" Eric asked innocently before they broke into laughter, staggering a bit and clutching each other in the warm summer darkness. Eric's arms tightened around her slim midriff covered by a thin T-shirt as her hands slid up his strong arms and clasped behind his neck. They kissed deeply before Eric slowly pulled away.

"I love your kisses, but I'm supposed to be in charge tonight. Instead, I let you seduce me away from my duties."

Marissa rolled her blue eyes. "Your duties? I think you really mean your *charges.* You're the cop from Philadelphia home on a summer vacation, and at twenty-five you think we're a bunch of kids and you are the *man.*"

Eric looked at her solemnly, frowned, and then said, "You're absolutely right. I am the Man—with a capital *M*, please."

"Oh my! Delusions of grandeur."

"Recognition of responsibility."

"You're no fun," Marissa pouted.

Eric kissed her ear and whispered, "I can be tons of fun, and *you* of all people know it."

"If you mean what I think you mean, I'd better be the *only* person who knows it," Marissa whispered lazily in return, tilting her head so the ends of her dark blond hair touched Eric's hands on her waist, half-closing her eyes, and pressing her lips against his. The kiss was slow and passionate. Marissa felt as if they were all alone in the world and incredibly lucky—both young, healthy, in love, committed.

Then Eric pulled away slightly, looked in her eyes, and groaned. "Oh hell. Sometimes I wish I were still a teenager who never heard of the word *dependable.*" He removed his hands from her waist and placed them on her shoulders, gently pushing her back a step. "We should have joined the others at least twenty minutes ago, sweetheart, not lolled around by ourselves. We're being rude."

Marissa's smile disappeared. "Rude? I hate it when people hide behind excuses, especially you with me, Eric. Just say you're worried about Gretchen."

"She is my little sister."

"And she's twenty-one, just like me, your *fiancée.*"

"Except that she's not worldly-wise like you," Eric said patiently. "She's shy and fragile and not great at taking care of herself. She's a musical prodigy, but in every other way . . . well, she's Gretchen."

Marissa wanted to say something to make Eric stop acting like the father of a little girl. She could think of nothing, though, probably because Gretchen had been her closest friend most of her life and to a certain degree Marissa understood how Eric felt. Gretchen had always reminded Marissa of spun sugar—sweet, delicate, and almost ephemeral. Marissa felt protective of Gretchen, too, but she thought Eric's concern for his adult sister bordered on preoccupation.

Eric picked up the one empty beer can lying near them. "Alcoholic," he teased. Still annoyed, Marissa ignored him. "Is your head spinning? Can you remember your name?"

Oh, all right, Marissa thought. She didn't want to concede, but she also didn't want to start a fight after their romantic evening. "I know my name, but I'm not sure I can recall where I live," Marissa said lightly. "Meanwhile, you are disgustingly sober."

"I am the pilot of your father's very expensive cabin cruiser tonight. By law the pilot cannot drink, my dear. Also, if I had a couple of beers, I might completely lose my sense of direction and we'd end up in Jamaica two months early for our honeymoon."

"Our vacation to Jamaica last year was the best trip of my life," Marissa sighed. "I would *love* to end up there two months early, whether we're married yet or not."

Eric threw an arm over her shoulders. "You're so busy with wedding preparations, two months will be gone before you know it. Now, walk fast, girl. It's time for everyone to be back at the boat."

Marissa stood still and said reluctantly, "Uh, Mr. In Charge, I don't think anyone is at the boat. They said they'd meet us at what's left of Lucian Gray's estate."

"What? Why?"

"They wanted to explore it because it's weird and interesting and they're curious."

"It could be dangerous. No one said anything to me about stumbling around those ruins at night."

"We're keeping secrets from you. It's a conspiracy," Marissa said dramatically. Eric didn't smile. "Okay. Gretchen knew you'd object. And obviously, you do."

"I don't like being lied to, Marissa." Eric sounded quietly angry.

"We didn't lie to you. We just didn't tell you." Marissa had expected him to be annoyed. She hadn't expected him to be angry. "I didn't even know the others planned to explore the ruins until we were getting off the boat. Gretchen wanted to see where the pipe organ sat before my grandfather donated it. She begged me not to tell you, and from the look on your face I can see why." Eric continued to stare at her. "Okay, blow up at me if you want. I don't see the harm—"

"She's *my* sister."

"Really? I didn't know that. I guess that gives you the right to hover over her like she's a child," Marissa huffed. "This is absurd. The island is only a quarter mile long and the buildings are smack-dab in the middle of it. I think we can find our group with no trouble and then you can yell at Gretchen."

"I don't yell at my sister."

"You just embarrass the hell out of her."

"My parents didn't want her to come tonight. I assured them if she could, I'd take care of her!"

"Does that mean holding her hand all night so she doesn't wander off? Your parents have brainwashed you into thinking you are your sister's keeper and you've become more like her jailor!"

Marissa slipped her feet into sandals and began flapping away, mad at Eric for acting so foolish about his sister and mad at Gretchen for asking Marissa to do something she knew would make Eric angry. What an end to a wonderful evening, Marissa fumed inwardly.

In a moment, Eric caught up to her, carrying the soft blanket on which they'd sat, talked, and cuddled less than half an hour ago. A silvery crescent moon shone in the warm night as they followed a path toward the church in silence.

Suddenly Eric said, "I shouldn't have blamed you. It's my fault for leaving Gretchen alone."

"You didn't. She's with Tonya, Andrew, and Dillon. And before you tear into Dillon, I know you think your sister likes him too much and you don't trust him." Eric remained silent. "We couldn't invite Andrew and not invite his brother, Dillon. Also, if Gretchen has the hots for Dillon, she's never told me, and I'm her best friend."

"Marissa, I am *not* the only person in town who thinks Dillon Archer is trouble, and she's been with him a lot lately."

"You've been in Philadelphia, Eric. Who's your news source?"

"She dated Will Addison for months. What happened? Did he dump her?"

"No, Eric, Will did not *dump* her. In fact, I think she broke off things with him. Don't ask me why, because she didn't tell me. She's not as open with me as she used to be. All I know is that lately she's spent some time with Dillon Archer."

"So she *is* in a relationship with Archer!"

Marissa stopped. "Oh, for God's sake, Eric, you act like she's twelve! You might not think she's as worldly-wise as I am—and I'm not sure that was a compliment—but she's certainly not a fool."

"But she's—"

"Gretchen. I know."

"That's not what I was going to say." Eric looked at Marissa in frustration. "I was going to say she's been acting different lately." He paused. "She's remote. Edgy. Sad."

Marissa had her mouth open, ready to snap back that Gretchen seemed different because she was becoming a woman, not just Eric's adoring little sister. His last three words drew her up short, though. *Remote. Edgy. Sad.* Marissa had to admit that she'd noticed Gretchen's behavior seemed unusual the last few months. She hadn't been eager to go places with Marissa and had let a couple of other friendships completely lapse. She no longer played the piano upon request, usually making an unconvincing excuse, and she'd often seemed distant, almost secretive.

A few weeks earlier, Marissa had asked Gretchen if anything was bothering her. Gretchen had said she had a lot of pressure on her because of the coming year's concert circuit and she was nervous. In addition, her mother had been pressuring Gretchen to practice six hours a day and they'd been arguing over the impossible schedule. Marissa had easily accepted the explanations— she'd been too excited about her upcoming wedding for Gretchen's distraction and occasional irritability to dampen her happiness.

"Well?" Eric asked. "Haven't you noticed a difference in her?"

Marissa didn't want to discuss Gretchen with Eric. She loved Eric, but Gretchen was her best friend and repeating their conversations to Gretchen's brother seemed like a betrayal. What Gretchen wanted Eric to know Gretchen should be the one to tell him.

"What I've noticed is that our romantic evening has become all about your sister," Marissa answered shortly.

They walked in silence until Eric finally grudgingly said, "I'm sorry."

Marissa let a few seconds pass before she said, "Me, too. I'm sorry that we argued, not that I didn't tell you about Gretchen seeing Dillon Archer. She's old enough to make decisions without asking you."

"I guess she is," Eric said flatly.

As they entered what Marissa had always thought of as Lucian's enclave, she felt as if a damp veil of misery lowered over her. She closed her eyes and could almost smell smoke lingering after the conflagration that had destroyed the house and slave quarters.

After a few seconds, Eric said, "I like the rest of the island, but not this place."

"I don't, either. Neither does Dad."

"Then why doesn't he sell the island?"

"He says no one has ever expressed an interest in buying it. Besides, the island is eroding. In a hundred years, it will be underwater."

"I suppose the local historians consider that a loss," Eric said.

"They do. I'm not certain how I feel." Marissa took his hand, forgetting that she'd been exasperated with him five minutes ago. "Not much is left of Lucian's house."

· They looked at the foundation stones of what had once supported a beautiful Greek Revival house. Grass and weeds now grew where exquisite rugs had once lain on gleaming wood floors. The foliage would have taken over the whole island if Marissa's father had not hired a landscape team to keep the flora under control.

Marissa said, "I gave the key to the church to Andrew. I see light in there."

They quickly crossed the ground to the tall white church with its steeple and spire pointing to the star-filled night. Marissa's father kept the church maintained and always locked against vandals. Three steps led to the well-preserved interior with beautiful stained-glass windows depicting the Easter Cross, the Descending Dove, the Cross and Crown, and the Five-Pointed Star. An aisle separated eight rows of pews. The pulpit stood on a raised platform, and above the pulpit was a balcony.

The others had clearly prepared to light up the church, but even six powerful Maglite flashlights did a poor job of chasing away darkness in the church tall enough to house the organ on a balcony. Someone had either found or brought several candles whose flames sent shadows crawling up the walls to the balcony where the magnificent organ had sat . . .

And Gretchen stood barefoot atop the tall, narrow rail.

Marissa and Eric jerked to a stop and Marissa almost cried out before Eric's hand quickly covered her mouth. "Don't startle her," he whispered.

Marissa nodded and Eric removed his hand. They heard Tonya's voice edged with fear: "Gretchen, you've shown off enough for tonight. Please come down now."

Someone on the balcony pointed a handheld flashlight at the slight, golden-haired girl holding out her arms for balance as if she walked a tightwire. She flinched and yelled, "Turn off the light!" The light blinked off.

"Eric, do something," Marissa hissed, her heart pounding against her ribs.

He ignored her for a moment. She felt his entire being focus on his sister before he whispered, "We don't want the flashlight glaring on her, but we can barely see her from down here. You go up to the balcony as quietly as you can. I'll stay here and talk to her."

Marissa nodded, slipped off her noisy sandals, and hurried to the stairs leading to the balcony. "I'm the king of the world!" Gretchen shouted.

"You've watched *Titanic* about twenty times," Eric called back. "Don't you know Leonardo DiCaprio is king of the world? Besides, you happen to be a girl. You can't be *king* of anything."

"Wonder what Mom and Dad would say if they saw me?"

"You'd give them the scare of their lives." Marissa recognized Dillon Archer's voice, which was deeper than his older brother Andrew's. "You're giving me the scare of *my* life."

Gretchen giggled. "You wonder what's gotten into this mousy little girl."

"I know what's gotten into you," Dillon answered. "Too much beer."

Gretchen laughed loudly. "Yes! And it feels *great*!"

Marissa reached the back of the balcony and stepped onto it next to Andrew Archer, who stood at an angle from Gretchen. "She just climbed up there before we realized what was happening," he whispered to Marissa.

Gretchen turned her head and narrowed her eyes. "Ah, do I hear my very, very, very best friend, Marissa? Are you telling secrets to her, Andrew?"

"No secrets, Gretchen," Andrew said. "I don't know any secrets."

"*I* know secrets. Big, surprising secrets." Gretchen had begun to slur. "Certain people should be v-verrry nice to me or I'll tell."

"Hey, Gretchen, we're headed back for the boat," Eric called casually. "If you don't get down, we're going to leave you behind."

"Fat chance. You watch me like a h-hawk. Drives me crazy." She paused, and then yelled furiously, "I'm not a lil' girl, Eric!"

"I know," he answered evenly. "Tonight Marissa gave me a lecture on that subject. I'm sorry I didn't notice you grew up."

"You n-noticed *she* grew up!"

Dillon walked softly beside Gretchen, staying parallel to her. "You're gonna run out of railing, pretty girl. What'll you do then?"

"I'll turn round and walk back!"

Gretchen was two-thirds across the railing, her right side facing Eric. Tonya stood about three feet away from Dillon, facing Gretchen's back. "Honey, we're all tired and we all want to go home, so please come down," Tonya said.

Gretchen took another unsteady step. "D'you believe you know everything 'bout your friends, Tonya? 'Cause if you do, you're wrong. You might *think* you know—"

Gretchen began to sway and Marissa stepped ahead of Andrew, getting about four feet away from Gretchen's back. If Dillon could reach up far enough to grab Gretchen around the thighs, he could pull her off the rail, Marissa thought frantically, her mouth dry, her palms wet.

She felt as if her thoughts had communicated themselves to Dillon when in the dim light on the balcony Marissa saw Dillon rise on his toes and slowly lift his hands upward and outward toward Gretchen. Thank God, Marissa thought, feeling as if she might faint from fear for her friend. He was going to seize Gretchen's thighs and jerk her down onto the balcony. The way she was teetering, it was her only chance. Dillon is going to save Gretchen's life, Marissa almost whispered. Dillon is going to save—

She couldn't even scream as she saw Dillon's raised left hand curve loosely around Gretchen's upper thighs while his right hand shot swiftly between her denim-covered legs, flattened against her right thigh, and *pushed*. He stood still for just an instant and then leaned forward as if desperately trying to grasp the slender spun-sugar girl plunging off the balcony.

Gretchen landed with her back stretched across the old pulpit. Her small feet dangled from one side, and her head hung from the other with her face turned slightly, so her amber eyes stared blindly at her brother.

I

Four and One-Half Years Later

1

Marissa Gray strapped her seat belt, turned the key in the ignition, and glared at the large, fluffy flakes of snow cascading on her windshield. "Oh, great," she muttered angrily.

"What's wrong?" Marissa looked at her beautiful older sister, Catherine, rapping insistently on the closed passenger's window. "Are you too scared to drive?" Catherine called.

Marissa pushed the automatic opener and the window purred halfway down. "I'm not scared, Catherine; I'm pissed off. The snow is falling faster, I'm the reporter who was supposed to be at the Addison party ten minutes ago, and I haven't even left home!"

"Oh, to heck with the Addisons." Catherine's long brown hair blew in the wind and her eyebrows pulled together above her light blue-green eyes. "Evelyn Addison wants you there early so she can name every single gourmet dish at the buffet and have that new photographer take her picture *alone* with the magnificent Christmas tree—no annoying guests trying to crowd into the shot. Of course, that's if she hasn't gotten too wide to entirely block the tree from the photo."

Marissa laughed. "Shame on you! She's our esteemed mayor's wife. Where's your respect?"

"It vanished when you said you were driving to the Addison house in your ridiculously small, *convertible* sports car."

"I have enough sense to put up the car top, Catherine."

"The tops of most convertibles aren't as sturdy as those of hardtop cars and you know it. Besides, a blizzard is coming."

"The weatherman didn't say anything about a blizzard. He said a heavy snow is predicted around two in the morning."

"*Heavy snow* is weatherman code for a *blizzard*, and of course well-behaved blizzards always arrive exactly when the weatherman predicts they will. James has a Lincoln with a *very* sturdy roof. Why don't you wait and go with us?"

"Oh, that would be fun," Marissa said dryly. "Me tagging along with my sister on a date. Besides, I told you I'm already late."

Catherine folded her sweater-covered arms. "I'm freezing!"

"Well, that's not *my* fault! You wouldn't be freezing if you'd go inside instead of standing in the driveway badgering me!" Marissa closed her eyes for a moment, fighting for patience. "Look, Catherine, this is our first Christmas since Mom died. Maybe we shouldn't have decided to spend it in the family home, but we did and now we both feel at sea. Everything is so different and not in a good way. You're twenty-eight, though, and I'm twenty-five. You're my older sister, not my *big* sister. You don't have to take care of me." Catherine didn't answer. "I know driving on snow terrifies you, but I'm only driving eight miles and I'm wearing my seat belt."

"You have to drive on the three worst miles of Falls Way to reach the Addisons'." Catherine sighed and looked beyond the car, batting her eyes against the snow. "I have a very bad feeling about you tonight, Marissa."

"Oh, Catherine!" Marissa burst out, then reminded herself she was speaking to the only remaining member of her immediate family—her sister, whom she'd always admired and loved. She softened her voice. "You worry about me too much, Catherine. You worry about everyone. It's endearing, but it must be exhausting for you. And frankly, trying *not* to worry *you* is exhausting for other people. You can't keep everyone at home under your wing like a mother bird. Can't you ease up at least one night?"

Catherine raised an eyebrow. "I never thought of myself as a mother bird. A crow?"

"A skylark. She makes the most beautiful song."

Catherine tilted her head, smiling. "When all else fails, try flattery. Okay, I guess I do clutch at other people, trying to hold them near me, as if *I* could keep anyone safe," she said grudgingly. "But it's so hard to shake these feelings of responsibility for you. Mom has been gone for only four months and Dad for three years . . ."

Marissa had learned over the years that simple reason couldn't stop Catherine's worrying. Diversion was the only answer.

Marissa started with sincerity: "I promise not to drive too fast and to be extra careful. I'm not worried about the weather conditions and I'm looking forward to having a good time. This year the Addison Christmas party is supposed to be the biggest ever." Marissa paused and frowned, moving on to distraction. "But Catherine, you're having your very first date with James Eastman tonight and look at your hair! The curl is falling out and the ends are frizzing. It will look *awful* if you don't get inside and fix it before James comes."

Got her! Marissa thought as something close to panic flashed in Catherine's eyes. Catherine seemed to think she'd hidden the crush she'd had on James since she was a teenager. Marissa had always known, though, and now almost giggled that the thought of not looking perfect for her first date with James temporarily banished everything else from Catherine's serious mind.

"Oh my God!" Catherine usually pretended oblivion to her striking appearance. The act would have been shattered if anyone had witnessed her whipping her hair over her shoulder and looking at the damp strands in near horror. "Look at it! What'll I do?"

"Your hair isn't soaked. If you get inside immediately, you'll just have time to spray it and put it on large hot rollers for five minutes. Five minutes only!" Marissa ordered urgently.

"You don't think I need to wash it and start over?"

"Absolutely not. Just use the rollers and it will look beautiful." Still, Marissa couldn't resist adding, "Oh, I tried on Mom's pearls you were going to wear tonight, but I can't remember where I put them. You'll need to look for them."

"You can't *remember*!" Catherine cried in dismay.

"I'm sure you'll find them. Maybe I left them in my room . . ."

"Honestly, Marissa, you're impossible! I don't know how you hold on to a job. Well, you should leave before the weather gets worse." Catherine was already rushing for the front door, grasping her wet hair, touching her throat as if searching for the pearls she feared she'd never see again. Marissa grinned. She'd placed the pearls in their padded velvet box on Catherine's dresser. "Bye," Catherine called absently over her shoulder. "Don't drive too fast. Be—"

The wind carried "careful" away just as the big front door slammed behind her.

She'll race up that staircase faster than the speed of light, Marissa thought, imagining Catherine's relief at discovering her addle-brained little sister hadn't stuck the pearls under the bed or in the refrigerator. Marissa knew that Catherine, who was finishing the last few months of internship needed to receive a license in clinical psychology, didn't truly think her sister was as capricious as she acted. Catherine's habitual fretting nearly drove the airy Marissa wild, though, and she couldn't resist occasionally pretending to be a complete flyby-night, hoping the repetition would eventually break Catherine's habit of overreacting. Besides, within twenty minutes Catherine would be worrying about her again. Marissa knew overconcern was in Catherine's nature, a deep part of the way she loved.

Marissa closed the car window, then looked in the rearview mirror for a quick appraisal of her own appearance. She'd long ago accepted that she wasn't a classic beauty like Catherine, but she could certainly hold her own. Her long dark blond hair, brightened at the stylist's with golden highlights, miraculously still held graceful waves in spite of its exposure to the brisk wind.

No liner or mascara had smeared around what her mother called her "sapphire" eyes. Red lip gloss gave her a more glamorous look than the usual peach or pink without looking too harsh. So far, so good, Marissa thought in satisfaction. Now if she could just endure the party without spilling something on her pale blue dress or getting a run in her ridiculously expensive sheer stockings she would consider the evening a success.

Marissa turned up the car heater and began to back slowly down the slight incline of the driveway. Her red Mustang didn't feel quite as steady as usual, which meant a paper-thin sheet of ice had already frozen over the snow. If she'd left only fifteen minutes earlier, Marissa thought in annoyance, she could have descended the tricky driveway before the top layer of snow began freezing.

Marissa knew traffic would be light tonight with everyone already warned about the bad weather. Nevertheless, people would attend Evelyn and Wilfred Addison's Christmas party, which had become an institution in the city, even before Wilfred Addison's grandfather had been the mayor. The daunting Evelyn, whom Marissa was always tempted to call "Your Majesty," felt the only acceptable excuses for missing her party were death and perhaps a calamitous matter occurring in an intended guest's personal or business life that might make for awkward party chatter.

Evelyn Addison also expected full coverage of her party in the *Aurora Falls Gazette*. After a badly written brief article and one small, blurry picture had infuriated Evelyn last year, this year the editor had placated Evelyn by promising a longer article and assigning it to Marissa Gray. Marissa—a relatively new reporter at the *Gazette*—was a member of one of the few families in Aurora Falls that Evelyn considered equal in social standing to the Addisons. Evelyn had been friends with Marissa's parents and known the Gray girls all of their lives. Her affection for Marissa seemed to have jumped several notches when Marissa promised that this year the *Gazette*'s new, award-winning photographer would be taking the pictures of the event.

Well, Evelyn should be pleased, Marissa thought as the steering wheel turned loosely on the icy road. I'm out here fighting the elements to reach her soirée in time. But it's my fault, she admitted mentally. If I hadn't changed my mind about my earrings at the last minute and misplaced my perfume, I'd be on time. Not that my appearance matters, she dismally reminded herself. Tonight was business. She hadn't gone on a date since returning home six months ago, and she doubted that Mr. Wonderful would magically appear at the Addison Christmas party in Aurora Falls.

Marissa looked in the rearview mirror for a glimpse of the falls she loved. In 1770 a handsome, wealthy, eccentric young man from New York named Sebastian Larke had organized an unofficial expedition south along the Orenda River, the third-largest river mapped in North America. Larke claimed he had a "calling" to find a sacred place he'd seen in a dream. The charismatic Larke had no trouble acquiring followers.

In the spring of 1771, the Larke expedition happened upon the falls. Record keepers of the trip wrote that on a June night they'd heard a distant roar that sounded like a waterfall near the Orenda River. Larke had insisted they make camp without going near the sound. Early the next morning, they had found Larke nearly half a mile away sitting beside wide, horseshoe-shaped falls later measured at a magnificent 124 feet high. According to one of the original journals, "the sun shone like a heavenly prism through the thick mist created by the plummeting water. Sebastian sat perilously near the edge of the falls, his eyes closed as glorious, golden sunlight surrounded him."

According to the journal, Sebastian had then confessed the Christian God had not sent him on this journey as he had let his followers assume. He claimed Aurora, the Roman goddess of the dawn, had asked him to search for her sacred waterfall. Believing the beautiful waterfall he saw with the dawn light shimmering through the rushing water was the one for which he'd searched, Sebastian had promptly named it Aurora in her honor. He had then plucked a white multi-flora rose from one of the many hardy bushes growing nearby and dropped the rose into the falls as an offering.

Nearly a hundred people stayed with Sebastian even after learning they had not been following the orders of their Christian God. Sebastian had spent the next twenty years unmarried and devoted solely to building a village for both the Anglos and the Indians around the falls. Now Aurora Falls was one of the few major waterfalls in the United States not enclosed within a state park and Sebastian's village had become a city of over forty thousand people.

The story of Sebastian Larke had always intrigued Marissa, especially when she was young and imagined him movie-star handsome, idealistic, *and* heroic. She was certain he'd longed for someone to love—someone brave, loyal, and understanding of his imaginative spirit. Someone with dark blond hair, very blue eyes, skinny legs, and a birthmark on his left shoulder blade that resembled a waterfall if you looked at it nearly cross-eyed. Marissa laughed softly in remembrance of her fantasy. Now was not the time to keep glancing back at the magnificent falls lighted green, red, yellow, and blue for the holiday season, though. Headed out of town, away from the lights of close-spaced houses, Marissa knew she needed to concentrate on the road, which was becoming more slippery by the minute.

A guardrail ran along the two-lane highway, separating it from a steep bank sloping sharply down to the Orenda River. Better lighting for this strip of road known as Falls Way had been a main topic of the seemingly endless city council meeting Marissa had covered for the *Aurora Falls Gazette* two nights ago. One man in his eighties had declared in a strong voice that more lights would be too expensive and they would create a teenage hangout where teenagers *did* what teenagers *did*. When a sneering young man around thirty asked him what teenagers did, the elderly man replied snappily, "It's a shame a fella your age needs to ask," bringing on loud laughter from the crowd.

On the opposing side, a woman who looked like a rainbow in a fuchsia and turquoise suit, her dyed red hair upswept, declared she wouldn't have had her second wreck on Falls Way last summer if the city provided adequate lighting in that area. Someone else suggested she might have been able to keep better control of her car if she'd called a taxi instead of driving home after a long evening spent in the Lonesome Me Tavern, a remark she had ignored with dignity so rigid Marissa had thought the woman's neck might break.

Finally, the wife of the town's sheriff, Jean Farrell, with her dowdy clothes, humble manner, and meek voice, sent the meeting into near pandemonium by politely stating that not only did Falls Way definitely need improved lighting, but also the first order of business *must* be to replace the old, weak guardrail between the highway and the Orenda River. She acknowledged the project's cost would eliminate the money the city had set aside to build a new baseball diamond in the park. However, if the city didn't begin work on the lights and the guardrail soon, Jean said pleasantly but firmly, she would take the matter to the governor, who everyone knew was not only her friend but also her cousin.

Almost laughing aloud at the memory of what the elderly man later called "one firecracker of a meeting," Marissa met another car going in the opposite direction and absently noted it was the first vehicle she'd seen in a couple of minutes. The car following her had turned left, and without the shine of its head-lights in her rear window she realized exactly how dark this stretch of road was at night.

The snow fell harder. The car chilled quickly. She'd forgotten her gloves and her fingers stiffened. On such a bad night, fewer people were traveling on Falls Way than usual and the highway rapidly grew slicker. Marissa was an exceptionally good driver, with quick reflexes and twenty-fifteen vision, but driving in this weather was nerve-wracking and Marissa decided that as soon as she reached the party she'd promptly ask for a drink. A double. She'd accept anything alcoholic and stimulating except fattening eggnog. Evelyn Addison would probably be annoyed that the party wasn't Marissa's immediate concern, but Marissa didn't care. Evelyn wouldn't have been driving in the slippery snow.

Or rather, ice. Both the defroster and the wipers were on high. Marissa leaned forward, squinting through her windshield. She'd turned her headlights on low beam, knowing high-beam light would refract off the snow and ice and create a blinding glare, but her range of vision was still alarmingly small.

Marissa glanced at the speedometer. Forty. She certainly wasn't driving too fast. She usually traveled Falls Way at sixty. Still, she slowed her speed another five miles per hour. Thank goodness the Addison house was less than two miles away, she thought, beginning to feel less certain of her ability to handle bad road conditions. Maybe Catherine had been right to expect—

Suddenly, only about fifteen feet ahead of Marissa, her headlights caught a blur of movement near the guardrail. A deer? she wondered. Then, to her shock, the form began to climb over the guardrail, although *climb* didn't seem to be the right word. As Marissa watched through her continually slush-splattered windshield, the figure looked as if it was slithering over the ice-covered rail, moving with smooth, sinuous, frighteningly unnatural ease. Once clear of the guardrail, the figure stood up tall in a long, dark coat, seemed to glide into Marissa's lane, and stopped directly in front of her.

Marissa gasped and pushed on her horn at the same moment. The figure didn't move. In the gleam of Marissa's headlights, she could see a pallid human-shaped face surrounded by a hood. In spite of the weather, she saw enormous black-rimmed eye sockets and, inside of them, the gleam of dark, almost inhuman eyes staring steadily at her. Her own hands trembled, but the figure never flinched as once again Marissa hit the horn, long and hard.

Marissa fought the urge to slam on the brakes, knowing doing so would throw her into a spin. Instead, she steered to the left, intending to go around the person who was obviously drunk or crazy. On her cell phone she would report the incident as soon as she'd eased back into her own lane—

Except a semitruck bore down on her in the left lane. The truck driver's horn blared. The truck was so close Marissa could see the driver's horrified expression. Now she had no time for deft maneuvers on ice. Immediately Marissa hit her brakes, simultaneously jerking the steering wheel to the right.

In a moment, she realized she'd dodged both the truck and the pedestrian, but her car was spinning out of control on the ice. Back in the correct lane, she fought the wheel, but the car had a life of its own, slewing rapidly to the right.

A thousand thoughts seemed to scramble through part of Marissa's brain while at the same time another part maintained an odd tranquility. The tranquility shattered when her Mustang smashed into the guardrail. Sparks of metal grating against metal flashed in the darkness before she heard the groan-snap of the old, weakened guardrail bending and splitting. Marissa finally screamed when the guardrail gave way and her car plunged down the steep, rough bank toward the Orenda River.

2

"This weather will discourage some of the guests." Catherine looked with concern at the cascade of snow on the windshield.

"Not if they know what's good for them. Evelyn Addison keeps very close track of her R.S.V.P. list. Only God knows what kind of social disasters might befall someone who misses her Christmas party."

Catherine stole a look at James Eastman sitting behind the steering wheel of the silver Lincoln. Even in the dim light of the instrument panel, she could clearly see the sharp angles of his profile, the sturdy chin, the straight nose, the strong forehead. He wore his black hair short at the sides with a sharp part and the top combed neatly to the side. Years ago, Catherine decided he had the physical perfection of a young Sean Connery. Still, she'd been shocked when at twenty-one she'd acknowledged her powerful attraction to the son of the Gray family's lawyer. She'd told no one except her mother.

Catherine had idolized her lovely, youthful, joyous mother and confided almost everything to her. No matter how startling or embarrassing Catherine considered the information, Annemarie Gray had never gotten angry, lectured, laughed, or, most important, betrayed a secret. At this moment, Catherine knew her mother would be overjoyed she was on a date with James. Annemarie had always said someday he would open his eyes and see Catherine as a woman, not just one of Bernard Gray's daughters.

Someday and an ex-wife later, Catherine still recalled the pain of her devastation when James had married a woman he'd met while attending law school at Tulane in New Orleans. Because her friendship with James had seemed so casual, Catherine had thought only her mother had known the unhappiness she hid beneath her smile the day the family attended James's wedding at the beautiful New Orleans home of the bride's family. Annemarie had squeezed Catherine's hand when the beautiful dark-haired bride, Renée, walked down the aisle, and Annemarie had stayed close to her daughter during the reception, helping her keep up her façade of cheerfulness that the entire Gray family was not only attending the wedding but also spending a few days in one of their favorite cities.

The first year of the marriage had seemed peaceful. The next year had been a bit bumpy, according to the local gossips. At the beginning of the third year, Renée told anyone who would listen she was miserable with workaholic James, she couldn't stand his overbearing parents, she hated the dullness of life in Aurora Falls, and she would *not* bear the three children James wanted. In October, Renée had left town so fast she seemed to vanish in a puff of smoke.

Afterward, a stony-faced James wouldn't talk about Renée at all, but his mother told friends she had gotten in touch with Renée's parents, who claimed she had not returned to her home in New Orleans—she'd merely called them a week before her departure from Aurora Falls and told them she was getting a divorce. Her behavior infuriated her staunch Catholic parents, who had told her she would not be welcomed back to their home. Apparently, in a fit of pique Renée had claimed she would never speak to them again.

When the news reached Annemarie, she'd hugged Catherine in unashamed jubilation. "James will be hurt for a while, but mostly he'll be humiliated," Annemarie had told Catherine. "When he emerges from his fog of misery, he'll see who has been right under his nose for years!" She'd paused. "Honestly, I think Renée must have cast some magic spell on him. When I looked in her eyes at the reception, I knew she was wrong for him. James has intelligence, depth, and a warm, kind soul. She was pretty but predatory and cold to her bones."

"Are *you* cold?" James asked.

Catherine's gaze flashed to him. "What did *that* mean?"

James tossed Catherine a startled look. "I'm comfortable, but is the car warm enough for you? What did you think I meant?"

"I thought . . . oh, I don't know. I wasn't even thinking about you." Catherine closed her eyes and wondered if she could have said anything ruder. "I'm sorry, James. That came out wrong. I'm jumpy tonight. Marissa is covering the party for the newspaper and she was running late, as usual, so she took off in her little convertible sports car, which she'll drive too fast. The weather is getting worse and I'm worried to death about her."

"It's sweet of you to care so much," James said softly, then more heartily, "Don't worry about her, Catherine. She'll be fine." He smiled ruefully at Catherine. "I thought you were already wondering how you'd get through a whole evening with me."

Are you crazy? Going to this party with you is my dream come true, Catherine almost burst out, but took a breath. "I'm sure we'll have a wonderful time, James. I'm pleased you invited me to join you." I sounded like a character from a Victorian novel, Catherine thought in frustration. She tried again: "James, I'm sorry I seem so strange tonight. I'm a worrier by nature and maybe because Mom died such a short time ago I'm especially overprotective of my sister now. She's impetuous, the risk taker, the live wire in the family."

James grinned at Catherine and she thought she saw a shade of relief in his dark eyes. "Then she'll fit right in at the party. Last year's turned out to be a bash. Evelyn Addison had a bit too much eggnog and did her rendition of My Heart Will Go On at the grand piano. Twice. And Evelyn put *her* heart in the song. If Céline Dion had heard her, she would have dropped dead in horror."

Catherine giggled, picturing Evelyn, whose grande dame act fell to pieces after too many drinks. Her husband usually kept an eagle eye on her to prevent such scenes, but someone must have cornered Wilfred. James went on, "As a dramatic conclusion to the party, Wilfred Addison the Fourth, Evelyn's pride and joy, put his very drunk twenty-seven-year-old self behind the wheel of his car, pushed hard on the accelerator, and rammed into the rear of Harmon Siders's Ford—his first new car in fifteen years.

"Harmon had been bidding his host good night at the door, but when he saw what had happened he came roaring down the porch steps threatening to beat the living daylights out of young Will. The way he moved, you would have never guessed Harmon is in his eighties. He bashed his cane twice on Will's door before anyone could stop him. Young Master Will just sat cowering in the car looking like a little boy waiting for his mother to rescue him."

By now, Catherine had bent forward, lost in laughter and completely free of her self-consciousness, which she knew had been James's intention. "My God," she gasped. "Mom wanted to spend last Christmas in Baltimore with her only sister and I'm glad we did that for her, but I'm sorry I missed all the fun at the annual Addison party!"

"I noticed you weren't there," James said casually. "I only came because Dad insisted. I didn't even bring a date. I was sort of hoping I might happen to meet up with you. Of course, *you* would have had a date, but maybe you would have taken pity on a poor, lonely guy who had to come to a party with his parents.

I felt like a fifteen-year-old ..." James's voice trailed off. He gently lifted his foot from the accelerator, carefully slowing the car on the icy road, and leaned forward, peering grimly through the snow-smeared windshield.

Catherine frowned, seeing the blurry flash of lights. She asked in a small voice full of dread, "What's wrong?"

"Damn this weather!" James swore softly. "There's been a wreck."

2

1

Wake up, sleepyhead. I've made blueberry pancakes. Your father and Catherine will eat all of them if you don't get out of bed and run to the kitchen.

"Run . . . run to kitchen. Pancakes. Have to run—"

Marissa tried to roll off the bed, but something held her tightly at the waist. When she struggled, the pressure increased. Slowly she opened her eyes to a strange world where white confetti fell all around her. She blinked several times and peered through the confetti. Beams of blurry light revealed tall columns with thin white arms reaching into the night. She let out a whimper of rising hysteria as she saw what seemed to be strings circling around her, moving swiftly, scraping against the windows, wrapping her in an icy cobweb cage.

"No! No! *No!*"

Marissa slapped her hands over her mouth, cutting off what she somehow knew were useless screams. Quiet. She must be quiet, she told herself. She must be quiet and *think.* Her father's words came back to her: *Reason is always more useful than panic.* How many times had he repeated that wisdom to her and Catherine? Enough for Marissa to remember it now.

She closed her eyes and tried to draw deep breaths, but she could only take in small breaths of the cold, stinging air. After a few moments, Marissa opened her eyes and forced herself to stare at the strings she'd thought were entwining her in a cage of ice. They weren't strings—they were long, skinny tree twigs and lengthy bare vines. A strong gust of wind set them wildly flaying her car and lashing at the windows as if they wanted entrance. The noise was unsettling, but Marissa managed to keep her nerves somewhat steady, although she still didn't know where she was or what had happened.

Marissa dropped her hands from her face to her lap, where they landed on a piece of limp but strong white nylon or plastic. Several spots of dark liquid splattered the material, one drop falling as she watched. She ran a sore tongue around the inside of her mouth and tasted coppery liquid. It had also spread warm and plentiful on her upper lip before more dripped onto her lap. She gingerly touched her face. Blood spreading from a sore tongue, blood running from her painful nose. Marissa decided she'd bitten her tongue and the discharge of an air bag, now lying deflated in her lap, had broken her nose. At last her mind cleared and she realized she'd had a car wreck.

Her body slanted hard to the right. Marissa forced herself to make another calm measurement and decided the car must be tilted about ninety degrees. She ran the palm of her cold, bare hand over her abdomen to find a length of sturdy nylon webbing holding her in place and another crossing her chest. Seat belts. They had saved her life. Now she needed her cell phone to call for help . . .

Except she'd put the phone in her gold clutch purse, which lay on the backseat, its rhinestone clasp winking faintly in the glow her headlights cast around the car. Marissa stretched her arm toward the backseat but couldn't reach her purse. Tears rose in her eyes. The seat belts had locked.

The car let out an ominous creak and she stopped moving, even breathing. Her tears dried as her panic flared. Certainly the truck driver would call in the incident, Marissa thought, trying to calm down. He would. He definitely would—

If he'd seen it. She'd already passed the front of his truck when she went into a spin. But what if he was the type who was more interested in meeting a deadline than getting into a mess with the police over some woman driving erratically? What if he was the kind who just didn't care? What if he only wanted to get to a warm motel room, kick off his shoes, and watch television?

"*Stop it!*" Marissa told herself aloud. Her headlights were on. The highway wasn't deserted. Someone driving on Falls Way would look down the riverbank and see the lights. Help *would* come. She must believe that or she'd start screaming and kicking and completely lose what good wits she had left.

I'll think about what happened, she told herself. I'll concentrate on every detail of what caused this . . . situation. I won't think about how I'll get out of it; I'll think about how I got in it. That's what Dad—ever-sensible Dad—would tell me to do.

First, what had caused her to wreck? Had she slid into another car? Turning as far to the left as her neck would allow her, she saw no car. Had she lost control and crashed into that useless piece of guardrail? She shut her eyes tightly, trying to remember. No, she'd been driving slowly, so slowly . . .

Her eyes snapped open. I saw something on the road and I tried to dodge it by . . . by how? I pulled into the other lane, but there was a semitruck, for God's sake, and I swerved back to my lane and slid into the guardrail and then—

Tap. Tap. Tap!

Marissa jerked her head to the right and struggled for breath. A white blur at the window sharpened into the long face Marissa had seen on the highway. Gaping black eyes dominated inhumanly pallid skin—eyes seemingly sunken too far back into the eye sockets to belong to anyone alive. Three painted black tears trailed down the right side of the face, the third one beside the gray lips. Marissa was clearheaded enough to know it was a mask with long dark and white hair escaping from beneath the hood—hair rough, tangled, and dry, the hair of a long-dead corpse.

Fear tightened Marissa's throat painfully. She couldn't scream. She could barely breathe. Although she realized the face outside was a mask, its immobility unnerved her. It looked like a human skull. Wind caught loose strands of long hair and coated them with snow and ice, turning them into a stiff, grotesque frame for a skin-stripped face.

Marissa fought the urge to struggle in the locked seat belt that earlier had saved her life but now made her a prisoner. Her thoughts skimmed back to a late summer day when she was nine, happily running in the woods with Catherine and their friend Tonya Ward, and had landed beside a den of young rattlesnakes. Marissa had been wearing canvas sneakers and no socks. Immediately the mother snake's tail had rattled before her head rose, poised at the bare flesh above Marissa's ankle.

Catherine and Tonya had stopped, looking back at Marissa, who'd shrieked, then gone stiff at the sound of the rattle. Catherine had begun screaming at the top of her voice, but coolheaded Tonya had ordered Catherine to *shut up* and firmly told Marissa, "*Do not move.*" After what seemed an interminable time, the snake stopped rattling and lowered back to its passive coil. After two or three minutes, Tonya had told Marissa to pretend she was in slow motion and take tiny steps until she'd escaped the danger of the mother snake.

Right now Marissa felt as if she were looking into the inscrutable eyes of that poisonous, deadly snake. Marissa's body instinctively stilled. She didn't open her mouth to cry out. She didn't allow her gaze to waver. She felt as if her heart had stopped beating. She and the being outside merely stared at each other like figures carved in stone—Marissa hurt, cold, and trapped; the figure covered in a black rain slicker, its face impassive, and its eyes as unfathomable as the eyes of the dead.

Then its fingers began scrabbling at the handle of the car door.

2

A cold lump settled in Catherine's stomach as soon as she spotted the semitruck pulled to the side of the road, flares set around it. A brown sedan had parked behind the semi and a blue SUV sat on the other side of the highway in front of what Catherine dreaded most to see—a sizeable, ragged-edged gap in the guardrail.

James drove past the aperture in the guardrail, slowly pulled in front of the SUV, and stopped. "I'm going to see what's happened," he told her calmly. "I'm leaving the car on so you'll have heat. Will you be all right?"

"I'm not staying in the car!" Catherine's voice shook. "Maybe Marissa—"

He clasped Catherine's hand and squeezed it. "And maybe not Marissa. Maybe not much of anything. This guardrail is so old and weak it might have just cracked in the cold and collapsed on its own."

Catherine looked at him disdainfully. "That's the kind of story you would tell a child, James Eastman, and I can't believe you even *tried* it on me! How stupid, how insulting, how utterly . . . utterly—"

He'd unlatched his seat belt, opened his door, and jerked his hand away from hers while she ranted. "Yeah, okay, I'm awful. You have tears dripping off your chin. *I* am going to see what happened. *You* are going to stay in the car."

He slammed the door and walked away from the Lincoln toward another man, never looking back at her. Catherine huddled in the warm car, pulling a tissue from her tiny purse that didn't hold much more than a tube of lipstick, a compact, and a cell phone. James in his black cashmere coat walked quickly toward a burly figure wearing jeans, boots, a billed cap, and a heavy denim jacket. The man glanced her way and Catherine saw that he looked on the verge of collapse. His whole body shook. One hand continually wiping his eyes, the other hand nervously taking off and putting on his cap. He must be the driver of the semi, Catherine thought, trying to feel sympathy for his obvious distress, but she kept shuddering, imagining his hulking truck meeting Marissa's small, sporty car.

Finally, the truck driver produced a large flashlight and almost charged toward the opening in the guardrail. James and another man each took one of his arms, trying to stop him. Let him go! Catherine thought in fury. Let him look! Maybe it isn't

Marissa at all. I'm sorry for anyone who did wreck, but *please* don't let it be Marissa.

Catherine couldn't stand it. In a flash, she jumped from the car and ran toward James, maneuvering ice and snow in her spike-heeled shoes. "What's happening? Are the police coming?"

"You should have been an ice dancer," James said as she stopped precisely in front of him without a wobble. He clasped her shoulders. "I told you to stay in the car."

She glared at him and nearly snarled, "James, how-bad-is-it?"

"Well, we can't tell much about it," James said unconvincingly. "The truck driver had a cell phone. A police unit was near—they should be here in a minute. It seems a car swerved out of its lane and almost collided with the truck and ended up going over the bank instead." James lowered his voice. "The guy in the jacket is the truck driver. He's a mess—blames himself. He won't wait for the cops. He's determined to go over the bank to see if . . . to see the car."

"I don't care about the damned truck driver," Catherine hissed. "What kind of car went through the guardrail?"

"He couldn't really see; it happened fast, the weather—"

"James!" Catherine watched his dark gaze trying to avoid hers. "It was a red Mustang, wasn't it?" she asked flatly.

James finally looked directly into her eyes, drew a deep breath, and tightened his hold on her shoulders. "Yes, Catherine, it was."

3

The cavernous eyes never wavered from Marissa's as the hands scratched at the car door. Marissa didn't break the gaze, giving no sign she knew whoever was outside was trying to get inside. To get inside and do what? Stab her? Strangle her as she lay twisted and trapped in the car she'd cherished?

Her left shoulder had begun to ache from the pressure of the seat belt holding her body as the car had hurdled, bounced, and jerked to a stop. Or what felt to Marissa like an *unsteady* stop if she wasn't imagining the slight rocking motion caused by her would-be visitor beginning to pull forcefully on the handle of the door.

The handle of a *locked* door! The thought flashed into Marissa's mind like a blinding flare. When she'd lived in Chicago, before moving back to Aurora Falls, where people rarely broke into automobiles, locking the car doors had become second nature to her. In or out of the car, she always locked the doors, and she'd done so this evening while Catherine stood at the car window spouting warnings.

Marissa's mental bubble of triumph burst when the being outside pulled even harder on her car door and Marissa realized it had given up on opening the door and was now trying to make the car lose its delicate balance. The Mustang began to sway. Although Marissa felt as if she might faint, dimly she thought of how ironic it would be to survive a near crash with a semitruck and a perilous dive down the icy river-bank only to die by having some child's nightmare monster pull the car into the Orenda River. If the car went into the river, she would die. Underwater, car doors wouldn't open unless the cabin of the car had filled and the pressure had equalized. She didn't think she could hold her breath that long.

Marissa couldn't even prepare for the worst by opening a window—the *thing* was outside trying to get in the car. She could open a window underwater, but trapped by the seat belt she couldn't reach the automatic window opener. Yes, her situation was quite entertaining, Marissa thought, so dizzy with pain and fright she felt almost goofily drunk. "This would make a good story, but who'll write it if no one knew about the monster?" She laughed almost hysterically before she choked on the blood running from her nose.

Abruptly her twisted amusement at the situation vanished and Marissa crashed back into a world of darkness and snow and something grotesque outside the car trying to kill her. For a moment, she wondered if she might be slipping in and out of consciousness. No grotesque thing was trying to kill her. She'd half-slept in the cold and had a child's nightmare. Night terrors. She'd been prone to them when she was very young.

Then Marissa's tormentor pulled so hard on the car that it grated on the snow and the front end shifted downward. The seat belt jerked harder on her left shoulder, increasing the pain. Marissa looked directly at the figure, and deep in the cavernous holes in the mask she saw darkened eyes narrow a fraction and triumph flitter in their murky depths. Did the monsters of children's imaginations smile? She couldn't remember about her own, but if she lived through this ordeal, she'd ask a child, because *this* monster smiled . . .

And then vanished. Marissa felt as if someone had blown out a candle. Her tormentor was there and then it wasn't. Where could it have gone? Could it have ducked below the car window? Was it creeping behind the car?

She tried to twist in her seat, but she was aching, shivering with cold, and frightened almost senseless. Suddenly a bright light shone beside her face. Her hands flew to her eyes and she cried out, terrified of what horror was surely to come. Then, drawing a ragged breath of tepid air, she burst into silent sobs when a man shouted, "You can stop holding your breath, Catherine! Marissa's alive!"

3

1

Even in the frenzy of her wild fear, Marissa detected something familiar, almost comforting, in the voice of the man who'd said her name. She tried to wrench her body to the left so she could see him, but with his flashlight shining directly into her face all she saw was the curve of his cheek, the shadows of wavy hair around the rim of his cap, a pair of dark eyes, and a hint of his mouth.

"Can you lower your window, Marissa?"

She shook her head no. Her throat tightened as tears began pouring down her face. "Can't reach."

"And Mustang doors are nearly impossible to open with a slim jim." She could vaguely see his smile and suddenly she knew him. "That's all right. Just don't move around any more than necessary. Are you hurt?" His words blasted through the night as if a concrete wall separated them. "Think anything is broken?"

"Nose. Shoulder hurts. Can't feel the rest of my body." His smile turned stiff and false, and she knew he was thinking paralysis. "I can move my legs and arms. I'm numb from the cold."

She could see his face relax and the smile return to normal. Normal? How did she know how his normal smile looked? She hadn't seen it for over four years.

Marissa finally blinked away her tears and calmed down enough to concentrate on her rescuer. Eric Montgomery. Tall, good-looking, smart Eric Montgomery. Back in the days when Marissa was best friends with his younger sister, Gretchen, he had an easy, wildly attractive smile, mischievous brown eyes, and appeared to be in unfailing high spirits. No one seemed immune to his charm, especially girls. But he'd been hers—hers alone. She'd thought they'd be married and have a child by now.

Eric's life suffered a dramatic change after his sister died, though. He'd left his job in Philadelphia and returned to the police force at Aurora Falls. He'd shut out Marissa and almost everyone else in his life. Now he was described as aloof, chilly, serious. Everyone said he was still "blue steel sharp" in the brains department, though, and he seemed utterly devoted to Aurora Falls, which had earned him the position of chief deputy at such a young age. Since Marissa had returned home this past summer, though, she'd seen him only from a distance and he'd given her a brief, dismissive wave.

Her throat relaxed enough for her to yell frantically, "Did you see it?"

Eric frowned. "Did I see *what*?"

"It's on the other side of the car."

"You say someone fell out of your car?"

"*No.* But something is out—"

Too late. Eric had already begun tramping and stumbling through the slick, snowy undergrowth, headed for the opposite side of her car. Marissa closed her eyes. What would that thing do to him? Was it crouched, waiting for him to circle the car so it could push him down the rest of the rugged bank to the river?

While she waited almost breathless for the sounds of an attack, she heard only wind whistling through icy branches. "Nothing over here, Marissa." His voice boomed as he circled the rear of the car and came back to her window. "Catherine said you didn't have any passengers. Maybe you imagined it."

"No! Something, someone—"

Eric either didn't hear her or decided to ignore her. "Catherine and James Eastman are up on the highway. So is the semitruck driver you scared half to death. He says you pulled right in front of him. Don't worry, though. We're going to get some equipment out here, put some chains around this car, and pull you up to the road in no time."

"With me in the car?"

"Even if I could get your door open, I wouldn't want to risk hurting you by getting you out of the car first. You're at a bad angle. The Emergency Services guys will be here in about ten minutes. They'll get you out safely. Trust me."

Just as he yelled for her to trust him, the rear of the car shuddered, slid downward at least four feet, and skewed until it hit a tree. Eric took a step back in surprise. Marissa gasped and drew in on herself.

Eric shined the flashlight on the tree. Marissa glanced at it, realizing in numb, clearheaded horror its diameter probably measured three inches at the most and it couldn't hold the car for long. Eric, so close yet nearly lost in a veil of snow, gaped as already the tree began to crack and the car once again shifted slightly.

"I didn't touch the car when I went around it! It shouldn't have moved!" Eric bellowed.

"The *thing*! It *moved* the car!" Marissa managed to yell through her shock.

"What thing? What are you talking about?"

Stunned with disbelief, Marissa shouted, "If you didn't see anyone *beside* the car, you must have seen them escaping! Someone in a hooded coat, long white hair—"

"Nobody is beside your car, Marissa. I didn't see anyone or signs of anyone around the car." Eric sounded as firm as anyone could while snow and ice battered his face. "You must have jolted the car loose when you were thrashing around inside."

In spite of her terror, the fire of anger blazed through Marissa. She suddenly wished she were wearing sturdy boots and his ankles were bare so she could kick him several times. While he had done nothing except blunder uselessly around her car she had forced herself to remain stock-still. Yet in his typically male mind, she fumed, Eric had pictured her flailing until she made the car even more unstable. And apparently he hadn't even seen what kind of creature had caused this uproar.

A mixture of fear, dread, and pure frustration welled up within her, and sounding like a fifteen-year-old, she managed a high-pitched angry scream: "You jerk!"

"You say you're hurt?" Eric sounded distracted. He leaned down and looked through her window; his expression was more alarmed than earlier. "Don't panic. We'll get you out of this. Just hold very still."

Inside she burned to ask him what the hell he thought she'd been doing for the last fifteen minutes, but two men struggling down the riverbank to join Eric sidetracked her attention. They moved away from the car, lowering their voices, frowning, and from the tail of her eye Marissa saw Eric give something small to a tall, slender man standing beside another one built like a fifty-year-old oak.

Eric finally turned and bawled, "Marissa, you still okay in there?"

"I can *hear* you," she called back acidly, still riled by the idea that Eric didn't give her credit for knowing to hold still. "You don't have to *bellow*! My God, they can hear you in Greenland! I'm stuck in here trying to hold my nerves together, trying to not think about what could happen to me at any minute, and you're making"—she shuddered and, to her horror, began sobbing—"everything worse, dammit! I'm s-so scared that I can't stay in c-control much longer and you just keep *shrieking* for me to hold still . . . and . . . and . . ." Marissa completely dissolved, terrified, wanting to scream her fear, to kick and batter her way free of this prison, but knowing movement would probably result in her death.

"I do not *shriek*!" Eric returned furiously, but after a moment he called in a lower voice, "Don't cry. I'm sorry, Marissa. I just wanted to make sure you heard me."

Ashamed, Marissa tried to control her hysteria. "I—I'm sorry, too. I'm so helpless and—" In spite of her sobbing, Marissa thought she heard something. Appalled, she went quiet for a moment, listening. Then she yelled, "Eric, I can feel the car moving and the tree is splitting! . . ."

"I want you to stay as calm as you can," he called immediately. "We don't have time to get chains around the car and drag it up the riverbank. I have seat belt cutters, but we *have* to get your door open. I want you to try to reach the door lock controls."

"I *can't*."

"You *can*. Give it another try."

Marissa reached with her left hand, but her fingers couldn't reach the door lock button. "I told you I can't reach it!"

"I was watching you, Marissa. You almost made it. The button was only about an inch away from your middle finger. If you don't open that door—"

"I could die in here. I'll try." Marissa twisted a fraction and reached for the control. Pain shot up her shoulder, making her gasp, but her middle finger nearly touched the edge of the button. She reached farther, this time crying out from the screaming strain on her shoulder, but she managed to move her finger a fraction farther. She pushed and heard the blessed click—the car was unlocked!

"Thank God!" Eric said loudly as he opened her door. "I have to lean across you so I can unlock the other door. I'll put as little of my weight on you as possible." Marissa managed to nod. His face reddened with the task of leaning to the other door while trying not to press against her. Quickly he clicked open the other lock, then drew back. "We're not the emergency squad, but we have to cut you loose and get you out of there. All right?"

Marissa realized they must be certain the car was going into the river. She nodded again and said, "Hurry."

Marissa took a deep breath and felt as if the men outside the car were doing the same. She clasped her nearly numb hands but didn't close her eyes. Eric might motion to her—she needed to see. Nevertheless, bitter wind stung her eyes shut for a few seconds when the men slowly, carefully opened her car doors, a move Marissa knew could change the car's balance one fatal inch. Someone slipped a sturdy arm around her waist. "Don't stiffen up, Marissa. Try to relax against me for a minute," Eric murmured in her ear, and she felt better knowing *he* was the man holding her.

The slender man leaned in the opposite open door and gripped the belt crossing Marissa's lap. The burly man stood in front of the car, clearly watching for signs that it was sliding out of control.

"*Now*," Eric ordered. Instantly the men began to serrate the seat belt's tough nylon—nylon that had saved her and now might cause her death. Wind blew and the spindly tree creaked. Marissa silently begged that the tree would hold for just a few more minutes.

The men worked frantically for less than a minute before the tree cracked sharply, the sound seeming to echo through the frozen night. Eric roared, "Get away from the car!" His arm tightened around her and he pulled with tremendous force, completely cutting off her breath. They rocketed back from the car, landing on a soft bed of snow, Eric heaving for air beneath her, Marissa—too shocked to cry—lying motionless on top of him.

Eric managed a raspy shout to the man who'd been on the opposite side of the car: "You okay over there?"

"Yeah." The man gasped as he scrambled through the snow, escaping the area of the vehicle. "But the car—"

"There it goes!" the burly man yelled as Eric rose up on one elbow, still holding Marissa in a near-death grip as they watched the Mustang smash through small brush, rip frozen vines from the ground, fling snow from its tires and under-carriage, and finally roll almost gracefully into the icy water of the Orenda River.

2

Two hours later, Catherine, James, and Eric sat in the Grays' large family room. The Emergency Services team and the backup police had arrived just minutes before Marissa's car rolled into the river. Eric had ordered the deputies to take the truck driver's statement, deliver him to a local motel, and offer to verify to the man's company on the phone that the wreck was not the driver's fault. The man's hands still trembled and the semitruck cab sat askew, the cab half-buried in the earth and snow, but he'd still helped to save Marissa. Eric had wanted to help the driver all he could.

Catherine had accompanied Marissa to the hospital in the ambulance while James and Eric took separate cars. An hour later, Marissa had calmly endured X-rays and a CT scan to check for a concussion and given blood to be tested for drugs or alcohol. Catherine looked as if she was going to faint with relief when doctors determined that miraculously Marissa had suffered only a battered but unbroken nose, and strained shoulder muscles and tendons.

Upon hearing the news, Marissa had loudly demanded to go home. When the doctor told her that would be "inadvisable," she burst into a deluge of tears. Finally, everyone had given in to her roller-coaster emotional state, she'd signed her forms to leave without medical consent, and James drove her and Catherine to the Gray house.

The other deputies had told Eric that headquarters was a zoo on this icy night with all the drivers who had collided with telephone poles and mailboxes. Along with them were two competing sets of teenagers who'd decided to try their skills at breaking and entering on a night when so many people were at parties, which left their homes empty. Police had apprehended the amateur teams and now both the young burglars and their enraged parents faced the crimes with maturity and dignity by yelling at one another and at the cops. Given the chaos at headquarters, Eric announced he would accompany a still weak, panicky Marissa to take her statement about the wreck in the peace and familiarity of her home.

Back in the safety of the lovely house where she'd lived most of her life, Marissa could hardly believe that less than two hours ago she'd been trapped in her Mustang and hanging on the bank of a river with someone jostling the car, trying to send it into the dark, frigid waters of the Orenda. Now she sat on a heavily padded couch in the warm family room of the Gray home, huddled in a floor-length heavy white velour robe. Catherine had insisted Marissa wear the pair of giant fuzzy white slippers with rabbit faces and floppy ears she knew were Marissa's favorites. She'd also wrapped Marissa in a blinding neon red and yellow afghan made by their grandmother. Marissa could see herself in a mirror across the room, though, and in spite of all her colorful insulation, she still looked pinched and frozen.

Tonight, the big room with its calming cream, cinnamon, and soft dusky blue color scheme looked like the scene of a party. Lighted Christmas wreaths hung at every window, and tinsel and lighted candles decorated the mantle of the large cherrywood hearth in which a cheerful fire burned. In what usually was an empty corner now towered a huge pine tree glittering with countless miniature lights and the lovely, fragile ornaments and decorations Annemarie Gray had collected throughout the years. As Catherine bent to light two large candles on the coffee table, James said, "Catherine, the room looks beautiful, but I'm afraid we're going to have a fire hazard if you light another candle."

Catherine glanced around her. "Oh. Well, maybe I am overdoing it, but it was so cold and dark on that bank and it seemed we were there for hours. I can imagine how poor Marissa feels."

"I'm still cold, but I don't think I'll thaw out until around daylight no matter how many candles we light." Marissa tried to smile at everyone, embarrassed by her less-than-poised crying jag at the hospital. "I would certainly like to have a drink, though." She looked at Eric. "It's all right for me to have alcohol now that my blood has already been drawn for testing, isn't it?"

"It would be if you weren't taking pain pills," Eric said mildly. "Alcohol and pain pills don't mix."

Marissa glared at him and James added loudly, "Marissa isn't the only one who'd like a drink. I'd love to have a Scotch and soda or a bourbon and Coke or . . . well, anything!"

"Of course. I'm so used to Mom taking control, although I'm glad she's not here tonight . . ." Tears rose in Catherine's eyes and she nervously fluttered off toward the kitchen, yelling back, "I think we have booze of every kind. Oh! What a thing to say with the chief deputy sitting right here! I sound like we're running a roadhouse. It's just that we bought extra liquor for guests and people give bottles as gifts." She paused. "I didn't even ask what everyone wanted. Marissa, where are the cocktail glasses? I thought Mom kept them . . . damn!" A kitchen cabinet door slammed.

"I think our hostess needs some help." James stood up. "Marissa, what would you like?"

"A Coke," she said glumly.

James smiled warmly. "Fine. Eric?"

"I'm still on duty. I'm afraid it will have to be coffee," Eric said politely. "Instant will be fine."

Marissa and Eric were old news in the romance department. Four and a half years ago, she'd worn an engagement ring given to her by Eric. Most of Marissa's life, her closest friend had been Eric's younger sister, Gretchen—a sweet, quiet blonde who lived for music. Her talents had begun emerging when she was barely more than a toddler. She played the violin and the piano and sang. Gretchen had already begun her concert career when at age twenty-one she died from a fall in the church on Gray's Island—a fall Eric and Marissa had both witnessed.

Immediately after Gretchen's death, Eric's lighthearted buoyancy, his irresistible charm, had vanished. He'd been on the fast track in Philadelphia law enforcement but came back to Aurora Falls to be near his shattered parents and join the Aurora city police in a much less prestigious position than he'd held in Philadelphia.

And he'd broken off his engagement to Marissa.

At first, Marissa had felt numb after what had been a crushing blow. For years, everyone had expected Marissa Gray to marry Eric Montgomery. Marissa's mother had begged her to give him time to straighten out his emotions, to not close the door on their romance, but Marissa knew Eric too well to believe a few months or even a year would set things right. So she'd applied for a newspaper job in Chicago. The hours had been long and the pay had been bad, but she hadn't cared. All she'd thought about was that with Eric back in Aurora Falls she must leave.

After two years, she'd told herself she'd completely recovered. She came home only at Christmas and for a week each summer. Her father had died of a heart attack during her second Christmas visit. Eric attended the funeral with his parents, but he and Marissa hadn't spoken and had even avoided each other's gazes. When she'd realized she couldn't even look at him without feeling as if a fist were squeezing her heart, she knew she hadn't gotten over him at all.

Still, Marissa wondered if the Eric Montgomery she'd loved existed anymore. Over the years, she had gotten calls from friends in Aurora Falls and she knew Eric never attended parties, hung out with old friends, played tennis with his father, or took his mother on the motorcycle rides that used to set her screaming and laughing with fearful joy. If he dated, no one in town knew about it.

People said his breezy handsomeness had disappeared. He still had the strong, classic facial features, of course, but most of the time he looked thin lipped and solemn; on bad days he appeared almost forbiddingly grim, his face rigid, a permanent furrow between his eyebrows. She wondered if his devilish smile and killer dimples still existed. He'd lost the mischievous, almost rakish glint in his dark brown eyes. He still wore his wavy blond hair a couple of inches longer than most men his age would have, but the Eric she'd known seemed to have disappeared. Even when he was staring right at you, you felt as if the essential Eric Montgomery was lost somewhere in the mists of time with Gretchen.

Now, in the smothery, overly decorated room, Marissa floundered for the kind of thing she would say to someone she'd known so long, but she felt as if a pane of thick glass separated her from Eric. He saved her embarrassment by not looking directly at her. He was withdrawing a pen and small notebook from his jacket when fifty pounds of blond love, warmth, and happiness bounded into the room carrying a small stuffed teddy bear. The dog jumped up on the couch beside Marissa, who hugged her and rubbed her ears.

Eric looked up from his notebook and allowed himself a small smile. "You're still a dog lover, I see."

"This is Lindsay." Marissa giggled as the dog dropped her teddy bear long enough to give Marissa a sloppy lick on the chin and carefully sniff the gauze and tape paramedics had applied to Marissa's bruised but no longer bleeding nose. "I got her at an animal shelter in Chicago about two years ago and named her for Lindsay Wagner, who used to play the Bionic Woman on television. She's exuberant and has a passion for stuffed animals, as you can see." Marissa smiled as Lindsay the dog snatched up her teddy bear again and gave it a good shaking. "This house is full of her toys."

"She looks like a good dog." Eric sounded stiff although he still wore that small, tight smile. "I'm sure she's a lot of company when Catherine isn't here."

"When I came home this summer, Mom fell in love with Lindsay." Marissa could feel a wave of desolation at the thought of her lost mother and looked down at the golden dog cuddling next to her. "She is a smart, loving, very special girl."

Eric nodded slowly, then said lightly, "Oh, Marissa Gray, I'll bet you say that to all the dogs."

After a jarring moment of surprise, Marissa glanced at Eric to see a hint of his old, familiar grin. Eric Montgomery, man of little humor, had actually been teasing her. Marissa felt as if the wall of glass between them had just developed hairline cracks. She was so startled she simply looked at him and blessed Catherine, who came chattering into the room carrying a tray of drinks and snacks.

"This isn't the usual way we take statements," Eric said seriously a few minutes later, his eyebrows drawing down toward the line between his eyes, the charming smile vanishing, "but considering your *insistence* on getting home, Marissa, it will have to do for now."

Marissa caught his disapproving edge on the word *insistence*. People in Aurora Falls often talked about Eric's demand for proper protocol. He lacked the casual authority of Sheriff Mitchell Farrell, so popular and admired he'd been elected sheriff time after time since Marissa's childhood. Three months earlier, he'd turned over his duties to Chief Deputy Montgomery before going home to die of cancer. Although many citizens didn't like Eric's cool formality, Sheriff Farrell's confidence in Eric's abilities earned their confidence, if not their affection.

"I'll need you to come to headquarters on Monday morning for something more formal, Marissa," Eric went on almost sternly, as if he thought she wouldn't cooperate.

"I'll be there," Marissa replied coolly.

"Okay, start at the very beginning, when you were headed for the Addisons' house." Eric's voice was courteous but businesslike. "Catherine said you were late and probably going to drive too fast."

Catherine flushed and looked at Marissa. "I didn't say you *would* go too fast, just that you might because you were late."

Marissa felt a prickle of annoyance with Catherine but kept her expression pleasant. "She always worries that I drive too fast," Marissa said to Eric. "The weather was bad, though, and I wasn't going to take any chances just to reach Evelyn Addison's house on time. I drove below the speed limit."

Eric nodded.

"By the time I neared the place where I wrecked, the snow had increased and I slowed down to thirty-five miles an hour," Marissa continued, her throat tightening. She looked at Lindsay, who was trying to tuck the teddy bear under the afghan. "That's when I saw . . . something. It climbed across that icy guardrail so easily! Then it walked into my lane, stopped, and stared at me." Marissa raised her eyes and looked at Eric with near defiance. "It seemed to be *daring* me to hit it."

Catherine, James, and Eric stared at her. Marissa thought even Lindsay, who'd successfully hidden her toy, was looking at her with especially probing dark brown eyes. "Well, it's true!" Marissa burst out defensively.

"Are you certain someone didn't run in front of you and freeze?" Catherine asked Marissa, and then quickly turned to Eric, speaking as if she were explaining a child's behavior. "The snow was obviously worse than Marissa had expected and she got frightened and confused and couldn't see clearly. Someone must have just run out in front of her and froze."

"That is *not* what happened," Marissa snapped.

Everyone's gaze fastened on Marissa again as Eric said, "But visibility was *very* poor. With all that snow and your headlights on low—I presume you know to turn your headlights on low so they won't—"

"Refract light on the snow and half-blind me. Yes, I know that, Eric, and my headlights were on low beam."

"But you still say you saw a person."

"It wasn't just a person stupidly trying to cross the highway in a snowstorm. It was someone dressed up like a Halloween ghoul who climbed the guardrail and deliberately stood in front of me!"

"I see," Eric said in the careful voice one would use with a hysteric.

Her own tension and the doubt she saw in three pairs of eyes suddenly made Marissa flashingly angry with everyone in the room. She glowered at James and Catherine, then fastened her gaze on Eric and burst out, "You're all looking at me like I'm crazy, but I'm in full possession of all my faculties just as I was minutes before I had the wreck. That's why I am *certain,* Mr. Chief Deputy, that someone walked onto the lane of a highway, then deliberately stopped in front of my car!"

Before Eric could answer, Marissa drew a deep breath and continued, seething, "You also might remember, Eric, that I have twenty-fifteen vision."

Eric tilted his head slightly and said coldly, "I do remember that, Marissa. I remember very well that you have above-average vision."

Oh God, Marissa thought. Her excellent vision—how she'd mentioned it to the police when Gretchen died, how little attention they'd paid, how she'd had no time to make them acknowledge its importance. Her throat tightened, and for a moment she didn't think she could continue talking to Eric. Then she made a decision. She'd failed to convince everyone of what she'd seen then. She wouldn't fail now.

Marissa drew a deep breath. "I just had my eyes checked two months ago and my vision is still twenty-fifteen. That's why I believe you can trust the accuracy of my description of this 'person of interest,' as you cops say, in spite of the bad weather." She looked straight at Eric and spoke firmly. "The man—I assume it was a man—was tall. He wore a long, dark, coat—by *long* I mean down to the ankles—with the hood up. The coat was shiny—obviously made for wet weather. Very long, ragged dark and white hair hung to his chest from beneath the hood.

"Inside the hood was a mask," Marissa charged on, even though she could see Eric wanted to ask a question. "The mask was loose and rubbery, something that completely covered the head, not a little plastic thing held on by a string around the back. The eyes in the mask were huge, made to look like deep holes in the skull." She paused. "Actually, the mask looked a lot like the one the killer wears in the movie *Scream,* but not exactly. I couldn't see the person's eyes at all at that time. I *did* see him walk into my lane and take a stance, legs slightly apart." Her voice began to tremble. "It—he—made absolutely no move to evade the car. He just stood motionless, staring right at me."

Marissa ended with another glare at Eric, then turned her gaze to Lindsay and gave her ears such a vigorous rubbing the dog yelped. Marissa murmured, "I'm sorry, baby," and laid her head on the dog's neck so no one would see the tears flowing into her eyes.

Another wave of uncomfortable silence washed through the room. All Marissa heard was the crackling of the flames in the fireplace, and humiliation filled her. Was she five instead of twenty-five? Temper and tears. Lord. She couldn't raise her head and look at anyone.

At last, Lindsay craned her head sideways far enough to lick away the salty tears from Marissa's face. The dog seemed to be putting her whole heart into the task and Marissa feared Lindsay planned a full-body bath. She looked up, managed a "Thank you, Lindsay," gently pushed the dog's ardent face away, pulled a tissue from the pocket of her robe, and began wiping her face.

Immediately Catherine stood over her holding a foil-wrapped antibacterial wipe. Marissa looked at it and burst out with a weak, teary giggle. "Gosh, Catherine, do you keep these tucked down the front of your dress?"

Catherine gave her a deadpan look. "At all times, in case a dog decides to wash my face."

Laughter, a bit edgy but still laughter, circled the room. Marissa wiped her face with the cold, astringent wipe and sniffed mightily. "I apologize to everyone for my tantrum. I'm afraid my manners aren't quite up to par tonight."

Two voices spoke at once. "It's all right, sweetie—you were almost *killed*!" This from Catherine. "Yes, you're safe and sound. Those few tears were just aftershock." This from James. In a moment, a soft, deep voice said slowly, "Go ahead and cry all you need to, Marissa. Sometimes crying is all that helps. I ought to know." Marissa lifted her gaze to see Eric giving her a look of deep understanding that touched her more than any words of sympathy ever could.

3

At three A.M. Eric Montgomery stood on the edge of Falls Way looking at the jagged path Marissa Gray's car had left on its shattering trip down to the Orenda River. The emergency crews had abandoned the area, and the carloads of sightseers were safely at home by now. Flares still marked the presence of the semitruck as well as the gaping hole in the guardrail. The blinding snow of a few hours ago had dwindled to a diaphanous veil. Behind Eric, a few scattered houses clung to the hill overlooking the river. Red, green, blue, and yellow Christmas lights glowed from some of them, reflecting on the dark, icy water that had almost turned Marissa's sporty car into her coffin.

Eric pictured Marissa wearing her huge bunny slippers, her nose buried under a mound of gauze and adhesive tape, and the garish afghan wrapped around her as she clutched her dog and defiantly insisted something resembling a ghoul had walked in front of her car on Falls Way. Someone else might think she'd had a few drinks before she left for the party. Eric knew Marissa would admit if she'd had even *one* drink before she left the house and she wouldn't make up a ridiculous story about a monster to explain why she wrecked.

Eric believed Marissa had seen *something*—maybe a deer or a big dog—and in the near whiteout caused by the snow she'd dodged the animal and gone sailing through the guardrail. She'd been knocked unconscious, then awakened to find herself literally hanging on the steeply sloped riverbank, trapped by her seat belt, waiting for help while snow, ice, and cold wind battered her car. Her fright and semi-consciousness had caused her mind to create a malevolent creature trying to get at her in the prison of her Mustang.

That sounded good, but Eric had trouble accepting it. Marissa had always been imaginative. He used to think she should have become an author of suspense novels instead of a journalist. Still, when she was young and he'd met her when she came to his house to visit Gretchen, Marissa had struck him as an outwardly high-spirited girl with a levelheaded core—a girl who would never confuse fiction with reality. She was far more mature than his sister, Gretchen, seemed to have her feet firmly on the ground, and tonight had been remarkably fearless.

Eric had rarely spoken to Marissa since Gretchen's death, but he'd kept track of her and hadn't heard anything to make him believe Marissa had changed. She admitted now that after the wreck at first she thought she was seeing a monster trying to get in the car. When her mind had cleared, though, she realized the "creature" still lurking by the car was actually a person in wild disguise. Eric sighed. All he could do was hope on Monday when she gave him her formal statement she would be rested and recovered from her initial panic and give a plausible statement with no mention of a creature or a monster.

Eric took a deep breath of the chilling air. A towboat pushed five barges down the river. Moving slowly and quietly, surrounded by mist and the last feathering of snow, they looked almost magical. Eric closed his eyes, recalling with almost jolting clarity hot summer days when the sun glared off the water and he relaxed almost to the point of drowsiness aboard Bernard Gray's cabin cruiser, the *Annemarie*. Ironically, the woman for whom Dr. Gray named the boat suffered from severe seasickness. She never went boating but urged her husband, who spent long days performing surgery, to enjoy himself on weekends.

Sheriff Mitch Farrell, Dr. Gray's cousin, went on the boat whenever he could. He laughed uproariously, drank endless amounts of soft drinks, and ate more than his share of sandwiches and potato salad from the coolers Mrs. Gray sent along, and his nose always turned bright red because he refused to wear sunblock. His wife, Jean, seemed content to stay at home tending to her flower and vegetable gardens.

Dr. Gray had loved young people, so aside from Mitch Farrell, his passengers were always his daughters, Catherine and Marissa, Eric and his younger sister, Gretchen, and Will Addison—charming despite his slight air of entitlement. Sometimes Dr. Gray included his daughters' friend Tonya Ward—a showily pretty girl who at sixteen seemed designed to wear a bikini and managed to be sexy, funny, flirtatious, and refined all at the same time. Gretchen had admired Tonya. So had local boys Dillon and Andrew Archer when their father allowed them to come along, which was seldom, because their father kept them nearly chained to Archer Auto Repair.

In spite of the cold, Eric removed his hat. Maybe their father had been right, he thought as the breeze caught his slightly long, wavy ash-blond hair and tossed it to one side. Dillon had been seventeen and Andrew nineteen years old the first summer they'd been allowed to go out on the boat. Dillon's dark coloring, striking blue eyes, and muscular build had made him far more attractive than Andrew with his almost white-blond hair worn in a crew cut, his tall, lanky body, and his unfortunate gawkiness.

Andrew had been almost silent during their first outing. Eric could tell he'd been awed by the beautiful boat and everyone's courteous and welcoming behavior. At fourteen, Marissa and Gretchen had worn their first two-piece bathing suits that summer and painted each other's toenails, which had brought on gales of adolescent giggling from them that baffled Eric. They'd even gone to Gray's Island a couple of times, where Dillon had seemed especially interested, almost entranced, by the church with the sun shining through its beautiful stained-glass windows.

Eric now felt like an old man remembering the fun and the laughter of what seemed a long-ago summer. Dr. Gray had encouraged everyone to go waterskiing if they weren't afraid. Eric could tell Andrew wanted to give it a try but was afraid he'd do something wrong. He always seemed afraid he'd do something wrong.

Dillon had much more confidence. His manners were excellent and he'd even tried waterskiing and done well the very first time. He'd talked to everyone, even Marissa and Gretchen, asking if they were going to paint every toenail a different color, which brought on another attack of giggles. Dillon had asked Catherine if she was looking forward to entering the University of California at Berkeley in the autumn, and he'd told Tonya to avoid taking a class from a teacher named Blume when school started in the fall. He was pleasant, charming, and polite. Still, Eric hadn't been able to shake the feeling that Dillon was being extremely watchful, as if coolly assessing everyone, and the feeling had made Eric uneasy.

Eric's attention now snapped back to the river. The towboat and barges had moved on, the remaining mist and snow closing in and making them invisible. They had vanished, Eric thought winsomely. They'd vanished like the *Annemarie,* which had been in storage since Dr. Gray's death.

Another blast of freezing air let Eric know he was being foolish to keep standing like a statue beside the road. But one memory held him immobilized—a bitter memory that chilled his already nearly numb body.

As Eric recalled, it would have been the Archer boys' third outing when Andrew had seemed more relaxed and Dillon had acted right at home. Both guys had laughed at Sheriff Farrell's jokes and Andrew had talked to nearly everyone without blushing. He had worn sunglasses, which hid the permanently insecure look in his light blue eyes, and with his new tan and slightly longer hair he'd looked a tad more appealing. For the first time in Eric's life, he'd seen both Andrew and Dillon Archer act young and carefree.

Late in the afternoon, Eric had gotten a cold can of Coke from the cooler and placed it beside Dillon, who wore only cutoff jeans and lay stretched full-length on his back, his well-formed body turning a nice shade of light golden brown. Dillon had looked up at Eric with his brilliant blue eyes, smiled almost blissfully, and said, "Thanks, Eric. You know, I hate to sound like an idiot, but all of this is so great I feel like I've died and gone to heaven."

Well, if there was any justice in the world, Dillon Archer hadn't gone to heaven, Eric now thought, bile rising in his throat after all these years, because on that bright and beautiful day he had been looking into the eyes of a murderer.

4

1

They stood in Catherine's ivory and sage green bedroom, one getting dressed, the other slumping drearily in front of the vanity mirror. "Thanks so much for going in with me to give my statement."

Catherine pulled a tan wool sweater over her head and threw Marissa's mirrored image an amazed look. "Did you think I'd send you there alone after you just had a car wreck Saturday night? Honestly, Marissa, you make me sound downright cold-blooded."

"You kept warning me not to go by myself in my Mustang Saturday night."

"So now I'm going to punish you for not obeying me? If I remember correctly, you told me to remember that we're not kids and I'm simply your older sister, not your big sister who gives the orders—not that I ever could give *you* orders. You've never been exactly pliable."

"You mean I'm stubborn."

"I thought I was being tactful."

"You were." Marissa sighed and leaned closer to the mirror. "Oh gosh, my face! I have bruises around my eyes, I have a long scratch on my jawline, and I shudder to think what my poor nose looks like under these bandages—"

"Enough!" Marissa jumped. Catherine rarely raised her voice. "You have been fretting over your looks since Saturday night. Even Lindsay is getting tired of listening to you."

Marissa looked down at her constant companion, sitting beside her with a red rubber ball in her mouth. Marissa stooped to stroke her on the head. "She loves me no matter how battered I am. You can't blame me for not wanting people to see me when I look like I've been in a boxing match."

"Well, at least you still have all of your teeth. It could be worse." Catherine walked toward her, smiling. "After we stop at the hospital and they take the bandages off your nose, you'll brighten up with some lip gloss and we'll put concealer under your eyes and blush on your cheeks."

"But my nose—"

"It isn't broken. It can't look *too* bad. And just think of—"

"Don't you dare say 'think of what you could have looked like.' That isn't going to make me feel one bit better."

"You're right. Imagining how things could have been worse never makes me feel better, either." Catherine ran a wide-toothed comb through her shining hair and reached down to remove a piece of lint from her brown wool slacks.

"I wish I were as tall and graceful as you," Marissa said forlornly.

"Oh, for God's sake, Marissa!" Catherine looked at the dog, Lindsay. "Your mother has a big case of feeling sorry for herself today, do you know that?" Lindsay cocked her blond head and Catherine's gaze shifted back to Marissa. "I'm five-seven; you're five-four—a perfectly respectable height. I have what people politely call a 'willowy' figure; you have 'curves.' My hair is straight as spaghetti and you have natural waves. Your eyes are as blue as . . . as the Adriatic Sea."

"Catherine, you've never been to the Adriatic Sea."

"Well, I know it's considered the bluest sea. Your eyes are like sapphires burning from inside with dazzling blue fire, your skin is like the finest porcelain, and your teeth are like pearls. If we lived a few hundred years ago, men would write poetry to your beauty. They would—"

"Lock you up for being insane."

Marissa and Catherine both burst out laughing, then flopped back on the bed as they continued to giggle. Lindsay watched them curiously.

"Oh, my gosh," Marissa finally gasped, pulling free and wiping tears from her cheeks. "We haven't laughed like that since Mom died."

Catherine nodded, pushing her hair behind her ears and dabbing at mascara smears beneath her eyes. "I know."

"What's gotten into you?"

"Everyone thinks you're the court jester of the Gray family, but I have a sense of humor, too."

"I didn't realize I was considered the Grays' court jester, but I guess I could be worse things." Marissa paused and looked at Catherine with narrowed, slightly bruise-encircled eyes. "If things had gone differently Saturday night, I'd attribute this good mood of yours to your date with James. But you can't tell me you had a wonderful time with him. I completely ruined your evening."

In an uncharacteristically lighthearted gesture, Catherine lightly kissed Marissa's forehead. "Although you scared me half to death, you did *not* ruin my date."

"Oh? Did something happen after Eric left and I went to bed?"

"Don't be ridiculous. I'm the shy and serious sister, remember? Now put on one of those heavy faux fur coats of yours. It's time for us to go and it's freezing outside."

Marissa settled onto the seat of Catherine's sensible sedan, fastened her seat belt, flipped down the visor, and looked in the mirror at her bandage-free face. "Oh no," she groaned. "Just fifteen minutes ago the doctor told me I look fine."

"You do look fine." Catherine started the car and crept to the exit of the hospital parking lot, even more wary of driving on snow since Marissa's wreck. "You look fine for someone who was punched in the nose by an air bag less than forty-eight hours ago. Give your poor face a chance to heal."

Marissa groaned again.

"I don't mean to hurt your feelings, Marissa, but this fixation on your looks makes you sound vain and shallow."

"Thank you, Catherine," Marissa said dully. "My feelings aren't hurt at all."

"I'm trying to make a point. You sound vain and shallow, but you're *not* vain and shallow." Catherine paused. "I believe you're obsessing about your appearance rather than thinking about what almost happened to you Saturday night."

"My sister the psychologist."

"Yes, I'm both and I know you very well." When Catherine stopped at a red light, she broke her two-handed grip on the steering wheel, reached over with her right hand, and clasped Marissa's gloved left fist. "You're holding in your emotions so tightly it must hurt. I sat by your bedside most of Saturday night. You had one nightmare after another. Once you got up and started to run. I grabbed you and you said, 'Mommy,' threw yourself against me, and started sobbing."

"I don't remember that happening," Marissa said meekly.

"I know. It was another moment of the normal human weakness you try to hide. You always try to act like the tough girl. Right now you're trying not to cry. I can tell."

"I don't want to cry!"

"Okay, then don't. I'm just saying that although you're tough in many ways, you don't have to act as if you're indestructible. You're not, and thank goodness, because if you weren't vulnerable, if you didn't have a soft side, you wouldn't be Marissa Gray."

"Whom everyone knows and loves."

"That's right."

"Well, somebody sure as hell didn't love me Saturday night," Marissa declared. "Because no matter how many times people tell me the wreck was an accident, I know somebody wanted me dead!"

Which was exactly what she repeated at police headquarters fifteen minutes later. Although she sat in Eric Montgomery's office, he'd left open his door and after her loud declaration the large outer room fell into complete silence. Marissa could feel her sister blush, but Eric simply gazed at her with steady amber eyes and an expressionless face. Finally, he asked formally, "Do you know of anyone who would want you dead, Marissa?"

"Well, no, of course not. I would have reported someone threatening me or stalking me. But this person walked right in front of my car—"

"And you don't think that could have been an accident?"

"A person dressed up like it's Halloween walked deliberately in front of my car on an icy highway and you think it was an accident?" Marissa's voice rose. "That's ludicrous!"

"You think this person wanted to kill you," Eric said calmly, "yet you just admitted he walked in front of your car on an icy highway. Doesn't that sound more as if he wanted *you* to kill *him*?"

"Why would I kill him? I don't even know who it was!"

"Maybe he'd planned a suicide."

"A suicide? Dressed up like a ghoul? Following the car halfway down the riverbank and trying to jostle the car loose so it would fall in the river? Or do you believe he hoped to commit suicide by having the car fall on top of him?"

"Marissa, you're shouting," Catherine said gently. "I know you're upset, but you might be taken more seriously—"

"If I act nonchalant?"

"If you stop sounding on the verge of hysteria." She gave Marissa an almost warning smile and said softly, "You sounded more rational after the wreck than you do right now."

Marissa started to snarl back an answer, looked at Catherine, then at Eric, and closed her eyes. "Are you all right?" Eric asked. Marissa nodded as she heard noise begin in the outer room— papers shuffled with too much fervor, questions asked loudly, and the copier beginning to shoot out papers, comments made in unnaturally formal voices. The staff was trying to act as if all was well and they hadn't been listening. They were acting *careful,* she realized, as if perhaps they should fear the mental state of the woman in the office with Chief Deputy Montgomery. Marissa exhaled what seemed like every ounce of air in her body and sagged in her chair. She was deeply embarrassed and felt beaten, as if all the fight had gone out of her with that nearly bottomless sigh.

"Yes, everyone, I'm all right," she said weakly as Catherine and Eric gazed at her in concern.

A young female deputy with dark brown hair, a thin, ascetic face, and dark blue eyes appeared in the doorway with a Styrofoam cup. "Coffee, Ms. Gray," she said abruptly, setting it down on Eric's desk in front of Marissa and smiling. "We only had enough left in the pot for one cup, and you seem to need it most. I'll put on a fresh pot. Oh, we only have artificial cream and sweetener, too. I don't know how you like your coffee, Ms. Gray, and this isn't the best in the world."

"I want fresh coffee, too, Robbie." Marissa recognized the loud, nasal voice of Deputy Buddy Pruitt. "On the double!"

"Go make your own," the deputy snapped back before giving Marissa a gentle smile. "I hope this makes you feel better."

Marissa smiled almost shyly, realizing how she must have sounded to everyone at headquarters. "Thank you."

"Yeah, thanks, Robbie," Eric said as the deputy left the room. "That's Robbie—Roberta—Landers, one of our newest deputies. Nice, intelligent, competent kid," he added with the paternal air of a sixty-year-old man. "She can hold her own with male deputies who don't always make things easy for her."

"Like Buddy Pruitt?" Marissa asked softly. "Her father is a reporter at the newspaper. He's talked about Robbie." Marissa sipped the bitter-edged coffee, forced herself not to grimace, and after a moment smiled shamefacedly at Catherine and Eric. "I'm sorry," she said steadily. "I've been trumpeting like an elephant since the wreck. I'm being ridiculously belligerent because I know how unlikely my story seems. Unlikely? *Crazy* is more like it. Sometimes I wish I'd made up something about an animal running in front of me so I wouldn't sound like a lunatic. I couldn't do that, though, because it just isn't true."

She leaned forward. "Eric, someone was out there and they didn't freeze from fear in front of my car. They stood deliberately still. And even if I had any doubts, those doubts would have vanished when *it,* he, whatever, hadn't followed my car over the riverbank and pecked on the windows, fiddled with the door handle, tried to pull the car the rest of the way over the bank and into the river, for God's sake! When you came down the bank to check the situation, even you didn't know what made the car suddenly begin to move—I hadn't so much as twitched; you hadn't touched the car; the wind had stopped for five seconds. You didn't see anyone, but you have to admit in that chaos someone could have scooted under the car unnoticed. Besides, you weren't even looking for anyone, because you couldn't hear what I was telling you about someone being outside the car!"

Eric held up his hand. "Take a breath, Marissa. You're talking so fast you're going to pass out." He looked right into her eyes, but she could tell his mind was back at the car Saturday night.

Marissa gathered her thoughts, drew a breath, and spoke calmly: "I'm a good driver, Eric. I'm skillful, calm, reliable"—she smiled and said loudly—"and just for the record, everyone, not at all prone to seeing monsters on the highway."

A few people in the outer room snickered and Eric finally grinned. It was a small grin but a grin nevertheless.

Eric seemed to relax in his chair, his back curving a bit, his fingers beginning to tap silently on the desktop. "The only other witness we have to the wreck is the truck driver. He said you seemed to be dodging something before you went into that spin. He didn't think you'd just dozed off and drifted into his lane or you wouldn't have regained your skills so fast." Eric paused. "I've been to the site twice. The snow, the brush, and the ground are all a mess. We can't get decent prints, but—"

"Mrs. Farrell!" Robbie exclaimed. Marissa turned around to see Jean Farrell, the sheriff's wife, enter the outer room of headquarters. She looked back at Eric and waved.

"But I'm not discounting that some people are almost as compelled to pull pranks at Christmas as they are at Halloween,"

Eric continued. "Although I'll have to say, this one had a hell of a lot of nerve. I'm going to be watching for him."

Marissa burst into a wide smile and almost jumped up. Eric looked alarmed, as if he feared she was going to fling herself across the desk at him. She saw the look and didn't feel the least insulted. Chief Deputy Eric Montgomery was too detached for his own good, she thought. A little shock once a day wouldn't hurt him a bit.

"Thank you so much, Deputy," she said sincerely and loudly, still smiling for all she was worth. "I feel so much better now that I know you're making this a priority case!"

Eric's eyes widened. "A priority case? I didn't say anything about a *priority*—"

"How great to see you here! I haven't seen you at all for weeks." Robbie jumped up from her desk, rushing to Jean. "Here, let me help you with those packages. How's Sheriff Farrell today?"

"Robbie, thank you, dear. I was on the verge of dropping everything," Jean Farrell said. "Hello, Buddy, Jeff, Arlene, Tom. Jeff, isn't the baby about due?"

"Another week, Mrs. Farrell. We'll be starting off the new year with a new baby."

"Oh, that's wonderful! Well, I decided to bake a coffee cake last night and I just couldn't stop baking! I brought sugar cookies, banana bread, spice muffins, and some butter for the muffins."

"How nice of you!" Robbie said. "Everything smells wonderful!"

"Old habits die hard, I guess." Jean smiled sadly. "I always enjoyed baking little whatnots for headquarters at Christmas. It wouldn't have felt like the holiday season if I couldn't have done some baking for you this year. As for your question about Mitch," Jean went on, handing the foil-wrapped trays set in boxes to Robbie and another deputy offering his services, "he had a bad night, but he's sleeping this morning. He'd love hearing you call him Sheriff, but he hasn't been the sheriff for months now."

Eric rose from behind his desk and walked out to greet the woman with brown and gray hair cut unflatteringly short, a wool coat at least one size too big, and tired gray eyes. Marissa marveled at how the last few months had aged the sturdy, strong-boned woman. She knew Jean Farrell was in her late fifties, but she looked seventy. Last year that coat would probably have fit, but she'd insisted on taking care of her invalid husband herself and she'd lost weight.

Jean's face had always been remarkably smooth—the envy of women who frantically fought wrinkles—but now her cheeks had slightly shrunken and all of her facial skin looked like pale, crinkled crêpe paper. She'd never worn much makeup, but today she'd made a slapdash attempt with a dull mauve lipstick, which made her look gray. Soon the burden would be too much for Jean alone, Marissa thought, although the woman didn't seem to think anyone could care for her husband, Mitchell, as well as she could.

"It's good to see you, Jean," Eric said, smiling his small smile and shaking her thin hand. "I was meaning to drop by and visit Mitch last week, but I'm never certain when a good time is and I don't want to call and maybe wake him up."

"And I never know when he'll be having a good day for visitors, so I'm no help." Jean smiled ruefully, as if she *should* know when a man in the final stages of pancreatic cancer would be up to having guests. She also refused to get a cell phone so people could call the house without the chance of waking up Mitch.

Marissa had known Jean all of her life and admired her for being warmhearted, patient, and a lover of children, although she had none of her own since the death of her three-year-old daughter, Betsy, over twenty-four years ago. Jean never had another child, but she wasn't perpetually depressed or without a sense of humor. She kept herself busy, enjoyed doing things for other people, and seemed to love having Marissa stay with her when Annemarie took Catherine for her music lessons a couple of miles away from the Farrells' house.

Marissa remembered summers in her childhood when she'd faithfully "helped" Jean plant seeds and bulbs and listened to her explain all about the flowers, even telling Marissa their Latin names. Jean had made Marissa feel grown-up and had taken her mind off the fact that Catherine had some musical talent while Marissa had absolutely none. All of the Grays had been fond of Jean, and Jean's dying husband, Mitchell, was not only a cousin of Bernard Gray's but also one of his closest friends. As boys, they'd been nearly inseparable.

"I hear you're doing a fine job since Mitch had to leave," Jean said to Eric, whose family was also close to the Farrells. "I'm certain you'll be elected sheriff, and that will please Mitch so much."

An uncomfortable moment of silence spun out. Everyone present knew Mitch would be gone before election time. Marissa could feel the tension lessen when Eric smiled and said, "All I'm thinking about for the present is keeping up Mitch's standards."

Jean looked past Eric. "Hello, Catherine, Marissa." Her long, plain face solemn, she walked to Marissa and hugged her, her wool coat smelling of lavender, her signature scent. "I'm so sorry I couldn't come to see you yesterday, but the roads were still a mess and I couldn't get anyone to help me with Mitch . . ."

"You explained on the phone yesterday," Marissa said, hugging the woman closer. Jean felt as close to a mother as Marissa had now. "I really just needed sleep and your good wishes."

Jean held Marissa away from her. "Well, you look only slightly the worse for wear, but it must have been horrifying. I didn't tell Mitch. I just praised the Lord you managed to live through that ordeal."

"I wouldn't have if not for Eric," Marissa said with warm spontaneity, not caring that she caught a salacious grin on the face of Deputy Buddy Pruitt. How the rat-faced incompetent little man had held on to his job for nearly ten years she could never guess. "I was trapped by the seat belt and Eric pulled me out of the car just seconds before it slid into the river."

Jean looked appalled. "Good heavens, I didn't know *that*! And I heard you say Eric is going to make this a priority case." Jean smiled at Eric. "You deserve a medal, Eric."

"Just doing my duty," Eric mumbled, looking half-annoyed at Marissa and half-embarrassed by Jean's praise.

Jean's dulled eyes gazed at his red, lowered face and suddenly they twinkled. "I don't know what's happening to the Aurora Falls gossip mill, leaving out that we have a hero in our midst! Work will have to be done to get the grapevine back to par!"

"Well, not work by you," Tom said kindly. "You have too much on your plate already, Mrs. Farrell, taking care of Mitch and spending so much time trying to get the city to act on renovating that bad section of Falls Way. No offense to you, Miss Gray," he said, gesturing at Marissa with a spice muffin in his hand, "but the positive side of your wreck is that it brought more attention to the problem. They can have all the city council meetings they like about the matter, which you get a gold star for attending, Mrs. Farrell, but that wreck was front-page news!"

"The newspaper left out the most excitin' part, though. They didn't talk about the big old monster chasin' her," Buddy Pruitt drawled as he leaned over his desk and scraped dyed red sugar off his cookie onto white paper. From behind, his large ears looked almost perpendicular to his head. "Or I guess it was standin' in front of you, Marissa, then it chased you down the riverbank and Superman saved you just before the thing pushed your car in the river. Wow! They got somethin' in Point Pleasant, West Virginia, called Mothman. Guess now we've got Marissa's Monster!"

Every pair of eyes settled on Buddy, giggling and scraping at colored sugar on his cookie until he finally seemed to realize no one was laughing. He spun in his swivel chair, his prominent front teeth bared beneath a nearly nonexistent upper lip, looking around in mild confusion. Then his little eyes turned hard. "Guess no one around here has a sense of humor."

"No one has a sense of humor about a wreck," Jeff said, and turned away.

Jean gave Buddy a long, freezing look. "Buddy Pruitt, you should be ashamed of yourself!"

"You can be a real jerk, Buddy," Robbie said quietly.

Buddy glared at Robbie, and then looked at Eric. "You gonna let a *woman* talk to me like that?"

Eric paused as if he were giving the matter serious thought. Finally, he gazed calmly at Buddy and said, "Yes, I believe I am. Deputy Pruitt, why don't you find something more useful to do than scrape sugar off your cookie here at police headquarters? I think some people forgot to put money in their parking meters. The matter needs your attention, right away."

Buddy snorted, shot to his feet like a jack-in-the-box, grabbed his jacket, threw his audience a murderous glare, and headed for the front door. "Don't worry, Buddy. Something thrilling might happen," Jeff called. "I've heard *Dillon Archer* has come back to town."

Buddy hesitated for a breathless moment, then straightened his shoulders and slammed out of the building.

2

"I hate the car I just rented," Marissa announced.

"I thought you'd decided to stop acting like a whining child."

"I'm almost finished," Marissa said. "I just need about five more minutes. Did I tell you I hate the car you talked me into renting?"

Catherine smiled. "I know you do, but it's safe. It will be sort of like riding around in a little bank vault."

Marissa groaned. "Oh, that sounds sporty, Cathy." She knew Catherine hated the nickname Cathy. "It's not as if my Mustang can be repaired. It's a goner."

"Good. I'm glad," Catherine snapped in honor of the "Cathy."

"So I'm going to buy a new Mustang convertible as soon as I get my car insurance money." Marissa smiled. "Okay, I'm done.

Bad, whiny, childish Marissa has slipped back into the tunnels underground."

She sipped her white wine and looked out the restaurant windows at the panoramic view of Aurora Falls. "It's really nice of you to bring me out to lunch." Marissa looked at the pine-paneled walls, the small chandeliers with their scrolling bronze arms and cream-colored etched-glass globes, the Christmas tree decorated with colorful toy-like ornaments, the pine-encircled candles at each table. "Especially because you picked the Larke Inn."

"Even if the big dining room isn't open for lunch?"

"I wouldn't care if we had to eat in the kitchen. I love this place."

Catherine laughed. "I think you expect Sebastian Larke to come walking in and claim you as his one and only. Still have that mad crush on him?"

"It's dulled from an inferno to a simmer, but I fear he'll always be the only man for me," Marissa said dramatically.

Catherine gave her a knowing look. "I seriously doubt that. Anyway, you've had a rough weekend. I also thought after your session at police headquarters and because you haven't had a pain pill you might enjoy something to calm you down or lift your spirits, or whatever wine does for you."

"Both. I'm also very hungry."

"I'm sure you are," Catherine said casually as she dug into her garden salad, "especially after making that end run around Eric Montgomery by thanking him for making your investigation a *priority case* so Jean would hear. You know how close the Montgomerys have always been to Jean and Mitch, and I think Mitch considers Eric the son he never had. Eric will do just about anything not to let Jean down. That was a brilliant move," Catherine finished without approval.

"I know I wasn't fair to Eric. I'm thoroughly ashamed of myself."

"You don't look like it. You look like you're going to jump up on the table and do a tap dance."

Marissa laid down her salad fork, her smile fading. "Actually, I'm ambivalent. I *am* ashamed of taking advantage of Eric in an awkward situation, but I don't want my car wreck written off as the result of an icy road or careless driving. Somebody deliberately caused the wreck, someone dangerous, Catherine. Maybe it was just a prank—as I said, I don't know anyone who'd want to kill me. But this prankster had fun *and* he got away. I don't think the kind of person who did this to me will be satisfied with one success. Unless Eric catches him, he won't stop, and maybe the next person won't be as lucky as I was. Is it so terrible of me to use any means I can to stop another accident or maybe even a death?"

The tightness in Catherine's face slowly eased. She took a drink of her own wine, glanced out the window at the falls, then looked at Marissa. "Okay. I don't approve of your method, but I understand why you ambushed Eric. Don't push him too hard, though, Marissa. He's got a lot on his mind with Mitch Farrell dying."

"I know. He always admired Mitch so much. When he majored in criminal justice and went to Philadelphia, he had visions of bringing some of Mitch's ways to a police force in a city of over a million people."

Catherine nodded. Then she picked up her fork and looked down at her salad for a moment before asking almost reluctantly, "Marissa, how do you feel about seeing Eric again? You can tell me to mind my own business . . ."

"But I won't. You spent hours talking with me, trying to cheer me up, after Eric broke off our engagement. Naturally, you're concerned." Marissa paused, frowning. "Honestly, I don't know how I feel. When he said he was coming to our house Saturday night to take my statement, at first I was too shaken by the wreck to feel much about him. After we got home, I felt awkward. I could hardly look at him." Catherine glanced up and Marissa looked at her earnestly. "But he's changed so much, he's like a different person, Catherine. This morning I realized I didn't feel the old hurt that stayed with me for so long. Is that weird?"

Catherine smiled. "In all my years of school I've never been taught what exactly constitutes 'weird.' Personally, I think it's both understandable and positive. Have you spent any time with Eric since Gretchen's death?"

Marissa drew a sharp breath. "It still upsets me to hear anyone mention Gretchen's 'death.' Dillon Archer *murdered* her. Even though he never stood trial, was never even arrested, I saw it happen."

Catherine frowned. "Do you think Dillon *might* be in town?"

Marissa tried to speak in a nonchalant voice, although her pulse had quickened. "You know rumors spark up every six months. No, I'm not worried. I don't think he'd dare come here—at least not for a long time."

"Or with Eric Montgomery acting as sheriff."

"One of the last things Eric said to me before he broke our engagement was that he knew I was right—Dillon had murdered Gretchen. He was in that church, too. He just couldn't see as well as I could. He trusted my version of events, though." Marissa took a small bite of salad, thinking. "You asked me if I've spent any time with Eric after Gretchen's murder. The answer is no. Not even immediately after the murder."

"How was that possible?" Catherine asked.

"After someone called the police and the Montgomerys, the rest of the night on Gray's Island was complete confusion. Eric's parents were hysterical—he stayed with them. We were giving informal statements to the police and the next day we gave our formal statements. I called Eric and he sounded so distant, almost dazed. I offered to help prepare for the wake, but he said no.

"He didn't speak to me at the wake," Marissa continued. "His parents looked like stone figures and barely spoke to me. Then I noticed they barely spoke to Eric, either. That seemed so strange. I would have thought after losing one child, they'd cling to him. Instead, they seemed to be shunning him."

"They were probably blaming him for what happened," Catherine said softly. "They expected him to take care of Gretchen as if she were a toddler. It wasn't fair."

"No, it wasn't. But he tried his damnedest." Marissa took a sip of wine. "And then . . ." Marissa felt the sting of tears rising in her eyes. "And then Eric came to our house three—exactly three—hours after the funeral and told me he didn't want me anymore."

"He didn't say *that*."

"No. He was courteous and that hurt more. He said he'd decided we were too young, we needed time to recover from Gretchen's death . . . I said we could postpone for six months, even a year, but he said *no*, it would be better to go our separate ways. I tried to give him the ring and he wouldn't take it, so I grabbed his hand and stuck the ring in it. He just looked at me and the man I saw behind those beautiful brown eyes was not the man I'd fallen in love with years ago. Then he walked away."

"So, since Gretchen's death, he's slowly been changing into the man he is now and you never had even one talk with him. Marissa, people told you he'd changed, but that isn't the same as actually facing it—facing him. I believe that's why you weren't terribly uncomfortable in his presence Saturday or today—he was Chief Deputy Montgomery, not your Eric."

"Well, if it isn't the Gray girls!" Neither woman had noticed the mayor's son, Wilfred "Will" Addison, approach them. He wore a long blue and coffee brown wool scarf with his camel hair coat, dark wash jeans, and a navy blue V-neck sweater over a pale blue shirt. His wavy brown hair fell in the deceptively casual cut that cost a fortune, and the skin on his slender, elegant face was almost as taut at twenty-seven as it had been at sixteen, except for the tissue paper crinkles beginning around his eyes.

Will's features were faultless from the high forehead to the straight nose, Marissa thought vaguely, yet she didn't remember him setting female hearts racing when they were younger. Was it because he went to private schools and acted slightly superior to those not in his social class? Or was something missing in that perfect face? Strength? Genuine animation? A smile that usually never reached his dark gray eyes?

"How great you both look," Will went on without a pause for one of them to speak. "Yes, even you, Marissa. A puffy nose and bruised eyes can't ruin that pretty face!" His smile disappeared. "Seriously, I felt awful when I heard about the wreck. What a horrible experience, but thank God you escaped relatively unscathed. I tried to send flowers the next day, but the damned florist won't deliver on Sunday."

"It's the thought that counts," Marissa said.

An awkward silence followed before Catherine asked, "Why don't you join us if you're not meeting anyone?"

A look of relief, rather than pleasure, flashed in Will's eyes. "I have no lunch date, which seemed unfortunate until I stumbled across the loveliest ladies in Aurora Falls. I'd love to join you."

Will whisked off his coat with flare, sat down beside Catherine, immediately signaled a waiter, and ordered a martini. Then Will grinned mischievously at Marissa. "You should know you've sent Mother into a real tailspin. You ruined her party—no newspaper story, no pictures for the *Gazette*, and word of your wreck reached the gala about an hour into the festivities. First the mood fell to the floor, and then people began leaving. She's mad as hell at you, Marissa, but she can't say so without sounding like a heartless bitch."

"Oh, what a quandary," Marissa mourned in exaggeration.

"Isn't it? The troubles that woman has! But Mother always carries on."

Marissa and Catherine laughed, although they couldn't miss the sarcastic edge beneath Will's banter. Evelyn Addison's suffocating love of her son, as well as his resentment of her, was no secret.

Will looked at Catherine. "You're more gorgeous every time I see you. What, or should I say *who*, is new with you?"

Catherine's lips parted slightly and her cheeks grew pink. Both sisters immediately knew Will had heard about Catherine's date with James Eastman, and they guessed Will's next comment would concern him.

Marissa jumped to the rescue: "Poor Catherine has been so busy taking care of me that she hasn't had time for anything else. She's really been a saint, Will. I don't know what I would have done without her. This morning she went with me to police headquarters so I could give my formal statement about what happened."

"Oh, that must have been fun." His bright smile quivered before blazing back to life. "How is our humorless chief deputy?"

"Fine. And Eric can be charming if he forces himself."

Catherine, who so far had done nothing but smile, suddenly began talking: "Will, when we were at headquarters, we heard something disturbing. Do you know anything about Dillon Archer being back in town?"

The color fled from Will's face as he raised his eyebrows. "No. Did Eric say Dillon was here?"

"No. Jeff Beal," Catherine said as Will reached for his martini before the waiter had time to set it on the table. "He's a deputy. He just told Buddy he'd heard Dillon was back in town."

"Dillon Archer back in Aurora Falls—it's just damned silly!" Will said loudly. "My God, this is the last place he'd come unless he's gone crazy. Why would this Jeff person even say that to Buddy?"

Marissa watched Will gulp a third of his martini. "Buddy, as usual, made some remarks he thought were funny. I suppose Jeff's had enough of him and shot back a remark about Dillon Archer being back in town."

Immediately Will's expression relaxed slightly. "Oh. Well, that explains things. Jeff wanted to embarrass him. No one has forgotten that Buddy was supposed to be watching Dillon and the idiot let Dillon talk him into going out fishing." Will took another sip of his martini and smiled crookedly. "So poor old Buddy got knocked unconscious with a paddle by Dillon before he dived into the river never to be seen again. Buddy Pruitt will *never* live down that one!"

"A lot of people think Mitch Farrell should have already arrested Dillon when that happened," Catherine said.

"Farrell hadn't arrested Dillon because he didn't have any hard evidence against him," Will answered sharply.

"He had my sister's formal statement."

Color flooded back to Will's cheeks. "Yeah, what Marissa claimed she saw." Catherine gave him a hard stare. "I mean I know Marissa was sure of what she saw, but as I remember, things were mixed up with Tonya what's-her-name saying she saw something else and—hell! It was a long time ago. I don't remember all the details and I didn't mean to imply anything bad about you, Marissa. I'm just babbling—" Will's suddenly desperate gaze circled the dining room. "Hey, there's Kenny Wicks. I haven't seen him in like . . . forever." Will rose, grabbing for his coat and the martini glass. "It was great talking to you girls. Well, Merry Christmas and all that stuff!"

Marissa and Catherine watched as Will hurried across the room, carelessly ruffling a few women's well-coiffed hair with the coat thrown over his arm. He reached the table where Kenny Wicks sat with an attractive blonde, smiled for all he was worth, and sat down with them. Neither Kenny nor the blonde looked pleased.

"Will used to be so charming—almost debonair," Catherine said. "I haven't been around him much the last ten years, but he's lost a lot of that sophistication."

"Too much alcohol doesn't improve anyone's urbanity, and I know he's been hitting the booze since his late teens and even harder after Gretchen's death," Marissa said.

"I know they dated for a while. Even Evelyn approved of Gretchen for her darling Will."

Marissa shook her head. "They were close for a few months after Gretchen's death last Christmas." Marissa lowered her voice: "He was her first lover. To her, that meant marriage in the future. But she worried about his drinking, which only increased toward spring. She told me their evenings together would start out fine and end with him either stumbling out the door or maundering about things not being his fault and saying, 'I'm sorry; I'm sorry.' "

"Sorry for what?"

"Gretchen didn't know and he never gave any hints. She was worried about him, though. She wanted him to see a psychologist and do something about his drinking. She seemed almost frantic. I had no doubt she was in love with him and afraid he might do something to himself, accidentally or on purpose." Marissa shook her head. "Then out of the blue, she broke up with him and started seeing Dillon."

"She might have been running from what she thought was Will's self-destruction and started dating Dillon as a way of shaking up Will. As I remember, Will was almost as anti-Dillon as Eric. Maybe she thought Will would try to help himself rather than losing her or seeing her with Dillon Archer."

"I guess so. Will did seem to care for her. He wasn't passionately in love with her—at least I don't think so—but when I saw them together he was always tender and affectionate. And if she'd had just a few weeks longer, she might have had a positive effect on him. Unfortunately . . ."

Catherine looked over at him speculatively. Half of the people in the room glanced at the table of Kenny Wicks and his blond companion, whom Will was embarrassing with a loud voice and flourishing arm movements. "Well, I think he's already on his second martini today and it won't be his last."

"Jeff rattled Buddy by saying Dillon's back and we rattled Will by repeating it." Marissa paused thoughtfully. "Strange. When they heard Dillon might be in town, they each looked almost afraid."

3

Buddy Pruitt slumped through the movie theater lobby, looked at the posters promising him this movie would be a laugh riot, and wondered if *anyone anywhere* had even worked up a giggle during the one hour and fifty minutes of film. Well, that one guy in aisle five laughed constantly for the first twenty minutes, but the theater manager removed him when he spotted the guy raising a liquor flask to his mouth. With the exception of Mr. Entertainment, everyone else had seemed to be in the same state of mind as Buddy:

Crummy.

He thought it must be because he'd seen Marissa Gray today. Buddy hadn't liked her since Marissa was sixteen. They'd been at Tonya Ward's eighteenth birthday party. Tonya hadn't invited Buddy—Dillon had just dragged him along. Buddy hadn't been able to keep his eyes off Marissa with her long blondish hair and velvet low-slung jeans and sparkly T-shirt. She'd gotten close to him and he smelled her perfume, which proved the final blow for Buddy's self-control.

Buddy had grabbed Marissa and kissed her. In return, she'd smacked him so hard he'd slipped and fallen on the floor. Everyone laughed and it was the first time Dillon had gotten mad at Buddy—*really* mad. Buddy hadn't known Dillon liked Marissa—Dillon sometimes dated Tonya, but not Marissa. Anyway, afterward Buddy had felt bitter whenever he thought about Marissa, and he still thought about her a lot.

Yes, it was seeing Marissa that made him feel the way he did tonight, he decided. She'd come strutting into police headquarters in her fur coat, not speaking to him, acting like the whole world should stop for her . . .

Buddy closed his eyes and sighed. Even his thoughts wouldn't give him peace. Probably no one even remembered his burst of unbridled lust so long ago, he admitted to himself. He was upset because Jeff's young voice echoed relentlessly in his mind: "I've heard *Dillon Archer* has come back to town." Dillon Archer. Dillon Archer. How Buddy wished he'd never heard that name.

But he had. He'd heard the name; he'd called Dillon friend. Dear God, Buddy had considered Dillon Archer his *first* friend. Maybe Grandpa was right, Buddy thought. Maybe I haven't gotten more out of life because I don't know up from down.

Worse, maybe I haven't gotten more out of life because I don't deserve it.

Buddy jammed his hands into his pockets and tried not to shiver as he started toward home. He'd walked to work this morning, called home and lied to his mother, telling her that he had to work late, then gone alone to the movie. Spending every evening with her was becoming more than he could bear. The fact that he was twenty-seven and still living with his mother was bad—really bad when his mother clung like she did—but she was so alone. So was he, for that matter. He'd never had many friends. He hadn't had *any* friends until Dillon Archer had come along.

Buddy had been twelve when he'd met Dillon. He'd sweated through a dorky elementary school graduation ceremony feeling like a fool when his mother clapped madly for him as he scuttled across the stage in his paper graduation cap and gown and picked up a diploma printed on a school secretary's computer.

His grandfather had come with Buddy's mother. Buddy couldn't figure out why Grandpa had wanted to attend until the Old Man began snickering, muttering, and then outright laughing when Buddy crossed the stage. Bastard, Buddy had thought, his cheeks bright red. Grandpa had only come to embarrass him. Other people tried and failed to ignore the old geezer sneering and snorting at his ugly little illegitimate grandson, and Buddy had wished with all his heart God would strike him dead.

Then Buddy had seen Dillon Archer—unusually handsome and poised for an adolescent—sitting in the audience like a young prince and looking at Buddy's grandfather as if he were a squirming maggot. Like magic, on that beautiful day some of Grandpa's power to hurt Buddy had drifted away like foul air.

Now, a cold gust of wind lifted Buddy's overly thick hair that would never naturally lie against his scalp. After many experiments throughout the years, he'd learned longer top hair worked best for him. Every morning after his shower, he carefully massaged in heavy-duty hair gel, placed three long metal clips on the top hair and two clips on his particularly rebellious cowlick to hold everything in place, blew it dry, then left in the clips another ten minutes for a firm set.

One morning he'd been in a rush, forgotten to remove the clips, and worn them to work. Everyone at headquarters had fallen into hysterical laughter. Everyone except Eric Montgomery. With his own thick, loose curly hair, he'd simply muttered, "Getting my hair into any kind of shape is a pain, too. That's why I don't even try. It would be easier if you and I would just shave our heads, Buddy." Then Eric had gone on working without even the twitch of a smile. Dillon had usually been nice to Buddy, but to his surprise, sometimes Eric was nice, too.

Buddy turned down Oak Lane, which he'd always liked with its huge, billowing oak trees that everyone wanted to cut down because the trees shed literally thousands of leaves in the fall. This past autumn Buddy had taken about twenty photographs of the trees in their colorful glory—golden, dark purple, copper, lime, and yellow-edged emerald green. He'd taken four shots of his favorite tree—a huge old oak whose leaves had turned a uniform burnt orange. In the late afternoon autumn sky, the tree looked brilliantly aflame. His mother, Bea, had put them in an album she'd been keeping since he was thirteen titled "Buddy's Photograph Album" and she looked at them every night, marveling over his talent.

Not that anyone respected Bea Pruitt's opinion of talent, and with good reason. Intellectual matters were not Bea's strong point. Although Buddy loved his mother, he'd known since childhood she was sweet, kind, dumb, and silly. She dithered through her small circle of the world oblivious to her low intelligence and lack of perception. Luckily, other people's poor opinion of Bea's brainpower did not hurt her, because she simply didn't feel it. Unkind actions, judgments, and even subtle insults simply passed by her. She rarely left the house, but within its dingy walls she was usually smiling and happy. She didn't even sound bitter when she told seven-year-old Buddy she'd wanted to name him after her father, who had less than politely refused the compliment. Grandpa's attempt to wound Bea hadn't worked. Instead, she had cheerfully named her son after her beloved girlhood dog.

Another gust of wind blew up and Buddy felt it lifting his stiff hair like a banner. He automatically pushed down the hair, but it didn't matter. Large, lovely nineteenth-century houses once had lined the street. Most people had abandoned the houses after a flood twelve years ago, and hardly anyone lived here. Sometimes looking at the formerly opulent homes made Buddy sad; other times, he fantasized that his father had lived in a house like one of these in its prime.

Buddy had no idea who had fathered him. His mother told him the story of a handsome, charming, extremely rich man who'd fallen madly in love with her where she worked. She'd never explained why this wealthy ideal of manhood was shopping in the sewing department of Walmart, but she claimed their romance was short, sweet, intense, and he'd asked her to marry him. Supposedly, he had died in a plane crash only a month before they were to wed. She said his family did not communicate with her and Buddy because they'd wanted their son to marry a rich girl, and Buddy always acted as if he believed every word of her fairy tale.

They lived with Buddy's widowed grandfather, who had made every day of Buddy's life a misery. He was whip thin, leathery skinned, and had the conscienceless eyes of an alligator. Buddy had always suspected the man had two sets of eyelids. He'd nearly forbidden the boy to have friends, not that anyone wanted to be friends with Buddy anyway. Then Dillon had walked up to Buddy at the sixth-grade graduation and introduced himself. Grandpa had glared for all he was worth and Buddy had found it astounding that one fiery glance from Dillon's brilliant blue eyes weakened the confidence of his grandfather's gaze.

Buddy couldn't believe it when Dillon had asked him if he'd like to walk around and get acquainted. Buddy had followed like a frightened puppy. They'd eaten potato chips and drunk some vile punch. Dillon had explained he'd attended the ceremony because his father—Isaac Archer—had a niece who'd also successfully made it through the sixth grade.

Then Dillon had asked if the next day Buddy would like to see a tree house he and his older brother, Andrew, were building. Buddy had found being in Dillon's presence a bit heady, not only because he was so good-looking but also because Dillon was thirteen, an actual *teenager*, and already a student at the middle school, but the boys had become friends.

Guiltily Buddy now looked at his watch. He'd spent a lot of time driving around in a patrol car this afternoon, blowing off steam, and after the movie he'd walked with lagging steps toward home. Bea would be upset that he'd missed the first ten minutes of the reality show about fifteen people living in one apartment and fighting all the time. She loved television.

At least now, though, his mother could stay up as long as she wanted to, watching one inane TV show after another. Her father had forced her to go upstairs to bed at nine o'clock the same as Buddy, even when Bea was in her thirties. Grandpa had gone to bed whenever he pleased, but he had invariably crept back down the stairs to have at least one shot of whiskey, although publicly he violently disapproved of drinking.

Then had come the evening Grandpa had gotten furious with Bea. Earlier, when cleaning a cabinet, she'd dropped and broken his bottle of bourbon during the day and didn't have enough money to buy a replacement. When Grandpa discovered she'd destroyed nearly a full bottle of bourbon, he'd punched her in the face. Buddy had lunged at his grandfather and nearly knocked him down.

In return, he had marched up to Buddy's tiny bedroom, collected his little sketchbook full of Buddy's execrable but heartfelt drawings, his one volume about photography, and his small notebook with the few dreadfully bad poems Buddy had labored over for months. The man had carried it all to the backyard and burned it, making Bea and Buddy stand and watch.

Buddy now closed his eyes for a moment, remembering that day as if it had happened last week. Then he heard noises behind him and he jerked around to see a half-broken tree limb creaking in the stiff breeze that propelled crackly dried oak leaves down the street. Buddy shuddered slightly, then laughed aloud to reassure himself he was being imaginative and silly.

Almost against his will, his mind returned to that awful day so long ago when Grandpa had set fire to Buddy's most precious possessions. Buddy hadn't turned to Bea, who'd stood in helpless devastation. He'd run to Dillon. At first Buddy had been reluctant to tell Dillon the things Grandpa had burned—it all sounded so girly—but when he'd finally spilled all the details Dillon hadn't laughed. Buddy would never forget that far-off look in Dillon's intensely blue eyes when he had said, "This time the Old Man has pushed the limit." Buddy'd had no idea what Dillon meant, but then often he didn't. He'd just accepted that Dillon had a superior mind and would always know the right way to handle difficult matters.

The day after Grandpa had burned Buddy's treasures, he hadn't been able to get out of the house fast enough. June had come again and he didn't have school. He'd pulled on cutoff jeans and a T-shirt and, still barefoot, hurried for the stairs, scraping his ankle on the sharp hinge once used for a baby gate. He hadn't even noticed his bleeding ankle until he got outside and saw Dillon. Dillon's sharp eyes had honed in on the dripping blood and Buddy had explained what had happened. They'd used toilet paper from the gasoline station restroom to clean the wound, and neither had mentioned it again.

Then, around four when Buddy had to go home, Dillon gave him that long, intense look of his and said, "I've thought about the Old Man and I've decided what we're going to do about him." Dillon explained his plan. It sounded good at the time. Buddy had agreed to everything Dillon had wanted him to do, and for a couple of days he'd actually felt powerful. Let the Old Man say or do what he wanted, Buddy had thought swaggeringly. He and Dillon Archer were going to take care of him.

Buddy's grandfather drove a delivery truck, and on Wednesdays he had a longer route and more heavy equipment to unload at various stores. He always came home late, worse tempered than usual, and he went to bed early. At ten o'clock Buddy had heard Grandpa clump up the stairs, go to his bedroom, and slam the door.

For nearly an hour Buddy had lain still, almost rigid, listening to his old-fashioned alarm clock loudly tick away the last minutes of Grandpa's life. After he'd heard Grandpa begin to snore, Buddy slid from his bed and slowly opened his bedroom door he hadn't completely closed.

He'd fought the urge to run down the hall. If he was merely walking and his grandfather opened his door, Buddy could say he was going to the bathroom. He'd wanted to run, though, because the hallway felt completely alien—cold on a summer night full of shadows and the essence of . . . evil. He'd stopped short. He now realized his conscience had been talking to him. Why hadn't he listened?

But back then, he'd closed his mind to *all* thoughts and tiptoed to the top of the stairs. He held a strong length of hemp twine Dillon had gotten, boasting it was 170-pound natural-colored hemp. Some twine was dyed blue or red and would leave marks that could do them in, Dillon had said ominously. Buddy had merely listened, owl eyed.

That awful night, shaking, his breath coming hard and fast, Buddy had tied one end of the twine around the hinge for the baby gate and the other end about two inches above the floor on the newel post. Then he'd cat-walked to his room.

Buddy's old clock had ticked away another seventy minutes before Grandpa's snoring grew more irregular, he emitted the horrid hacking, gurgling sound that had always made Buddy shudder, then he groaned as he climbed out of bed. Grandpa had opened his door and walked heavily down the dark hall. He never turned on the hall light.

The sound of Grandpa's banging, clattering, bone-breaking, crashing descent down those stairs would stay with Buddy for the rest of his life. Grandpa hadn't screamed or shouted. He'd always worn just undershorts to bed, and tonight he hadn't even bothered with a robe. He'd landed on his back with his long bare, skinny legs sprawled up the steps. Buddy had slunk down the stairway and looked into his grandfather's face. The man's mouth had gaped and his yellowish eyes had been open and unblinking. "Thank you, God," Buddy had whispered. "It's finally over."

Then Grandpa had moaned.

5

1

Even now, Buddy shuddered violently at the memory. He'd almost screamed when his grandfather moaned, his body still motionless but a flicker of awareness in his pale eyes. That's when Dillon had stepped out of the closet not ten feet away. Buddy had nearly screamed again, but Dillon had moved with the speed of a panther, put a hand over Buddy's mouth, and said, "Don't be afraid. I've been here ever since you were eating dinner." He'd smiled kindly and said in an almost hypnotic voice, "I wanted to be with you in case anything went wrong. I'll take care of you, Buddy."

Dillon had glanced up the stairs. "Where's your mother? Didn't she hear the Old Man fall?"

Buddy, trembling and dripping sweat, shook his head no. He had taken a couple of shallow breaths and managed, "Sleeps like the dead." That did it. He'd almost fainted at using Grandpa's phrase, but Dillon had shaken him and said, "Hold on. I *need* you."

Dillon Archer needing Buddy was probably the only thing in the world powerful enough to have made him keep himself from slipping into a peaceful faint. He'd nodded to Dillon and rubbed his wet hands on his pajama bottoms. He and Dillon had leaned over Grandpa and peered into his eyes. The Old Man had blinked, and Buddy rocked back onto his bottom. He couldn't tell if Grandpa had recognized him or Dillon, but the man's gaze seemed to shift slightly, fearfully, toward Dillon.

Buddy's heart had been beating so hard it hurt his ribs, but Dillon seemed unfazed. With remarkable concentration, he had watched a rivulet of blood run from the corner of the Old Man's dry lips to his chin before he'd croaked, "Help me."

Dillon had looked at the Old Man calmly and said, "Okay." Then Dillon had taken Grandpa's head in his hands, lifted it slightly, and jerk-twisted it so fast Buddy wouldn't have known what he saw if he hadn't heard bone snap. "There now." Dillon had sounded satisfied. "You're not in pain anymore, Old Man, and you can't cause Buddy pain anymore, either. I call that fair and square."

Buddy had been too shocked to utter a sound. He'd sat rigid when Dillon looked directly into his eyes and said gently, "This seals our friendship for life." When Buddy didn't answer, Dillon asked louder, "Well, doesn't it?"

Buddy had nodded.

Dillon was all business. "Take the hemp off the hook and the post. Make sure *every* strand of hemp is off that hook. Then flush it down the commode. *Don't* forget to flush it—it's incriminating evidence. Go back to bed. When the cops come, act surprised, but don't scream and cry and all that crap. Everyone knows you hated him. You'd be overacting and they'd think something was suspicious. Got all that?"

Buddy had nodded again.

"Okay, then." Dillon had stood up, peeked out a front window, and decided to make his escape. He'd opened the door, stepped onto the porch, looked back into Buddy's frightened eyes, and smiled. "Remember, this makes us pals for life. Friends *never* tell on each other," he'd said softly with just an undercurrent of menace. "Don't ever forget it."

So Buddy had carefully removed the hemp, checked the hook to make certain he'd left no strands, flushed the twine, gone to bed, and numbly lay awake until his mother screamed. He'd called Emergency Services because Bea was so frenzied she couldn't put together a comprehensible sentence, and when the ambulance came Buddy had acted shocked but not grief stricken. Later, Grandpa's death had been ruled an accident, and Buddy Pruitt had lived in fear and guilt the rest of his life.

Now, fourteen years later, Buddy still awakened from nightmares about Grandpa lying stretched out on those stairs saying, "Help me." No one in town except Bea mourned the old man after his death. Only Dillon had come to the funeral with Bea and Buddy. Buddy didn't hear a word the minister said. Grandpa's moan and the sound of Dillon snapping the old man's neck echoed so loudly in Buddy's mind he could hear nothing else.

Like now. True, it was almost nine thirty at night on a little-traveled street, but usually when he walked this street at night he could still hear a few birds chirping before they bedded down. Sounds from elsewhere also drifted over—sirens, the whistle of the nine-thirty train, at this time of year stores blasting Christmas carols out to the street. Now there was nothing—nothing except newly fallen dead leaves crackling as the bitter wind drove them over the remains of snow and ice. They sounded remarkably like bones snapping. Like Grandpa's neck snapping.

Buddy shivered but decided looking around would indicate, if only to himself, that he was frightened. Dillon Archer—damn him—wouldn't be frightened. Much as he hated it, Dillon was still Buddy's model of fearlessness and bravura. So, Buddy merely lowered his head and picked up his pace, although his heart beat faster and a feeling of cold, dark dread washed through him.

Suddenly an arm encircled Buddy's neck, yanked him sharply backward and fiery pain shot up his back. His vision dimmed as the pain branched out, scorching, raging, running rampant throughout his body, sending him to his knees. His skinny frame shook, and something twisted deep within him, tearing organs, grating against his ribs, sending a torrent of warm blood down the flesh of his back and past the belt that surrounded his small waist.

Buddy tried to scream, but the arm held his throat so tightly, all he could do was whimper. That's all I could ever do, he thought distantly as the gouging and tearing continued inside him. That's all I was ever good for, he thought with fuzzy sadness whispering through the pain. A whimper.

He felt as if he was being dragged; then someone unzipped his jacket and a hand darted inside, maybe looking for something, maybe leaving something ... he wasn't certain ... and then left his jacket partly open. Buddy waited a few moments, then tried to get to his knees, thinking his attacker had left, but the effort was too great and he collapsed. Someone snickered. He looked up and saw no one, but he realized he was beneath the tree that glowed glorious burnt orange in the autumn. He closed his eyes and dreamily pictured his mother's face—bovine and full of love. Finally someone beside him spoke:

"Say hello to Grandpa, Buddy. He's waiting for you."

2

The bedside phone rang and Marissa, hanging on the cliff edge of sleep, groaned and answered.

"You kilt him!" a woman screeched. "You *murdered* him because you always expected him to act like you're some kind of princess, and when he wouldn't you *kilt* my poor Buddy!"

Marissa lay in stunned silence for a moment before looking at the caller ID. *Unknown 555-3476.* "Who is this?" she asked.

"It's Bea. Who else would it be?"

Marissa blinked several times and focused on the clock by her bed. Two fifteen. A woman had a nightmare and simply picked up her phone and began punching numbers, Marissa thought, her shock fading. "I'm sorry, ma'am, but I think you have the wrong number."

"I'm Bea Pruitt and I don't have the wrong number. It's right here! He was carryin' it on a piece of paper close to his heart!" She broke into heart-twisting sobs. "It's got your name and phone number on it. *Marissa Gray,* it says. I heard when you came to see the sheriff today Buddy made a joke and you threw a fit. You tried to hit him. You threatened to kill him! Maybe he was gonna call and apologize to you or maybe he was meetin' you and that's why he didn't get home in time for our favorite TV show.

"Anyway, I know who you are. You're that doctor's daughter who works at the newspaper," Bea continued. "Your mama was nice to me a couple of times, so he and me went to your mama's funeral, and I saw you. You're the mean one with blonde hair that hit him a long time ago. Today he teased you and you got so mad that you kilt him tonight! You're not as smart as you think you are, though. I watch murder shows, so I know about evidence. You left murder evidence right on him and I'm gonna give it to the police as soon as they get here and then your goose is cooked!" She drew a deep breath and choked out, "My poor Buddy!"

Marissa's hand tightened on the phone as realization dawned. "Are you talking about Buddy Pruitt?"

"How many men named Buddy did you kill tonight?"

Marissa sat up in bed, her stomach clenching. "My God, Buddy Pruitt has been murdered?"

"Don't you take the Lord's name in vain and don't you even *try* to sound innocent. You can't fool me. You won't fool the police!"

For a moment Marissa's mind went blank. Buddy Pruitt had been murdered? Why? How? *Where?* Finally, she knew what to ask. "Ms. Pruitt, where are you calling me from?"

"I'm with Buddy. I wouldn't leave him all alone! I'm with him here at his favorite tree. You knew it was his favorite tree, didn't you? He must have told you sometime. Maybe he gave you a picture of it when it turned all orange in October?"

"What tree, Ms. Pruitt? Where is the tree?"

The woman began talking vaguely, recalling the earlier hours of the night. "When he didn't come home tonight and our TV show was on, I knew somethin' was wrong. I waited till after midnight and then I came out lookin' for him. I don't usually come out at night—I get lost. But I had to find Buddy. I walked awhile and then I thought about his favorite tree here on Oak

Lane." Ms. Pruitt sniffled. "I found him layin' almost right beside it in the big mess of moldy leaves mixed with snow where you'd tried to hide him. So we're here. Just me and Buddy by his tree," she ended miserably.

Marissa's mouth had gone dry. She asked gently, "Ms. Pruitt, are you using your cell phone?"

"No. I don't need one of those. I'm usin' Buddy's. It was layin' a ways from him, but I found it. Then it took me a while to figure out how to use it even though Buddy's shown me a bunch of times, but I finally called nine-one-one like Buddy told me to do if there was ever any trouble. And then I found that piece of paper with your name and phone number—" She choked on more sobs. "That paper's got blood—my Buddy's blood—on it, but I could still see the writin'. You didn't count on me havin' such good eyes, did you? But it's too late for you just like it's too late for Buddy." Bea's voice trembled. "The police are on their way!"

"I'm certain they are. You stay put, Ms. Pruitt. Don't wander off—stay with Buddy."

"Don't wander off! You think I'd leave my little boy all bloody . . . and dead . . . in a mess of leaves . . . He's so cold . . . He was comin' home to me, but before he could get there—"

Ms. Pruitt broke the connection. Marissa drew a deep breath, reached for the glass of water she always kept by her bedside, and drained it. By this time, Lindsay had jumped up on the bed and, sensing Marissa's tension, had brought her a toy rooster for comfort. Marissa put the rooster on her lap and pulled Lindsay close to her while she dialed 911. Marissa identified herself and explained the situation, verifying that a woman had called for assistance on Oak Lane and an ambulance should arrive shortly.

Marissa then called Andrew Archer, editor of the *Gazette*, and gave him the information. "I'll go immediately," he said, and Marissa heard his wife, Tonya, protesting in cranky sleepiness. Andrew seemed to ignore her. "You stay home, Marissa. You don't officially begin work again until tomorrow."

"It *is* tomorrow, Andrew, and I'll meet you on Oak Lane."

Twenty minutes later, wearing jeans, a heavy sweater, boots, and a down-filled coat, Marissa left a note for Catherine, who'd apparently taken the phone extension out of her bedroom and hadn't heard the call. Marissa simply wrote:

There's been an accident on Oak Lane. Andrew and I are going to the scene. I'll be back as soon as I can.

She picked up her notebook, tote bag, and tape recorder and turned on a living room light, although a family room lamp burned as well. Maybe the lights wouldn't fool anyone into thinking people at the Gray house were sitting up alert and prepared to face down a killer, but she didn't want to leave Catherine obliviously asleep and alone in the house. Lindsay was not a trained watchdog, but Marissa knew she would begin barking if anyone tried to enter the house. Marissa locked the front door and dashed to her rental car.

Ms. Pruitt had said she and Buddy were at his favorite tree on Oak Lane. Marissa had no idea which tree on Oak Lane was Buddy's favorite, but as soon as she turned onto the narrow street she saw the swirling red lights of an ambulance and a police patrol car. She parked half a block away from the scene, not wanting to get in anyone's way or call attention to herself and be ordered to leave.

Marissa carefully walked on the dirty ice and snow, not yet removed by street cleaners because of Oak Lane's nearly non-existent traffic. As she neared a patrol car, she heard a woman's wails cutting through the noise of police speaking loudly and chatter coming from official radios.

"No, I *won't* let go of him. Don't you even *try* to make me let go of him! Didn't you hear me? He's my boy—my Buddy! My poor, poor little Buddy!"

Portable lights turned the scene a startling blue-white. Two police officers drove stakes into the cold ground and attached yellow tape, but their efforts to preserve the crime scene were useless. A plump woman Marissa knew must be Bea Pruitt crawled frantically on the bloody snow around her son, pulling down the tape, scuttling back to the body, clawing and swatting at anyone who came near, ignoring pleas for her to let officials examine Buddy for evidence.

"You don't need to put your rough hands all over my boy lookin' for clues!" she yelled, her face smeared with Buddy's blood. "I've already done it nice and gentle." She waved something small, limp, and white at them. "That trashy blond Marissa Gray kilt my boy. Here's your evidence. Her name and phone number. She might as well have left her callin' card. You go put her in jail and stop tryin' to poke and prod at Buddy. And don't you *dare* take pictures of him like this! He'd die of shame and my poor boy's been through enough today!"

Marissa came to a halt as horror washed through her. Bea Pruitt looked like an animal pitifully trying to protect her injured young from relentless predators surrounding her. Marissa had never met Bea and didn't like Buddy, but the pathos of the scene filled her eyes with tears and made her want to run back to the peace and comfort of her home, away from the bloody snow, the crazed woman, and the crumpled body of Buddy Pruitt, who looked much smaller in death than in life.

Mesmerized by the dreadful scene, Marissa didn't see Andrew Archer walk up to her. "I told you to stay home."

"And you knew I wouldn't." Marissa looked up at Andrew. He'd changed dramatically since those days when he and Dillon had gone out on the *Annemarie*. Andrew was no longer all long, clumsy arms and legs and big, naïve blue eyes in an unnaturally pale face. He wore his light hair in a stylish, if conservative, cut, not the unflattering crew cut he used to sport, and his body looked trim and yet fit, as if he worked out. The last few years had hardened his face. He now had cheekbones, a stronger jawline, and a look of experience in those formerly innocent eyes. "This is awful," Marissa said, unable to keep the distress from her voice. "That poor woman. What are they going to do about her?"

"Obviously they have to get her away from the body. The only way I can see that happening is by giving her a tranquilizer."

"How can they do that?" Marissa asked. "She won't let them near her. Are you suggesting they use a tranquilizer gun?" Marissa sighed. "That sounded like I was making a joke. I wasn't. I'm just appalled."

"I know." Andrew looked at her. "So am I."

At that moment, Eric Montgomery yelled for everyone to back away from Ms. Pruitt. Those surrounding her stopped, but they didn't retreat. Once again, this time with a firmer edge to his voice, Eric ordered people to withdraw. Another few seconds passed as the police and paramedics looked at Bea panting, her long hair hanging in her face, her expression almost feral, and they began to move away. The world seemed to stop as Bea Pruitt looked at the gathering of officials, her gaze challenging them to come near her and Buddy. She was exhausted, though, and after only a couple of minutes she sank from her hands and knees to a sitting position.

Eric didn't move as he called, "Ms. Pruitt, I'm Eric Montgomery. Has Buddy ever mentioned me to you?"

"Well, of *course*," the woman answered disdainfully. "He didn't like you as much as he did Sheriff Farrell, but he said you weren't bad at your job."

"I'm glad to hear Buddy had a fairly good opinion of me. And you should know we all thought Buddy was a fine deputy, Ms. Pruitt."

The woman looked at Eric suspiciously. "That's not what he told me. He said you people at police headquarters laughed at him."

Eric smiled. "Now, Ms. Pruitt, you know Buddy could be overly sensitive. Sometimes we joked around with each other and nobody cared. Sometimes when we joked with Buddy, though, he took it personally. Everyone at headquarters thought Buddy was a good deputy."

Ms. Pruitt hesitated and then asked, "You did?"

"Well, sure. He worked there for almost ten years. You don't think Sheriff Farrell would have kept Buddy on the force so long if he wasn't good at his job, do you?" Bea Pruitt simply looked at Eric, but Marissa could see that the woman was thinking about what Eric had said.

"Buddy probably would have gone on being a shining example in law enforcement for many more years, but his life was cut short." Eric shook his head sadly. "We need to examine his . . . him so we can look for evidence. We'll be as gentle as possible, Ms. Pruitt, but we need to know who did this to Buddy."

Ms. Pruitt had seemed to be calming down, but suddenly she yelled, "I *know* who did this to Buddy! I told you! I've got the evidence right in my hand—a note with that Marissa Gray's phone number on it!"

"Yes, I know you have that note. But as I'm certain Buddy must have told you over the years, we can't convict someone of murder on the basis of a note. Besides, we might find even *more* evidence." Eric took a deep breath. Marissa could tell remaining calm and placating in this situation was beginning to take its toll on him. "That note will have to be sent to the crime lab and I'm sorry, but we do have to examine Buddy's body. Buddy would understand that it's the law."

Ms. Pruitt hung her head and began weeping. Eric continued, "What would help us most is for you to go sit in the ambulance for now. You must be freezing, Ms. Pruitt. Meanwhile, we'll look at Buddy and the crime scene, and then we'll carry him gentle as a baby and put him in the ambulance with you."

Although Marissa knew part of Eric's speech was insincere, unless he had completely changed from the man she'd once loved, the gentleness and compassion in his voice were genuine. No matter how much trouble Bea was causing, Marissa was certain he empathized with someone trying to protect the person she loved most in the world, even if that person was dead. Unexpected tears rose in Marissa's eyes as she remembered Eric keeping everyone away from his sister's body hanging over the pulpit, not allowing anyone to touch her because they might injure her neck or her back or any part of her body, because he could not accept that she was dead.

"You can ride with him to the hospital," Eric called to Bea. "Will that be all right with you, ma'am?"

"Is it a good idea for her to accompany the body to the hospital?" Marissa whispered to Andrew.

"It's the only way they'll get her to go peaceably. Don't worry—they'll separate her from Buddy at the hospital. A doctor will make sure she's all right physically and sedate her. I'm sure they'll keep her at the hospital tonight. Look at her—she certainly can't go home, even with a friend."

All the while Eric had been talking to Bea Pruitt, he'd also been inching closer to her. He stood only about a foot away from her now and he held out his hand. "Please come with me, Ms. Pruitt."

The woman looked at the body of her son, wiped her eyes on the sleeve of her coat, and reached for Eric's hand. "Okay. But you have to promise me you won't hurt Buddy."

"I promise."

"And promise me you'll go arrest that Gray woman."

"We'll certainly be talking with her. Come on now, Ms. Pruitt," Eric said quickly. "The sooner you go sit in the ambulance, the sooner we can get our work done and bring Buddy to you."

Andrew took Marissa's arm. "We're not close and she's partially blinded by the lights, but I don't want Bea to catch sight of you." Marissa knew Andrew could feel her arm trembling. "Why don't you go home for now? Once they put Bea in the ambulance, she could break free and start running or . . . well, I don't know what, but her seeing you could have disastrous results." He smiled at her. "There's nothing you can do here, so try to get some sleep so you'll be alert tomorrow. And come in an hour later than usual in the morning. I don't want you nodding off at your desk."

"Andrew, I would *never*—"

"Go home now, come in an hour late, or you're fired."

"Yeah, sure," Marissa mumbled, managing to grin at him. "You just scare me silly, you know that?"

"My wife says the same thing." Andrew grinned. "Now *go!*"

6

1

Although Marissa had reset her alarm clock to go off an hour later than usual, Catherine shook her awake after she'd slept a mere twenty extra minutes. "Marissa, you must have turned off your alarm clock," she hissed. "You're running late."

Marissa moaned and muttered, "You don't have to whisper when you're trying to wake me. Besides, Andrew said I could come in an hour late this morning."

"Oh, I'm so sorry. I'll just tiptoe out and you go right back to sleep."

Lindsay had already begun picking out toys from one of her wicker baskets, preparing for the day, and the smell of gourmet coffee floated into Marissa's room. "Never mind. I'm awake. Forty more minutes of sleep aren't going to make my mind any sharper than it is now, which isn't saying much."

"This morning I saw your note." Catherine looked both dismayed and eager as Marissa threw off the blankets and pulled on her velour robe. "What happened last night?"

"Please go downstairs and fix me a big mug of coffee while I wash my face. Then I'll give you all the details."

Ten minutes later, Marissa took a gulp of steaming coffee, looked at her sister, and announced, "Buddy Pruitt has been murdered and his mother says I did it."

Catherine gaped and asked loudly, "Buddy Pruitt the deputy?" Marissa nodded. "He's been murdered?" Marissa nodded again. "By you?" Marissa stared at her. "Oh, of course not by you. I meant why does his mother think you killed him?"

Marissa spent the next five minutes explaining the situation to Catherine as she rummaged through the cabinets until she found the aspirin bottle. "I'm reorganizing the kitchen," Catherine said, and Marissa inwardly groaned. Now she'd never be able to find anything. She gulped two pills while her sister absorbed the details of the previous night. When Marissa sat down again, Catherine looked at her calmly.

"Gee, I expected more of a reaction. Do you hear about murders nearly in your own backyard every day?"

"I'm training myself to remain expressionless. I'll probably be hearing quite a few shocking stories in my practice." Catherine took a drink of coffee and shook her head. "Buddy Pruitt. I haven't thought about him for years, then we saw him yesterday, and last night he was murdered."

"His mother thinks seeing him at headquarters set off my raging homicidal impulse."

"You said he was murdered on his way home. How did she know he saw us? Did he call her and tell her?"

"I have no idea what Buddy Pruitt could have done. He might have dashed home and told her. Eric sent him out before we left headquarters."

"Yes, he did." Catherine frowned. "I don't believe you should go in to work today. You're still recovering from the wreck and you were out in the middle of the night. You look terrible."

"Catherine, you sweet talker!"

"Oh, Marissa, you know—"

"I know what you mean, but I missed yesterday and at the *Gazette* office I might learn more about the murder." Marissa stood up. "So I'm going to fix another mug of coffee, go upstairs, and begin the hopeless task of making myself look halfway professional."

2

Marissa arrived five minutes late to find the *Gazette* offices seeming to crackle with electricity. Everyone moved faster, talked more, held telephone receivers, and furiously took notes. As soon as the door closed behind Marissa, every set of eyes seemed to find her. Unnerved, she didn't go to her desk as usual. She headed straight for Andrew Archer's small office. He, too, was on the phone but waved her in when she knocked lightly on the door.

"Did aliens land last night?" she asked as soon as Andrew finished his call.

"We had a murder. Did you forget?"

"I certainly didn't, but I'm not used to all of this frenetic activity caused by one murder."

Andrew smiled slightly and told her to sit down. "I keep forgetting that you've come to us from a Chicago newspaper. I imagine they have quite a few more murders in a city of almost three million there than we do in Aurora Falls."

"To say the least. Have you learned any more than we did last night?"

"The word is out that Buddy was carrying a note with your name and phone number on it."

"Oh. So that's why I got all the stares when I came in this morning."

Andrew nodded. "Ms. Pruitt kept yelling about it. No wonder every bystander picked up that piece of news. Anyway, Eric Montgomery is supposed to have a press conference around eleven a.m. He'll tell us what the medical examiner learned from the autopsy. Of course, he already knows, but he told me firmly about half an hour ago we'd know when everyone else does. I wish you still had some influence with that guy." Andrew stopped abruptly and turned bright red. "God, I'm sorry, Marissa."

"Eric and I ended a long time ago." She airily waved away Andrew's apology, hoping he hadn't seen her tears last night as she'd watched Eric's gentle handling of Ms. Pruitt. "We don't have long to wait for the press conference. People at the *Gazette* knew Buddy. Does anyone here have an idea about who would want to kill him?"

"Kill him? No. Kick him, shake him, dunk his head in a toilet? Probably. Buddy Pruitt was not the most charming man in town, you know."

"As a matter of fact, I did know. We had a one-sided run-in at the sheriff's office yesterday, which makes his mother certain I murdered him." She paused. "I wonder how Bea knew there was tension between Buddy and me at the sheriff's? I also have no idea why Buddy would have my number."

"He wanted to ask you out for a date?"

"Andrew Archer, I remember when you used to be too shy to say hello to me without blushing. Now I get this suggestion from you? Buddy wanted to date me?"

"I've gotten bolder with the years." Andrew smiled. "Besides, you couldn't blame Buddy for trying. Maybe he thought you'd been pining for him since you came back to town."

"Well, I'd better get to my desk before gossip starts about *us*. Also, Eric will be holding the press conference in an hour and a half. I should get some questions ready," Marissa said, starting to stand up.

"Uh, Marissa, I want Hank Landers to be the lead reporter on Buddy Pruitt."

"But I—"

"I know, but you were at the crime scene, Ms. Pruitt called *you*, and people know about the note on Buddy's body with your name and phone number. You just have too many connections with this case."

Marissa dropped onto her chair. "Andrew, if you think I can't be impartial because I didn't like Buddy, you're wrong."

"Tonya told me you wouldn't take this well." Andrew looked almost mournful. "I know you can be impartial. But the note and Ms. Pruitt bother me. Everyone will want to know why he was going to call you. And Ms. Pruitt keeps babbling about you being mean to Buddy at police headquarters yesterday. You can see how the public might think there was something between you and Buddy, bad blood. Bea Pruitt is in the hospital on a seventy-two-hour psychiatric hold, but when she gets out if she's still certain you killed her son God knows what might happen." He sighed. "I'm sorry. You can get mad at me if you like, but I can't risk your safety, Marissa, and I won't risk the reputation of the newspaper, either."

Marissa counted to ten, letting the wave of anger pass and reason return. Andrew was right. She wanted to cover the Buddy Pruitt case because she hadn't covered anything of significance since Andrew had hired her, but this particular case should not be hers.

Still, she couldn't keep the disappointment out of her voice when she said, "You're the boss. What would you like for me to work on today?"

"The upcoming performance of the Aurora Falls Choristers Friday evening, the Doggie Santa Claus Costume Competition Saturday afternoon, and the obituaries."

Marissa looked at him. Andrew remained straight-faced, but laughter danced in his eyes. "Yes, sir! And may I say that days like this are why I went into journalism."

3

The morning dragged for Marissa, who felt chained to her chair and the telephone. The only excitement arrived with Hank Landers returning from Eric's press conference. According to Eric, Buddy Pruitt had been stabbed three times in the back, destroying his kidneys and spleen. The murder weapon had been a knife. Apparently, the attack had occurred on the sidewalk and the attacker had dragged Pruitt's body onto the lawn of 1834 Oak Lane. As of yet, the police had no leads.

"In other words, we don't know any more than we did last night," Marissa said to Andrew while Hank wrote the story.

"We know the killer used a knife."

"What a surprise! Smooth or serrated blade? The police aren't going to release that information yet or maybe at all. We don't even know if they found the knife. They certainly know more than they're saying. But I know they have to withhold some details to ask all those nuts who always come in confessing to a crime." Marissa sighed. "Buddy was such a pain, but harmless. And friendless . . ." She saw the look in Andrew's eyes become wary. Of course, she thought. Buddy's only "friend" had been Dillon, Andrew's brother. She decided not to mention Dillon now. He was best left forgotten. "Well, the day isn't over. Maybe the police will release more information this afternoon."

"Don't forget—Hank's daughter Robbie works as a deputy. We have a spy."

"And you know Hank is far too admirable to make his daughter spy for him. Besides, from everything I've heard, Robbie is a good girl, Andrew. We don't want to corrupt her."

He winked at Marissa. "A spy with a crush on Eric Montgomery. Anyway, you're right—my finer nature won't let me stoop to using her for information."

After Andrew returned to his office, Marissa headed for the coffee machine. At least the coffee was better here than at the police headquarters, she thought. For that blessing everyone owed Tonya Ward, or Tonya Archer, who had married Andrew last summer, to the surprise of most people in Aurora Falls. They'd certainly kept their romance on the down low. Annemarie, who hung on to the city's gossip ring for as long as possible, told Marissa they were seeing each other, and two weeks later they had eloped.

Marissa felt as if she was dragging every word she wrote from her sluggish, sleep-deprived mind. Shortly before noon, she was back at the coffee machine for her third cup when Tonya swept through the *Gazette* doors. Marissa hadn't seen Tonya since the day after Gretchen died, and even then they hadn't spoken, their stories of Dillon Archer's actions being polar opposites.

Marissa wandered back to her desk, taking time to see that Tonya was still slender and wore her russet-colored hair long and almost straight. She barely nodded to a couple of reporters, then hurried into Andrew's office and closed the door. He looked up in surprise and Tonya pulled a red envelope from her purse and shoved it at him. He reached for it, but she pulled it back, waving her arms, her voice growing loud enough for people outside the office to hear. One of the female reporters looked over at Marissa and winked before she lowered her head. Marissa did the same, acting as if she were working diligently while she strained to hear actual words, not just Tonya's heated diatribe. In less than five minutes, a pink-faced Andrew had risen from his chair, grabbed his coat, and quickly steered Tonya outside.

4

Andrew had nearly pulled Tonya from the *Gazette* office half a block down to a cozy dim little restaurant named The Grille and shoved her into a booth. He sat down across from her and said sharply, "Let me see the picture again."

Tonya's eyes narrowed. Her face tightened while color heightened in her cheeks. She didn't move. Andrew looked at her and took a deep breath. "I'm sorry I reacted that way, honey," he said in a beleaguered voice. "I was up half the night, everyone's having hysterics over Buddy Pruitt's murder, and then you came charging in with that picture. I don't think you know how loud you were talking, but I apologize for yanking you out of the building. I have the manners of a gorilla."

Tonya relaxed and even smiled. "I don't know how gorillas act, but you're forgiven anyway. I get loud when I'm excited or upset. I should be the one apologizing, though. Half the people in the office were looking at me."

"Never mind them. May I see what's inside the envelope?"

Tonya opened her purse and withdrew a square red envelope suitable for a greeting card. She handed it to Andrew. He skimmed the front with its typed address **Mrs. Tonya Archer,** not **Mr. and Mrs. Archer.** The flap had been tucked inside the envelope, not licked and glued. Andrew pulled out a photograph of Tonya and him decorating their Christmas tree in front of the picture window of their new house. The picture had been taken at night, but they'd turned on every lamp in the living room, including the Christmas tree lights, and their beaming faces showed clearly. Andrew turned over the picture:

Hope you're enjoying your new life, Tonya.

D.A.

"Well?" Tonya asked anxiously.

"You think this is from Dillon."

"Of course I do! Don't you?"

The waitress came by and both Tonya and Andrew ordered a hamburger and coffee, although she asked for decaf. After the girl left, Andrew went into a deep study of the photo again. Tonya thought she would scream.

"Andrew, he knows where we live!"

"Will you please lower your voice?" he asked tightly. "Aurora Falls only has a population of around forty thousand people. We're not hard to find. Besides, his knowing where we live isn't important—"

"Isn't important!"

"Tonya, you have to calm down. You're going to get one of your headaches," Andrew said kindly.

"One is already starting."

"Then take some of your medication now. The doctor said the pills work better if you take them when the headache is beginning than when it's already going full force."

Tonya smiled as she searched her purse for a small pill container. "You make the headaches sound like locomotives, and that's exactly what they feel like."

"Well, I might not be an F. Scott Fitzgerald, but I have a writer's imagination of sorts. I just wish we could find the cause and stop them."

"Maybe they'll stop as quickly as they began." Tonya swallowed two pills with a gulp of water and almost choked. She grabbed her napkin, coughed heartily for a moment, then looked at Andrew with regretful hazel eyes. "I'm embarrassing you."

"You're worrying me. Sweetheart, you're going to pieces about a photograph someone took of us decorating our Christmas tree."

Tonya frowned. "That's not all I'm going to pieces about. Someone intruded on our lives, caught us in an intimate moment—"

"Decorating a Christmas tree isn't exactly intimate, Tonya." Andrew smiled.

"It was to me. I've told you we never had a Christmas tree after Dad left. Mom said the trees made too much mess and were silly. Your dad never allowed the family to have one. This is the first one I've had for years, your first one ever, and we bought and decorated it *together*. Didn't that mean anything to you?"

Andrew sighed. "Can't you see how happy I look in that picture? Do you think I've suddenly changed my mind since Friday night when we put up the tree?"

"No." Tonya kept her gaze downcast as the waitress brought their coffee and left. "But when I think of someone outside *watching* us—"

"We realize we should have drawn the draperies. Simple as that."

"No, it isn't simple. What about that message inside? It's a threat, Andrew. It's a threat from Dillon!"

Tonya knew Andrew wouldn't talk to her as if she were a child, attempt to tease her out of her fear. He would try to make her feel calm, though. Calm and safe, and that's what she desperately needed.

"I admit 'Hope you're enjoying your new life, Tonya,' is meant to be sardonic, but I don't think it's a threat." He paused. "You have a strong personality, Tonya. You've laughed about it. You don't mince words, and while I love that quality in you, someone else might not. This could have come from someone you pissed off and didn't even know it."

"Like a clerk in a store?" Andrew nodded. "A clerk who would go to the trouble of standing outside in the cold until they could get a picture of us being happy together, put a *sardonic* question on the back, and then stick it in our mailbox?"

"People are crazy." Andrew's gaze flickered. "I didn't even notice that there was no stamp."

"Andrew, Dillon's been to our *door!*"

This time Andrew couldn't help laughing. Tonya stiffened, offended, but Andrew couldn't stop. Finally, he was able to down a gulp of water and get control of himself. "Tonya, you sound like someone in a horror movie. Quite a few people have come to our front door and we're still alive and well." He paused. "But you're afraid Dillon was at our door."

Their sandwiches arrived and they went silent until the waitress left for the third time. "Yes. Your brother, Dillon. Look at the card. How many other people do we know with the name *Dillon*?" Tonya asked earnestly.

"Honey, it's signed 'D.A.,' not 'Dillon.' You're letting your imagination run away with you. But what if Dillon did put the picture in the mailbox? He had an offbeat sense of humor—he'd think that was funny."

"Well, it isn't! Why aren't you more upset?"

"Why are you *so* upset?" Andrew ignored his sandwich, reached across the table and took her hand. "You know you can tell me anything."

Tonya's gaze wavered as her mind raced. How she wished she *could* tell him anything, but she was afraid his love wasn't strong enough to make him forgive her. "Everyone is saying Dillon is back," she began. "I don't think so many people could be wrong."

"I don't know how many people are saying Dillon is here—no one has said it to me. It would be stupid for him to come to Aurora Falls where so many people think he murdered Gretchen Montgomery unless he wanted to clear his name, but even if that's what he's trying to do, why would he want to hurt or scare *you*? You told the police he was trying to pull Gretchen off the rail onto the balcony to save her. *Marissa* said he pushed Gretchen to her death. It was your word against hers and you didn't say anything that would cause him trouble."

"But you know how respected the Grays are in this city. Everyone would have believed Marissa."

"The law looks at everyone as equal," Andrew said seriously. "In a court of law, your word would have been as good as Marissa Gray's."

Dear Andrew, Tonya thought. He was idealistic, a trait she both loved and found naïve. Sometimes, she thought he *couldn't* be as unsophisticated as he sounded. It was an act. Other times, Tonya was certain of his sincerity. She knew she was jaded, though. She found it nearly impossible to have faith in others and it made her overcritical. She'd decided months ago that if Andrew could believe so fervently that the justice system was always fair and people's fates didn't always depend on the esteem of important people, she would cherish rather than try to destroy his trust.

Tonya stared at her husband for a moment and then gave him a weak smile. "You're right—the levelheaded one as always. I guess I've had visions of Dillon escaping from Buddy and then just going wild, literally crazy."

"Dressing up in a monster outfit and trying to cause Marissa to wreck? Coming home to murder Buddy, his friend?" Andrew shook his head. "I've always thought Buddy probably didn't make it too hard for Dillon to get away. They probably cooked up the scheme together." He squeezed her hand. "Tonya, sweetie, I'd be the first to agree that Dillon was rowdy, a trouble-maker, and he had a bad temper. Sometimes he seemed fierce. He wouldn't *kill* someone, though, unless it was self-defense."

"You don't know that!"

"Tonya, he's my *brother*."

"Yes, he's your brother. If he did manage to clear himself of killing Gretchen, would you want us to be one big, happy family with him going along cheerfully causing trouble for us and being a bad influence on *our* son?"

"When we have two sons and a daughter."

"Oh really? I'm beginning to feel like one of Henry the Eighth's poor wives. 'Give me an heir and a spare and a pretty princess to marry to the king of a rich country or it's off with your head, woman!' "

"It's not all that bad. I plan on giving you plenty of time, not jumping the gun or anything." Tonya smiled and Andrew continued, "Tonya, Buddy didn't have anything to fear from Dillon and neither do you. Someone simply started a rumor that Dillon is back in Aurora Falls, and a week or two afterward Buddy was murdered. The people who linked the two things are now losing their minds, certain Dillon is a crazed murderer loose on the streets. It's a sort of mob mentality."

"And I became part of the mob just because of a weird Christmas card. I'm smarter than that. Aren't I?"

"You are the smartest woman I know."

"The smartest *woman* you know?"

"The smartest person I know in the whole, entire universe. Now eat your sandwich."

Andrew lifted his sandwich and was about to bite in with gusto when Tonya tilted her head. "Andrew, why did you hire Marissa Gray when she said your brother murdered Gretchen?"

Andrew looked like he wanted to groan and laid down his sandwich. "She's smart, she's young but shows signs of becoming an excellent reporter, with wonderful credentials, and I always thought she and her sister were fairly great people. I also don't believe she *lied* about Dillon pushing Gretchen. She and Gretchen were *so* close, like sisters, that I think the shock of that night caused her to think she saw something she didn't." He paused. "I've never discussed this with her, but after all this time to calm down and really analyze what she saw I'd bet you a hundred dollars she'd no longer swear she saw Dillon push Gretchen."

"I'm glad you have so much faith in her, but I think you'd better count on having a hundred dollars less to spend on my Christmas gift."

Andrew laughed and then slowly grew sober. "My God, *you're* not going to ask Marissa what she saw the night of Gretchen's fall, are you?" Tonya remained silent. "Tonya, let this whole thing alone. You're right—this is our first Christmas together and I want it to be perfect, not spoiled by dredging up all that awful business with Gretchen. *Promise me.*"

Tonya looked at him intensely, then relaxed and smiled. "Nothing is going to ruin our Christmas. I promise."

7

1

As Marissa finished her last obituary, Andrew casually walked to her desk and said softly, "Time for you to go home."

"Home? It's not four fifteen. Did I mess up an obituary? Offend a judge on the board of the Doggie Santa Claus Costume Competition? Drink too much expresso?"

"The latter. You've been running on empty since about noon. I should have made you take the day off, but I knew you'd argue. Anyway, I don't want you fainting from exhaustion. I'll get a reputation for being a slave driver." Andrew grinned. "Take the extra time, Marissa, and don't fight me. I promise the paper won't collapse without you, even if you are one of our finest reporters."

"That's not fair—ending an order with a compliment."

"Life isn't fair," Andrew said, walking away. "Get used to it."

Secretly Marissa could have kissed Andrew for letting her go early. She *was* exhausted. She also had an errand she wanted to do before evening fell so maddeningly early in the winter. She knew many people considered her audacious, but she wasn't daring enough to run around at night with a murderer on the loose.

Exhausted, again furious at the sight of her clunky rental car, and depressed by the weather, Marissa gritted her teeth and drove to the florist nearest the *Gazette* offices. Once she stepped inside, the gloomy, pewter-skied day disappeared as a world of red, green, gold, and silver surrounded her. Wreaths hung every-where—pine, balsam, cedar, fir—emitting delectable scents and decorated with pine cones, red and plaid ribbons, crab apples, and red berries. "Good King Wenceslas" played just loud enough to be pleasant. The tangy smells, the lights, and the music raised her spirits.

Marissa spent at least half an hour looking at real and artificial wreaths as well as beautiful table enhancements. Moving on to the living, potted Christmas decorations, Marissa dithered mentally for a few minutes and then decided on Prestige Red poinsettias growing in a gold foil-wrapped pot with a green velveteen bow. When she left the store, she felt as if she'd stepped out of a fairyland so she could visit a place that always gave her an ache in her heart.

Marissa thought Aurora Falls Cemetery was one of the loveliest cemeteries she'd ever seen. Just outside the city, the waterfall formed a beautiful backdrop for the cemetery and provided the ever-present sound of rushing water. On most days, sunshine gleamed on the falls creating a rainbow of color. Marissa's parents were buried here, but it was not their graves she'd come to visit.

She drove through the stone-columned entrance and turned right on one of the narrow roads curving through the cemetery. As she neared a towering, dense blue spruce tree, she slowed, hesitated, then pulled slightly off the road and stopped behind the police cruiser.

He didn't even glance at her until she said, "Hello, Eric," as she held her pot of poinsettias and looked at the man crouched at the grave of Gretchen Montgomery.

His blond head snapped up. He blinked twice as if coming out of a trance, then returned Marissa's gaze stonily. "I didn't hear you drive up."

"I know." He started to rise, but Marissa crouched quickly on the opposite side of the grave and spoke, hoping he wouldn't leave: "Gretchen loved Prestige Red."

Eric, hat in his hand, frowned at her. "What's Prestige Red?"

"Poinsettias." She placed the large pot near the headstone. "This shade is Prestige Red."

Eric looked at the beautiful, vibrantly red plant. "Why didn't I know that?"

"I don't think most girls discuss their favorite shade of poinsettia with their brothers. It isn't as if you didn't know her birth date."

"Or her death date."

Well, I stepped right into that one, Marissa thought regretfully. She wouldn't give up, although she didn't want to ask about Buddy. She didn't want Eric to think she was pumping him for recent information about the murder. "Do you have any leads on who might have caused my wreck?"

"No. I told you the blizzard destroyed any physical evidence he might have left." Eric paused as if deciding whether he wanted to talk to her. "We went over the area as thoroughly as we could."

"I didn't think you'd be able to find anything." She paused. "Catherine was really unhappy with me for causing such a scene at headquarters on Monday, but you know how I get when I'm passionate about something."

Eric's golden-flecked brown eyes seemed to bore a hole through her own until he said with quiet fury, "You certainly weren't passionate about seeing Dillon Archer kill my sister."

Marissa felt as if Eric had punched her in the abdomen. She only had enough air to whisper, "*What?*"

"You heard me. You *saw* Dillon push Gretchen off that balcony, but when the police questioned you the assertive, confident, tenacious girl I'd known for years vanished. 'It happened so fast,' " he mimicked what she'd said to the police. " 'The light was bad.' 'Tonya was closer to her than I was.' It's no wonder Mitch Farrell didn't arrest Dillon on the spot." His voice grew louder: "And now here you are with your poinsettias as if they matter to my sister whose *murder* you could have avenged!"

Fury and shock washed through Marissa. Eric started to stand up, but Marissa leaned across the grave, reached out, and with strength she didn't know she possessed placed her hands on his shoulders and then pushed him flat to the ground on his rear. "How *dare* you imply I didn't do everything I could for Gretchen that night?" she nearly shouted. "How can you mock me, claiming I said the light was bad, things happened too fast, Tonya was closer than I was to Gretchen? Dillon, Tonya, and Andrew were harping on those things, not me!"

"You could have sounded like you *meant* what you said," Eric flared. "No ifs, ands, or buts. No wavering. You could have sounded like you *knew* what happened!"

Marissa drew a deep breath, seething. "Eric Montgomery, I told the truth. Did I acknowledge that the lighting was bad? Yes. It was. Did I argue when Tonya said she was closer to Gretchen than I was? No, because Tonya *was* closer. But I knew what I saw, I told the police what I saw, and I did *not* waver."

Eric still sat on the cold ground and turned his head away from her. Marissa kneeled, leaned over the grave again, her knees digging deeper into the snow, took hold of his chin, and forced him to face her. "Are you even *listening* to me? I told the police *exactly* what I saw," she said between clenched teeth. "I saw Dillon lean closer to Gretchen, I saw him reach out with both arms. I thought he intended to grab her around the thighs and drag her down, but he only put his *left* arm around her. With his right hand, he *pushed* her. Then he did a lot of flailing around as if she'd fallen in spite of his efforts. I've gone over this hundreds of times in my mind. I *saw* what he did and I'll never say differently.

"Afterward, Tonya told the police the light was bad in that loft—there were a couple of flashlights and candles only—which was true," Marissa continued. "She said she was standing closer to Gretchen than I was, which was also true. She swore she saw both of Dillon's arms close around Gretchen's thighs and pull her toward the loft. That was not what happened and I *said* so to the police."

"But not with any fervor."

Marissa was stunned. "So you were furious with me because I wasn't strident enough to suit you?" Eric turned his head. "Look at me, dammit!" Eric's gaze slowly returned to her. "No,

I didn't scream that Tonya was wrong because I would have seemed hysterical and I didn't want the police to dismiss me as a horror-stricken girl not sure of *what* she'd seen. I admitted that the light was dim in the loft, but I told them about my above-average vision. I told them Tonya was closer to Gretchen than I was but only by a couple of feet. I wasn't going to lie."

"Oh, God forbid that you sully your soul by lying!'"

"God forbid that I sully my credibility. And I wasn't the only person on the balcony."

"Oh yes, Andrew was there. Andrew, Dillon's *brother*."

"Andrew who said nothing except to agree that the light was bad. That's all he said to defend Dillon, his own brother. I think he saw what I did. I always have. But he managed to lose himself in all the commotion that night."

Eric withdrew behind his eyes. Marissa knew the expression well. He was no longer looking at her. He was lost in the labyrinth of his mind. She glanced up to see a couple placing a small gold and red wreath on a grave. The woman sniffled into a handkerchief. The man glowered at Marissa and Eric. Marissa didn't resent the expression. A cemetery was no place to have a shouting argument, but for the first time since Gretchen's death Eric was *really* talking to her, spilling out his feelings—his hurt, his resentment, his blame—and Marissa would do nothing to stop him, no matter how many people they offended.

Finally, she said, "Eric, Mitch Farrell came that night. He's known me for all of my life. He knows my vision is especially keen. He knows I wouldn't accuse someone of pushing Gretchen off that railing unless I was positive that's what I saw. He also knew Tonya and Dillon. Neither one of them had a spotless reputation, especially Dillon.

"Eric, I knew Mitch's questions weren't going to end that night in the church. I knew he'd question us again and again and, as crushed as I was about Gretchen, my answers weren't going to change one tiny bit. They were only going to become clearer when I could better demonstrate that small difference in the placement of Dillon's hands that made all the difference."

Marissa sighed. "But Tonya told the same story as Dillon. Mitch was stuck with conflicting eyewitness versions. Dillon didn't have a shining reputation around here, but he'd *never* been arrested or even brought into police headquarters for questioning. Mitch didn't have time to do a thorough investigation that night, but he did assign twenty-four-hour surveillance on Dillon, which protocol didn't demand."

"Yes, he assigned that idiot deputy Buddy Pruitt, Dillon's *friend*." Eric took off his hat and ran his right hand through his hair. "I've always admired Mitch Farrell. He's the reason I decided when I was twelve I wanted to be a cop. He was sharp and meticulous and relentless. Except for the night my sister was killed."

"Did you expect Mitch to come to Gray's Island, arrest warrant for Dillon Archer in hand? He did have conflicting accounts of Gretchen's fall."

Eric looked at Marissa. "There's no point in going over this again. Intellectually I know Mitch did all he could. All I can blame him for was having Buddy Pruitt as his watchdog." Eric put his hat back on and gave her a hard look. "But what about us?"

"What *about* us?"

"We should have been in that church, Marissa, but you suggested breaking away from the pack for a while to enjoy the stars. When I'd say we should go find the others, you'd say, 'Just a few more minutes, just a few more minutes.' Well, those minutes turned into an hour and look what happened!"

Marissa gaped at him. "Eric Montgomery, I didn't have you tied to posts in the ground. You could have left any time you wanted. You stayed and you're blaming *me*! All these years you've been picturing me as this seductress, a Greek siren luring the sailors to the treacherous rocks. I cannot believe it!"

"Marissa, you're shouting."

"Are you worried about your public image? Well, I don't care! The idea that I could have been in love with a man so weak he'd be manipulated by a couple of playful pleas from a woman for him to stay with her when he should have been looking for another one who was in danger is beyond insulting!"

"I didn't say that."

"You didn't use those exact words, but it's what you've been thinking."

Eric looked at her angrily. "Do *not* tell me what I'm thinking!"

"Swear to me it never crossed your mind that if Marissa hadn't been asking you to spend some 'alone' time with her, you would have gone to the church earlier and saved Gretchen." A wave of guilt flashed over his face. "Yes, it has. And I'll tell you again, you were never so malleable, so weak! You wanted to stay with me—alone—for a while. You weren't worried that Gretchen briefly went off with the others. Only when you realized more time had passed than you realized did you get worried! And you knew so much time hadn't passed because I was begging you to stay with me. It passed because you didn't want to leave me any more than I wanted you to leave. Do you hear me? You didn't *want* to leave so you could babysit your sister like you had most of your life!"

Eric glared at her, took a deep breath, and rose so fast he swayed slightly. Something crunched under his shoe as he stepped forward to catch himself. "Oh, hell, what now?" He lifted his foot. "It's a little box on Gretchen's grave."

"A box? What's in it?"

"I don't have X-ray vision, Marissa, but who the hell leaves a Christmas present for a dead person?"

The man standing near tossed them one final searing look and then led away his weeping wife. "I don't know who leaves a gift," Marissa said, lowering her voice too late. "If you'll move your big foot away from it, we'll see."

The box, slightly crushed, measured about two inches by two inches. Wrapped in gold foil paper, it bore a small red bow but no name tag.

Marissa glanced over the collection of bouquets, wreaths, and her own pot of poinsettias on the grave. "I've never heard of leaving a gift at a grave. I mean . . . who's going to open it? Do you think we *should* open it? After all, we both know Gretchen was murdered. Isn't it evidence?"

Eric stared at it as if mesmerized and said after a moment, "Gretchen's death was ruled an accident, not a homicide, so this can't be considered evidence." Eric continued to stare at the partly mashed box. "I'm getting a very strange feeling about it. I'm going to open it." To Marissa's surprise, he whipped latex gloves from an inside pocket of his coat and picked the box up. He untied the simple bow, peeled back the Scotch tape already coming loose in the cold, and slipped a navy blue box out of the gold paper. He opened the lid of the box, and on a bed of cotton lay a silver and moonstone ring.

As soon as Marissa saw the contents, all thoughts of their argument vanished from her mind. "Her *ring!*" she gasped.

"I haven't seen this ring since she died," Eric said slowly. "Mom was determined she would be buried wearing this ring because it meant so much to Gretchen, but she couldn't find it anywhere."

Eric handed Marissa a latex glove and she lifted the ring from the cotton. Even in the dimming light, the marquise-shaped stone glowed with a pale rainbow of colors. It was bezel set in silver decorated with scrollwork. "She wore this on her index finger."

"It could be a ring just like hers."

"It isn't. When my family went to Mexico, I bought rings for Gretchen and me. We vowed we would never take them off." Marissa held out her hand to show the ring on her middle finger. "It was to exemplify our friendship, but it was also to celebrate Gretchen getting her driver's license. *Finally* on her third try." Marissa laughed softly. "We'd all just about given up hope of her ever passing the driving part of the exam."

"But you know the artist made more than two rings like this," Eric insisted.

Marissa shook her head. "Not *just* like this." She removed hers and handed it to Eric, then turned the other ring so he could see the inside of the band: ∞. "The same symbol is on each ring. It meant we would be best friends for infinity."

2

The several halogen lights placed around the cemetery did not ease the nervousness Marissa felt as late afternoon turned to twilight and Eric held Gretchen's ring in his hand. He withdrew a small plastic bag from his pocket, placed the ring back in the box, and dropped everything into the bag. "You and Catherine would have made a great team," Marissa said shakily. "Prepared for every occasion. Antibacterial wipes, latex gloves, evidence bags . . ."

Eric seemed far away, although he answered, "When I was seven, I never went out without my yo-yo. Now it's latex gloves. Habits change, I guess." He frowned at her. "Why *infinity* instead of *eternity*?"

"Eternity seemed so common. Everybody says it. *Infinity* relates to the idea of 'without end.' I thought it was unusual and perfect." Eric stared at her and she sighed. "Okay, Catherine knew all about the infinity symbol and suggested it. She knows just about everything in the whole world."

Eric continued to stare at Marissa for a moment, then started laughing. "Do you know you sounded like an eight-year-old girl jealous of her big sister?" Marissa didn't crack a smile, although she realized in embarrassment that's exactly how she'd sounded. "Speaking of Catherine, it's six thirty. Won't she be worried about you?"

At that moment, Marissa's cell phone went off. "Yes, Catherine, I'm fine," she said, pulling a face at Eric. "I took a detour on the way home. I should have told you. I'll be there in fifteen minutes."

"Catherine is going to make someone a fine mother some-day." Marissa smiled. "Loving, protective, encouraging, and maddening."

"Yeah, probably." Eric's voice had grown vague as he looked grimly at the evidence bag again. "We should be going. I need to get this back to headquarters and you need to assure your sister you're alive and well."

He didn't walk her to her car, which she'd parked directly behind his. He gave her a slight smile and told her to have a nice evening. He sounded as if he'd stopped someone on the road for going a bit too fast. The same thing he'd tell anyone, Marissa thought. He'd finally been opening up to her, telling her all the things he hadn't when he broke off their engagement, sounding like the Eric she'd known and loved, but finding the ring had sent him right back into his shell.

Marissa could have been annoyed with him, but the ring was such an important and unnerving discovery, she realized she had nothing more to say, either. She was too shocked to make conversation, too shaken to discuss the matter calmly and logically.

Someone had wanted Gretchen's ring found on her grave. Was it a message, or had it been put there strictly for shock value? What if somebody had simply opened the box and taken the ring? Did that mean someone was watching, making sure nothing like that happened? Had someone watched Marissa and Eric tonight? Had the watcher been satisfied that *they* had found the ring?

The idea of someone seeing them bent over the grave, opening the box, comparing the ring to the one on Marissa's hand, sent a shudder through her. She hadn't even thought about it in the cemetery. While they lingered at Gretchen's grave, Marissa had been concentrating on the ring and what Eric had revealed of his feelings about her—feelings he'd harbored for so long. She regretted that he hadn't finished.

She stopped at a red light. At least she thought she regretted it. Most of what he described was pent-up anger and blame, all directed at her. He'd decided she hadn't been forceful enough when she talked to the police. On a hot summer's night on Gray's Island less than an hour after Gretchen's hideous death, he thought Marissa should have defeated Tonya's version of the incident and had the police leading Dillon away in handcuffs.

Eric also seemed to blame Marissa because they'd spent an hour away from the others. Yes, she had asked him several times to linger with her under the beautiful night sky, but when had Eric Montgomery ever let her dominate him when he felt a matter was important? In those cases, he'd always trusted his own judgment, admitting if he'd been wrong, but not shamed or embarrassed.

When the light turned green, Marissa pushed hard on the accelerator. Eric hadn't been fair to her then and he wasn't being fair to her now, dammit. He'd felt guilty, but he'd also pushed his self-blame onto her. He still didn't have a kind word for her. Just recriminations. The farther Marissa drove toward home, the more wounded and angry she felt.

3

When Marissa neared her house, she saw James Eastman's silver Lincoln parked in the double driveway and the porch light glowing. She almost groaned. She was mad and hurt, but she'd have to act polite for the sake of James. Catherine would detect her mood immediately.

Marissa parked by the curb and stared at the rose garden her mother and Jean Farrell had planted on the large side lawn. Annemarie had known little about growing roses and Jean had seemed happy to help her start her garden with eight bushes. Marissa remembered her father and Mitch digging eight holes with Jean standing beside Mitch and Bernard giving directions about depth and width. Then she'd sent the men into the house. One by one, Jean had set the plants in the ground, lecturing Annemarie about the magnificent tea rose, the floribunda, and the miniature rose. Every time Annemarie had attempted to plant one herself, Jean had nearly flown at her, telling her how she was doing it wrong—she was using too much mulch; she hadn't used enough bonemeal; she was tamping the dirt around the roots too forcefully.

A twelve-year-old Marissa had simply stayed out of the way, watching and smothering smiles. Then she saw it coming. The women had sat on the ground, Jean going strong with her carping and corrections when finally Annemarie's mouth tightened, her eyes narrowed, and suddenly she picked up a dirt clod and threw it at Jean. The woman had been so startled, she'd simply stared agape at Annemarie. Marissa's eyes had widened and she'd waited for Jean to jump up and stomp angrily into the house. After a moment, though, Jean had closed her hand against the loose dirt nearby and tossed a dirt clod at Annemarie, who'd promptly returned fire. Then Annemarie picked up the bucket of water sitting next to her and dashed it onto Jean, who gasped, shook her hair out of her eyes, reached for another full bucket, and drenched Annemarie. At this point the men had come out of the house to see both of their wives, wet, dirty, and laughing until they cried.

The rose garden expanded as Annemarie learned everything she could about the growing of roses. Within three years, the side lawn was a breathtaking explosion of red, pink, yellow, and white. In the weeks before Annemarie died, she'd frequently looked out her window at the beautiful roses and they made her smile. They certainly wouldn't now, Marissa sighed inwardly. She'd carefully prepared them for winter and knew they be glorious again in the summer, but at this time of year they simply looked bare, lonely, and forlorn like most of the other flora.

"Well, I can't stay here daydreaming and worrying Catherine," Marissa said aloud. "Going in couldn't be worse."

At least she didn't think so until she reached the front door and faced an extremely large pine wreath bedecked with silver ribbons and figurines her mother had thought looked like angels. Marissa always thought the figurines resembled ghouls instead and believed she'd carefully hidden the eye-sore. Apparently, she hadn't hidden it well enough.

As soon as she stepped inside, Lindsay ran to her and presented a stuffed cow as a welcome home gift. Marissa bent, took the cow, and rubbed her chin on Lindsay's head. "Just what I've needed all day!" she declared, holding on to the fat cow.

"Oh, you're home!" Catherine cried, jumping up to help Marissa with her coat as if she were an invalid. "I searched this house from attic to basement until I found the big wreath Aunt Ida made when we were kids. I thought you said it was lost. Did you notice it?"

"How could I help it?" Marissa answered, hoping her voice didn't betray her sarcasm. She'd have to try harder unless she wanted to betray her falling spirits. "Hello, James. How nice to see you!"

He'd stood when she walked in, just as men had done fifty years ago when a lady entered the room. "Hi, Marissa. When you were late, Catherine was certain you'd had another wreck."

"I should have called her."

"You look exhausted and cold," Catherine said, inspecting her from head to toe. "Why are your knees so red?"

"I've been kneeling on the snow." Catherine looked as if she was going to ask if Marissa had visited their parents' graves, so Marissa quickly glanced at the fireplace. "Ah, nothing makes you feel better on a cold winter evening than a crackling fire. How nice to come home to one." She sighed and nearly dropped onto the large brown armchair that had been her father's. "Do you two have plans?" Marissa asked.

"We're going to the Larke Inn for dinner," James said. He hesitated. "Can we talk you into joining us?"

Which you'd absolutely hate, Marissa thought. "No, it's been a hard day and I don't have much appetite. All I can think of is how much I'd like a glass of wine."

"I'll get it," Catherine piped. "You sit right there. You look pale."

"With red knees." As soon as she vanished into the kitchen, Marissa's eyes twinkled at James. "Mother hen."

"I think it's endearing." Marissa felt a tiny burst of joy. James already sounded fond when he spoke of Catherine.

"She loves the dining room at the Inn."

James's face brightened. "I didn't know. I guess I made the right choice."

"It also shouldn't be too busy on a Tuesday night."

"That's what I thought when I called Catherine right after noon. According to my mother, it's insulting to ask out a lady without proper notice, but the idea just hit me. I'd like for us to have a cozy, uninterrupted dinner, which is impossible on a Friday or Saturday evening."

"Does Catherine look annoyed at being asked out improperly late?" Marissa asked, smiling. "I think your mother needs to progress with the times."

Catherine came back in the room and brought Marissa a glass of white wine. She looked beautiful in a heather green long-sleeved cashmere sheath dress with high-heeled black pumps. Her hair lay in waves down her back and she'd used just enough subtle liner to create mesmerizing blue-green cat eyes. Marissa caught a whiff of her own J'adore L'eau perfume when Catherine leaned forward to give her the wine.

Marissa beamed. "You look gorgeous, Catherine."

"Doesn't she?" James asked enthusiastically. "That dress looks so soft on her she's just begging to be fondled." Time seemed to stand still for a moment. Then Catherine turned crimson, James flushed, and Marissa burst into uncontrollable laughter.

"That's the first time I've laughed all day," Marissa said, setting down her wine so she wouldn't spill it. "James, you are a master of words."

"I speak more appropriately in court," he answered dolefully. "And I can't remember when I last used the word *fondled*."

"The word sneaked past the filter between your brain and your mouth. I think it's a perfect description of her dress." Marissa couldn't stop grinning. "Shouldn't you two be on your way to dinner? Even on weeknights, near Christmas the Larke dining room fills up, and I know the two of you want privacy," Marissa said with an exaggerated wink.

Catherine glared at her. "If I didn't know better, I'd think that wasn't Marissa's first glass of wine tonight, or even her fourth. However, I think she has a good idea. We should go now, James, and leave my sister, who is *so* delighted with herself, alone all evening so she can giggle like a fourteen-year-old in peace." Catherine yanked a brown wool coat from the closet, sending the hanger swinging. "You got a few Christmas cards today, Marissa. They'll probably send you into gales of laughter."

"Okay. Good night, you two."

Catherine didn't speak. Behind Catherine's back, James grimaced and muttered, "Good night."

"Have a great time." Marissa turned to look out the window behind her chair. James took Catherine's arm and helped her into the car as if she were both delicate and precious. Marissa smiled. She felt wonderful seeing her sister treated with gentility and admiration by the man of her dreams. Marissa glanced at Lindsay, who sat at her feet with her head cocked. "I don't think those two are the *least* in need of a love potion, girl."

Marissa thought of selections for dinner, but every one of them would result in a pile of dirty dishes, so she checked to see that they had plenty of Diet Coke and ordered a pizza. While she waited for the pizza, Marissa changed into a pair of sweatpants, a fuzzy sweater, and her bunny slippers. It had been colder in the cemetery than she realized and she still felt chilled and drained. No wonder, she thought. Her clash with Eric had shocked, pained, infuriated, and yet enlightened her. She'd had no idea of the maelstrom in Eric's mind concerning her that had caused him to break their engagement after Gretchen's death. At last, she knew why she'd lost Eric. He'd been an idiot to blame her for not disputing Tonya's defense of Dillon more vociferously, but at least finally Marissa had an answer. The answer made her angry, but knowing it also gave her a sense of peace.

The ring was a different matter. She looked down at the marquise-cut moonstone glowing pale blue on her finger even in this room's dim light. Gretchen had squealed with delight when Marissa presented her with the lovely ring, then squealed again when she saw that Marissa wore one just like it. Marissa slipped her ring from her middle finger and squinted at the symbol engraved inside. ∞. Infinity. They'd thought their connection would last through infinity. But someone, probably her murderer, had decided Gretchen would not wear the ring that had been a sign of her and Marissa's bond.

Marissa shivered in spite of her warm clothes and slipped the ring back onto her finger. She would not consider the significance of finding the matching ring at Gretchen's grave, she thought sternly. She just couldn't handle it tonight.

Marissa glanced at the large, beribboned box on a table near the front door and remembered Catherine mentioning that she'd gotten a few Christmas cards. A diversion, she thought in relief. She headed for the box like someone drowning, and while she waited for the pizza, stomach growling loudly, Marissa sat down on the floor with Lindsay beside her and glanced at the cards lying on top. Two from girlfriends she'd had in Chicago, one from a guy she'd broken off with a couple of months before she returned to Aurora Falls, one from a great-aunt who always called her Matilda, one from Tonya and Andrew Archer, and another with no return address and no postmark.

Marissa opened the last one slowly and withdrew a postcard. On the front was a picture of Aurora Falls on a dreary day, obviously meant to show the various florid-leaved autumn trees against the white water and gray sky. At the top of the falls someone had drawn the figures of a man and woman holding hands, obviously poised to plunge into the frothy water below. The picture alone chilled her. Then she turned over the postcard and saw a typed message: **Together forever, Marissa**. The card was signed with a simple *D.A.*

"Dillon Archer," Marissa whispered.

Abruptly pictures flashed in her mind like a slide show: the ghoulish character slithering over the guardrail, eyes seeming to burn in its skull, the car plummeting over the hillside, vines like icy tendrils appearing to creep around and imprison the car, the skull at the window again as the character diligently worked at the door handle, trying to reach her.

Dillon, she thought again. The card was a reminder that Dillon felt forever connected with the woman who'd accused him of murder and he intended to murder in return.

Marissa tossed the card in a desk drawer and slammed it shut, abruptly feeling alone and turned to ice by knowing someone was watching her, hating her . . .

And waiting for another chance to kill her.

8

1

Marissa jumped when the doorbell rang. After she'd peeped out the family room window as well as the peephole in the front door, she finally opened the door to a boy of about sixteen with acne. "Pizza for Gray?" he asked a bit uncertainly, surely having noticed the peering she'd done before she would accept the pizza she'd ordered. She handed him money she had left lying on a nearby table, told him to keep the change, slammed and bolted the door. She watched him stroll down the front walk toward the pizza truck, shaking his head and laughing.

Marissa carried the pizza to the kitchen and opened the box. It smelled heavenly, but she'd suddenly lost her appetite. Then her stomach growled again, a reminder that she'd eaten only a candy bar at work, and she decided she had to stop thinking about the ring and the Christmas card long enough to force down at least one slice.

Marissa first fixed a bowl of dog food for Lindsay, who began eating as if she hadn't eaten for days. Then Marissa set about trying to force down some nourishment for herself. When she was halfway through her slice of pizza, the doorbell rang again. Marissa stiffened. Catherine and James wouldn't be home so early and Catherine certainly wouldn't ring the doorbell. Who else . . .

"Oh, how ridiculous!" Marissa said aloud. Lindsay, chomping greedily at her own dinner, looked up at her. "I hardly think a murderer is going to ring the bell. I'm acting like a fool." She walked with determination from the kitchen but couldn't help grabbing a knife lying on the counter.

Marissa looked through the peephole, sighed with relief, and opened the door. Eric Montgomery stood in front of her holding his hat, blond curls blowing in the wind, his cheeks reddened from the cold. He glanced at her hand.

"May I come in?" he asked. "Or do you intend to hack me to pieces with that paring knife?"

Embarrassed, Marissa looked down at the dull three-inch blade on the knife clenched at her side. She put her hand behind her back and said, "Oh, I just had it in my hand and forgot to lay it down."

Eric raised his eyebrows in an "I don't believe one word of that" way. "I'm probably the last person in the world you want to see after our earlier encounter."

She hesitated. "Why are you here?"

"If you'll let me in, I'll tell you."

"I don't want to fight with you anymore."

"I don't want to fight with you anymore, either. May I come in?"

Marissa sighed loudly. "Oh . . . all right."

"Thank you, and may I say you're mighty gracious, ma'am."

Marissa shut the door just as Lindsay rushed in, ready to save her now that she'd licked her doggie bowl clean. She looked at Eric and emitted a long, low growl. Eric stooped and rubbed the ears of the valiant watchdog, which immediately stopped growling.

"What's wrong?" Marissa asked anxiously. "Do you know where the ring on Gretchen's grave came from? My God, no one else has been murdered, have they? Catherine! Has something happened to Catherine?"

"Thoughts rush like missiles through your mistress's mind, don't they?" Eric asked Lindsay before he stood up. "And you've always told me Catherine was the panicky one. No, Marissa, nothing of note has happened. I just . . . well . . ." He looked down and for a moment she thought he was going to shuffle his feet. "We didn't finish talking earlier—"

"Fighting."

"I wouldn't say we were *fighting*."

"I would."

"Okay. Can we compromise? We were *arguing*." Marissa gave him a noncommittal look. "Anyway, we didn't get to finish—"

"I don't want to *argue* anymore."

"Dammit, Marissa, will you just let me get out what I'm trying to say?"

"Fine. Go ahead. Make it quick."

"Now I feel like I'm in the fourth grade and I've been called to the front of the class for bad behavior." Marissa stared at him stonily. "I want to talk to you. At least I did when I came over, but if you're going to be too mad to even listen to me, I'll just leave."

Marissa almost grabbed his arm as he turned toward the door, shocked by her response. She immediately tried to look blasé. "You don't have to leave. I think we were having the fight, argument, whatever, we should have had over four years ago. So stay and let's finish it."

"Well, that sounds like a promising beginning. Any place in particular you'd like for me to sit?"

Eric seemed slightly more relaxed, almost friendly, and Marissa felt her muscles loosening. "If you haven't eaten, I have a very large pizza in the kitchen I ordered because Catherine is out with James. Would you like to help me with it?"

Eric smiled. "I thought I smelled pizza as soon as you put away your weapon and let me in. I'd be happy to have some."

They walked into the high-ceilinged kitchen with its shining wood floor and linen-colored glass-fronted cabinets. At one end of the kitchen, three-quarters of a wall composed of windows stood behind lowered pale yellow semi-opaque Roman blinds. In the summer, the windows provided a striking view of the rose garden. Six padded chairs sat around the large island covered with a brown-gold quartz top with a simple wrought bronze-finished chandelier above.

"I always liked this kitchen," Eric said, barely entering the room, obviously ill at ease. "The kitchen at my parents' house is large but only has two fairly small windows. Mom also insisted on a kitchen table too big for the room and little rugs Dad and I always trip over."

"Did you go home and take a mood-improvement pill or something?"

"Is there such a thing?"

"I don't know, but you're certainly acting different than you did in the cemetery."

"I had some time to get my temper under control, to 'compose' myself, as my mother would say."

"Okay," Marissa said warily. She turned and opened the refrigerator. "How are your parents?"

"They don't go out much. I thought that would have changed by now, but I believe it's become a habit. They were invited to about a dozen Christmas parties and don't plan on attending any of them."

"They didn't go to the Addison party?"

"No. And frankly, I don't see as much of them as I'd planned to when I came back from Philadelphia." A shadow of sadness washed over Eric's face and he looked at the floor. "I don't think they really want to see that much of me."

"I'm sure that's not true." Marissa realized she'd sounded as if she were merely saying the proper thing. She quickly looked into the refrigerator. "We have Coke, Seven Up, milk, tonic water—"

"Beer?"

Marissa looked at him. "Do you intend to drink on duty, Chief Deputy?"

"I'm not on duty, although I've asked to be called if anything happens."

"Have a seat at the table or the island. Want your beer in a glass?"

"No, ma'am. I take mine straight from the bottle."

"I'm having Diet Coke. It makes no sense—a pizza with a million calories and a *diet* drink." As Marissa fixed the drinks, Lindsay looked at her plaintively. "No beer or Coke for you. Just bottled water. Will that suit you?"

It did, along with a bacon strip treat. Lindsay then parked herself beside Eric's chair, clearly hoping he was a messy eater who tended to drop pieces of pizza on the floor.

Marissa also supplied plates, forks, and napkins. Then she sat down across from Eric and wondered what she was going to say. She'd run out of small talk.

Eric solved the problem for her: "I see you're still wearing your mother-of-pearl ring."

"Moonstone, Eric. I never take it off unless I do something with my hands I think might damage the stone."

Eric took a deep sip of beer. "Why moonstone?"

"One year Gretchen and I got interested in gemstones and their meanings. Moonstone means 'beloved by the moon.' Hindu mythology teaches that moonstone formed moonlight. It's a sign of feminine wisdom and in Hindu represents the female aspect of the crown. It's also supposed to give us insight and emotional balance. And I learned that on my own. Catherine didn't tell me."

Eric looked at her intently. "Insight, emotional balance, and wisdom. Maybe I should wear moonstone."

"It represents *feminine* wisdom, Eric," Marissa said patiently. "Heaven knows what might happen if *you* wore it!"

He grinned. "The way my luck has been running, I certainly shouldn't tempt the fates, or Gods, or whatever. Now, however, I know why you and Gretchen were so much smarter than I was." He took another gulp of beer, then reached for a piece of pizza. "Did you and Gretchen show these rings to other people?"

"Well, they could see the rings on our fingers—they're large rings. But we never took them off and showed the infinity symbol. It was to be a secret just for us." She smiled. "Teenagers."

"Not just teenagers. You're wearing yours. You must still love Gretchen just like I do."

"Of course I do, Eric! Not a day goes by that I don't think about her and sometimes I still cry over her. I carry her picture in my wallet. During the years I was in Chicago, I couldn't force myself to go to a piano concert because I knew I'd fall apart not seeing Gretchen up on that stage . . . And—"

Eric held up his hand. "Okay. I get it and I'm sorry I said what I did. It was really stupid." He took another bite of pizza, gazing straight ahead as if he could find something to say to change the mood by staring at the cabinets. Finally, he came out with, "Can you remember the last time you saw Gretchen wearing the ring?"

Marissa thought for a moment. "No. I'm sorry, but when you get so used to seeing something on a person—like glasses, for instance—you don't notice anymore." She paused. "I helped her off the boat the last night, though. She was right-handed, so she would have given me that hand, and I would have noticed if the ring was gone. At least I think I would have." She sighed, rubbed her temples for a moment, then burst out, "Photographs! Do you have any photographs of her taken shortly before . . . the boat trip?"

"You mean her murder," Eric said flatly. "I didn't have many and I left all my pictures of Gretchen and—well, you—at my parents' house. My mother would have dozens of pictures of Gretchen, though. She took photos all the time."

"I remember. Then all you have to do is look through them—"

Eric shook his head. "I told you—our relationship has never been the same since Gretchen's death. Mom and Dad haven't disowned me, but things are different. Tense. Strained. The three of us seem to be weighing what we say before we say it." His gaze dropped. "I only see them about once a month. There's a distance, a chill toward me, especially from Mom. I can't ask her to let me see her collection of pictures, especially those of Gretchen. She blames me even more than Dad does for not sticking by Gretchen's side that night and for letting her get drunk."

"And you've always blamed me."

Eric suddenly looked up into her eyes. Marissa saw a maelstrom of emotion behind his gaze for a few moments, then resolution. "I did blame you at first and I did a damned good job of blaming you for months—longer."

"Until tonight?"

"No. I began to come to my senses about a year ago."

"So why were you so angry with me at Gretchen's grave? Why did you say I was at fault for not being adamant enough with the police and that I'd kept you with me when you should have been with your sister?"

Eric hesitated. "I believe I'd stopped blaming the Marissa in my memory a while ago. When you came back to care for your mother, though, I was faced with the real you again and the blame seeped back. I was shocked and I decided to stay away from you. I'd still be keeping my distance if it weren't for your wreck. But you did have a car wreck and I realized how I would have felt if you'd died. Not guilty, but as if I'd died, too. Then at the grave, all the blame and anger and resentment I'd felt after Gretchen died spewed out of me. Just listening to myself made me realize how wrong I'd been to push the responsibility for Gretchen's death on you as well as myself." He gave her a slight smile. "By the time I got home, I realized that for the first time in over four years I felt clean and light. You were right—Gretchen was a woman. I didn't do anything wrong by treating her like one. I have a right to be happy. I'm not just a monument to my little sister."

They stared at each other for a moment. Marissa felt like he was looking into her soul, the way she used to feel. But it had been such a long time since she'd been comfortable with that invasion, at ease with her vulnerability. Her muscles tightened slightly.

"Wow . . . You realized how you felt about me *and* yourself while you were yelling at me in a cemetery?" she asked hesitantly.

Eric looked at her unflinchingly, his mouth slightly open, before he let out a whoop of laughter that surprised Lindsay into a barking fit. He laughed until a tear ran down his left cheek, and after Lindsay quieted he said chokingly, "Yes. I've never been a master of the moment. I suppose I could have picked a better spot than a graveyard to announce my feelings at the top of my voice." He spent a moment wiping at his cheek with a napkin and then said, "You were always the only person who could make me laugh that way."

"I'm glad, but the bad news is that I don't think the couple standing at the grave beside us will be voting for you for sheriff in the fall."

"I don't care about them. I don't even care if I lose the election. At least I don't right at this moment."

Lindsay cocked her head toward the covered windows and barked, startling both of them before they laughed.

"All three of us are of the same opinion." Marissa glanced down. "I'd really like to get off this subject, but there's something about Gretchen that night I've always wanted to tell you but never got the chance." She looked up and saw wariness creep into Eric's gaze. "Your parents treated her like a child and I think she accepted it from them because most parents always think of their children as too young to know what they're doing. But Gretchen couldn't accept it from you. She knew how you thought of her and she hated it. I've wondered if she wasn't trying to prove something to you that night with the beer and Dillon. She was showing you she'd do as she pleased no matter what you thought."

"You're probably right," Eric said softly. "She didn't even like beer, but the lab tests came back showing she'd had far over the legal limit."

"That's something else I've thought about, Eric. We brought a twelve-pack of beer on that trip. I had one. That left eleven beers for four people. Do you think everyone else had just one beer, leaving the other seven for Gretchen? I don't believe so, especially considering how much Dillon and Tonya liked beer. I'm certain someone brought more liquor, maybe because they *wanted* to get Gretchen drunk."

Eric looked down. "That's crossed my mind, too, Marissa, but even if someone encouraged her to drink liquor and she didn't want it, she wouldn't have drunk it. Gretchen could be extremely stubborn. I also don't think someone tricked her by pouring liquor into her beer—she would have tasted it and she would have stopped drinking. She *meant* to get drunk that night, but I can't believe Gretchen would voluntarily drink herself into half oblivion just to prove to me that she'd do what she pleased. She had a reason, Marissa."

"I know. She may have had a secret demon she was trying to drown. She was troubled that summer. She said she was nervous about her concert schedule and I accepted her explanation that it was worry over her performances. Maybe she'd learned something about Dillon, something he'd realized shortly before we went to the island. Usually, if that were the case, she would have told me immediately. I'm ashamed to say I didn't make myself very available to her that summer, though. I was lost in myself and you and our wedding plans."

Eric flinched slightly. "Two more months and we would have been husband and wife. But I wouldn't let that happen. I *couldn't* let it happen, Marissa. I regret the way I broke off our engagement, but I don't regret breaking it. I would have destroyed our marriage with my misplaced anger, my guilt and depression that were too big a burden for me to carry. I would have tried to push some of that off on you and picked fights over anything and everything." Lindsay barked again and Eric smiled. "Another agreement from the four-legged contingent."

"I think I was partially to blame, Eric. I knew Gretchen better than anyone except you and I knew something was not right with her that summer, but I didn't try to help her."

Eric looked at her. "The bottom line is that if either of us had responsibility for Gretchen, it was me, not you. But even I shouldn't have had responsibility for her. She was twenty-one years old. She was a woman." He paused and took a deep breath. "Marissa, *please* forgive me for my past behavior. I don't blame you for one thing that happened that awful night and I was a complete fool to have *ever* blamed you."

Marissa didn't break eye contact with Eric, but she swallowed hard to hold back tears. Thank you almost made it past her lips before she reminded herself she didn't need to thank Eric. What had happened to Gretchen *hadn't* been her fault. Nor had she downplayed to the police what she'd seen Dillon do—push Gretchen's leg so that she lost her balance. Eric had finally granted the truth he'd tried to dodge for so long, and for that he needed acknowledgment.

"I'm glad, Eric," Marissa said softly. "I'm glad you don't blame me, that you aren't angry with me, that you'll *talk* to me." She smiled. "I've missed you."

"And I've missed you." His voice sounded warm. "*So* much."

Their gazes met and held. Under the strong kitchen light, the gold flecks in Eric's eyes seemed brighter, the gold-tipped brown lashes longer. His eyes narrowed slightly and his breath quickened. Their hands, each gripping the granite top of the island, slid closer and touched softly, tenderly. Their lips could only have been an inch apart when Lindsay burst into frenzied barking and raced to the windows, teeth bared.

Eric jumped up and followed her, jerking aside the blinds. "Good God!" he exclaimed. "The rose garden is on fire!"

2

Shock rocketed through Marissa, rendering her motionless, her mouth slightly open. Through the semi-opaque blinds, she could see the soft glow of fire; through the space where Eric had pushed the blinds aside, she saw yellow and red flames leaping in the cold darkness of night.

Lindsay jumped up and down, spraying saliva on the window with her frantic barking. Eric jerked a cell phone from his pocket and dialed, giving Marissa's address, telling someone to bring one of the smaller trucks. Finally, he turned and started out of the kitchen with a quick, "You stay here," to her. That snapped her from her trance. In seconds, she'd vacated her stool and nearly trampled on his heels as they ran for the front door.

The three of them, Lindsay making as much noise as possible, exploded onto the porch, down the steps, and around to the rose garden. A thin layer of snow lay on the ground and nothing else burned—just the sixteen rosebushes Annemarie had planted and nurtured for years. Tears rose in Marissa's eyes.

Sam Patterson dashed out of the house next door and joined them several feet away from the fire. "What happened?"

"We don't know," Eric said. "I suddenly saw flames. Someone used an accelerant and confined the fire to the rose garden. You didn't happen to see anyone, did you?"

"No," Sam said dolefully. "The wife and I were at the other end of the house. Then our dog started raising hell."

"So did Lindsay." Marissa shivered and folded her arms. "That's what she was barking at earlier, Eric, but we didn't pay any attention. If we'd just looked out the window, we would have seen who did this."

"But we *didn't* look out the window." A fire truck pulled up almost directly behind them. "Thank God that was quick, although I don't think either house was in danger," Eric said to Mr. Patterson.

The man nodded and looked back at his home. "Well, I have to report what I know so far or the wife will be out here lickety-split. She'll kill me if I don't get back and tell her *something*. I see her hovering on the porch now. Talk to you later, Marissa," he called as he dashed back to his house where the dreaded curious wife awaited answers.

A firefighter loomed beside Eric, who said, "The fire isn't large, but the hose, buckets, everything we could have used to put it out ourselves are stored for winter. Plus, I'd like for you to be around in case any other embers spring to life." The firefighter nodded and returned to the truck while Marissa saw more neighbors coming out onto their porches.

"You'd better go back inside," Eric said to her. "You don't even have a jacket and your lips look like they're going to turn blue. You also need to get Lindsay out of the way. I know you don't want anything to happen to her."

Marissa looked at him, nodded, and then motioned to Lindsay, who obediently followed her into the house despite the exciting commotion outside. She walked into the family room and dropped onto her father's recliner, hardly aware of her movements, blind to her surroundings. All she could see was the fire devouring her mother's rosebushes—a fire set by someone who hated Annemarie or who hated Marissa?

"Mom is dead," Marissa said aloud. "The Christmas postcard, the fire outside of my home, and, most horrible, the deliberate attempt to send me into the river. Someone hates *me*." Lindsay sat at her feet, tilting her head as Marissa talked. Marissa looked at her and smiled. "We'll show whoever is watching that we're not too scared to watch, either."

She shrugged into her down jacket, traded her damp bunny slippers for a pair of boots, and hooked Lindsay's leash to her collar. At the last minute, Lindsay picked up her stuffed cow and together they faced the fire in the night once more.

"I thought I told you to go inside," Eric said as Marissa walked up beside him.

"I did. Then I came out again." Eric looked at her in annoyance. "It's *my* lawn, Eric. I'd like to know what's going on out here."

"Did Lindsay want to know what's going on, too?"

"We're a team."

A firefighter yelled, "Okay!" and someone shut off the hose. Marissa gazed at the small, blackened sticks dripping with water. They looked even more pathetic than they had earlier in the evening when they'd simply sat in bare winter sleep. She wanted to cry, but she wouldn't, not in front of Eric. She'd have time to cry later.

One of the firefighters approached Eric. "The accelerant was kerosene. Makes for a nice, steady fire, not an explosion like gasoline." Eric nodded. The man held something out to Eric in a gloved hand. "I found this about four feet away from the fire." He held it out and Eric took it in his own gloved hand. "I don't think it was meant to burn."

Marissa looked down at a plastic doll about eighteen inches long and wearing a pink dress. Its blond hair was barely mussed

and it stared at them with sapphire blue eyes. A piece of folded
ivory stationery had been tucked inside the pink sash of its dress.
Eric turned on his flashlight as he withdrew the paper, unfolded
it, and read:

> *For Marissa*
>
> *Tyger! Tyger! burning bright*
> *In the forests of the night,*
> *What immortal hand or eye*
> *Could frame thy fearful symmetry?*

9

1

Marissa swayed but righted herself before Eric could try to catch her. "Dillon," she said faintly. "Dillon is the Tyger. Dillon set the fire. Dillon wants to kill me. He won't stop, Eric; he'll just keep after me until—"

"That's enough," Eric said abruptly. "Inside. Right now!"

Eric gave her a slight push and she moved like a sleepwalker, still clutching Lindsay's leash. Once inside the house, Eric locked and flipped the dead bolt on the front door. He pushed her down onto the recliner and strode to the kitchen, holding the doll and the paper. First he yelled, asking where the ziplock plastic bags were; then he yelled again, asking the location of the vodka. Marissa still sat motionless in the chair, clutching the leash, when he returned with two glasses.

"Vodka and tonic," he said. "One for you, one for me. You don't get both."

"I really don't want a drink—"

"Yes, you really do. Drink up or I'll arrest you."

Marissa took one small sip. After that went down, she took a gulp and Eric beamed. He went back to the kitchen and brought in Lindsay's water bowl. "No vodka for you, but you did a lot of panting outside. You must be parched."

"Eric, you're trying to keep your tone light so I won't freak out, but it's not helping. That doll is supposed to be me and Dillon put it next to the fire! My God, he'd been gone for over four years when I moved here to take care of Mom. I never dreamed he'd come back for me!"

"Calm down," Eric said gently. "We have no proof that Dillon is even here, much less that's he's come back to Aurora Falls to get back at you for accusing him of murder."

"No? Well, just take a look at what came in the mail today!" Marissa jumped up and opened a desk drawer, pulling out the postcard she'd received earlier in the day. "Look at it, Eric!"

Eric handled the postcard by the edges, carefully looking at the hand-drawn figures at the top of the falls and then turning it over to read the typed message: **Together forever, Marissa** and the signature: *D.A.*

"Dillon Archer," Marissa said loudly. "*Dillon Archer!*"

"I heard you the first time, Marissa. You said this came today?"

"Yes. When I got home, Catherine and James were here. She said I'd received several Christmas cards. It was in an envelope and I'm sure she didn't pay much attention to it."

"An envelope without a stamp. Hand delivered." Eric looked beyond her, his gaze lost in thought. Finally, he said, "I can see Dillon writing something like 'Together forever,' but 'Tyger! Tyger! burning bright—'"

"I don't picture Dillon reading William Blake, either, but that's such a well-known stanza and it's one that would appeal to him." Eric looked at her. "Don't you think it would have been something he liked, something he'd remember?"

"I don't know Dillon's tastes in poetry, but I can imagine him liking this better than some sweet love poem."

"Me, too. I suppose it's because of what he did to Gretchen. 'What immortal hand or eye / Could frame thy fearful symmetry?'" Marissa closed her eyes. "Eric, in one day I've received a morbid but romantic picture of Dillon and me at the falls and later an effigy of me lying beside a fire," she said softly. "I think he's telling me that I'm *his*, whether by choice or by force."

2

Almost immediately, Eric's cell phone rang. He swore and then announced there had been an attempted armed robbery of the convenience store on Chadwick Street with shots fired. He had to leave immediately after making Marissa promise to lock and dead-bolt the door and spend the evening in the house and not even take Lindsay out for a quick visit to the lawn before bedtime. "And if anyone calls about the fire, I'd brush it off as a prank," he said earnestly. "We don't want to stir up a lot of excitement. After all, if Dillon *is* behind this, it's just what he'd like."

"You think I need surveillance?" Marissa asked anxiously.

"Yes, but I won't have anyone free until tomorrow night. Until then, I want you to use this." He held out a can of Mace. "I'm sure you can read the directions by yourself. And Marissa, don't go *anywhere* without it and keep it handy—not in the bottom of your tote bag buried under all that stuff you women carry." He smiled, looked as if he were going to kiss her, then quickly turned and headed for the door.

After he left, Marissa's thoughts roiled. Could Dillon Archer really be responsible for her wreck or for the fire? Who else? She would never say she didn't have an enemy in the world—she believed everyone had at least a few people who didn't wish them well. But people who wished her dead? She could only think of one.

Marissa realized her cold hands were trembling. She couldn't draw a deep breath and she felt the muscles pulling between her scalp and her back with enough force to break her neck. She knew this feeling well. It would lead to one of the migraine headaches she'd experienced ever since Gretchen's death and she would *not* give in to one of those migraines now, she decided. They blurred her senses and she needed to be completely alert.

Marissa took a Maxalt for the headache. She'd recently read that some doctors administer Botox for migraines. She might try it, she decided. If the Botox didn't help her migraine, it would at least give her the forehead of a fifteen-year-old.

In case the Maxalt didn't work, she needed a distraction. Marissa turned on the television and flipped through six different shows but couldn't concentrate on any of them. So much for cable TV, she thought. She picked up a fashion magazine and discovered she hadn't the least interest in patterned tights or flared coats.

She wandered to the stereo, glancing at some of the CDs her mother had listened to until the last month of her life. Marissa smiled. Annemarie had loved to dance to the rock music that had been popular when she had met Bernard. She'd told Marissa he would dance whenever she wanted back then. Only after they'd been married a couple of years had he told her dancing to rock music made him feel like a fool and Bernard Gray had officially retired to the sidelines of the dance floor.

Annemarie hadn't, though, and often she danced with her daughters, telling them dancing could usually banish a bad mood. Marissa picked a CD and in a few minutes was absent-mindedly swaying her hips and moving her feet to Billy Idol's "Dancing with Myself." Lindsay, used to these displays, sat on the couch with a stuffed frog in her mouth, being an attentive audience.

Marissa had just begun to concentrate on the song instead of thinking about her rose garden when suddenly Lindsay barked and ran to the front door. Oh God, no, Marissa thought. Not another semi-calamity. Lindsay wasn't barking frantically as she had earlier, though. She barked the way she usually did when people approached the house, even before they'd knocked or rung the doorbell. Sure enough, seconds later the doorbell sounded. Marissa jumped and her heart picked up speed. She should ignore the bell, she thought. Except that Catherine might have forgotten her key. If she and James were returning, though, their date had been short.

The doorbell rang again and Marissa couldn't ignore its pull. "I'm worse than Pavlov's dogs," she said aloud. She lowered the music and moved slowly to the door, picking up a fireplace poker along the way. She looked out the peephole and on the lighted porch stood Tonya Archer, formerly Tonya Ward, whom Marissa had known since childhood. She saw no one else on the porch. Tonya looked around as if thinking of leaving and Marissa impulsively unbolted, unlocked, and opened the door.

"Hi," they said simultaneously, exchanging nervous smiles.

Tonya's smile stayed fixed. "I'm sorry I didn't call earlier, but I was afraid you might not want me to come. I don't know how you feel about me, but I'd really like to talk to you. We haven't talked much since . . . well, for years."

"We haven't talked at all." A short mental battle went on in Marissa's mind before she opened the door farther. "Come in."

Tonya stepped in almost tentatively and then looked down at Lindsay standing armed with her stuffed frog. "This is Lindsay, Tonya. She doesn't bite."

"Lindsay!" Tonya laughed and stooped to pet the dog's head. "Don't tell me—you named her for Lindsay Wagner, the Bionic Woman!"

"I can't believe you remember."

"My God, Marissa, you watched the reruns and talked about Lindsay Wagner all the time. You even had a poster of her on your bedroom wall."

"Well, I've finally taken it down," Marissa said sheepishly. "It was yellowing around the edges."

"But I'll bet you didn't throw it away."

"You're a mind reader. It's safely tucked away in my closet, where some archaeologist will find it hundreds of years from now and put it in a museum."

Tonya laughed and stood up. At five foot six she was taller than Marissa, and when she slid out of her coat Marissa saw that Tonya had gained a little weight, but it did nothing to spoil the enviable figure of her teenage years. She wore fashionably tight jeans and black boots. Her auburn hair hung thick and straight over the shoulders of her lavender turtleneck sweater. She looked remarkably attractive, yet her large hazel eyes seemed harder, the planes of her face sharper, than the last time Marissa had seen her.

Marissa waited for Tonya to say something about the fire in the side yard, but either she'd parked on the street and hadn't noticed it in the dark or she'd decided not to mention it. Instead, Tonya cocked her head. "I hear Billy Idol. You were dancing, weren't you?"

Marissa blushed. "No, I was just listening—you know, moving around to the music."

"That's called dancing. How many times did you and Catherine and your mother and I dance in this room?"

"Too many to remember." Marissa finally laughed. Then her laughter died, replaced by a sad smile. "It's been a long time since we've danced or even talked together, Tonya."

"That's why I simply *had* to see you tonight," Tonya said earnestly. "I've been thinking so much about you since your mother's death and your move back from Chicago. I didn't try to talk to you at first—I knew you were dealing with your mother's illness and I was caught up in my love life." She smiled. "I know most people were surprised when Andrew and I got married."

"*I* certainly was. I didn't even know you two were seeing each other, but Mom was very sick in the late spring and early summer. I didn't go out much and not many people came to visit. They knew Mom was too sick to enjoy company. Anyway, when I told her about the marriage she was surprised but pleased."

"Really? She was always so kind to me." Tonya smiled, more to herself than to Marissa. "Andrew and I eloped. No fanfare, and a quick honeymoon in New York City. Andrew said if we spent much time there, I'd spend every dollar we had on clothes. He had to get me home—fast!" They giggled. "Honestly, Marissa, my marriage has made me even happier than I'd hoped."

"I'm glad," Marissa said sincerely.

"Is Catherine here?"

"No, she's on a date." Tonya's eyebrows rose. Marissa waited a few seconds and then decided keeping her sister's new relationship undercover was silly. "She's having dinner with James Eastman."

Tonya frowned. "James Eastman? Did Renée finally come back to town to get the divorce she wanted so badly?"

"No. James had a thorough search made for her, but no one could find her. He was able to divorce her on the grounds of desertion."

"No one could find her? I thought she'd go running back to Mommy and Daddy in New Orleans."

"They didn't want her. We all think she's probably with another man, only this one is rich."

"Maybe rich, but certainly not better looking than James. Oh well, the few times I was at an event she graced with her presence she struck me as a shallow snob and she looked at me like I was dirt under her feet. If she gave up James, though, I'll bet she'll regret it. Her loss, not his. I'm glad he's dating again."

Tonya's smile faded. "I know you're wondering why I'm here. I'm nervous as hell and I can't keep up the small talk. I've been thinking so much about you and Catherine, it's almost Christmas and Andrew is working late, and . . . well, tonight just felt like *the* night I had to try to fix things between us. I know we had some serious trouble, but it was years ago and it isn't as if we were deliberately trying to hurt each other. I don't believe it's something we can't work out, Marissa. Please say we can try."

Tonya's big hazel eyes looked pleading, her mouth trembled slightly, and a shallow crease appeared between her eyebrows. Marissa couldn't remember Tonya Ward ever acting anxious and pleading. The change in her manner struck Marissa as not only odd but also suspect, as if Tonya wasn't telling the whole truth.

Marissa teetered on the edge of maintaining the shield that had existed between them since Gretchen's death. If she was polite but cold, Tonya wouldn't persist. She would leave, and maybe that was best.

Then Marissa remembered how important she'd felt when she was young and this pretty, popular girl *two* years Marissa's senior treated her as if she were an equal, as much a part of the friendship as Catherine. Suddenly Marissa felt a wave of affection for the Tonya with whom she'd spent so many happy days on the boat, trailed along with her and Catherine to movies, traded so many secrets.

Traded so many secrets.

"You're right." Marissa felt slightly guilty. She felt too doubt-ful about Tonya to yearn for comradeship. At the same time, Marissa couldn't help wanting time to scrutinize this woman who hadn't spoken to her for years and now suddenly, almost desperately, wanted closeness. Marissa managed to speak warmly: "We shouldn't let ourselves drift apart. Have a seat on the couch. I have a nice fire going and the room is cozy. I'll turn off the music—"

"No, I like the music," Tonya said quickly. "It reminds me of your mother."

"Good. Me, too. Would you like a glass of wine, a soft drink, coffee, hot chocolate—?"

"Hot chocolate sounds good on a cold evening." Tonya smiled. "With lots of marshmallows if you have them!"

"I'm sorry I didn't call after your car wreck," Tonya said later as she and Marissa sat down in the family room with their hot chocolate.

"Andrew did."

"But it seemed as if *I* didn't care. Andrew tells me every-thing he knows that's going on with you, but still I feel cut off."

"We've been out of touch since Gretchen died, Tonya. We haven't spoken since then except to say 'hello' and that was ages ago." Marissa paused. "I tried to talk to you when I saw you around town, but you always seemed to dodge me."

Tonya looked cornered for a moment, shifted her gaze to the fire, and then said without conviction, "I didn't know how to handle matters after Gretchen's . . . accident. Our versions of what we'd seen differed so much."

"They really differed very little—just enough to make Dillon someone trying to save her or purposely kill her."

"Is that still what you remember?" Tonya asked hesitantly. "That Dillon pushed Gretchen?"

Marissa waited a moment and then nodded. "I can see him push her thigh as if it were yesterday, Tonya."

Tonya continued to look into the fire while she sipped her hot chocolate. Finally she said, "We saw things differently. The light was so bad, we were all scared, but I was closer to Dillon than you."

"And you didn't see his hand *push* against her right thigh?"

"I saw him reaching around both thighs, or trying to, and one arm was around her, but the other arm hadn't reached it and Gretchen started tottering and slipping—her feet were sweating—and then she . . . she just fell."

Marissa's gaze searched Tonya. She looked truthful, yet something in her voice sounded false, flat. Marissa's defenses went up, but she tried not to let them show. "Tonya, while we were still on Gray's Island, we each told the police what we'd seen in the church. Andrew claimed he was too far back in the shadows to see much of anything. Eric was on the main floor and could hardly see anything in that bad light. You and I were the eyewitnesses and our stories didn't jibe. There was an investigation, but with Dillon gone the investigation didn't lead to his arrest."

Tonya finally looked at her. "Why are you telling me all of this when I already know? I was *there.*"

"Just to make certain that this time we're on the same page, not arguing over what happened after . . . the fall."

"We are."

"Okay." Marissa took a deep breath. "Let's agree that the lighting was bad, we were standing at different angles, and we saw things differently. Let's forget the last four and a half years, act like there's never been a rift in our friendship, and you tell me *why* you really came to see me tonight."

Tonya flushed, seemed to fumble for something to say, and finally blurted, "Marissa, I thought you were glad to see me."

"I *am* glad to see you."

"Then why do you sound so hostile?"

"I'm not hostile. I just want you to be honest with me. I've known you a long time, Tonya, and I know when you're not being completely truthful. You want to renew our friendship, but there's more to this visit."

Tonya set her mug on an end table. "I should go."

"No!" The volume of Marissa's voice startled both of them. "I'm sorry. I didn't mean to shout." Marissa closed her eyes for a moment and then looked at Tonya repentantly. "This has been a bad day for me." She hesitated. Should she say something about the postcard? The fire?

Marissa made up her mind in an instant. No. She hadn't even talked to Tonya for years. The last time they were together was when Dillon had pushed Gretchen to her death, only Tonya told the police he'd tried to save her. Tonya would no doubt hear about the fire tomorrow, but Marissa intended to keep the postcard and the "Tyger" note confidential. "I'm sorry if I haven't made you feel welcome, Tonya. Your visit surprised me and it was only natural that the awful night on Gray's Island came up. We've talked about it, though, so now we can move on to something else."

Tonya's face had lost color and she ran her right hand through her hair the way she'd always done when she was agitated. "You're right. Gray's Island was the elephant in the room. And I admit that I was nervous about dropping in on you." She glanced at her watch. "Are you expecting Catherine and James soon? Or does she sleep at his house?"

"Tonya, this is only their second date. Catherine does *not* sleep at James's house."

"You don't have to sound so prickly, like you're talking to someone who'd spend the night with any man who'd buy her dinner!"

The venom in Tonya's voice stunned Marissa. "Tonya, that's not what I was implying. I wasn't implying anything, really, except . . . well, you know Catherine."

"Oh yes. A lady to the end of her days. She's probably still a virgin. I wonder how James is handling *that* after being married to Renée?"

Marissa fought for composure. "Tonya, are you angry with Catherine about something?"

"No. Well, just for being with James, I guess. I had a couple of dates with him a lifetime ago. I wasn't good enough, though. He married Renée." She laughed harshly. "If he thought he was getting a lady, he made a big mistake. A big *humiliating* mistake. Luckily for James, Renée seemed to vanish into thin air just like Dillon." Her gaze drifted past Marissa. "But I don't think Aurora Falls has gotten rid of either of them."

IO

1

"What makes you think Aurora Falls hasn't gotten rid of Dillon?" Marissa asked, trying to sound artless. After all, Tonya was married to Dillon's brother. She might know more about Dillon than anyone besides Andrew.

Tonya seemed to shudder slightly and then smiled unconvincingly. "I don't know. I guess it's because he was born in this town and he'll always be part of it. I mean look at us—we haven't seen him for almost five years, but he's dominating our thoughts at our big reunion. Dillon seems like a part of this place and he's causing trouble, just like now, whether he's dead or alive."

"Do *you* think Dillon is dead?" Marissa finally asked gently.

Tonya blinked twice, then seemed to shake herself back into the moment and began speaking with airy unconcern: "Oh, I have no idea. Andrew hasn't heard from him since Dillon left town, but of course he wouldn't. Dillon used to make fun of Andrew for being such a straight arrow, and he is."

"Does Andrew think Dillon caused Gretchen's death?"

"He refuses to talk about that subject. He talks about Dillon sometimes—how mean their father was to both of them but especially Dillon, how much worse things got after their mother died, the good times they had on the *Annemarie*. He mentions how much they both liked Mitch Farrell playing 'big brother' to them, taking them places occasionally, showing them how to do some woodworking. You remember Sheriff Farrell had that whole building full of woodworking equipment. He made all kinds of stuff like cedar chests and . . . oh, I don't know what all.

"Old Mr. Archer probably wouldn't have let anyone else take the boys places, but Sheriff Farrell could be intimidating. And he could have put the word out and ruined Archer Auto Repair." Tonya's voice had grown vague, almost maundering. "Old Mr. Archer was furious when Andrew left for college. Andrew worked his way through school."

"I know, Tonya. He'd already graduated summa cum laude when I went to Chicago."

"Oh, that's right." Tonya waved her hand absently. "I'm getting time mixed up. Andrew loved college. Can you imagine loving college? I knew it wasn't for me. I know Catherine *really* loved it. How about you?"

"It was all right," Marissa answered tersely. She didn't want to say anything that would disrupt Tonya's train of thought and possibly reveal something about her state of mind, because at the moment she was still trying to get a fix on the woman sitting across from her, a Tonya whom Marissa felt she'd never met.

Tonya seemed to be rambling as she gazed into the fire: "I was friendly with Dillon when I was around seventeen. We were *friends,* that's all, but Andrew doesn't want to hear a word about it, not that there's anything to tell. He always felt inferior to Dillon and I guess he had a crush on me even back then, but I didn't know it. I'm glad I didn't, because I thought he definitely wasn't for me and I might have tried to discourage him by saying something to hurt his feelings." She drew a deep breath and continued, "So I don't know a thing about Dillon. I never want to see him again. He's Trouble with a capital *T.*"

"I'm sure Andrew understands you were friendly to Dillon— you were friendly to everybody." Tonya's gaze jerked from the fire to Marissa. "When I said you were friendly to everyone, I just meant you were always pleasant, not flirtatious, with every guy in school, Tonya."

"Some men can't differentiate between pleasant and flirtatious. That was the problem."

Marissa glanced at Tonya, who seemed to be growing stiffer by the moment. Marissa decided to keep babbling. "Frankly, I didn't think about Dillon much during the years I was gone. School kept me busy and I thought I'd be getting married when I graduated. Then things changed and I went to Chicago instead of getting married. But the last month, Dillon has been on my mind. I suppose it's just natural to wonder where he is after almost five years."

Tonya's voice suddenly hardened. "Look, Marissa, I know you're trying to patch up things with Eric, and maybe you think feeding him information about Dillon will help, but you might as well stop questioning me. I don't have any information about Dillon."

Surprise overtook Marissa, and for a moment she could think of nothing to say. Finally, she came out with, "What makes you think I'm trying to patch up things with Eric?"

"I think half the town has heard about him coming here after your wreck and you going to see him two days later—"

"I had to give a statement, Tonya."

"He's been here quite a bit."

"He has not! I don't know who's been telling you all of this, but your source is unreliable. He hasn't 'been here quite a bit,' as you put it. There is *nothing* between Eric and me."

"I guess that's why you're getting so snippy with me."

"I'm not—"

"You are and I think it's time for me to go." Tonya stood, her hair shining like copper in the light of the fire. "I hope we can renew our friendship, Marissa, but I can see it's going to take some time. And I have no interest in whether or not you're seeing Eric again. I don't know why you got so upset when I brought up the subject."

"I didn't get upset."

"Yes, well, whatever you want to call it." Tonya abruptly turned from annoyed to casual. "It's been . . . interesting seeing you again, Marissa. Maybe the next time we talk, we can find a more cheerful topic than Dillon Archer or the love life you're claiming you don't have." She was halfway to the door with Marissa trailing after her and Lindsay bringing up the rear.

"Andrew told me not to 'spring' myself on you this way. He said you'd be defensive and it would probably be best if I just let things drift for a while. I see that he was right."

"Tonya, I didn't mean to upset you or make you angry or interrogate you or offend you in any way," Marissa said as Tonya put on her coat. "I told you I've had a rotten day. It's my fault tonight didn't turn out so well. Can't we try again?"

"Perhaps someday." Tonya had put on a haughty air along with her coat. "I did enjoy seeing you before things got uncomfortable. And Marissa, I hope you won't go whining to Andrew about our less-than-successful visit."

"*Whining?*" Marissa's emotions abruptly swept from regretful to indignant. "Do you think I'd run to your husband and *whine* like a twelve-year-old?"

Tonya gave her a long look. "Honey, I have no idea what you might do. I never did."

2

Andrew had been right, Tonya thought as she started the drive home. He had said she shouldn't spring a visit on Marissa. She should arrange something casual, maybe invite Marissa out to lunch and keep the conversation light before having a serious talk with her. But Andrew didn't know all of the reasons Tonya had wanted to talk to Marissa. He didn't know how upset she was, how sleepless, how many disastrous scenarios she'd imagined. Tonight she had gotten so agitated she'd decided time was desperately short and she needed to talk with Marissa *now*. So Tonya had made the mistake of going to the Grays' house on impulse and she'd been so nervous she'd made a mess of the visit. Worse—a disaster. Marissa no doubt thought she was crazy and would start talking about Tonya to everyone she knew.

Tonya burst into tears. Dammit, she should have listened to Andrew even if he didn't know everything about her life, she thought as she drove with extra care on streets that still bore traces of dirty snow and ice. After all, in his calm, unobtrusive way, he'd managed his own life so much better than she had her own. She loved Andrew more than she had thought herself capable of loving a man who was neither dashingly handsome nor well fixed in the money department. For years, she had pursued that kind of man—pursued and generally lost to a woman younger, prettier, or more socially superior than Tonya Ward. Acting charming in the subdued, cultured way she'd been practicing since she was an adolescent had become so tiring, she'd thought of abandoning the whole project and resigning herself to being the mistress of a man who would at least "keep" her, even if he'd never propose.

Then Andrew had asked for a date. She now blushed in shame to think she'd accepted mostly because he'd invited her to dinner at the Larke Inn, which she loved. She'd expected to enjoy getting dressed up, eating excellent food in the elegant ambience of the dining room, and perhaps catching the eye of one of the city's prominent bachelors or ex-husbands while not having to worry about impressing Andrew.

Instead, Andrew had amazed her with his polished demeanor, perfect manners, and only slightly less than handsome looks. He'd been alternately witty, serious, genuinely interested in what she had to say, and—stunned as she was to admit it when she got home—he'd been the most charming man she'd gone out with for ages. Later, she'd discovered he was a better-than-average lover—slow, tender, yet passionate and definitely experienced.

Within two months, Tonya realized being with Andrew gave her a feeling of safety and stability she hadn't known since her father had died when she was twelve. A month later, *she* had proposed to *him*. A stunned Andrew couldn't accept fast enough, nor did he object to eloping. After all, he had no family and she had only a mother who'd lost interest in her years ago. Tonya had been unbelievably happy for five months and three days after she'd learned she was pregnant. She hadn't told Andrew yet—she was saving it as a surprise for his birthday on Thursday. He would be thrilled.

And Tonya would be ecstatic except for one thing—Marissa Gray had come back to Aurora Falls in June and decided to stay.

When Marissa had returned to take care of her mother, Tonya had been certain she would leave for Chicago or some other big city after Annemarie Gray died. But Marissa had lingered, and in October Andrew had come home and announced that she'd decided to stay in Aurora Falls and he'd hired her. He was jubilant—he said Marissa was an excellent reporter, a natural, a wonderful addition to the *Gazette*.

Tonya felt as if a storm had shattered the summer sky when she learned blond-haired, confident, inflexible Marissa Gray had invaded the beautiful life she'd built for herself. Marissa knew too much about her—things she could bring to light or begin harping about, like Gretchen's death. Things that could humiliate both Tonya and Andrew—maybe even make Andrew realize what a mistake he'd made in marrying her. And now, after the picture of her and Andrew decorating the tree had arrived, Tonya feared Dillon was back in town. He'd been Tonya's friend, or so she'd thought, but she now believed Dillon was far from being a friend—she feared he was dangerous and maybe even insane. As soon as Tonya learned she was pregnant, she knew she had to start fervently protecting her world. First, she had to know if Dillon really had come back to Aurora Falls. Her next step was to find out how much Marissa knew about Tonya's past. The last was to rebuild her friendship with Marissa, who could destroy all Tonya had accomplished.

Distracted, Tonya had taken a left turn instead of a right, sending her down the less-populated Harper Street rather than the road leading back to the highway. She hadn't driven on Harper Street for years and couldn't help looking at the modest home now painted soft blue with white shutters, much more tasteful than when it had been yellow-green and brown and belonged to Edgar Blume.

Edgar Blume was a name that drifted through her mind at least once a day and always produced a chill. She hadn't seen him for ten years, yet with sickening clarity she recalled his small, seeking eyes, the greasy hair combed across his bald spot, his foul breath when he so often leaned over her desk to "help" her with a math problem, his ever-present body odor, and his perpetual look of superiority.

Back in high school she'd managed to dodge him fairly well until she'd brought calamity down on herself by cheating on an algebra test in his class. She remembered running to the bathroom after the class and crying stormily. Marissa had followed her and she'd blurted out what she'd done. Marissa had been sympathetic but couldn't help her. The next day Blume had confronted Tonya and threatened to report her for cheating to the principal, a report that would end up with her being expelled and humiliated, a report he'd told her would not happen if they could "talk" about the matter. Only Blume was using *talk* as a euphemism.

Tonya had thought of turning the tables and reporting Edgar Blume to the principal for sexual harassment, but her female English teacher had lodged a similar complaint against her a year earlier and another incident had occurred two months ago, when the principal had warned Tonya if this happened again he would expel her. She knew that if she got herself kicked out of an ordinary public school she would never win the attention of the guy on whom she'd set her sights: Will Addison—good-looking and son of the prosperous and socially prominent mayor. Even if things didn't work out with Will, the humiliation of the expulsion would follow her for years.

Tonya had been certain she could bear Edgar Blume for one brief encounter—after all, she'd endured a repulsive stepfather for almost a year—but Tonya knew her attractions. One sweaty rendezvous would not satisfy Blume. He would want more and more and eventually he would get careless or brag and then *everyone* would know. Tonya had felt as if she'd rather die.

Tonya pulled herself back to the present when, with relief, she made another right turn and got herself on the road leading to the highway. What a stupid mistake to turn onto the street where Blume had lived, she thought. She'd traveled these roads a hundred times. She was so edgy, so frightened, she felt as if he'd somehow drawn her there to remind her of him, of everything that had sprung from her hideous evening with him, of everything she now could lose.

The wind suddenly picked up and the limbs of a thick evergreen near the street swayed as if the whole tree was going to blow in front of her. She slammed on her brakes, cringing as the seat belt tightened on her abdomen. Tonya feared the strap had hurt the baby and felt on the verge of tears again. Ten minutes, she thought. If she could keep her wits, she could be home in just ten minutes, but even that seemed like an eternity.

Nausea sprouted and grew in Tonya's body. She rolled down a window and took a deep breath of sharp, icy air. Then another. A deep coldness settled in her body and she quickly closed the window and turned up the car heater. Already she was experiencing morning sickness and she felt as if she might have to stop by the side of the road and throw up, but it wasn't morning. "Be sensible, Tonya," she said aloud. "The baby isn't making you sick, thinking about Blume is, so stop it. *Immediately!*" God. She'd sounded just like him. *Immediately* had seemed to be his favorite word.

She stopped at a red light, put in a CD, and tried to sing along with "Save Me" by k. d. lang. Lyrics she sang every time she drove now deserted her, though. All she could think about was walking to Edgar Blume's house on that February evening, opening his back door, smiling as he rushed her into his darkened kitchen, grabbing for her and rubbing his hands all over her body. He'd brushed his teeth, but toothpaste couldn't cover the putrid breath. She'd forced herself to ignore it and steer him into the living room so fast he forgot to lock the kitchen door— the door where Dillon Archer had promised her he'd enter the house within ten minutes. Dillon had been her casual, secret sex partner on and off since they'd met aboard the *Annemarie* and he hated Blume even more than Blume hated him.

"I brought this," Tonya had said flatly, holding up a bottle of red wine. Dillon had given her the wine and told her not to sound happy when she presented it. Blume was supposed to get the idea she'd brought it to help numb her senses.

Blume had looked at the bottle dubiously. "Ruby port? Is that what you teenagers are drinking these days?"

"One day in class you said you liked it. I tried it. It's heavy and sweet."

" 'Heavy and sweet' sounds like you're talking about cough syrup, but at least you're trying to please, aren't you?" She'd shrugged. "My wife's mother is sick and she's with her for the night. Took the kid. But this isn't a party, Tonya."

Tonya had given him an icy glare. "You think this is a party for me? Pour us each a glass and I'll be more relaxed. Or forget the wine and I'll be more than happy to leave no matter what the consequences."

"You aren't going anywhere if you want to stay in school and keep a little dignity in this town. Get in the bedroom—the big one. I'll fix the damned wine."

The wine. To this day Tonya could not bear the sight of port wine. In fact, she rarely drank at all. Drinking loosened her tongue. What was that old saying? "Loose lips sink ships." No truer words were ever spoken, she thought, laughed aloud, and abruptly stopped. My God, she was driving in an empty car on an icy night and laughing with an edge of hysteria in her voice. Was that what a visit to Marissa Gray had done to her?

No, this was what remembering that night with Edgar Blume was doing to her. After all these years, he could still make her sick, afraid, haunted.

Dillon had told her to touch as few things as possible in the bedroom and to leave as little of "herself" as possible, so she'd only stripped out of her jeans and sweater and slipped under the blanket. "Here," Blume said harshly, handing her a glass. "Why are you still wearing a bra?"

"Can't you give me a few minutes to loosen up? And you've got *all* your clothes on."

He'd promptly begun to strip and Tonya could have kicked herself. She couldn't bear to look at him. She sipped the wine she hated and told herself to think of something else. But in a moment, Blume had stood in the dim bedroom light in all his glory—sinewy, white as a corpse, and hairy. He'd gulped down his wine, made a face that indicated approval—Dillon had known not to go cheap with the evening's refreshment—and once again told her to take off all her clothes.

"Not until I get more wine," Tonya had said, trying to sound calm when everything inside her shook.

Blume's small eyes had narrowed even more. "I told you we're not having a party."

"But we could have." He'd looked at her, blinking rapidly. "You know I wouldn't be doing this if you weren't forcing me, but you are forcing me and if you're not satisfied, I stand to lose a lot. I'm not stupid . . . Edgar. You said your wife won't be coming home tonight. We don't have to hurry. I really liked that wine. It made me feel warm and sexy, but I could feel sexier, do whatever you want. See? I'll make it good for you in bed and you'll make things good for me at school." She'd paused, amazed at her imitation of composure. "Get some wine for *both* of us. Nice big servings. I'll give you a night you won't forget."

He'd looked at her dubiously for a moment as if wondering if she weren't pushing the wine on him. She had thought her heart might beat out of her chest because that's exactly what she had been trying to do. But apparently Blume assured himself that he had opened a new bottle of wine and that Tonya was asking him to get their second glasses.

He'd put on a robe—thank God—and left the room. He'd returned holding two drinking glasses full of wine, wine she knew Dillon had spiked minutes earlier. She'd taken a sip. Blume had gulped half of his. What came after had been fast and brutal. He'd disposed of her bra, torn her cotton panties, clutching her breasts with crushing hands, rolling frenziedly on top of her. Tonya had briefly wondered if this was what it felt like when a bear mauled you, tossing you from side to side, drenching your face in saliva, tearing hairs from your scalp. She'd been on the verge of screaming when he'd stopped as if suddenly frozen. His eyes had widened, he'd smacked a hand to his chest, and his whole body had stiffened.

"H-heart," he'd muttered, rolling off her. "My heart. Digitalis in bathroom." Tonya had lain motionless, staring at him. "On . . . counter . . . bathroom. Hurry."

Tonya had remained absolutely still and he'd realized she had no intention of helping him. He'd begun crawling off the bed, gasping, when Dillon had walked into the room, his handsome face graced by a calm smile.

"I don't think digitalis is going to help you, Blume," he'd said softly. "It doesn't do much when you've ingested a fair amount of Viagra. Oh, also cocaine. Not a good mixture for a man with a weak heart."

Tonya hadn't known what Dillon intended to do beyond putting something in the wine, which was why he'd warned her not to pour any and make Blume suspicious that she'd "doctored" the drink. Blume would drink wine he thought only he'd poured from a sealed bottle.

"I remembered my brother, Andrew, talking about when you had a heart attack back when he was in your class," Dillon had said, coming to the bed, holding on to the skinny, wild-eyed man. "And Tonya isn't the first girl you've forced into bed. You like variety? Control? Or doesn't the wife want anything to do with you anymore? No wonder."

Dillon had then looked at Tonya. "Put your clothes on; pull off that sheet you were lying on and the pillowcase. Then go. Get rid of the bed stuff—cram it down a storm drain. I'll take care of everything else here."

"Dillon, what if he lives?" she'd asked, terrified.

"He won't." Dillon had given her a slow, lazy smile. "You're safe. I'm seeing to it that you'll be safe. And maybe you can do the same for me someday. That's what friends do for each other. They pay each other back for favors, Tonya. Always remember that."

Tonya had gotten into most of her clothes, stuffed her underwear in her purse, grabbed the bedding, and run from the room, not looking back as Dillon held down the groaning Blume. She'd slipped out the back door and tried to keep away from the streets except to find a storm drain. The bedding and her little bit of clothes had gone in easily. She'd started walking fast, although her lungs felt empty. She was only two blocks away from Blume's and veering away from the road when headlights caught her, a car slowed down, and Marissa Gray had yelled, "Tonya? Is that you?"

Tonya had felt as if she might pass out and stood absolutely still for a moment. Marissa didn't have a driver's license yet. She was with someone else. Tonya had stiffened her spine and walked to the car to find that Annemarie was the driver. Thank God, she'd thought. Annemarie liked her.

Tonya had told Annemarie and Marissa that her mother was in a bad mood, which the Grays knew was code for drunk, and Tonya had gone for a long walk just to get away from her. She knew she was breathlessly chattering, her hair was a mess, and she didn't even want to think about how her facial skin must look, especially her lips. She'd hoped Annemarie and Marissa would chalk it all up to Tonya's distress over her mother's anger.

Annemarie had offered to take her home, and when they'd arrived Tonya's mother had been gone. "Well, thank God I don't have to listen to *her* anymore tonight," Tonya remembered saying, although the woman had been gone all evening. Tonya had given the Grays a terse "good night," run to her front door, slammed it behind her, and waited until she saw Annemarie drive away before she'd buried her head in a couch pillow and screamed until she had no voice left.

The next day brought no news, but the day after the principal announced Edgar Blume had died of a heart attack. The shock over Blume's death had quickly been overcome by the rumors that Blume's wife had been out of town and Blume was found naked in bed along with a pair of a woman's black lace panties— rumors that Tonya knew were Dillon's touch. Worst of all, she'd seen Marissa looking at her guardedly. Of course she would remember how close Tonya had been to Blume's house when she and her mother had picked up Tonya.

Within four days the news that Blume had been doing cocaine and taking Viagra crept through the city. Tonya had known police hadn't released all of this information—Dillon had been spreading the word. It had worked. Blume's reputation as a strict but scrupulous teacher lay in ruins. His reputation as a loving and faithful husband had shattered. A month after his death, when the mention of his name resulted in snickers, Mrs. Blume had left the city with her young son, although their house wouldn't sell for two years.

What if that happened to me? Tonya now wondered. What if someone ruined my life, the baby's life, *took* Andrew's life? Tonya felt drenched in guilt and shame. In spite of the cold, she suddenly began to perspire. She wondered if she should pull to the side of the road—if she wasn't safe to drive—but she was too close to home. Someone might stop to ask if they could help her—she, who didn't deserve anyone's help—and delay her arrival at the sanctuary of her and Andrew's small, cozy house. Andrew. Concentrating on the kind of man she'd married would banish this nauseating shame. She must keep in mind that as embarrassed as Mrs. Blume must have been, her husband had been responsible for everything that had happened. He'd brought humiliation down on the family. He'd driven Tonya to do what she had done to him. Andrew was incapable of such ruthlessness. Andrew would always keep her and the baby safe.

Ever since she married Andrew, she believed she, too, had helped preserve a future with Andrew and their child, although she hadn't known it at the time. She'd kept her promise to Dillon to return his "favor" to her. It had happened when she'd least expected it, years after Dillon had saved her from Edgar Blume.

The group she'd called friends had all been in their twenties. Gretchen had been acting strange, but then Gretchen was a genius and Tonya had heard geniuses were all weird. She hadn't known what Will Addison had seen in her or why he'd dated her for four months. Gretchen's sudden relationship with Dillon puzzled Tonya even more. At twenty-one Gretchen still seemed nothing but a thin, mildly pretty, strange little girl who was a complete cipher to Tonya. But Tonya hadn't cared about Dillon's current sexual interest. She'd only been relieved and light-hearted that Will Addison was on the market again.

Then, finally, had come that beautiful night when they'd gone to Gray's Island on the *Annemarie*. Tonya had been walking toward the church when Dillon had lightly caught her arm and pulled her close to him. "Remember the night when I told you friends always pay each other back for favors?" he'd asked softly.

A bud of fear had begun to bloom in her stomach, sending quivering vines throughout her body. The warm night had turned cold and dark, and the moon and stars had slowly dimmed until they'd almost reached oblivion.

"Well, tonight is the night for you to return the favor I did for you." Dillon had unobtrusively stroked her arm. "You'll know the time. And you'll do what's right—for me."

She'd looked up at him—at those mesmerizing blue eyes and the confidently sensuous face—and she'd known she would do what he wanted. Tonya had seen Dillon at his worst—or had the night at Blume's actually been his best?—and she'd known she would obey. She had too much to lose otherwise, and Dillon would make certain she'd pay for disobedience. She believed he'd make her pay more than she believed anything else in the world.

Tonya had felt a moment of panic when Marissa and Eric had deserted the rest of the group. She had no sexual feelings about Eric and everyone knew he'd been in love with Marissa for years, but he had a way of making people feel secure. Tonya had trusted Eric Montgomery and wanted desperately for him to stay with the group.

But he hadn't.

Parker Street at last, Tonya now thought with the nearest feeling to joy she could muster. She turned onto the relatively new street where development had just begun. Only five houses so far, and she thought she would start crying again when she saw the small one-story rectangular home that was her haven. She'd insisted it be repainted yellow from its original dusky blue-gray. Tonya had wanted something bright and warm that would remind her of happy summer days, and Andrew had thought her yearning for a house the color of sunlight cute and endearing.

Tonya had forgotten to leave on the porch light and the house sat in shadows but she probably wouldn't have noticed if she weren't so anxious tonight. She pulled onto the driveway, pushed a button on the automatic garage door opener, then drove too fast into the garage and almost hit the back wall. Her hands shook as she closed the garage door and opened the door leading into the kitchen. The cheerful little room seemed unusually dark and cold. Imagination, Tonya thought. She needed lights and something to drink. Her throat had grown tight and raw. She felt as if she could barely swallow, but the desire for cold water, juice—*anything*—overwhelmed her.

She knew exactly where the light switch was without looking. She flipped it. Nothing. The room remained coolly dark. Tonya almost ran back outside to her car, and then told herself she was being silly. The damned lightbulb had burned out. Of all times!

She dropped her keys in her purse, walked farther into the kitchen, and set her purse on the counter. Tonya started to take off her coat and then stopped. The house felt so cold that she wondered if something had gone wrong with the furnace. Oh, that would be great, she thought, getting angry. They couldn't get it fixed until tomorrow, meaning they'd have to spend the night at her mother's house. She had taken off for Las Vegas with a man she barely knew and Tonya wasn't certain she had the key. Hell, she and Andrew might end up at a little motel. The Larke Inn was too expensive.

She stalked to the kitchen, furious with Marissa for upsetting her earlier, furious that she'd taken a wrong turn and driven by Edgar Blume's house, furious with the furnace that might be broken. She knew she shouldn't take a tranquilizer, but just one couldn't hurt, she reasoned. Something mild, she told herself, although she knew one mild tranquilizer wouldn't help. Maybe two, even three—

As she stood motionless in the kitchen, trying to decide what to do, she had the uncanny feeling that the house had begun to breathe, to become conscious, to *live*. Tonya closed her eyes and drew air into her lungs. She was being ridiculous. She could always call Andrew and tell him to come home immediately, but she didn't want to be a clinging wife. She didn't want him to think she was weak, paranoid, suffocating—

A whisper of movement came from the living room. Tonya stiffened and then forced herself to walk slowly to the doorway and ask, "Who's there?" Only cold quiet answered. A dim bluish glow from a streetlight revealed most of the room and furniture that looked strange in the cool, distant lighting. She didn't hear a thing.

"Tonya, you're not supposed to take tranquilizers, but if you don't take one—just one now—you're going to pass out from nerves," she said aloud for company. She turned and headed back into the kitchen. "This has been the worst night I've had for a long time. If I hadn't let Buddy Pruitt's death spook me, I could have stayed calm and done a much better job of befriending Marissa again, of making her forget when Blume died, when Gretchen died . . ."

She grabbed a flashlight she kept in a drawer beside the kitchen sink. She turned it on and it bloomed with brightness. Tonya scanned the kitchen and then screamed when she saw a bottle of ruby port wine sitting on the counter. She could see Edgar Blume, his face contorted in agony, clutching his chest, as he'd lain on the bed, held down by a smiling Dillon. She reached out to touch the bottle and then quickly drew back her hand. Andrew wouldn't have bought this, she thought.

Someone had brought it in during the last two hours, wanting her to see it. Or *waiting* for her to see it.

Tonya started to turn in order to pick up her purse with her car keys inside, but an arm closed around her left side and something slid smoothly into her throat at the base of the Adam's apple. Blood spurted all over the yellow cabinet tops and splattered on the refrigerator. Tonya reached for her neck, trying to cover it with her hand, but something like a spike stabbed between her fingers and tore into her neck again.

By now, Tonya tried to scream, but only a gurgle emerged. Then, abruptly, someone let go of her body. She staggered, choking, and then folded to her knees, still trying to wrap both hands around her neck to stanch the pool of blood forming around her on the vinyl floor.

She couldn't breathe around the blood bubbling in her throat. She grew dizzy. The kitchen and her attacker began to whirl around her, faster and faster. Weakness and languor crept through her body, but she could still think—think that even if her attacker left her right now, she didn't think she could make it to the cell phone in her purse, and certainly not the phone in the living room.

This is it, she thought numbly. I've spent twenty-seven years trying to find happiness and finally I have it with Andrew Archer and a baby, and it's all going . . . going . . .

Tonya fell sideways, drenching her right side in blood, still holding desperately to her neck. If only Andrew would walk in right now and call an ambulance. But Andrew wasn't going to arrive and save the day, she thought with what she had left of bitter mental laughter. She'd had her brief window of happiness and now it was closing, just like her eyes. She'd lie here on the kitchen floor, drifting into death. She'd picture her baby in Andrew's arms. That's what she'd picture, she thought with growing cloudiness, trying with all the will she had left. The baby . . . the sweet baby . . . Andrew and the baby . . .

Instead, all she could see was Gretchen Montgomery, drunk on the beer and other alcohol Dillon had kept pushing on her. Gretchen drunk and standing barefoot on a high, high rail in a church. Dillon Archer inching closer and closer to her until he reached out with both arms, placed a hand on her thigh, and *pushed*, just like Marissa had said. But Tonya couldn't tell the police the truth because she owed Dillon a debt and if she hadn't paid her debt, she probably would have ended up like Gretchen—broken, dead, and looking at the world with unseeing eyes.

But she'd kept her promise and she was dying just like Gretchen anyway. Why? she wondered with her last bit of consciousness. Why?

II

1

The alarm sounded like an air-raid siren to Marissa the next morning. She jerked up in bed, grabbed the clock, and searched frantically for the "off" button. She'd tried the more mellow radio alarm clocks, but the sound of music—even if it was fairly loud—never woke her, so she stayed true to the twin bell clocks she'd used since childhood. Although she and her sister both slept with their doors closed so the alarm wouldn't awaken Catherine, the method was not always effective, and Marissa didn't want to wake Catherine this morning. Marissa had gone to bed before her sister returned home with James last night and she wanted to leave for work before Catherine awakened this morning and avoid telling her about the rosebushes, the "Tyger" note, and Tonya's bizarre visit.

In forty-five minutes, Marissa drank the coffee left in her mug and popped the last piece of toast in her mouth. The crisply blue day sent bright light through the kitchen windows, although she'd kept the blinds lowered so she wouldn't have to look at the ruin of her mother's rose garden; it made Marissa feel as if someone had bludgeoned Annemarie. And herself. After all, she knew the blue-eyed doll represented her. She was glad Eric had taken it, the note, and the postcard away as evidence.

She had to stop thinking about the fire, she told herself. *Anything* else would be better. Marissa glanced down at her navy blue wool skirt, cornflower blue turtleneck sweater, two long strands of faux pearls, and two equally long gold-tone chains. Her engraved bangle bracelet sparkled in the sun, and she checked to make sure her big hoop earrings hadn't tangled in her hair and then looked at Lindsay, whose expression said she hoped ardently for one last dog biscuit. The expression never failed. The dog was beginning to crunch with gusto when Marissa's cell phone rang.

Her purse lay on the counter nearly beside her, and for once, she immediately located the cell phone amid the myriad assortment of objects she needed to get through her day. She glanced at caller ID and felt a slight leap of joy, although she knew this could be more bad news.

"Good morning, Eric."

"You sound chipper. Getting ready for work?"

"Of course. I managed to shower, dress, and eat without waking Catherine. This Christmas is supposed to be a break from all the work she does at school, but so far I don't think she's getting much rest. I didn't want to tell her about the fire last night or early this morning. I want her to sleep as late as possible."

"You're a kind, considerate soul, Marissa Gray."

"I know. I'm expecting to be presented a medal for my goodness at the Christmas parade." She paused. "You didn't call just to see if I'm ready for work."

He drew a deep breath. "Marissa, Tonya was murdered last night."

Numbly Marissa looked outside, shielding herself from the news by watching a brilliantly red male cardinal hop from twig to twig on the big oak tree. Would he fly away or just spend the morning sightseeing from the Grays' yard? Then she felt her hand trembling and the shield shattered. Eric's news finally hit it like a hammer blow. "T-Tonya? *Murdered?*"

"Yes. Andrew found her. He said he'd had to work late. She was in her kitchen and someone stabbed her in the throat. Puncture wound, the doctor says. Must have gotten one of the jugular veins. I'll have to wait for the ME's report to know."

"But that couldn't be. She was *here!*"

"There?"

"Yes. About half an hour after you left, she arrived without calling. I guess she didn't notice the flower garden. If she did, she didn't mention it. She said she wanted to patch up our friendship. She stayed for about a half hour, but she was nervous and quick to take offense and she was rambling about Dillon and finally she left in a huff and told me not to go *whining* to Andrew about her being here."

"Good God!" Marissa could hear Eric draw a deep breath. "She was wearing a coat when Andrew found her. She must have just gotten home, which means—"

"Someone was waiting inside for her?"

"They weren't there when Andrew got home. He's a wreck."

"Of course he is. I didn't see them together often, but I know he was so in love with her. And vice versa, from what I heard last night."

"He won't be in to work today. I think someone called the guy who retired as editor and Andrew replaced. He'll fill in."

"Oh. Sure."

"Marissa, are you all right? You sound so vague."

"I'm just trying to take it all in."

"I think everyone is. Marissa, have you talked over everything that's happened with Catherine? Does she know all about Tonya's visit?"

"No. I'd gone to bed when she came in."

"Good. I don't want her to know about Tonya right now. Will she be home this evening?

"As far as I know she doesn't have plans."

"Then I'd like to ask a favor from you."

"Anything I can do to help, Eric."

"I need to get a time line on Tonya's murder, and the time Andrew says he returned home. Also, you said Tonya's visit was strange. I want to hear all the details, and I'd like to keep this stuff between the two of us for now."

"All right. I won't say a word to her. You took the postcard and the doll and the 'Tyger' note, so she can't accidentally run across them. Only you and I know about them. She'll see the rose garden, though."

"No getting around that. You'll have to tell her about the fire. Leave out the doll and the other stuff for now."

"Was that the favor you wanted to ask of me?"

"No. I didn't get any sleep last night and I'll be working all day, so here's the favor. I wonder if you would meet me at headquarters about five thirty. Outside, of course. We don't want to set off the gossipmongers here. Anyway, we'll go back to my place and you can tell me everything you can remember about times, things you and Tonya discussed—anything that might help. That way we'll have complete privacy."

"Catherine will pester me to death wanting to know why you want privacy with me."

"I've already thought of that. I think it's best she knows where you are in case something happens and she needs you—us. Tell her I want to go over details about your wreck again. I know by six o'clock or so I'll be tired and in need of a shower to wake up my brain. And I have some files at my apartment I'd like for you to read."

Marissa didn't hesitate. Eric's tone told her he had nothing in mind but business for tonight. He wasn't trying to lure her to his apartment for a romantic interlude. "I understand. You said you'd want to eat. So will I. I haven't worked on my cooking skills the last few years, so I can't go into your kitchen and whip up something wonderful in a jiffy."

"You certainly couldn't. I have beer, a jar of mustard, some shriveled hot dogs, and some milk I'm sure has gone sour. We'll stop and get something. How about Kentucky Fried Chicken?"

"I love it."

"I remember. See you later, Marissa."

2

The offices of the *Aurora Falls Gazette* were almost eerily quiet. People sat at their desks, working efficiently, but they all had a look of shock and bewilderment. In the mornings, Marissa always walked by Andrew's office and waved. Today, she saw a much older man with weathered skin and thick white hair sitting at Andrew's desk. She recalled that Peter Hagarty had been the former editor. She didn't know him and would have stopped in his office to introduce herself, but he held the phone in his hand as he took notes, his forehead furrowed.

Marissa sauntered to the coffeemaker Tonya had given to the *Gazette* not long before Andrew hired Marissa. As she poured a cup of the aromatic blend, the call from Eric repeated itself in her mind. He'd said Tonya had suffered a puncture wound in the neck damaging a jugular vein. She'd probably died in a pool of blood. Marissa cringed. She'd seen Tonya just twelve hours earlier and her features remained sharp in Marissa's mind. Tonya had looked so young last night, she thought. So young and . . . blooming. Many people said a woman looked blooming when she was—

Marissa nearly dropped her cup before she got back to her desk.

Could Tonya's odd behavior last night have had anything to do with a pregnancy? People said a woman's hormones went wild during pregnancy. Marissa sat down and took a sip of hot coffee and then another, as if they could clear her head. No, she thought. Maybe hormones were partially responsible for Tonya's mood swings but not for the whole conversation. Why was she so hell-bent on renewing the friendship? She didn't want me stirring up trouble, Marissa decided. She wanted the whole issue of Gretchen's death forgotten. Could it be that if Tonya was pregnant, she didn't want her child ever to hear something that made it doubt its mother?

Peter Hagarty, looking harried, opened his door and called, "Marissa Gray?"

She hurried to his office and he shut the door. "Hi. Pete Hagarty," he said, extending his hand. "Sorry I couldn't introduce myself earlier."

"That's all right. I'm Marissa and I've always heard good things about you." She paused. "And boy, did that sound like apple-polishing."

He laughed, a rumbling sound deep in his chest. "Maybe from someone else, but you're too good a reporter to need to flatter me." His laughter stopped as quickly as it had begun. "You know about the Tonya Archer murder. I want you and Landers to cover it. Just because it's the murder of your boss's wife, don't walk on eggshells—"

"I'm sorry to interrupt, Mr. Hagarty, but Tonya Archer was a friend of mine." She hesitated. Eric had told her not to mention what Tonya had said during her visit last night, but Marissa's reporter's ethics overrode her desire to please Eric. "She was at my house last night."

"*What?*" Hagarty boomed so loudly people outside his office looked at them through the glass. "Tonya Archer was at your house last night?"

I just said that, Marissa thought, but she tried to keep any annoyance from her expression. "Yes, sir. I wish I could help today, but unfortunately, I'm connected to the murders of Buddy Pruitt and Tonya Archer. Tangentially to Buddy, but as far as the police are concerned—"

"Damn. The police are out to get me."

Marissa didn't know whether he was serious. He stared out the window, making a steeple with his fingers. Then he let out a huge sigh and looked at Marissa with sympathy. "My wife would smack me over the head with an iron frying pan for what I just did—thinking about how things aren't working out for me when your friend has just been murdered. I'm sorry, Marissa."

"Thank you."

"You and Tonya were good friends?"

She tilted her head and looked at him cannily. "Always the reporter, aren't you?"

"You caught me. Just think—a week ago we were known for being a low-crime city. Now . . ." He raised his arms. "Well, I do have a story you can cover." The expression in his gaze lightened. "Hold on to your hat—it's a big one."

Marissa laughed. "I would, but I'm not wearing a hat."

"On January fifth, the Friends of the Library are holding a book auction to raise funds for the new library. They're going to have refreshments and entertainment. My wife is one of the Friends and instructed me to see that we do a decent story about it, not some little blurb on the last page. The president of the Friends is Susan Montgomery—the chief deputy's mother—but my wife says she doesn't like talking to the press. Shy or something. So I guess you could talk to my wife—"

"I can talk to Susan!" Marissa blurted, remembering Eric saying things were uncomfortable when he visited his house. He didn't want to ask to see albums. Marissa didn't, either, but she wouldn't be crushed if her request was denied. "Susan's daughter was my best friend. I know the Montgomerys very well. I think I could get a decent interview from Susan. She'd be relaxed around me—she's known me since I was a little girl—and if I have a tape recorder going, she might start talking and forget her stage fright. I'm sure I can get *something* helpful from her!"

Mr. Hagarty leaned back in his chair, put up both hands, and said, "Whoa! My God, Marissa, you *do* have the heart of a reporter! Not shy about going after the big stories, are you?"

Marissa laughed. "We're not exactly talking about an interview at the White House."

"No, but . . ."

"Mr. Hagarty, this wouldn't be the same as my covering a news story about Buddy Pruitt or Tonya," Marissa said earnestly. "It's more of a feature story. I wouldn't be breaching ethics."

He frowned before bursting out, "Why not? My wife told me we have to treat Susan very gently because she lost her daughter, but if you knew that daughter, if you were friends with the family—"

"I did know Gretchen. I know the whole family. I will be my absolutely most tactful and gentle. After all, the story isn't about

Gretchen. I don't think I'll have to bully Susan into talking about the city library."

"You might have to be a little forceful to get her to agree to an interview."

"I know. And I will if I must, but I can do it gently." Marissa was already rising from her chair. "Please, Mr. Hagarty, let me do this story. I'll call Mrs. Montgomery this afternoon and set up a time for the interview as soon as possible. January fifth isn't far away."

"You're right. Get to work. And Marissa?"

"Yes?"

"Could you call me Peter? Or even better, Pete. I have a problem with a whizz kid like you calling me Mr. Hagarty— makes me feel like an old fogey."

Marissa smiled. "I don't think I'll have a bit of trouble calling you Pete."

"The *Aurora Falls Gazette*, Marissa Gray speaking."

Catherine nearly shouted over the phone: "Marissa, how could you leave this morning without telling me Tonya was murdered last night?"

"I wanted you to get as much sleep as possible before you heard the news. Who told you?"

"Will Addison! He called this morning and was shocked that I didn't know. We haven't been close to Tonya for years, but she was our friend since we were children! I don't understand what you were thinking, Marissa, letting me just sleep the morning away when you *knew* Tonya had been murdered!"

"You've already burst my right ear drum. Can you lower your voice?"

"What? I'm sorry, but I'm upset." Her voice grew even louder: "And what the hell happened to the rose garden?"

"Catherine, you are beyond upset. Take a couple of breaths before you have a stroke. Now, you said Will Addison called you about Tonya. What time did he call you?"

"About eleven o'clock."

"I found out about Tonya more than two hours earlier. That was two hours you were able to sleep and enjoy your morning. You couldn't do anything for Tonya. I thought I could do something for you—give you a peaceful morning. Your visit home has been pretty much of a disaster."

"Well, I guess I understand your thinking," Catherine said reluctantly. "I could never have kept my mouth shut—I would have been up the stairs and had you awake within ten minutes—but you've always been much more coolheaded about everything than I am. I get so distressed."

Which is partly why I'm not going to tell you now that Tonya visited me last night, Marissa thought. That news can wait, especially because Eric doesn't want the news generally known. "As for Mom's rose garden, someone poured kerosene on the bushes and set fire to them."

"Who? Why?"

"Those are the questions I, the reporter, am supposed to ask. We don't know who did it. Eric was there—"

"Eric! Why?"

"To talk about something that happened earlier yesterday. I'll tell you when I have more privacy. Anyway, we were sitting in the kitchen and the blinds were down. Lindsay kept barking and at first we ignored her; then she got really frantic and Eric pulled aside a blind and we saw the fire. The fire department sent a small truck to put it out and a firefighter told us the accelerant was kerosene. Of course, Eric is investigating, but he hasn't turned up anything yet."

"Mom's poor flowers," Catherine mourned. "I'm glad she can't see them. I also have my doubts about this being a prank, happening so soon after your wreck."

"Maybe that's why someone decided to do it. They thought I'd be more frightened after the wreck."

"Maybe." Catherine was obviously unconvinced.

"If you hadn't called me, I was going to call you in a few minutes anyway," Marissa said quickly. "I won't be home for dinner tonight. Eric wants to go over a few things with me."

"And you're going to a restaurant to do that?"

Marissa braced herself, knowing how Catherine would interpret the information. "No, we're going to his apartment. Eric didn't sleep at all last night and he hasn't stopped for two days in a row. He said getting out of that uniform, taking a shower, and relaxing would help him concentrate. Taking a shower to relax before we talk. Talk about evidence and . . . well, stuff like that." Marissa rolled her eyes. "This isn't a date or anything, Catherine. It's strictly business."

"Did I say otherwise?"

"No, but the tone of your voice spoke volumes." Feeling ridiculously juvenile, Marissa asked quickly, "Will you give Lindsay her dinner?"

"I will. What television shows does she like? We'll have a *whole* evening to occupy ourselves."

"Not a *whole* evening, Catherine."

"Uh-huh."

"Don't be silly. I won't be gone all evening." She paused. "Why don't you call James and ask him to keep you company?"

"Call James! I just saw him last night! He'll think I'm desperate and he'll run for the hills."

"I doubt that, but at least be certain to keep the doors locked."

"Because you're expecting more trouble?"

"No, because it's a good idea." Marissa needed to change the subject. "Why did Will call you?"

"He invited me to lunch. He said his mother had some presents for us—I guess she feels guilty because we're orphans—and he said he could bring them over and then take me out for a leisurely meal."

"Is he giving James a run for his money?"

"No. Will and I have been friends for a long time—not close friends, but friends. You know that. We'll just do some catching up."

"Have a good time," Marissa said. "And pray he doesn't bring his mother along."

Catherine laughed. "I don't think I have to worry about Evelyn Addison today."

3

"Oh, Will, I haven't come to Antonio's for years!" Catherine exclaimed as they stepped through the door of the Italian restaurant. "It looks just like I remember it, though," she said, gazing at walls designed to make the restaurant look like a wine cellar, the cozy booths covered in a moss green suede-like fabric, and the copper-plated ceiling, the hand-carved mahogany bar.

Will smiled. "I haven't been here for a couple of years, either. Of course, neither one of us has spent much time in Aurora Falls lately."

A waiter showed them to a booth, told them the specials of the day, and took their drink orders. Catherine ordered a white wine spritzer. Will ordered his usual martini.

"So you'll be getting your degree in the spring?" Will asked.

"Yes. I've finished my course work and now I'm actually working, although under supervision. If all goes well, I'll get my license in May."

"And go to work in a hospital?"

Catherine frowned. "I used to think that's what I wanted. Now I believe I'd like to join the practice of a friend."

"Would this friend be male?"

"No, this friend would not. She's a few years older than I am and has a practice in San Francisco. The city is so beautiful."

"And so far away from home."

The drinks arrived and Catherine ordered Chicken Alfredo and Will, after much pondering, selected Spaghetti Marvelo. After the waiter left, will leaned across the table and told her, "I can't stand people who ask a dozen questions before ordering and then want this not overcooked and that not overcooked and a quarter-inch-wide piece of orange rind on the side. They drive me crazy! I was deciding if I wanted to get something with lots of onion and garlic so Mother would keep her distance tonight."

Catherine laughed. "Poor Will. Your mother adores you."

"I wish my mother had at least five other children to worry about—not just me. But I've given her plenty of reason to worry, I guess."

"I don't remember ever hearing that you'd gotten in serious trouble, Will. As for your higher education . . ."

Will grinned. "Stepped in it there, didn't you? No one wants to talk about my higher education. I've dropped out of three universities before they could fail me. Then last year—well, last year was what Mother calls 'a year of recuperation.' This semester I started all over in a new university—the only one that would have me, I think. I'm supposed to be a changed man."

Will reached for his martini, immediately downing more than could be considered a sip. Catherine looked at him. Only one year younger than she, he had some noticeable vertical lines across his forehead, a slightly crinkled look at the corners of his eyes, and a few gray hairs at his temples. He could smile and laugh and not look happy. The new university wouldn't work out for him, either, she thought. His "year of recuperation," which most people believed had been several months of rehab in Europe, hadn't helped. Catherine wondered what had happened to this handsome, intelligent, charming young man when he was seventeen or eighteen to change him so much.

Will narrowed an eye. "You're analyzing me."

"No, I wasn't." Catherine took a sip of her spritzer. "Well, maybe just a little."

Will stuck out his hand and turned the palm up. "What do you see?"

Her mouth opened slightly, she looked at the hand, and then she looked at the glint in his eyes. "Uh, that's not quite how we do it, Will."

"Oh, phooey," he said as if deeply disappointed. "No palm reading? No looking into a crystal ball? No phrenology?"

"Thank goodness no phrenology. I can just imagine feeling the bumps on people's heads all day."

"Yeah, some people have dirty hair. Then some people have filthy hair and *lice!*"

Catherine laughed. "Will you stop before my food comes?"

"Maybe if you won't completely break my heart by telling me you don't read tarot cards. *I* can read tarot cards, I'll have you know, and I thought if this latest university didn't see what a superior mind I have and asked me to leave, I could go into business with you. Not fifty-fifty, of course. You wouldn't need me for every case. But for the ones calling for tarot card readings I could be a lifesaver."

"If you don't stop, I think I'll make *you* my first patient." Catherine giggled.

"I'll stop teasing you if you'll answer a serious question." Catherine waited a moment and then nodded. "Do you think you'll ever come back here like Marissa did?"

Catherine frowned. "I don't know. When I left, all I could think of was seeing the world. Now I'm not certain how I planned to do that and work at my chosen profession, too, but it's what I wanted. Mom and Dad were alive and it seemed as if they would be forever. But they're both gone and I spent so little time with them the last few years. Now there's only Marissa. Of course she came back to take care of Mom—I would have helped, but they don't allow extended leaves in doctoral programs; still, I feel guilty that I wasn't here to help. And I think so often of those last months of my mother's life that I missed.

"At first Marissa said she was only going to stay here until we got all the legalities settled," Catherine went on. "Then she got a job. Now she says she should stay at least a year. Changing jobs frequently doesn't help you get another one. I feel there's more to her wanting to stay than her career, though. This is home to her." Catherine sighed. "She's been home since late June. She's had time to settle back into life here. Since mom's funeral, I've only been here for this Christmas break. I know we said we were *not* going to talk about any of the awful things that have happened this week, but they've made me wonder if I could make this home again. Right now, I have this strange feeling I'm in the horror house at the carnival."

"Well stated," Will said, finishing the rest of his martini. "This place is like a horror house. Or being trapped in a nightmare that won't let you wake up." He went silent. Catherine noticed the slight twitch beside his eye and he curled his fingers in and out of his damp palms.

"Hello, Catherine."

She looked up to see James Eastman standing beside the booth, his face solemn. "James," she said in surprise. "What are you doing here?"

"I came to have lunch."

"Oh yes, of course. What a stupid question. James, you know Will Addison, don't you?"

James gave him a stony look. "We've met several times. How are you, Will?"

"Same as always," Will said jovially. James's gaze fixed on the empty martini glass and Will tried unobtrusively to shove it away. "Won't you join us? Catherine and I haven't seen each other for ages. Well, actually, we saw each other Monday but only for a few minutes. We're just catching up on old times."

"Thank you for the invitation, but I've already had my lunch and I'm expecting a client at the office in ten minutes. I wouldn't want to interrupt your reminiscences, anyway." He gave them each a stiff smile. "Maybe another time. Good-bye, Will, Catherine," and he was on his way out.

Will looked at Catherine and raised an eyebrow. "Friendly fellow, that James Eastman."

"Well, he usually is," Catherine said faintly, feeling as if she'd done something wrong but not sure what it was. "Maybe he doesn't feel well or he's dreading the client he'll be seeing or—"

Will burst into laughter. "Or he doesn't like seeing his girl dining out with another man."

"His *girl*! Will Addison, I am not James's girl. We've had exactly two dates."

"*Two!* I only knew about the one in the Larke dining room. When was the other one?"

"Not that it's any of your business and not that it was really a date, but we were going to your mother's party together."

"Then Marissa had to blow things by having that silly wreck."

"You're awful, Will Addison. And I'm not James Eastman's *girl*."

"Judging by the look on his face when he saw you with another man, I think you'd better tell *him* you're not his girl. He became the town's most eligible bachelor after the lovely Renée vanished, but I don't think he'll hold that title for long. I believe he has again found love."

Catherine blushed. "You are too silly for words, Will. James is not in love with me."

"Are you in love with him?"

"What? That's ludicrous! Did you see that in your tarot cards? Will, really!"

"Settle down, Catherine. I just know when another man is feeling territorial."

"Oh, that was beautifully stated. I feel like the neighborhood female dog in heat."

"Equally lovely. Perhaps we should just run away and become poets."

Catherine was about to answer when they brought the food, smelling unbelievably good, and Will ordered another martini. Catherine closed her eyes and breathed in the hot chicken, Alfredo sauce, and Parmesan cheese. When she opened her eyes, Will was staring at her intently.

"You're the most beautiful woman I've ever seen," he said softly.

"Oh. Well, thank you." Catherine felt thrown off balance. She and Will had always shared a casual friendship without a hint of romance. "I suppose this wonderful food is bringing a twinkle to my eye and color to my cheeks."

"You think I'm leading up to a joke. I'm not. I've never seen blue-green eyes like yours, almond-shaped eyes, high cheekbones, perfect lips. You could have been a model. Or an actress. Instead, you used your impressive intelligence to propel yourself through a grueling course of training leading to a serious career. You don't know how much I admire that about you."

Now Catherine's cheeks were burning. Will looked at her solemnly, intensely, and his voice sounded slightly husky.

"I wish things had been different, Catherine. I wish *I* had been different. Maybe I could have pursued you and you would have taken me seriously if I hadn't always been a screwup."

"You're not a screwup, Will."

"Yes, I am. You're too nice to say it, but you know it. Still, you've continued to be my friend. Even when we were in our teens, when age differences mean so much, you always treated me as an equal although I was a year younger than you."

Nervously Catherine picked up her spritzer and took a large sip. She felt as if she'd come into the restaurant with one man and was now sitting with another. She'd never seen Will so serious, so . . . earnest.

"Will, I have to be honest. I think you're getting maudlin. You're handsome. You come from a family with money. You might have left a couple of universities—"

"Three."

"Okay, three, but a lot of young people bounce around before they decide what they really want to do in life. You're only twenty-seven. You have so many opportunities if you'll just take advantage of them. When I met you twelve years ago, you seemed ready to take on the world." She paused. "There's something I've always wanted to ask you." He raised his eyebrows. "Why did you change when you were seventeen? Before, you seemed genuinely to enjoy life. Ever since, you seemed to be pretending, acting. And you're not a good actor."

Will looked surprised and grabbed his martini. "If I changed, I wasn't aware of it," he said with complete lack of sincerity.

"Yes, you are. Did a girl break your heart?"

He said barely above a whisper, "A boy broke my heart."

"Oh." Catherine stared at him. "*Oh!* I didn't know it was that way for you. Why have you always kept it a secret?"

Will smiled. "I'm not gay, Catherine. I didn't mean a boy broke my heart in a romantic sense. I meant—"

"Well, for heaven's sake, of all the coincidences!" Will and Catherine looked up to see Evelyn Addison, Will's mother. "I didn't know you were having lunch together!"

Catherine beamed at Evelyn while Will rolled his eyes. He'd told Catherine his mother eavesdropped on phone calls whenever she got the chance. "Won't you sit down with us, Mrs. Addison?" Catherine asked.

"Well . . ." Evelyn pretended to think it over. "I believe I will. I've been doing last-minute Christmas shopping and I didn't know how tired and hungry I was until I walked in here." Catherine scooted over, but the tall, forty-pounds-too-heavy Evelyn shoved in beside Will, who looked as sad as if he'd lost his last friend in the world.

"How is Marissa, Catherine? I've been *so* worried about her." Evelyn frowned and tried to look as if tears were about to appear in those heavily made-up dark eyes. "Some people thought I'd be upset she couldn't cover our Christmas party for the newspaper, but of course I wasn't. All I cared about was Marissa's welfare."

Will rolled his eyes again.

"She's fine, Mrs. Addison. She had a close call—they pulled her from the car just before it rolled into the river—and she was in quite a bit of pain over the weekend, but she's all right now."

"Well, that's marvelous," Evelyn said absently. "Is she back at work?"

"Yes."

"Oh, wonderful! That she's well enough to work, I meant." Catherine felt pinned to the booth by the woman's probing eyes. She leaned forward. "Tell me something in confidence, Catherine. Working on the paper, has Marissa heard anything new about Tonya Archer's death? I can't believe she was murdered! She was known for being a bit loose for a while, but then she straightened up and married Andrew Archer, of all people. Anyway, Tonya's murder right after Buddy Pruitt's gives me chills!"

Catherine was saved from answering by the waiter stopping at their booth. Evelyn ordered tonic water with lime and asked for crackers immediately because she felt a bit nauseated. Oh, and could she also have a large glass of water with extra ice? And she'd *love* to have one of those delicious chocolate treats they gave you when you left. Maybe two, if it wouldn't be too much trouble.

Will sighed and ordered another martini.

12

1

Marissa waited until around three o'clock before calling Susan Montgomery. When Marissa introduced herself, Eric's mother hesitated before saying, "Hello, Marissa." No, How are you? No, It's nice to hear from you. When Marissa explained that she was calling about the Friends of the Library auction and reception and would like to do an interview, Susan's voice grew even stiffer.

"Marissa, I'm really not good at things like interviews. I'm sure someone else would be better—Irene Hagarty, perhaps. She's our treasurer—"

"I know," Marissa lied. "That's just the problem. The story would have so much more impact if you—the president of the Friends of the Library—could speak about how much the library means to the whole town and all your goals for an institution that benefits everyone."

Susan hesitated and then still balked. "I'm simply shy, Marissa. You know that about me. I'm not an articulate speaker—"

"You're much more articulate than you know. Besides, you will have me to edit for you. What if I promise to show you the article before we run it? That way you can omit anything you've said that you'd rather not have in the newspaper or add anything you'd like to add since we did the interview. The story will be just the way you want. That's your privilege as the president. Won't you please do this, Mrs. Montgomery? For the library?"

Marissa knew she'd backed the woman into a corner. If she said no, she'd sound as if she didn't really care about the organization—she just liked being president of a civic group. Marissa could almost hear Susan's mental battle before she said resignedly, "All right, Marissa. Could you come to my house around two o'clock tomorrow? We want to get news of the event into the paper as soon as possible."

"Oh, thank you so much, Mrs. Montgomery. I really appreciate this."

"You're welcome. And Marissa," Susan added dryly, "you haven't lost your touch for talking anyone into anything."

Marissa hung up, her face burning red at Susan Montgomery's knowledge of how Marissa had manipulated her, but she had to smile. At least she'd pulled off something that could help Eric and her learn more about Gretchen's last summer.

At five fifteen Marissa felt she'd done less work than anyone else at the *Gazette*, but she'd completed everything assigned to her. Eric had said to meet him at five thirty, so she knew she should be on her way. She glanced at Hank Landers, who was working frantically, and felt guilty that she couldn't help him. When all of this was over, she'd try to take more than her share of the load, she told herself as she put on her coat and headed outside toward her rental car.

Within five minutes after she'd pulled into a parking spot half a block away from police headquarters, Eric came loping out, jacket pulled high around his neck, head bent, looking neither right nor left. He hopped into Marissa's car, turned his back to the passenger window facing the sidewalk, and looked affronted when she burst into laughter.

"What's so funny?"

"You are just about the most suspicious-looking person I've ever seen. What's the matter? Did you slaughter everyone at headquarters before you made it to the getaway car?"

He gave her a look of heavy patience. "Do you realize you are involved in this case?"

"I do."

"Do you know everyone in headquarters—hell, half the town—knows we were engaged?"

"I didn't know, but it's good to get accurate statistics."

"Well, for one thing, I am not allowed to become personally involved with a material witness."

"Material witness! Eric, you know whoever caused my wreck was swathed from head to toe in a disguise. I didn't see what he really looked like!"

"Nevertheless, you're considered a material witness and I repeat, I'm not supposed to become personally involved with you. *Especially* romantically. And if people see me with you, that's what they'll think—that we're . . ."

"Romantically involved."

"Yes. I'm trying to prevent trouble at the worst, embarrassment at the least."

"All right. I'm sorry I laughed. I didn't know all the possible trouble that could come of our discussing the case outside of headquarters."

"Don't say 'discussing the case'!" Eric nearly shouted, looking appalled.

"I thought that's what we're going to do."

"We are, but we're not going to tell anyone."

"Okay. You can count on me, sir."

Eric picked up on the hint of laughter in her voice and gave her a stern look. "I mean it, Marissa. What we're doing could be a serious breach of procedure."

"I *get* it, Eric. Stop worrying. No one is paying any attention to us."

Eric was reaching for the door handle when someone pecked on Marissa's window. They both jumped as if they'd been shot and whipped around to see Jean Farrell. Marissa rolled down the window.

"I don't have a lot of time and I wanted to speak with both of you," Jean said. "I'm so glad I found you together."

Marissa knew both of them looked pink faced and guilty, but the fact that they were together in Marissa's car didn't even seem to register with Jean. She looked at Marissa. The woman's pale eyes were red rimmed from lack of sleep and her cheeks were sunken. "I know you're thinking I look dreadful, Marissa."

"No, I—"

"Yes, you were and yes, I do. But I don't think Mitch can last much longer, and I want him to know that I'm there," she said firmly. " 'In sickness and in health,' you know."

"But you need help, Jean. You're absolutely worn-out."

"She's right," Eric added.

"I know when I've reached my limit and I finally got someone," she said, addressing both Marissa and Eric. "A nice male nurse starts tomorrow. He'll come every morning at nine and stay until early afternoon. I have someone with Mitch now, but she's adamant about leaving by six thirty."

Eric frowned. "Don't you think you need someone full-time?"

Jean sounded reluctant. "Well, you know how tight the insurance companies are these days. I'm grateful for the nurse a few hours a day. I asked my neighbor to come this afternoon because I had a few last errands to do. Frankly, I don't think Mitch can hold on much longer. I've asked him to let me send him to the hospital, but he wants to die at home. We've lived in that house all our married life. We had our little girl, Betsy, there with us for three precious years."

Jean swallowed hard and began rubbing her hands, which bore scars from a lifetime of working outside and refusing to wear gardening gloves. A scar on the palm of her left hand was the worst, and she kneaded it vigorously. "I just can't drag him off to some sterile-looking hospital room with none of the things he loves around him.

"Marissa, Mitch loves you and Catherine and Eric so much and you love Mitch," Jean went on.

"Oh, we do," Marissa said through her own tears.

"Mitch wants to see all of you. He asked if I'd delay his morphine dose tomorrow evening and the three of you could make a short visit. Do you think you three could come together?

I don't want to string out the visits over two or three evenings—
it would be too hard on him and there might not be time."

Marissa took Jean's cold hand. "Of course I can come, and I
know that even if Catherine has plans she'll change them."

"I'll bring Catherine and Marissa if they'll let me," Eric said.
"What would be a good time?"

"Six thirty? I usually give Mitch some morphine at seven, but
I know he can hold off for at least half an hour." She smiled and
squeezed Marissa's hand. "Thank you, my dears. I hope you
don't feel like I'm stalking you, but I just happened to see you
pull up to the police station, Marissa, and Eric run out to the
car. It was my chance to tell you this in person. I know how
much seeing you will mean to my dear Mitch."

2

Although darkness had fallen, Marissa parked her car three
spaces away from Eric's. He carried the big bag with the barrel
of fried chicken and all the side dishes up to the second floor,
where he unlocked his door and almost shoved her inside. Then
he shut the door, drew shut the draperies, and turned on a lamp.

Marissa hung her coat in the closet and looked around the
small living room with its gray carpet, eggshell-colored walls
with no pictures, navy blue couch and one chair, bare coffee
table, small television, and an end table bearing the only lamp in
the room.

"Gosh, Eric, you went wild decorating this place, didn't
you?" she asked dryly. "All these colors, knickknacks, paintings,
framed family pictures, so much furniture—it makes me dizzy.
And exactly how close do you have to sit in front of that television before you can see anything? Would two feet be stretching
it?"

"There's a television show on Saturday mornings where two
people visit homes for sale and tell the owners how crappy their
houses look and that's why they won't sell. You should audition
for the show. You'd be perfect."

"Well, I didn't mean to hurt your feelings. I was just—"

"Giving your opinion, for which I didn't ask, by the way." Eric set the bag of food on the small kitchen counter. "Will you deign to eat here, Miss Interior Design?"

Marissa tried to smother a grin, sensing that beneath his teasing Eric *was* just the tiniest bit insulted. "Your apartment might not win awards for interior decorating, but it's so clean you could eat off the floor."

"How gracious of you to say so. Would you care to prove what you claim?"

"No, tonight I think I'll try to act like a lady, not like Lindsay."

"She seemed like a lady to me."

"She has lapses." Marissa looked at Eric's tired face and his slightly slumping shoulders. She opened the refrigerator door. "Ah, beer! Thank God!" She took out two cans. "Why don't you get out of that uniform, take your shower, drink your beer, and then we'll eat. You look like you've been run over by a truck."

"You just can't turn off the charm tonight, can you?" Eric asked, although he was beginning to grin. "When is it I'm supposed to drink my beer, ma'am?"

"Before or after you take off the uniform, in the shower, after the shower—whenever you like."

"And what will you do if I decide to lounge in a bubble bath and drink my beer slowly, like nectar from the Gods?"

"I'm certain you keep plenty of bubble bath around here, not to mention exotic oils. And this beer can looks like a container for honey mead, so just go to it. I'll watch TV. We can dine when you've finished your nightly beauty ritual."

By now the grin had deepened his dimples—the dimples she'd once found irresistible. "You make a great handmaiden, you know it?"

"Ah—I've always wanted to be a handmaiden, never having to think, getting to wear gossamer gowns with a wreath of flowers on my flowing locks, always at my master's bidding, being his lover whenever he wants me. Yes, I think it's the career for me." Marissa realized that Eric's grin had lessened and her own voice had slowed and deepened slightly. She forced a laugh. "Go take your shower, Chief Deputy, so we can eat. I'm starving."

"So am I," he said huskily as he turned and walked into another room, closing the door behind him.

Marissa stood staring at the door, trying to push down an almost irresistible impulse to follow him, take off the uniform piece by piece, lie down with him on the bed, run her hands through his soft hair the way she used to, encircle his lips with tiny kisses—

"Oh God," she whispered. "I won't let this happen again. I *won't*."

With that she popped open a can of beer, took a gulp, turned on the television, and forced herself to concentrate on a game show, not the gorgeous naked man in the next room.

3

"First of all, I'd like to know if you've found out anything about the moonstone ring left on Gretchen's grave," Marissa asked, sitting on the floor with a plate of chicken, coleslaw, mashed potatoes and gravy, and a beer in front of her on the coffee table. She'd always liked eating this way. Eric had opted to sit in the chair.

"Nothing, I'm afraid. Absolutely no fingerprints. That was to be expected. The lab is going over it for any traces of DNA. We won't find out about that for a few days."

"Damn," Marissa said forcefully. "I get so mad thinking that someone has had her ring all of these years—the ring I bought her, one part of the pair we were going to wear our whole lives."

"Almost like a wedding ring," Eric said softly.

"Yes, I guess it was."

"*Is.* We have it back now."

Marissa nodded but couldn't smile. "What about the post-card and the 'Tyger' note?"

"Once again, no fingerprints. Someone did the typing on the postcard on an old manual typewriter, though. We're not absolutely certain yet, but the type looks like that of a 1940s or '50s model Underwood."

"Who would still be using one of those?"

"I don't know who would be using one, but I'm sure some people have them as collectible pieces. I think Olivetti bought into Underwood in the early sixties." Eric poured more gravy over his mashed potatoes. "My parents have one. A 1949 Underwood. After he retired, my great-grandfather wrote a mystery story on it and the story was published, so he made everyone promise they'd never get rid of the typewriter."

"My gosh!" Marissa exclaimed. "I'd completely forgotten, but Gretchen had a copy of the story." She paused. " 'Midnight Movie'!"

"Right! He wrote some more, but no publishers bought them. Anyway, I'm sure we're not the only people in town with an old manual typewriter."

"No. The 'Tyger' stanza was written on a computer, but everyone has one of those, too." Marissa sighed. "Okay, my turn to tell you what I know about the case. Where do you want me to begin?"

"How about with Tonya's visit to you last night?" Eric took a bite of coleslaw. "Start from the beginning."

Marissa told him how surprised she'd been when Tonya showed up at the door. "She came around eight and couldn't have been more pleasant. She said Andrew had to work late and it was Christmas—I guess that meant she was feeling sentimental—and she wanted to patch up our friendship." Marissa saw Eric tense and knew he was thinking of when their friendship had ended. She plowed ahead. "We talked a bit about what we'd seen that night on the island. I wanted to give her the benefit of the doubt, but especially I didn't want to get in an argument, so I ended that topic with something weak about the dark and angles and our seeing things differently."

Marissa took a bite of buttery biscuit, not caring about calories, and chewed slowly as she focused on the evening. "Tonya talked about her relationship with Andrew and how surprised people were when they eloped and how happy she is—was." Marissa swallowed and looked at Eric. "Then she went off on a tangent about James dating Catherine. She all but asked if they were sleeping together. She talked about how much she'd disliked Renée and said Renée had vanished just like Dillon."

Marissa closed her eyes, trying to remember everything Tonya had said and wishing she'd had a tape recorder on last night. "Then I asked why she'd come to see me besides to simply renew our friendship and she became a different person. Offended. Really nervous. She talked about Dillon again and how they'd just been friends. They'd never been more than friends." Marissa sighed. "I'm not getting all of this in the right order, Eric."

"That's all right. At least you're remembering most of it."

"Well, after the last mention of Dillon, she made some remark about me pumping her for information about Dillon because I thought that would win you back. I was stunned and she said everyone in town knew about us. You'd been at my house a lot. She told me not to go whining to Andrew about our argument. Then off she went in a huff."

"Ummm," Eric mumbled thoughtfully. "Do you think everyone knows about us?"

"What's there to know, Eric? That we've talked as two people who know each other very well?"

"Do you believe that's what Jean thinks?"

"I don't believe Jean is thinking about much of anything except Mitch. Even if we were having a torrid romance, she wouldn't say a word. You know Jean—she's just like my mother about keeping confidences. I suppose that's why they became such good friends in their way." Tears rose in Marissa's eyes. "I'll never forget the day they planted the rose garden."

Eric laughed. "You told me about it. It's hard to imagine now, but Jean's life can be happy again."

"I wish my mother were alive to help with that job."

"My mother is. She and Jean were friends, too, although I don't think Jean and Mitch visited our house as much as yours, but maybe if Mom will reach out to Jean, it would help both of them." Before Marissa could say anything about having arranged an interview with his mother for tomorrow afternoon, Eric cleared his throat and said in a professional tone, "Okay, back to business. What time did Tonya leave your house?"

"I didn't look at the clock but I'd say it was around eight thirty. I told you it was a short visit."

"So she was at your house an hour at the most?"

"Less than an hour. I'm certain." Marissa paused. "Do those times coincide with the times Andrew gave you?"

"He said he had a lot of work to do at the office last night. There's a message from him on the home answering machine made around eight fifty to tell Tonya he'd be home within half an hour. We didn't find anything on her voicemail."

"Her cell phone didn't ring while she was here. Apparently Andrew wasn't trying to find her. Are you thinking the answering-machine message was used to set up an alibi?"

"If so, it was clumsy, because Andrew says he left the office at nine fifteen. The medical examiner puts Tonya's death at about nine. A phone message from his office at eight fifty wouldn't give him an alibi for her murder at nine. He *could* have made it home by nine. Of course, estimated times of death aren't as accurate as they are on television. They can't tell if someone was murdered at nine precisely or nine ten. Andrew called nine-one-one at nine thirty. The reports say that at nine fifty, her body temp had barely dropped."

Marissa frowned. "If she left my house at eight thirty, it wouldn't have taken her until nine to get home. I wonder where she went after she left my house?"

"Wherever she went, she didn't stay for long. She probably just got some coffee, although we haven't found anyone who claims to have seen her." Eric's gaze became more intense. "Did she tell you she was pregnant?"

"No!" Marissa took a breath. "But she looked a little heavier than I remembered her being, and today I wondered if pregnancy could have been responsible for her mood swings. Did Andrew know?"

"Andrew was in tatters about Tonya's murder, but when we mentioned the fetus, he completely fell apart. If he was acting, he's very good at it. Tonya was about seven weeks along. She would have had to tell him soon, and I have a strong feeling that part of the reason she came to your house to reconcile was because of the baby. Maybe she felt guilty ever since Gretchen's death but she didn't try to mend fences. Getting pregnant might have spurred her into action, though. She wanted a perfect family with good friends, no one to hold a grudge against her, no one who would ever tell her child that its mother absolutely had lied about a murder. The story of what happened to Gretchen was all a big mix-up." Eric shrugged. "Just a guess."

"But a good one," Marissa said, almost in awe. "My goodness, Eric, what a discussion you and Catherine could have!" She paused. "What do you think of Tonya's talking about Dillon?"

"Maybe she'd heard the gossip that he's back in town and that he tried to kill you." Eric paused. "There's something else . . ."

"What else? Tell me."

Eric stared at her for a moment as if making up his mind. "But this is confidential. I *shouldn't*—"

"Eric! I don't care what the rules are; Tonya has been murdered and whatever is going on involves *me*! Don't you think I have a right to know everything?"

Eric stared at her for another moment and Marissa was on the verge of shouting at him when he said quietly, "Tonya got a Christmas card signed 'D.A.,' too. It was a photograph of her and Andrew decorating their Christmas tree in front of the picture window and it said: 'Hope you're enjoying your new life, Tonya.' It was signed 'D.A.' "

Marissa felt as if her neck had been touched with ice. "She was frightened. That's why she came to see me. She probably wanted to know if I'd received something similar signed 'D.A.' She was just so nervous, she blew out of the house before she had a chance to ask."

"I think you're right. Andrew said she was really shaken up about it. Now he thinks he should have insisted she bring it to the police. Instead, he told her to just cool down. He'll never forgive himself."

"It wouldn't have helped. Would you have put her under surveillance because of one picture?"

Eric shook his head. "We have two people out with the flu as it is. I couldn't have justified surveillance for a picture signed 'D.A.' "

Marissa leaned forward, rubbing her neck muscles growing annoyingly tight again. "If Dillon is in the city, I can understand why he'd try to kill me. I'm the one who claimed he pushed Gretchen off the railing," Marissa said, "but why would he murder Tonya? And what about Buddy?"

Eric slowly chewed a piece of chicken. "Maybe Dillon didn't 'escape' the day after Gretchen's death. Maybe Buddy let him go."

"And that's a motive for murder?"

"The only long-term friend Dillon ever had was Buddy Pruitt. I always thought it was because he liked to control people. Dillon Archer loved to play God. That was easy to do with poor Buddy. Maybe he boasted to Buddy about some of the petty crimes he'd committed and gotten away with, or maybe there were worse crimes he confided to Buddy. I always sensed Buddy was afraid of him, Marissa, and maybe he had good reason to be. Maybe he knew more about Dillon than any of us did and Dillon decided it was time to shut him up for good."

"And Tonya?"

"Same reason."

"But she had more spine than Buddy. People couldn't boss her around like they did Buddy. She was spirited. She could even be aggressive at times."

"I agree, but could she act the same way with Dillon as she did with other people? Couldn't he have held something over her head, something he didn't want known and would punish her for revealing?"

"Edgar Blume," Marissa almost whispered.

"Edgar Blume? That high school teacher that died from an overdose? What about him?"

"I don't know. I've just always wondered . . ." She stopped rubbing her neck and looked at Eric. "You think Dillon Archer had a God complex?"

"Yes, I do. Your sister would have a more educated view of his psyche, but in my opinion Dillon wanted to have power over everyone he could. His father mistreated him. Everyone knew it. No one did anything about it, not even his mother. Abused children can grow up to be like Buddy or they can be like Dillon. They were a perfect pair. As for Tonya?" He shrugged.

"My God, I'd never thought of that before." A terrible thought crossed Marissa's mind and she shivered but said nothing.

"What is it?" Eric asked.

"Nothing."

"Marissa, tell me."

Marissa didn't want to hint that Gretchen could be guilty of anything, but she didn't have a choice. "Could Dillon have had something to hold over Gretchen's head? Is that why she left Will Addison and turned to Dillon? Because she was *forced* to be with Dillon?"

Eric's face went rigid. Marissa had been afraid to ask the question about his beloved dead sister, but they were talking honestly tonight. If she couldn't ask him now, she could never ask him.

Marissa hardly breathed as his gaze grew hard and she could almost feel the strength it took for him to control his answer. At last, he asked in a coldly angry voice, "What in God's name is it you think Dillon was holding over my sister's head?"

"I didn't say he *was*. I asked if there *could* have been something. After all, you're the one who said Dillon liked to play God, to have power over everyone, to be in control."

"I was in Philadelphia most of the year. You were my sister's best friend. I know she'd just graduated from Juilliard and the two of you weren't together throughout the winters, but you'd each been home during the summers. Wouldn't you know more about her life then than I do?"

"Yes, I should have." Marissa could hear the defeat in her own voice. "She spent a lot of time practicing for the fall concert tour. I was making wedding plans for August. I did get the feeling she was being slightly distant with me, but she was seeing Will and I was glad. I know many people thought Will was spoiled and wild and wouldn't turn out to be anything, but I never felt that way about him. Besides, as far as I knew, Gretchen had never had a serious boyfriend before Will.

"Suddenly she told me it was over. She wouldn't say why— she just said they weren't a good match," Marissa went on. "Then I heard she'd been seen around town with Dillon. When I asked her about him, she made a joke and said the reports of their romance were highly exaggerated. She'd only had a couple of casual 'friendly' dates with him. After all, could I imagine her with Dillon Archer?" Marissa sighed. "I wasn't as good a friend to Gretchen that summer as I should have been. I should have kept track of her, checked into these romances, pressed her until she told me why she seemed distant."

Marissa couldn't look at Eric. She suddenly felt as if what had happened to Gretchen *was* her fault. Something had been wrong with Gretchen that summer—her behavior was odd: her bouncing from Will to Dillon was beyond Marissa's understanding; her keeping her distance both physically and emotionally from Marissa was totally out of character. Yet I did nothing, Marissa thought. I blamed it all on nerves over her concert tour and the fact that she wanted to be more independent.

Eric slowly got up holding his plate, picked up Marissa's, took them both to the sink, and retrieved two more beers from the refrigerator. When he returned, he sat on the couch, leaned down, and said, "Marissa, would you like to sit on the couch like a grown-up?"

Marissa wasn't certain if it was his teasing tone or tension that threw her into a fit of giggles. After the worst had passed, she pushed away the small, light table, scrambled up onto the couch, and sat about four feet away from Eric, suddenly nervous, her legs pressed together, her hands clenched in her lap.

"I know we had one hell of a fight the other night at Gretchen's grave and I accused you of not standing up for her like you should have," Eric said gently. "When I came over to your house later, I said I wanted to finish that fight. I told you I no longer blame you for anything that happened the night she died. I wanted to clear the slate with that statement and it sounded superficial. Well, it was somewhat superficial. The truth is that I blame all of us for what happened to Gretchen and I always will."

Marissa stiffened. "All of us. Dillon, Andrew, Tonya, you, and me."

"And my parents and their friends and Gretchen's teachers—everybody who saw a beautiful teenage girl and treated her like she was ten because she was small, dainty, and soft-spoken. Even when she was twenty-one, she looked fifteen. Then there was her musical talent. She was a prodigy, so we all treated her like she was more fragile than crystal. We tried to keep her absolutely safe; we even tried to protect her from bad news—we might as well have wrapped her up in cotton batting and packed her away."

"I know," Marissa said sadly.

Eric took a deep breath and scooted closer to her, putting his arm around her shoulder. "I think the only person close to her who tried to tear away all that cotton batting was you," he went on. "Sometimes I got annoyed with you because I didn't think you were being careful enough with her. For a couple of years after her death, I kept telling myself there was something different about her that summer—something not good—and I blamed you for not finding out what it was. I was completely unreasonable. I now recognize that you tried to find out, but you had enough respect for her to give her privacy. She wasn't obligated to tell anyone, even you, every thought and every feeling she had, and you didn't badger her. My sister couldn't have had a better friend than you, Marissa. I know that. I truly believe it."

Marissa stared straight ahead, tears welling in her eyes. She was painfully aware of Eric's closeness and every breath he drew. His earlier apology for blaming her had moved Marissa. She'd known it was a big step for him. But the things he'd said tonight touched her heart because they were so strong, so genuine. Marissa realized the amount of soul-searching he must have done to be able to tell her how he felt and she knew the pain it must have cost him.

"I don't know what to say, Eric." Her voice quivered, weaker than normal. "I hadn't even talked to you for almost five years before my wreck Saturday night, and suddenly you're telling me you feel all of us were in a way to blame for what happened to Gretchen."

"I know. I sound like I've done a one-hundred-eighty-degree turn in less than a week, but I haven't. For two years I gave in to my anger over Gretchen—a stupid, childish fury. I was irrational and foolishly enraged. I guess I must have some sense, though, because slowly it began to work its way through all that unfair anger and forced me to look at things more clearly. It wasn't an easy process or a fast one—I fought it with everything in me, maybe because I preferred thinking we lived in a chaotic universe where no matter how hard I tried as an agent of the law, all my efforts were for nothing. Because there was no justice, no sense, in Gretchen's death, I decided there wasn't any justice or sense in the world." Eric made a small, derogatory laugh. "I was very cocky, wasn't I, thinking *I* understood the nature of the universe?"

Marissa smiled. "Don't make so much fun of yourself. You didn't think no justice existed in the whole world, just a small part of it. And I believe you can bring justice to that part, Eric."

"I can't do anything for Gretchen."

After a few moments of silence, Marissa said, "The more we've talked about her the last few days, the more I've thought about the way she was acting that summer. I was young, I was over-the-moon about our wedding, but I still noticed it. Now that I've thought about it more deeply, I'm more convinced something was really bothering her—something beyond nerves over a concert tour or anger at being treated like a child."

"What? Her breakup with Will?"

"I thought she was in love with Will. She never told me so, but her voice and the look in her eyes changed when she talked about him. You know how easily embarrassed she was, so I never asked her. She wasn't jealous over losing you to me. She was thrilled that we'd be a real family."

"So what was bothering her?"

Marissa sighed. "I don't know. I do know she was secretive that summer. She always told me everything about her life—what she was doing, what she thought. Not that summer, though." Marissa paused, trying not to sound triumphant. "Eric, I've arranged to have an interview with your mother tomorrow."

When his mouth dropped open, she explained about the event sponsored by the Friends of the Library, his mother's part in it as president, and how she'd almost bullied Susan into giving her the interview. "You and I talked about looking at the photo albums in reference to the rings, but maybe I can find out more about Gretchen in the house. Have things changed a lot there? Particularly Gretchen's room?"

"Gretchen's room is exactly the way she left it the night we went to Gray's Island."

"Knowing your mother, I guessed as much. If I get a chance to see Gretchen's room without your mother's presence, would you mind if I snooped around a little bit?"

Eric smiled at her kindly. "Of course not, but I've looked through Gretchen's room. I haven't seen anything unusual that would give us a clue about what was wrong with her."

"*You* didn't find a clue. I knew your sister's hiding places."

"Hiding places? Gretchen didn't have anything to hide," Eric said sharply.

"Everyone has a few things to hide, Eric. Certainly working in the law, you know that's true."

"I guess so. But Gretchen?" he asked reluctantly.

"Maybe," Marissa said to soothe his defenses. "I have been wrong two or three times in my life."

He looked at her and then laughed. "Okay. You know more about teenage girls than I do. Search the room if you get the chance. I just can't believe you got the chance so soon."

"Sometimes you have to make your chances, Eric. People don't always like you for it, but reporters get used to pushing their noses where others think they don't belong."

"I'm proud of you, but Gretchen always said you had a lot of determination. She said you couldn't be stopped once you'd set your mind to something." Eric slid across the four inches of couch that separated them. Unnerved, Marissa loosened her hands and looked down at her watch. "I should be going. I left Catherine all alone—"

Marissa turned her head quickly, so Eric's kiss just grazed her cheek. In a few moments, her voice cut through the silence: "What was that about?"

"We almost kissed last night and you didn't act offended."

"We leaned toward each other. It seemed almost out of habit." She faced him. "Tonight seemed like a setup."

"Oh." She expected resentment, irritation, hauteur. Instead, Eric laughed. "I lure a beautiful woman to my swanky apartment, I ply her with Kentucky Fried Chicken and beer, and then I sweet-talk her by telling her I don't blame her for my sister's death. I see how that could seem like a setup."

"Eric, it isn't funny."

"Yes, it is. You're just mad and you don't want to laugh." His entire face changed—the brown eyes danced, the dimples appeared, the worry line between his eyebrows disappeared, and the deep, joyous sound of his laughter filled the room. His effect on Marissa was exactly the same as it had been five years ago, but she didn't want him to know it. *She* didn't want to know it.

"I'm sorry, Marissa. I didn't mean for that kiss to be what it must have seemed to be. You know I . . . care about you. I have since you were about fifteen. And it felt so good to *really* talk to you again. Can we call it a misunderstood kiss of friendship?"

Marissa forced herself to smile while her emotions roiled. She was furious when she thought he was taking advantage of the situation, trying to lure her to his bed. She was devastated when he said he cared about her and the attempted kiss had been a "kiss of friendship." All at once, she wanted to curse and cry at the same time.

Abruptly she stood up. "Well, now that we've defined our relationship—"

"Defined our relationship—"

"I really do have to go, Eric," she rushed on as if he'd said nothing. "It gets dark so early and I don't like to think of Catherine alone in the house at night and after Tonya's visit last night God knows who'll come by tonight." She walked quickly to the closet and took out her coat. "I hope we got a few things straight. About the case, I mean. I'll do my best to look around Gretchen's room tomorrow. I can't make any promises, though."

Eric followed her to the front door and opened it to the icy December night. "I'll follow you home," he said.

She looked startled. "What for? I thought I answered all of your questions. And it's late."

"It's not late and I didn't intend to invite myself in once we got to your house, if that's what you're thinking. I want to make sure you get home safely, Marissa."

"That's not necessary. I'm going straight home. I'll use the automatic garage door opener from the locked car, drive the car into the garage, close the garage door, and then rush right in the house. Just like I always do." She gave him a quick, jittery smile that said, Don't you dare follow me. Aloud she muttered, "Have a good night," and hurried to her car. She glanced in her rearview mirror and saw Eric standing in his open doorway, watching until her red taillights turned right onto the highway. As she sped into the bitterly cold darkness, she wished she felt as confident about her safety as she pretended.

13

1

After Marissa left, Eric took another can of beer from the refrigerator, flipped the television back on, lay down on the couch, and smiled. He'd let Marissa go so easily because he'd already arranged for surveillance at her house. She would arrive to find Deputy Randall Crane parked in front of her house.

He took a sip of beer and half of it ran down his chin. He'd never been good at drinking while lying down, and after nearly choking on the beer that had actually made it into his mouth he muttered, "Damn," and sat up, wiping his chin with his hand. Eric hoped he hadn't done that in front of Marissa. Marissa had seen it happen many times before, though. Marissa knew almost everything about him, even how cold and unforgiving he could be sometimes.

Eric stood up and took another sip of beer. After circling the room aimlessly, he went to the picture window and stood motionless, staring out into the dark, thinking of Christmas five years ago—Gretchen's last. He'd had four days off and more than just trading Christmas gifts on his mind. He'd known how much Marissa loved Christmas, and along with a beautiful deep blue cashmere sweater he'd bought a one-carat engagement ring. He'd spent most of the way home practicing his proposal.

The large Montgomery home had been swathed in Christmas lights and this year his father had placed artificial reindeer in the front yard, including one with a glowing red nose. Whenever Eric came home to visit, his parents had always acted as if he'd just returned from a war. Bear hugs from Dad, kisses from Mom along with darting inspections of Eric's face meant to ferret out pallid skin, red eyes, or the beginnings of a fever. His mother would run her hands over his midriff to see if he was losing weight because he wouldn't eat properly. He'd always felt embarrassed and he'd always loved the attention.

Usually Gretchen had run to him and hugged him with the ferocity of a little girl, he now thought, taking another drink of beer. That visit she'd merely walked in during his parents' greeting, smiled tenderly, and given him a gentle hug—no laughing, joking, and messing up his already-messy hair. He'd thought her gracious manner was cute—she was trying to act more mature, like Marissa, although Marissa often gave in to her own juvenile, silly side and he loved it.

He'd been mentally only half-present for the family festivities, though. The rest of the time, he'd been thinking of the perfect proposal, hoping Marissa would like the square-cut diamond set in gold, wondering if she would want to immediately pick a date for the wedding. He intended to push for mid-August, when his best friend would be back from active duty overseas in the Army. He was almost certain she'd agree.

Eric turned his back on the cold December evening and began putting away food left over from his dinner with Marissa. He smiled at the thought of this being a seduction dinner. He hadn't meant it to be. He certainly wished he hadn't tried to kiss her. Having her sitting next to him, listening to her animated voice and her irresistible giggle, smelling the same perfume she'd worn years ago, he hadn't even thought before he'd acted. Kissing her had seemed the most natural act in the world and it had been damned stupid of him. He'd insulted her. Not so much that she never wanted to be alone with him again, he hoped. They'd spent a long time apart, though. He didn't know how to act around her, now. Now, he thought. Was he kidding himself? He'd acted as bungling five years ago, the night he proposed, as he'd acted tonight.

Eric smiled at the memory of what he'd been thinking of as "the momentous event." He'd made a reservation at the Larke

Inn dining room, making certain they got a table next to the wall of windows overlooking the waterfall and that they had a special table decoration—two white and two apricot-colored roses instead of the single rose in a bud vase. He'd dressed in his best suit, and when he'd come downstairs in his home his mother had gasped, saying she'd never seen such a handsome man in her life, sending his father and Gretchen into fits of laughter.

If Gretchen had known Eric was going to propose, she hadn't said anything, and he hadn't told her until the last minute, fearing she couldn't keep a secret from Marissa for even twenty-four hours. Everyone had come out on the front porch to wave him off, as if he were leaving for a world tour, and he'd been self-conscious yet too excited to mind as much as usual.

When he'd arrived at Marissa's, he'd talked to her parents for a minute; then Marissa had come down the steps in a sapphire-colored dress—the same color as her eyes—something knee length and soft, with a skirt that flared gently when she turned. Her light brown and golden hair rippled long and loose the way he liked it best, and he'd noticed she wore her mother's pearl necklace and earrings. He'd never seen Marissa look so beautiful.

His beautiful, smart, energetic, funny Marissa. How could he have ever thought he could live without her? What would he do if he lost her like he had lost Gretchen or Andrew had lost Tonya?

He thought for a moment and then went to the phone. Within seconds, he heard a young, crisp female voice: "Roberta Landers."

"Eric Montgomery."

"Yes, sir. I saw that on the caller ID."

"You don't have to keep calling me sir, Robbie," Eric said.

"All right, sir. I mean Chief Deputy Montgomery."

Eric rolled his eyes. "*Sir* is better than that. I sound like royalty. Anyway, I hope I'm not disturbing you."

"No, sir. I was just watching television."

"I have an assignment for you and I'd prefer that you keep it to yourself. That's why I'm calling you at home. Too many ears at headquarters."

"I understand, sir, and I won't tell a soul."

"Do you know what Dillon Archer looks like?"

"Well, yes. I mean, I know what he looked like when he ran away from Aurora Falls. I kept all the news clippings about him."

"Do you have them at your apartment?"

"Yes, but Dad covered most of the stories about Gretchen's death and Dillon's disappearance, so he'd have an actual photograph in his files at home. I could get one."

"No," Eric said quickly. "I don't even want Hank knowing about this. Tomorrow I want you to start canvassing all of the local motels looking for Dillon. Cut a picture from one of your newspaper articles to show. *Don't* mention his name. Just say he's someone we'd like to talk to as the witness of a minor incident. If someone recognizes him as Dillon Archer, just say something vague about us trying to close old files." He paused. "I don't quite know how to say this without offending you, but when you show the picture I want you to smile a lot. Giggle. Bat your eyelashes."

"Sir?" Robbie asked doubtfully.

"I know this sounds terrible, but I don't want you to seem smart. If you act sharp, if this seems like an important investigation, someone is going to connect Dillon Archer to the recent murders and the city will go wild. If they think you're just some cute little airhead I sent out on an unimportant errand, they might not pay too much attention." Robbie remained silent and Eric knew she was insulted. "Believe me, if you *were* some cute little airhead, I wouldn't be sending you on this particular assignment. You're smart, but you can act giggly and not too bright."

"Thank you, sir. I guess."

Eric finally laughed. "This is coming out all wrong, Robbie. I've never been a master of words. What I'm trying to say is that I trust you implicitly. I know you're the person for this job because it calls for special skills, which you have. It's important, Robbie." He paused. "It concerns the murders of Tonya Archer and Buddy Pruitt and the attempt on Marissa Gray's life in the car wreck. Perhaps other people are involved, but right now I'm most concerned about Marissa."

Robbie's voice immediately warmed: "I understand, sir." I understand you're probably still in love with her, the undertone said. "And if any of those people are mentioned in connection with the picture, I'll just look blank."

"Great. Concentrate on the less ostentatious places. I can't see Dillon marching nonchalantly through the Larke Inn lobby."

"I understand, sir. Thank you for trusting me with this assignment. I'll do the very best I can."

"I know you will, Robbie. And practice that giggle."

"I'm on my way to find my volumizing mascara and neon green eye shadow as we speak." Robbie giggled mindlessly and said in a slow, drawling voice, "Night night, Mr. Chief Deputy."

She hung up. Eric stared at the phone for a moment and then broke out laughing.

2

Marissa put her arm through his as they walked into the candle-lit dining room of the Larke Inn. With pleasure, Eric saw several people turn their heads to glance at the beautiful blonde on his arm. He gave the name Montgomery to the maître d', who escorted them to a table by the windows overlooking the water-fall—a table with a centerpiece of two white roses and two apri-cot-colored roses. Marissa noticed them immediately and murmured, "Ah," in delight. Eric pulled out her chair, looked away for an instant, and pulled out the chair a fraction more just as she started to sit down. She emitted a, "Whoop!" as she missed falling on the floor by no more than two inches. People looked, Eric turned crimson, launched into frantic apologies, and Marissa had begun giggling.

And giggling.

And giggling.

And . . . Eric opened his eyes. Dammit, he thought. He wasn't hearing Marissa giggling. He was hearing his phone ringing.

He picked up the handset and barked, "Montgomery here." He listened for almost five minutes and said, "I'll be right there." He replaced the phone, groaned, ran a hand over his eyes, and made a difficult decision.

It was two thirty-three in the morning when he called Marissa.

The phone rang. Marissa, wide-awake, looked at the caller ID that read: *Eric Montgomery,* picked up the handset, and muttered a sleepy, "'Lo."

"Marissa, it's Eric."

"Who?" Marissa asked, still sizzling over the "friendship" kiss.

"Eric Montgomery. *Eric.* Are you awake?"

"Oh well, I guess I am now." She hadn't slept at all, but she tried to sound half-drowsy, half-peeved: "What is it?"

"Marissa, this is serious. No one has been murdered, but we have a situation that involves you. I don't have time to explain, but I need for you to dress in something for outside wear. Your surveillance deputy, Randall Crane, is parked outside your house. He'll bring you and Catherine."

"Bring us where? What's happened?"

"I just told you I don't have time to explain. Randall will—"

"Pick us up. I got it," Marissa snapped.

Marissa hung on to the phone, her heart fluttering, perspiration popping out along her hairline. Eric sounded shaken. It took a lot to shake Eric. Fright had flooded through Marissa and she'd immediately become contentious. She always reacted the same way when she was frightened. Eric would have expected it, she thought.

Fifteen minutes later, Marissa and Catherine climbed into the patrol car. "Deputy Crane, what's happened?" Marissa asked as soon as they settled in the backseat. "Eric said no one has been murdered. Is someone injured? Why does he want both of us to come? I don't understand."

Catherine laid a calming hand on Marissa's thigh. "Please stop firing questions at the poor man. You're not giving him a chance to answer anything even if Eric wanted him to, which I don't believe Eric does." She leaned forward. "We appreciate the ride."

"You're welcome, although I wish it was under better circumstances."

He looked as if he could have bitten his tongue when Marissa fired out, "What *are* the circumstances? We're just supposed to go somewhere in the middle of the night because there's some kind of bad situation Eric can't explain and we don't know what we're in for or—" Marissa abruptly stopped talking, then asked in disbelief, "Are you turning into the cemetery?"

"Uh, yes, ma'am."

Marissa looked around in astonishment. Then she saw halogen lights shining on the area near a large weeping willow. As they drew closer, she noticed two patrol cars, a white truck that must hold a generator, crime scene tape, and—

The ruin of her mother's grave.

14

1

Marissa and Catherine sat like statues in the back of the patrol car, their faces expressionless and their eyes unblinking. Catherine reached over and clenched Marissa's gloved left hand. "They don't want us to go over . . . there, do they?"

"They can't make us. Eric won't let them," Marissa murmured in a daze.

But apparently he would. He walked over to the car and opened the door. The sisters drew closer together like little girls, huddling, drawing strength from each other, hiding from the horror. "Marissa, Catherine, you don't know how sorry I am to do this, but I have to ask you to look at something."

"*Something?*" Marissa felt sudden fury. "Why don't you just say 'your mother's grave'? I think we're past using euphemisms."

His voice remained mild: "I hated to ask you to come, but I felt you should. We have a Romeo and Juliet whose parents don't want them to see each other, so they made a brilliant plan to meet secretly in the cemetery. They were walking around quoting poetry to each other, at least according to them, when Juliet almost fell in an unexpected hole. Romeo pulled her back. Their first impulse was to run, of course, but they thought they saw someone—large and wearing a cape lurking around. They were certain this person or 'being' was waiting to kill them if they tried to leave the cemetery. So they called nine-one-one on a cell phone."

"And where did the cloaked 'being' go?" Marissa asked sharply.

"Vanished while they clung to each other shuddering. We haven't called their parents yet—the kids say they'll be furious and we didn't need four other people out here shouting. Enough is going on."

"That's an understatement," Marissa said bitterly. Then her lower lip started to quiver.

"Did the person dig all the way down to my mother's casket?" Catherine asked in a tremulous voice. "Did they break open her casket?"

Eric answered firmly and professionally, "Catherine, your mother's casket is in a vault and whoever disturbed the grave didn't even dig down to the vault. He only went down about two feet, maybe on purpose, maybe because the ground is so cold it's hard as a rock." He looked at both women. "I know this is hard on you, but it will be harder when people begin to gather, and even at this hour they will. Four or five already have. I wanted you to see this for yourselves, not hear about it tomorrow when local citizens have created a scene even worse than it is. Let's do this, ladies, the sooner the better."

Although Eric's voice wasn't harsh, he made it clear he wanted no further delays. He stood back and motioned for them to get out of the car. Marissa led the way, trying to look strong when she felt as if everything in her was quaking. She wished she could prevent Catherine from having to endure this ordeal, but Eric had been adamant about her coming along.

Two deputies and several people who appeared as no more than blurs stepped away when Marissa and Catherine neared the grave. The icy night lay silent and deep, making Marissa feel as if she were floating through a void without atmosphere, without a hint of other human presence. One of the cemetery lights shone harshly into the desecrated grave. Marissa walked as close to the hole as possible and kneeled.

She saw objects, but at first her jumbled thoughts could make no sense of them. Catherine stooped down beside her and gripped her gloved hand. "Marissa," she said softly, "I know it's cold, but I'm here with you. Neither of us has to be here alone."

At first everything seemed blurry. As much as it hurt, though, Marissa drew knife-sharp air into her lungs, held it for a moment, and then the objects took form. With a sense of unreality, she saw a dainty, puffy-sleeved satin and organza dress spread carefully on the cold dirt and a tiny matching cap placed slightly above the dress. The dress collar bore a small, gracefully embroidered pink *M*.

On the narrow bodice, in the location of the heart, spread a pool of red liquid pierced by an ice pick driven in to the hilt.

The world spun for a moment and Marissa gratefully felt Catherine's arms close tightly around her. Marissa blinked, regained her balance, and said to Eric in a thin, high voice, "It's my christening dress."

2

Eric paused and then asked, "Are you sure it's your dress?"

"Yes. My mother embroidered the *M*. She embroidered a *C* on Catherine's."

"The two of you didn't wear the same dress?"

"No. My parents believed we should each have our own dresses."

"Did your parents give you the dresses to keep when you became adults? Did you have yours when you were in Chicago, Marissa?"

"No. I had a small apartment then—I didn't have room for keepsakes."

"And I live in a small apartment now," Catherine said. "Mom said someday we'd both have houses with room for all the things she'd saved from our childhoods, but for now she had plenty of space for them at home."

Eric frowned. "So this dress has always been in the Gray home, Marissa?"

"Yes. Packed away with Catherine's, I suppose. We don't get out our christening dresses and look at them every time we visit."

"You never loaned your christening dress to anyone else?"

"No," Marissa snapped. "That would have hurt my mother's feelings. And besides . . . I just wouldn't want anyone else—even a sweet baby—to wear it. There you have it—I'm a selfish bitch."

"Oh, you are not," Catherine soothed. "You're the most generous—"

Eric spoke quietly but firmly: "Ladies, I hate to interrupt this beautiful moment, but let's not forget someone wanted to put Marissa's christening dress on your mother's grave and stick an ice pick through it." Marissa flinched. "Have there been any signs that someone broke into your house?"

"Of course not!" Marissa flared. "Don't you think we would have noticed?"

"Have you checked every window lock? Every door lock for traces that somebody skillfully picked one? Do you know who has keys to your house?"

"No one except Marissa and me," Catherine said, for the first time sounding stern. Marissa thought her sister might have had enough of Eric's unsympathetic tone. "Do you think we go around passing out keys to our home?"

"No, but I think your parents might have given a key to a neighbor in case they locked themselves out. That would be more likely after your father died and your mother lived there alone. She wouldn't have a husband to call and let her in if her keys fell out of her purse and she didn't notice or her purse was stolen or . . ." Eric huffed. "There are a dozen ways a perfectly competent person can lose keys. Whether there are lost keys, keys given to someone else, keys simply vaporized into space, we're getting your locks changed tomorrow. I should have done it a couple of days ago so something like—" he gestured at the grave—"this couldn't have happened."

For a moment, everyone present simply stared at him, wondering what to expect next. Marissa didn't give him a chance to speak, though. "There's a photograph lying beside my dress. I can't see clearly—my eyes are watery from the cold. May I pick it up? I'm wearing gloves."

Eric nodded. Marissa leaned forward and retrieved a four-by-six-inch color close-up. "We must have been on the *Annemarie,*" she said absently. She guessed herself to be sixteen in the picture. She wore the white bikini her father had thought too daring but she loved against the fabulous tan she'd gotten that summer. Her hair had been longer than now, almost touching her waist. Her eyes had looked dazzling as Dillon Archer—tan, muscular, and handsome—wrapped his right arm tightly, possessively, around her shoulders and gazed at her with ... affection? No, Marissa thought. Love.

On the back of the photograph was written: *M.G. & D.A.— Together Forever.*

15

1

"Good lord, Marissa, we've looked at every door and window in this house and I can't see *any* sign that someone even tried to get in here, much less accomplished it." Catherine and Marissa sprawled on the comfortable furniture of the family room, each drinking strong coffee. "I guess we were stupid to conduct a search as soon as we got home. Now it's dawn, we're exhausted, and Eric is going to send experts over here to go over the whole place."

"Both of us were too horrified to get any sleep last night anyway, even with surveillance. Besides, if someone had gotten in and took the dress, I wanted to be able to say *we* found out how." Marissa paused. "I know we're getting new locks, but you don't suppose they're going to put in new windows in the middle of winter, do you?"

"God forbid," Catherine groaned, then burst out, "Why did it take us so long to remember where the hell Mom stored our christening dresses?"

"I have a feeling my christening dress *has* been in hell the last few days," Marissa said grimly.

"I don't like to think about where it's been lately. I'd rather think of it wrapped in tissue paper and lying in a labeled box in the cedar-lined storage closet with mine. Should I feel inferior because someone only wanted yours?"

"If you felt inferior because yours wasn't stolen, I'll be *very* worried about you, and I have enough on my mind," Marissa murmured dolefully.

"No reason for worry. I think I'm taking everything very well, considering my reputation as the scaredy-cat sister." Catherine stood and headed for the kitchen. "I'm going to take some fresh coffee out to Deputy Crane, who's been sitting in front of the house most of the night for nothing."

"You sound almost disappointed that he *was* here for nothing."

Catherine stopped walking and frowned. After a moment, she said, "Maybe I am. At least if someone had tried to break in, the cop would have caught him and this nightmare would be over."

Marissa smiled regretfully. "I have a weird feeling that even if the person who defiled Mom's grave is the killer, the nightmare still won't be over for a long time."

"Marissa, you didn't need to come in at the regular time this morning," Pete Hagarty said when she arrived at the *Gazette* office. "You could have called and said you'd be in at noon. I know all about what happened last night."

"Of course you do. You're a first-rate newsman," Marissa answered. "Catherine and I were awake all night, though. If I'd stayed at home even an extra couple of hours, I wouldn't have slept."

Pete leaned close to her, smelling strongly of Old Spice. "Is it true *your* christening gown lay in the grave with an ice pick stuck in it?"

"Yes. Catherine's christening gown is still at our house."

"You have no signs of a burglary?"

"No."

"How about the photograph? I heard there was a photograph with the dress."

Marissa thought of the picture. Yes, Pete, she almost said. It was a photograph of Dillon Archer holding me possessively, both of us looking radiantly happy. Eric wasn't in the picture. Why? At sixteen, I already had a mad crush on Eric. Maybe he didn't feel the same about me.

Then she caught herself. Had she forgotten she was a news-woman? She was spilling information the police probably didn't want released. "It was an old photograph of me on Dad's boat. It seemed everyone was taking pictures on those boat rides, though. There must be a hundred of them."

They just weren't enlarged, pristine, and titled "Together Forever."

All day Marissa worked on obituaries and small, unimportant stories. She even wrote a couple of fillers. She knew an article about the grave desecration would appear in the evening paper, but she didn't know who was writing it and she knew she wouldn't be reading it tonight.

At one o'clock, Eric called to let her know he'd ordered new locks for her house, which would be installed during the after-noon, and that a basement window latch showed signs of tampering. "No footprints in the dirt, though, and no fingerprints."

"We went over *everything*. I can't believe we missed it," Marissa said.

"The latch wasn't broken and you could only see the damage from outside. Also, it should make you feel better to know the red liquid on the dress wasn't blood," Eric told her. "It was red food coloring and water. We also didn't find any prints on the ice pick. We might find something just under the hilt edge, but I doubt it." He sounded tired and disappointed. "I heard you and Catherine stayed up all night."

"Randall Crane told you, didn't he? Aside from looking for a way a burglar could have gotten in, we were also looking for our baby things—Catherine's christening dress, special little Easter and Christmas dresses, our baby books. We found Catherine's dress in the big cedar closet. Mom had wrapped it in tissue paper. I suppose she'd done the same with mine."

Eric frowned. "The dress doesn't smell of cedar."

"Then it's been out of the cabinet for quite a while or some-one took it to the dry cleaner's before putting it in the grave."

"I don't understand why our guy would do that, but we'll check local dry cleaners and see if they remember a christening gown." Eric sighed. "What about that photograph, Marissa? Was it yours?"

"No," she said definitely. "I mean, it might have been in the house, but I don't remember even seeing it before last night."

"How old were you in that picture?"

"Sixteen."

"I thought you didn't know anything about the photograph?"

"I remember my bikini. I loved it. Dad thought it was too revealing and didn't want me to wear it. He gave in rather than get in an argument with me. At the end of the summer, I spilled chocolate sauce from a sundae on it and the stains wouldn't come out. I thought losing that bikini was a tragedy."

"I'm sure Dillon did, too. In the picture he was looking at you like he loved you *and* your bikini."

"I don't know what that look was about, Eric," Marissa said honestly. "Maybe he *was* just attracted by the bikini, because he never touched me inappropriately, kissed me, or even asked me on a date. He was always nice to me. Very nice but nothing else."

"Nice." Eric sounded unconvinced. "Well, we have to keep the photo as evidence."

"Fine. I don't care if I ever see it again."

"Don't sound so put out. At least you found Catherine's dress. You don't have to spend this evening searching."

"I have to search for an answer about why *my* dress was taken but not Catherine's. I have to spend this *afternoon* searching for answers about Gretchen. I'm going to your parents' house at two, remember? If I make it to Gretchen's room, I'll be looking for anything that might tell me what was bothering her that summer, and it's not going to be as easy as looking for my baby clothes."

2

Susan Montgomery was a stickler about punctuality, so Marissa made certain she pulled her car into Susan's double driveway at one fifty-nine. Susan opened the front door almost immediately, hesitated for a moment, then gave Marissa a cool smile. "Hello, Marissa. It's been a long time. Please come in."

Marissa stepped into the foyer with its shining hardwood floor, curving stairs, beige brocade settee sitting beneath a large oil painting of an autumn landscape, and a bronze ten-light chandelier. Sun shone brightly through the sidelights and Marissa saw that half of Susan's curly blonde hair, so much like Eric's, had turned silver. Horizontal lines creased her forehead and she'd developed nasal-labial folds. Even her brown eyes seemed to have lightened a couple of shades. Her short hair had been perfectly styled, though, and she wore a touch of tan eye shadow, mascara, blush, and a muted pink lipstick.

Susan said with her cool smile, "You look nice on this cold day."

"Thanks." Marissa used to call the woman Susan. After all that had happened, though, she feared Eric's mother would take offense at informality. "And thank you for agreeing to the interview, Mrs. Montgomery."

"My pleasure. I'm devoted to this project and appreciate the publicity."

Susan Montgomery's remarkable composure rattled an already-jittery Marissa. The woman had rarely shown Annemarie's joie de vivre, but she'd never seemed carved from ice.

"We haven't seen each other for a while . . ." Marissa stepped into the foyer, dropped her tote bag, which she'd forgotten to fasten, and sent items skittering all over the gleaming wood floor. "Oh . . . dear. I'm sorry," she muttered as she began chasing pens, a steno pad, tubes of lip gloss, car keys, a portable tape recorder, a cell phone, and her wallet.

"It's all right." Susan picked up a large Snickers candy bar. "Still an addiction?"

Marissa blushed. Her love of Snickers bars used to be a joke with the family. "Yes. I wish they had support groups for Snickers addicts, but I've never found one." Marissa grabbed a wide-toothed comb lying by a wall. "I'm hopeless anyway."

"I believe there are worse addictions. I doubt if they're doing your health any harm, and from what I can see under that gorgeous faux fur coat they aren't hurting your figure, either."

Marissa realized her laugh sounded stiff. "I'm glad you like the coat. I'm also addicted to faux fur." Certain she'd gathered everything she'd spilled, Marissa stood up and swept back her hair from her face. "Coats, vests. Faux fur, I mean."

"I knew what you meant. I'll hang up your coat and we'll sit in the living room. Would you like something to drink?"

Yes, a boilermaker, Marissa thought. Maybe two. She'd seen Eric's parents at Gretchen's funeral and not again until her parents' funerals, where they'd each murmured, "Sorry for your loss," but they hadn't come to the house afterward. Marissa had known she would be nervous actually talking to Susan for the first time in over four years, but she hadn't guessed exactly *how* nervous she would be. The woman—dressed in beige slacks and a powder blue sweater set—seemed like an eerily composed, washed-out version of the slightly shy but warm Susan Montgomery Marissa had once known. She wanted to turn and run out the door. "No thank you. I'm not thirsty now, but I might be later," Marissa finally managed. "Or you might be. You'll be the one doing most of the talking."

"Well, I can't guarantee I'll do much talking." Susan hung up the coat. "I've never been interviewed before today. I hope I don't let down the other members of the auction committee."

"I'm sure you'll do just fine," Marissa said as they walked into a living room filled with winter light shining through sheer draperies. A beautiful subdued blue and gold patterned rug dominated the center of the room, and Marissa guessed that an interior designer had strategically placed new burnished gold and rose-colored furniture. Marissa retrieved her notebook and pen and set her tape recorder on the coffee table. "First I should get the names of the other people on the committee," Marissa said.

Susan rattled off eight names, only that of Irene Hagarty, Pete's wife, familiar to Marissa. "They made me president of the committee," Susan said. "I think that's because no one else would do it."

Marissa smiled. "I understand the auction is to help get funds for a new library."

For the first time, Susan laughed. "Heavens, no! We'd never get a new library if we depended on little events like this. We'd like to build an additional room to the library, one devoted to children. The shelves would all be low; we'd have colorful tables and chairs; every Saturday we'd invite a guest reader; later we might even hold a creative-writing class for the second-through-sixth-graders, although we'd be careful not to call it a *class*. That would sound like work. For now, we've been fortunate enough to have many authors donate their signed, first-edition books to be auctioned . . ."

Marissa devoted full attention to every word Susan said. Although shorthand was out of style, Marissa had learned it as a teenager, and what she missed she knew the tape recorder would catch. She conscientiously made eye contact with Eric's mother, but all Marissa could think about was Gretchen. Marissa knew across the hall from them a grand piano sat in a special music room—a space always called "Gretchen's Room." She remembered sprawling on the couch in the room, listening to Gretchen practice intricate and what had seemed to Marissa at the time endless classical pieces. Then Gretchen would burst into something by Jerry Lee Lewis and from somewhere in the house Susan would call out a reprimand edged with laughter. What good times those had been, Marissa thought.

"Do you have another question?" Susan asked, and Marissa came back to the present with a jolt.

"I'm so sorry. My mind wandered." Marissa flushed. "That is just inexcusable—"

"No, it isn't," Susan said gently. "You look exhausted, and well . . . Eric told me what happened at the cemetery last night.

I know he's not supposed to discuss those things and he's strict about maintaining rules, but he knew you had an interview with me today and he wanted me to understand if you seemed tired or distracted."

"Oh! Well, that was thoughtful of him. Actually, this has been quite a week for me. Probably the worst I've ever had except for when—"

Dillon Archer murdered Gretchen. Horrified, Marissa realized she'd almost said the worst thing possible. Susan, however, looked at her knowingly and, to Marissa's surprise, reached over and patted her arm.

"I understand, Marissa. I know how it is to feel shocked and literally beaten by the world." Susan paused. "I believe you felt that way before, when Gretchen died. You thought we all blamed you, and to be honest, we did. Partly. Eric, of course, was crushed. Looking back, I'm appalled at how my husband and I treated both of you. I think we drove him into breaking off your engagement."

"It was probably for the best," Marissa said, her voice shaky.

Susan closed her eyes and shook her head. "He doesn't blame himself so much anymore, thank God. He's probably told you so, but in case he hasn't, I will interfere and say it for him. As for his father and me—well, you have no reason to feel guilty or uncomfortable with us. We know Gretchen's . . . death wasn't your fault. You loved Gretchen like a sister and we thought of you as a daughter. We've missed you terribly, Marissa."

Marissa looked at Susan, astounded, and burst into heaving sobs. Her own parents were gone and she hadn't realized how much she'd missed the Montgomerys. She grabbed for her tote bag, fished through it wildly, and discovered the only thing it *didn't* contain was a tissue.

Marissa knew her supposedly waterproof eye shadow and mascara were running down her face. Susan leaned back and from an end table lifted a small box of soft tissues, which she handed to Marissa. "Good heavens, dear, I'm so sorry. I didn't mean to throw you into such a fit!"

Susan sounded so sweetly concerned and old-fashioned that Marissa began to laugh through her tears. Susan's brown eyes widened as she no doubt wondered what Marissa proposed to do next. Marissa buried her face in a tissue. "I'm sorry. Mom dying just a few months ago, seeing Eric and you, talking about Gretchen, enduring all the things that have happened to *me* this week—well, I guess it's just been too much," she cried before emitting a resounding hiccup.

"Goodness gracious, you aren't in good shape, Marissa. I knew it as soon as you walked in the door. You looked almost afraid of me. You're alarmingly pale. You shouldn't have worked this week."

"Appearances to the contrary, I'm okay," Marissa blubbered.

"No, you aren't. You need food—you are *so* slim—and you need something hot to drink." She drew a deep breath as if shoring up for duty. "I baked gingerbread this morning with that sweet sauce you and Gretchen used to like. Why don't I warm the sauce, pour it over a big piece of gingerbread, and fix a cup of coffee for you? Do you think that might make you feel better?"

"I think it would make me feel wonderful."

Susan beamed. "Then you pull yourself together and we'll eat and drink and have girl talk before we go back to my scintillating interview. I'm certain you remember where the downstairs bathroom is. You'll probably want to touch up your face."

" 'Touch up' might be putting it mildly." Although Marissa was terribly upset, she reminded herself she was here partly on a mission. She girded herself for a question: "Susan, would you mind terribly if I used the upstairs bathroom and looked at Gretchen's room? Eric said you haven't changed her bedroom and we spent so many happy hours there—I'd love to see it again."

Susan looked down. Here it comes, Marissa thought. The refusal. She might have forgiven me, but letting me go into Gretchen's room is just too much.

Susan raised her gaze. "I think Gretchen would like the idea of you being in her room again. I used to sit down here and listen to the two of you laugh and occasionally squeal the way adolescent girls do. She loved you, Marissa. You and Eric were the lights of her life. Go right on up and take your time."

Susan rose from the couch and disappeared into the dining room leading to the kitchen. Meanwhile, Marissa sat for a moment, trying to decide if she should actually search Gretchen's room. Susan had seemed so trusting, so certain that Marissa wanted to see the room only for sentimental reasons. What if she knew Marissa actually had another agenda?

Susan wouldn't understand, but Gretchen would, Marissa thought. Besides, Eric knew the plan and approved of it. They only wanted to discover what had been bothering Gretchen that summer, what had gone wrong in her world. Gretchen hadn't wanted them to know then or she would have told them. What about now, though? Marissa was absolutely certain Gretchen did not want to die when she did. No matter what was wrong back then, Gretchen would have wanted to live, to find love, to have a child, but she hadn't gotten the chance. Yes, Marissa thought, Gretchen would want those people closest to her to know what unhappiness had driven her to take the course leading to her death.

Marissa clutched her tote bag and ran lightly up the stairs to the second floor. Gretchen's room had been the third on the right overlooking a beautiful summer backyard. As soon as she stepped in, Marissa smiled. Gretchen had always called this the Pepto-Bismol room, and with good reason—almost everything was pink. White furniture sat on pink carpet leading up to pale pink walls. A deep pink coverlet decorated with white and pink stuffed animals lay on the double bed. It's good Lindsay isn't with me now, Marissa thought, or none of the stuffed animals would be safe. A picture of white, pale pink, and cerise flowers hung above the bed. The room would have been a little girl's dream. Gretchen had still been sleeping in it when she was twenty-one.

Last night having sharpened her searching skills, Marissa quickly laid down her tote bag and began opening dresser drawers. Underwear, nightwear, and scarves lay neatly folded and still smelling faintly of the vanilla sachet Gretchen always used. She'd even put each pair of panty hose into a ziplock plastic bag and lined up the bags according to color. Marissa noticed Gretchen had owned no fanciful patterned hose like Marissa wore right now—everything was either "buff" or "beige" or "suntan."

Marissa glanced at her watch and saw that six minutes had passed. She'd set ten as her limit. She rushed to the walk-in closet and opened the door. Once again, clothes had been organized—plastic-covered gowns Gretchen wore when she gave concerts, dresses, blouses, slacks, shorts, and T-shirts. Marissa shook her head when she saw two pairs of jeans bearing dry-cleaning tags. The insistence on dry cleaning must have been Susan's, Marissa mused.

One end of the closet bore shelves for shoes and a few drawers. Vaguely Marissa remembered a ten-year-old Gretchen telling her mother she wanted a cabinet at the back of the closet where she could store her shoes and jewelry. She'd seen such a unit on television when someone was making a tour of a movie star's home.

Susan had wavered, and Gretchen's father had almost refused because of the expense. Marissa had instructed Gretchen to make the request when Mitch and Jean Farrell had come to dinner at the Montgomery home. Gretchen followed Marissa's instructions, and as Marissa expected, Mitch had quickly volunteered for the job, saying it would be fun to make something like a movie star had in her closet and he could broaden his woodworking skills and lower the cost at the same time. The Montgomerys could hardly say no to such a generous offer.

What they hadn't known was that Mitch had installed a "secret cabinet" in the unit. Gretchen had told Marissa that Mitch said every girl needed a place to keep absolutely private items from parents, a statement Marissa later knew Mitch would not have made to anyone except a sweet, gentle girl like Gretchen who would never hide anything dangerous in the cabinet.

Marissa recalled that several weeks after Mitch had completed the unit she and Gretchen had been "hanging out" in Gretchen's bedroom, listening to music, talking about hair-styles and when they would *ever* be old enough for their mothers to let them wear makeup. Suddenly, after Gretchen had made certain her mother was out of the house, she'd pulled Marissa to the back of the closet and kneeled down in front of the storage unit. She'd hit a spot of what looked like solid wood and a door popped open. "Isn't it neat?" She'd beamed at Marissa. "It feels so Nancy Drew." Gretchen had withdrawn a few magazines like *Tiger Beat,* a much-treasured copy of Eric's *Rolling Stone,* a cigarette she planned to try someday, a few notebooks in which she'd written poetry and songs, ballads accompanied by lyrics, and an eight-by-ten picture of Leonardo DiCaprio. In later years, she'd added a metal storage box complete with padlock to her hoard. "You know how Mom snoops," she'd said darkly.

Drained of ideas of where to search for she-didn't-know-what in Gretchen's room, Marissa hit the corner of the secret wooden door with the heel of her hand. Nothing. Again slightly to the right. Nothing. Susan is going to hear me, she thought almost frantically. One more time she hit a spot on the left, and the door popped open.

Marissa gasped in relief, especially when she saw the metal storage box. She pulled it out and felt as if someone had stuck a pin in her balloon of joy. The thing still bore the padlock.

Gretchen had told her the combination to the padlock. She'd told her, made her repeat it three times, and tested her every couple of months until they were about fifteen. Marissa sighed in exasperation. She tried Gretchen's birth date, although she knew that was too simple. She tried her own birth date. Nothing. Eric's birth date. The lock held firm. Marissa closed her eyes, feeling as if she was going to cry again. Then she mistily recalled Gretchen announcing, "Nobody will ever think of this number! You know how Mom hates . . ." Hates what? What did Susan

Montgomery hate that her daughter had loved?

Horror movies! The answer popped into Marissa's mind so quickly she almost shouted it. Susan hated horror movies. She wouldn't allow Gretchen to see horror movies at the theater or on television, certain they'd give her nightmares. Gretchen had pretended to obey her mother's ban on horror movies and watched the movies on videos at Marissa's house. But what horror movie with *numbers* had Gretchen particularly liked? What had they watched over and over . . .

The Omen. 666.

Marissa's hands trembled as she turned the padlock, going to 6 one time, two times, three times until the padlock popped open. Marissa lifted the lid and looked at the single sealed manila envelope inside labeled in Gretchen's hand: *Gretchen Alice Montgomery—The End.*

16

1

Marissa stuffed the envelope into her tote bag, shut the padlock on the metal storage box and shoved it back in the cabinet, and then dashed into the upstairs bathroom. When she glanced in the mirror, a combination of tears, nerves, and triumph almost made her laugh. Black mascara streaks ran down her face, her bright lip gloss had smeared around her mouth, and her nose was pink. *Now it matches Gretchen's room*, she thought, and almost burst into flustered giggles.

She splashed her face with warm water, guiltily wiped away the remains of mascara with one of Susan's snowy white washcloths, brightened her face with lip gloss she applied with jerky fingers, and combed her hair back from her face. She decided the result was rather pathetic, but Susan Montgomery wasn't expecting a beauty queen. Just as Marissa dropped her comb back in her tote bag and zipped it so Susan would be certain not to see the manila envelope, the woman called from downstairs.

"Are you all right, Marissa?"

Marissa jerked open the bathroom door and nearly ran down the stairs. "I'm sorry I took so long. I just got lost in my memories."

Susan smiled. "Sometimes I sit in her bedroom and I do the same thing. My husband wants to remodel the room, but I won't allow it." She paused. "I hope your gingerbread and coffee haven't gotten cold, but if they have, we'll stick them in the microwave."

Ten minutes later Marissa and Susan sat at the kitchen table, eating gingerbread and talking comfortably as if the last four and a half years hadn't existed. As Marissa picked up the last bite of her second piece of gingerbread and sauce, Susan reached out and took her hand. She looked intensely at the moonstone ring.

"You still have it!" she exclaimed.

"I wear it every day," Marissa said, recalling that part of her mission at the Montgomery home was to look at photographs taken shortly before Gretchen died. In spite of her newfound ease with Susan, though, Marissa couldn't think of a graceful way of asking to see pictures of that time. Her link with Susan was too new, too tenuous.

"I had two made in Mexico and gave one to Gretchen when she finally passed her driver's test," Marissa said quickly. Susan nodded, indicating she clearly remembered, but Marissa needed more information. She smiled and tried to sound light, offhand. "I know she wore hers for years. I can't remember if she still wore it after her concert years started."

Susan looked at her in surprise. "You can't? Why, Marissa, I saw her cleaning it just a couple of days before . . . she died. It meant so much to her, she wore it even when she was performing. She told me she'd wear it all of her life."

2

After Marissa finished her interview with Susan, she went home instead of back to the *Gazette*. She would write the story the next day and Pete planned to run it in the Sunday edition. Glancing at her watch, she saw that it was five thirty. Jean had asked them to visit Mitch at six thirty, which meant Eric would be picking up Catherine and her around six ten. Just like his mother, Eric was a stickler for punctuality.

Marissa had no time to change clothes, but she ran upstairs to the bathroom to fix her face, Catherine and Lindsay pounding right behind her. "How did things go?" Catherine asked. "Was she mean? You've been crying."

"Yes," Marissa answered to the last question. "I went on a real bender with the tears. I'm probably dehydrated."

"Are you joking?"

"No. It wasn't because she was cold to me, though. She really couldn't have been nicer after the first few awkward minutes." Marissa looked at Catherine in her forest green wool slacks, matching sweater, and a beautiful cameo hanging from a single gold chain. "I see you're ready to visit Mitch and Jean."

"Yes. Looking forward to it and dreading it at the same time. Eric should be here soon."

"Which is why I'm trying to repair the ravages of my visit to Susan's. Will you hand me my eye shadow?"

"Which one? You must have twenty shades in this makeup box."

"Not *twenty*. I want 'Vanilla Shake.' I don't want to look like I'm going to a party."

Catherine began diligently looking at every eye shadow container and Marissa had an overwhelming urge to tell Catherine about her search of Gretchen's room. She knew Catherine wouldn't approve, though. Marissa immediately grabbed the right container. "I don't know how you find *anything* in this mess . . ." Catherine began organizing the eye shadows.

Marissa swallowed her irritation. "I can do this faster with a little privacy. Do you mind?"

"Oh, sure. I'm sorry. I was just worried. You don't have time to take a shower, though," Catherine called, stepping out of the bathroom just as Lindsay slipped in holding a stuffed lion. Lindsay always oversaw Marissa's makeup and hair sessions, as if she didn't trust Marissa to do things right.

The doorbell rang just as Marissa emerged from the bathroom, makeup replaced, waves added to the hair around her face, and Lindsay racing along behind, stuffed lion still firmly clenched in her teeth. Catherine had already opened the door and Eric stood in the family room, his expression a bit uncertain.

"Hi. Catherine says your visit with Mom went okay, but when you got home you looked like you'd been crying—sobbing, actually—and you had to run upstairs for repair work. Did Mom hurt your feelings or wasn't she nice to you or . . ."

Or didn't you find anything to help us find out what was going on with Gretchen the summer she died? Marissa could read the question in his eyes.

"Everything went fine, Eric. Your mother couldn't have been nicer. I just cried because I hadn't seen her for so long. I've missed her." She paused and looked meaningfully at Eric. "I think the visit may have been successful."

"May have?" Catherine looked confused. "What does that mean? You didn't get your interview?"

"I did. A very nice interview." Marissa smiled brightly at her sister. "I think we'd better be on our way, though. Jean is holding off Mitch's morphine injection until we get there and have a chance to talk with him a little. We don't want him to be in pain because we're dawdling."

3

To Marissa's relief, they were able to leave the surveillance deputy behind because Eric was the escort. Marissa hadn't realized how much safer she'd felt today knowing her every move had been watched, especially after the spectacle someone had made of her mother's grave. She had thought the surveillance would be annoying; instead, it had been just the opposite.

"I took Lindsay for a walk today," Catherine suddenly announced from the backseat.

Marissa craned her neck to look at her sister. "I thought you didn't like her."

"What made you think that?"

"You never play with her—"

Catherine drew herself up. "I would like to defend myself on the grounds that you've never seen Lindsay and me alone. We get along marvelously and today we had a wonderful time. When you're home, you expect all of her attention and she's very obliging."

The day had been a strain on an already-exhausted Marissa and a lightning bolt of irritation shot through her. "I do not expect all of Lindsay's attention! And you're starting to talk like James."

"Who called today to see how we're doing after last night and to explain his behavior the other day when he saw me having lunch with Will Addison."

"What behavior?" Marissa burst out. "What did James do?"

"Nothing. That was the problem. He wasn't friendly. At all. Today he told me he was just tired when he saw us, but I think he was a little jealous," Catherine finished with a small, satisfied smile. "We're going to a movie at an actual theater on Saturday evening. I think it's much more fun to watch a movie at a theater than a DVD on television."

"So does Lindsay. You two have become such friends, you can take her on your date," Marissa sniped.

"I don't think James is the only one suffering from jealousy," Catherine muttered, just loud enough to make sure Marissa heard her.

"Girls, would you please try to behave yourselves," Eric said in a harassed voice but obviously trying not to grin. "I can't separate you any farther unless I stick one of you in the trunk."

Mitch and Jean Farrell lived near the edge of the city limits in a small green house on a knoll overlooking Falls Way and the Orenda River. As they neared the house, Marissa looked at the bank leading down from the highway to the river. She knew the state road crew could not fix the guardrail so soon in the bad weather they'd suffered. For now, two reflective barrels blocked the hole left in the rail along with a tall slow sign.

"Do you think my car is still down there or has it moved with the current?" Marissa asked.

"It's probably on its way to Florida. Much better climate." Eric smiled at her. "Are you thinking of saving it?"

"No. Too much water damage by now. I've decided to let the insurance company buy me a new one."

"*Not* a convertible!" Catherine ordered firmly.

"The car being a convertible had nothing to do with the wreck," Marissa said. "You simply never know when a *monster* is going to wander out in front of you, whether you're driving a convertible or a hardtop."

Marissa thought many people would believe their sporadic joking and jibes during the drive was unfitting, but she knew they were all trying to brace themselves before they faced the morbid sight of Mitch Farrell dying. A minute later, they turned into the Farrell driveway leading to the house. In the summer, Jean's beautiful flower beds nearly buried it in a plethora of rich color. In the winter, the house looked small and lonely and bleak. Jean stood on the porch, wrapped in her large, flapping coat, waving to them. When they emerged from the car and reached her, she hugged each of them, tears in her eyes.

"I'm so glad you're a little early. Mitch will try to put on a good show, but he's not at all well today. I hate to be rude, but could we make the visit short?"

"Of course, Jean," Eric said. "We didn't intend to stay more than fifteen or twenty minutes anyway. Is that all right?"

"Yes. I think that will be fine. If not, I'll give you a signal." A tear ran down her cheek. "Or you'll see for yourself."

Jean's father had owned a hundred acres of prime land at the other end of the city. Many people said handsome Mitch Farrell married plain, shy Jean Curtis because Jean was an only child and Mitch knew someday she would inherit the land. After six years of marriage she did inherit the land, but she didn't sell a bit of it, saying she had a special plan for all hundred acres.

If Mitch had a problem with her refusing to sell the land, no one knew of it. He seemed content in his marriage and happy with Jean, if not madly in love with her. She, on the other hand, adored her husband, and everyone knew she wanted desperately to give him a child. After eight years of marriage she finally conceived, and no one doubted Mitch was delighted. At age thirty, Jean gave birth to Elizabeth Amanda Farrell—Betsy— who people said was just about the most beautiful, sweet-tempered toddler they'd ever known. Betsy died five days after her third birthday.

They still lived in the house Mitch's parents had left to him after they were killed in a car wreck, the house where he'd lived when he and Jean married. She still owned the hundred acres of land and everyone knew she regularly got offers for part or all of it, but she wouldn't sell.

As Marissa stepped into the small, claustrophobic two-story house, she saw that it looked as it had the first time she'd seen it, years ago. The old-fashioned furniture remained in exactly the same spots, the same faded rug covered most of the hardwood floor, and the walls were painted bisque that had begun to turn slightly yellow with age. Only two nondescript pictures hung on the walls, both looking as if they'd been bought at a discount store. The only difference Marissa noticed was the absence of a twenty-eight-inch-screen portable television that used to sit on a small rolling cart across the room from Mitch's lumpy beige recliner. As always, not a mote of dust dared show itself and Marissa smelled a medley of cleaning agents.

"We turned the dining room into Mitch's room," Jean said softly, as if preparing them for what they were going to see. "He has a hospital bed, and the IV hook, and a window right across from his bed. He wanted the television in there, too. He likes to keep it on all day and half the night. It drives me crazy, especially because I know Mitch can't really concentrate on it, but he wants it. He's allowed me to turn it off for your visit. I keep a baby monitor beside his bed when I try to sleep upstairs in our old bedroom, but lately he's not having good nights, so I sleep on the couch."

Jean lowered her voice even more and they all leaned toward her, trying to hear. "Now I want to prepare you for how he looks. Mitchell Farrell was the most handsome man I ever saw— even more handsome than a movie star—but he's lost a lot of weight. I think he's lost five or six pounds just in the last week. His cheeks have sunken and he's lost all of that beautiful black hair—well, it was turning gray, but it's gone. He's very pale.

Sometimes he talks straight and other times he mumbles and doesn't make much sense. You'll have to tell him who you are. He doesn't always recognize people right away."

"We won't look or act surprised when we see him, Jean," Eric said. "Marissa has had recent experience with this kind of thing."

Although my mother's appearance didn't change much until the last few weeks and she never had trouble recognizing people, Marissa thought. Mom went to the hospital seven days before she died, which is where Mitch should be. Jean says he wants to die at home, though. She's putting herself through hell to satisfy him, which doesn't surprise me at all.

Mitch moaned in a ragged, muted voice from the other room. Jean managed a pained smile. "His voice is especially rough tonight." She took a deep breath. "Well, he knows you're here. We'd better go in."

Marissa had felt anxiety earlier in the day when she went into Gretchen's room, but the dread had mingled with the sense of a mission. Going into Mitch's room filled her only with pure dread. She had not seen him for almost six weeks, not for lack of trying but because Jean had discouraged her, saying she thought seeing Mitch would disturb Marissa and Mitch. Eric told Marissa he hadn't seen Mitch for a month. They'd both wanted to visit, but now that the time had come, their steps lagged and the skin of their faces tightened with tension. Catherine took Marissa's hand in a firm hold.

Darkness already closed around the small house and two lamps emitted soft light in Mitch's room. He was propped on three bed pillows, and he wore a burgundy and blue pajama top buttoned as high as it would go. Jean hadn't wanted them to see his reed-like neck, Marissa thought. His hands—always large, strong, and rough from all the woodworking he did—now lay pale and quivering atop a patchwork quilt. He wore his wedding ring on the index finger of his left hand. Clearly, his ring finger had shrunk too much for it.

"Come in, come in." He motioned to them with a shaky arm. "So glad to see you."

"It's great to see you, too," Marissa said, vaguely wondering if he knew she was lying. The man looked like the cartoons of a caped, stalking Death.

Eric reached Mitch first, bent down, and hugged the man whose pale hands trembled above Eric's back. "You're a fine, strong man. Good-looking, too, Bernie. You still a doctor?"

"Mitch, this isn't Bernard Gray," Jean said quickly, clearly seeing that Eric was flustered by Mitch's first words. "This is Eric Montgomery."

Mitch squinted. "Well, I must need new glasses. Bernie doesn't have blond hair! Keepin' yourself busy these days?"

"Yes, sir, I am. I'm a lawman, like you."

Mitch frowned and looked at him even more closely. "Well, I'll be damned. I think I'm getting senile. You *worked* for me!"

"I sure did. Still do, really. You're still the sheriff, Mitch." Eric laughed. Marissa wondered if Mitch heard the strained, false edge of the laughter.

"I *am*." Mitch looked as if he'd just remembered something. "Oh lord, I've been forgetting to go to work! Jean, why didn't you remind me?"

Jean hovered at the foot of the hospital bed looking agitated and limp at the same time.

"I won't tell," Eric said quickly, and stepped aside. "Here's Catherine."

Mitch narrowed his eyes and Marissa knew he didn't remember Catherine. "My goodness, you've gotten as tall as Jean." He sounded as if Catherine were still a growing girl, not a twenty-eight-year-old woman. Then knowledge seemed to creep into his eyes. "Catherine. So pretty. You look like your mother, Annemarie."

"Thank you, Mitch, but I'll never be the beauty Mom was." Catherine bent and hugged him, holding on to the man for a few extra seconds, and Marissa saw a tear drip down his face onto his pajama collar.

When Catherine pulled back, Mitch tried to cock an eyebrow at her. The effect was pitiful. "Still get seasick, honey?"

"Oh, I never got seasick. That was my mother. Poor Mom—she would have loved to go out on the boat with us."

"Yes, we had ourselves some fun, didn't we? Both families *all* together and there was some other boy that came. I remember the time . . ."

Mitch launched into an imaginary tale that sounded as if it had come from *The Pirates of the Caribbean*. Mitch and Jean had always eaten Christmas dinner with the Grays and Marissa recalled the year before last Mitch telling them how he'd loved the movie and announcing with gusto he could have played the Johnny Depp role of Captain Jack Sparrow.

The memory was so painful to Marissa, she shifted her gaze from Mitch to a desk in the corner. In the muted light, she still managed to see small, framed photographs. Jean and Mitch on their wedding day; two pictures of their beloved Betsy, one as a baby in arms, one that must have been taken shortly before her death; a picture of Annemarie and Bernard; another of Catherine and Marissa as teenagers; one of the *Annemarie*; and one of Aurora Falls. Then Marissa focused on a particularly nice shot of the church on Gray's Island with the sun bouncing off the stained-glass windows and the white steeple soaring against an azure blue sky.

Marissa realized Jean was looking at her intently and her attention snapped back to Mitch. Apparently, he'd finally remembered Catherine.

"I'll be graduating from Berkeley this spring," Catherine was saying. "Nobody thinks I'll ever finish school, but at last I will!"

"You always were smart as they come. We're all proud you're gonna be a surgeon like your daddy."

No one corrected Mitch. Marissa could tell he was trying to show how sharp his memory had remained.

His gaze turned to Marissa. "And my beautiful Betsy with the sapphire eyes. Give Daddy a kiss, sweetheart."

Marissa felt as if something had sucked the air from the room. Everyone seemed turned to stone, while Jean gasped and Mitch's eyes rested fondly on Marissa. He held out both shaky hands, and without thinking Marissa stepped forward and grasped them in both of hers. "Hi," she whispered.

"Where've you been, baby? Playing outside? It's mighty cold now, but when summer comes, Mama and Daddy will get you a puppy. You love puppies, don't you, darlin'?"

Marissa swallowed hard, not knowing what to say or do. She smiled faintly and Jean said loudly but lovingly, "Mitch, dear, this isn't our Betsy. This is Marissa. She's Annemarie and Bernard Gray's daughter. You remember Bernard—you two had the same grandmother. Different grandfathers. You were cousins. Would that be first half cousins or half first cousins? I always get mixed up."

Marissa didn't know if Jean had simply boggled Mitch's thoughts with tangled family connections or if he was getting tired of her interruptions. "Don't try to fool me, Jean!" he said sharply. "I know my own little girl when I see her!" He pulled Marissa closer to his face. "Mama's trying to fool us, but she can't." He looked at Jean. "Did you already hide the Easter eggs? Betsy and I want to find them."

What little color Jean had left drained away and Marissa thought the woman might drop on the floor. Marissa said, "I love to hunt Easter eggs. I'll see if Mama has them hidden yet."

He gave her a weak smile and then fell into a violent coughing attack. Jean rushed to him, slipped her arm under his shoulders, raised him higher, and grabbed a few tissues from the box on the bedside table. Mitch coughed wretchedly for another couple of minutes, then took a sip of water from a glass Jean held out to him. He gasped for breath and Marissa thought they should be calling 911 when Mitch finally began to settle down.

Marissa and Eric glanced at each other while Catherine watched Mitch. After a minute, Catherine said, "Jean, I'll take over now. You look like you could use some water and Mitch will need some more water when he stops coughing."

Mitch looked at Catherine and nodded vigorously, a slight tinge of pink appearing in his cheeks. Marissa didn't know if it was from embarrassment or the exertion of the coughing fit.

Jean hesitated and then allowed Catherine to step in for her, handing her a fresh bunch of tissues. "I'll get the water," Jean murmured. She looked at Marissa. "Would you like a glass of water?"

My God, yes! Marissa thought. She started to walk around Mitch's bed toward the kitchen where Jean had disappeared. Mitch pulled away from the tissues, looked Marissa in the eyes, and tapped the small table sitting beside his bed. "What is it?" she asked.

"This is yours, Betsy. I made it for you."

"It's beautiful. Thank you." Marissa smiled and nodded. He'd begun to cough again as she walked into the kitchen. Jean stood over the sink in the kitchen looking out at the starless night. Her expression revealed calm defeat and Marissa couldn't stop herself from going to the woman, closing her arms around Jean's waist, and laying her head on her shoulder. "Jean, I'm so sorry. I don't know how you bear it."

"I'm not the one bearing it, honey. Mitch is."

"He's bearing the physical pain. You're the one whose emotions must be in tatters."

"He thought you were Betsy. All of these years I've known he thought of her all the time, although he rarely mentioned her. She probably would have looked like you if she'd gotten a chance to grow up. Instead I—"

"Shhh. Don't talk about Betsy now, Jean."

"It was just her and me in the house on a cold December night with snow falling so heavy." Jean's voice sounded distant, almost singsong. Marissa had a feeling Jean wasn't even aware of her presence. "Betsy loved the snow and I'd put her in her snowsuit and taken her out about five o'clock, before we lost the light. That didn't satisfy her, though. She kept talking about the snow. I got busy . . . the search went on all night. People kept telling me to go inside—my lips were blue. But I didn't even feel the cold . . ."

Annemarie had told Catherine and Marissa the story of Betsy Farrell's death. She'd shuddered and said she didn't know how she could bear such a loss, and Jean almost hadn't borne it, either. She'd had a complete nervous breakdown and become a recluse for over a year. Mitch had always stood by her, though, and never said a word against her. If he'd blamed her for Betsy's death, no one knew it.

Marissa gave Jean a squeeze. "Mitch is really going to need water. I'd like a glass, too. Shall I ask Catherine and Eric?"

"What?" Jean looked as if she were coming out of a dream. "Water? Oh yes. I made coffee and I have some milk. I should have shopped . . ."

"No you shouldn't have. We won't be staying long. You get some water for Mitch, and I'll fix glasses for the rest of us."

Five minutes later, as she returned to the bedroom, Marissa announced gaily, "Water!" She carried a tray of glasses full of lukewarm water and no ice. Eric and Catherine each gave her a quick look, then took their glasses and gulped as if they'd been dying for water all evening. Mitch's coughing fit seemed to have stopped, and Jean gently held a glass of water to his lips so he could drink.

"Wish I could remember what bourbon tastes like," he said in a growly voice, and even Jean laughed, although everyone knew she disapproved of drinking alcohol unless it was for medicinal reasons. Mitch had once joked to the Grays he'd nearly exhausted his imagination thinking up so many maladies that called for alcohol.

Mitch looked at Eric. "So you're going to be a lawman. I was, too. I used to be sheriff of a place called Aurora Falls. I don't recall if I retired or got fired."

Jean closed her eyes, but Eric played along: "You retired, sir. They'd never fire a sheriff like Mitch Farrell."

"Was I as good as him?"

"You *are* Mitch Farrell," Eric said, not so heartily.

Mitch shook his head. "I think it's time to move on to the next world when you can't remember your own name." He winced slightly. "I've got a pain . . . oh, to hell with my pains. Got 'em all over the place. They make me mad."

"Maybe you're getting tired," Jean said gently.

"I'm not tired!" Mitch's voice rasped and cracked. His pale eyes roamed the room and then fastened on Catherine. "How's Bernie?"

"Bernie? Bernard? Dad?" Catherine looked startled. Marissa could tell her sister was battling with lying to Mitch or telling him the truth—that Bernard was dead.

Mitch saved her: "Bernard. Hah! He hated that name. We all called him Bernie. We went fishing last weekend. I caught a . . . a . . . something."

"Fish?" Jean asked helpfully.

"Well, of course!" Mitch returned in loud irritability. "I recall now. It was a fifteen-pound bass."

Marissa knew little about fishing, but she remembered her father's joy when he caught a five-pound bass. Mitch must have caught a mutant, she thought, and smiled.

"It's true!" Mitch had thought she was smiling about his great catch. He looked at Catherine. "Annemarie, you sure didn't like cleaning that thing for me."

"Ummm, no. Fish are stinky."

"And you're way too pretty to be stuck at home cleaning fish, Annemarie." Mitch looked as if his body were slowly deflating. "Annemarie. Beautiful Annemarie." Then he fell into another violent coughing attack.

Jean looked at her three guests almost pleadingly. Mitch was failing. They'd stayed long enough. Too long.

Eric raised Mitch from the pillows, supporting him while Jean wiped at the man's cracked lips. When the coughing ended and he took a drink of water, he choked, coughed some more, and this time waved away the water.

"I wanna go fishin' with Bernie," he said in a thin, plaintive voice. "We had such good times. I got married. Good woman, Jean is. Good woman."

Eric made a show of looking at his watch and said, "Well, I guess it's time for us to go, girls."

"No!" Mitch tried to shout, his voice so gravelly Marissa knew that within five minutes he wouldn't be able to talk.

"I think we've tired you out," Eric said. "A nap will do wonders for you."

"It won't." Mitch started to cry. "It won't. Please stay."

Marissa looked at Jean. She was doing the smart thing by not continuing to argue with Mitch and get him more agitated. She'd begun injecting what Marissa guessed to be morphine into the port of Mitch's IV. Within a minute, Mitch seemed to quiet a bit, but he raised his left hand and motioned to Marissa. She walked to the left side of the bed and tried to take his hand, but he shook her off and tapped the table beside his bed.

"See this little thing I made?" he asked, nodding toward a pretty, octagonal table built of mahogany. On four of the eight sides he'd attached fancy antique-gold handles, and each of the other four sides bore a hand carved fleur-de-lis stained the same color as the handles. "I made this for you, my little girl."

Marissa didn't want to agitate Mitch by arguing that she wasn't Betsy. "I love it, Daddy," she said.

"I'm glad . . ." Mitch's eyelids drooped. "It's yours. You're . . . my little girl." His eyes popped open and he looked at Eric. "Boy, you gotta behave, and I mean it! No good is gonna come of the way you act!"

Eric looked shocked and then murmured, "I'll behave. I'll act better. I promise."

Mitch's eyes closed, but his head faced Marissa. "You'll always . . . be my little girl."

17

No one said anything on the way home from the Farrells' house. Eric pulled into the Grays' driveway, turned off the car, and the three of them sat in silence for at least a minute.

"Thank God that's over," Marissa said finally. "Seeing poor Mitch was worse than my wreck. I don't think I'll ever be the same."

Catherine stirred in the backseat. "We need coffee or drinks. Probably lots of drinks. Are you coming in, Eric?"

"Yes, if you don't mind. You have a deputy here on surveillance—you don't need me—but I don't think I can bear to go home to an empty apartment."

"You're very welcome in our home," Catherine said, already climbing out of the car.

So he isn't going to mention anything about wanting to talk to me about Gretchen, Marissa thought, relieved. Whatever was in the manila envelope Gretchen had hidden, Marissa wanted Eric to be the first to see it.

Lindsay waited for them at the door and as usual furiously wagged her tail when Marissa stepped inside. She bent, rubbed the dog's ears, and gave her an especially tight hug. The dog offered love and comfort, and that's what Marissa felt she needed more than anything.

Later, as everyone sat in the family room, Marissa said what she knew Eric and Catherine were thinking: "Mitch should be in a hospital even if that's not what he wants. After all, he's obviously not in his right mind, and I'm afraid Jean's getting so run-down she might have a heart attack."

"But you know how hard Jean has always tried to please Mitch," Catherine said. "Dad told me everyone was surprised when Mitch married her—she was plain and not even well educated. Everyone thought he married her to get his hands on her father's land, but Dad claimed her simplicity, her adoration of him, even her old-fashioned ways appealed to Mitch. He wanted children desperately, but he never complained when it took eight years for Jean to conceive Betsy. She died in Jean's care, but Mitch never said a critical word about her. He went right on being loyal and kind and supportive of Jean even though there could be no more children and, as far as Dad knew, all of that valuable land was still in Jean's name, not hers and Mitch's." Catherine sighed. "She is more than devoted to him. He is her whole life. I doubt if she would even think of doing something he wouldn't want, like being put in a hospital."

Eric looked up from a deep study of his bourbon and Coke. "Then consider how she must have felt when he said, 'Beautiful Annemarie,' then called Jean a 'good woman.' " He looked up. "Was he in love with your mother?"

"Eric, what an awful—"

"Our mother would *never*—"

Both women burst out so loudly Lindsay jumped and quickly grabbed her teddy bear for protection.

Eric leaned back and nearly yelled, "Hey! I didn't say they were having an affair. I just asked if Mitch could have been in love with your mother. She was beautiful, full of life and warmth and . . ." He looked at both of them. "Well, even I had half a crush on her when I was about thirteen. Mitch is a good guy, but he's human. He couldn't help comparing your mother to Jean now and again, especially when they came here to dinner so often. They attended the Fourth of July parties, too, if I remember right."

The sisters subsided for a moment, both looking far away. "I never thought of that," Catherine finally said. "How stupid of me never to have considered whether he could have fallen in love with Mom."

"You're not stupid and Mitch loved Jean," Marissa said decisively. She gave Eric a wounded look. "When you were thirteen, I thought you had a crush on me."

"Marissa, you were a skinny nine-year-old with crooked teeth."

"I had potential. I just needed braces."

"I was waiting for the braces to come off."

"You couldn't look past my braces to see how intelligent and sensitive I was?" Marissa asked hotly.

Catherine surprised them by laughing. "Nerves must be responsible for this ridiculous argument." They stared at her. "We have to accept that there is *nothing* we can do about Mitch and Jean, no matter how much we love them. We certainly can't guess what Mitch's feelings were for Mom. We *do* know that Mom was crazy about Dad and vice versa. So no matter how painful the scene was earlier, we need to let it—to let Mitch and Jean—go for tonight."

"You're right." Eric sounded defeated. "But this talk about who should be in the hospital reminded me of something I need to tell you, Marissa. Bea Pruitt was released from the psychiatric ward today."

Marissa was stunned. "Today! But it hasn't been seventy-two hours!"

"By law, a person can be held for up *to* seventy-two hours."

"She *needs* to be there," Marissa protested.

Catherine intervened: "If the opinion of two doctors is that the patient is safe to go home, then they go home, even if they haven't been in the hospital for quite seventy-two hours. Bea must have been very well behaved and convinced everyone she wasn't a danger to herself or anyone else."

"You should have seen her Monday night," Marissa snapped. "And her fury was directed at *me*!"

"To be fair, she'd been deeply shocked to find Buddy's body," Catherine said calmly. "Maybe after she'd been given a sedative that night, some tranquilizers for a couple of days, and had several talks with a psychiatrist, she calmed down enough to see reason."

"Wouldn't she have to be released into someone's custody?" Marissa asked hopefully.

"Not unless she's been declared incompetent," Catherine said.

"She hasn't," Eric returned. "She was always calm and happy living with Buddy. I hope if she's reached some state of tranquility without him, she can hold on to it."

Catherine nodded. "Only time will tell, to quote a cliché. She might be fine for a month and then lose it again. Or she might be all right the rest of her life."

"Or she might go around the bend now that she's free. Maybe she was just . . . I don't know . . . playing possum in the hospital so they'd let her out." Marissa sighed hugely. "Well, this just sucks."

"Beautifully put but true," Eric said. "Let's get our minds on something more cheerful than Mitch Farrell and Bea Pruitt. Maybe we should play Scrabble." Marissa and Catherine groaned. "Monopoly? Charades?"

Marissa glanced at Catherine and could see she'd picked up the vibe that Eric didn't intend to leave quickly. She yawned in the way that only Marissa knew was fake and said in a sleepy voice, "My goodness, I'm suddenly *so* tired. The alcohol must be affecting me—pleasantly, I must say." She stood up. "I think I'll go upstairs, get in my nightgown, and watch television." She trailed slowly to the stairs. "Thank you for taking us, Eric. Good night, you two. I mean three. Take good care of them, Lindsay."

After Catherine disappeared up the stairs, Marissa said casually, "I don't know how I expected your mother to act with me today, Eric, but after the first fifteen minutes or so being with her was almost like old times."

"I'm glad. Sometimes she's like that with me. Then she has a bad day and she's distant. Dad's mood seems more even, although he's quieter than before Gretchen died."

"I think talking can help a lot. Have you ever talked to them like you talked to me about Gretchen?"

He looked almost horrified. "No! They don't want me to talk about her."

"Maybe they don't want you to, but maybe they need to hear some things. I thought you broke off our engagement because you blamed me entirely for what happened to your sister. Instead, you felt most of the blame, shoved some of it off onto me without even knowing what you were doing, and broke off the engagement because you knew marriage for us at that time couldn't work. Professional psychologists like Catherine help people figure out those situations."

Eric nodded. "I know what people like Catherine do, Marissa. I didn't think she set broken legs."

"Just making sure. After all, we could use someone like Catherine in Aurora Falls."

"I believe we have a few people like Catherine in Aurora Falls. But you think we need another one? Particularly, your sister?"

"I wouldn't mind it." Marissa stopped talking and cocked her head. She heard Catherine's television. "I was waiting for that. I also don't think it would hurt if we had some music down here. Any requests?" Eric looked at her quizzically. "I acquired an envelope in Gretchen's room today. I don't want anyone to know what's in it until you do. And that goes for me, too."

"Oh. You're being cloak-and-dagger."

"I'm sure it's very private. Now pick some CDs and load them."

In a minute, Don Henley sang "The Boys of Summer" as Marissa handed Eric the sealed envelope. He stared at the words *The End* on the front of the envelope and finally began tearing it open. Marissa took Lindsay into the kitchen and gave her a bacon treat, then poured another glass of wine and took a quick sip.

Marissa wandered over to the wall of windows. A whimsical birdhouse shaped like a castle still hung in a nearby poplar tree and swung gently in the cold breeze. She couldn't bear to look at the blackened remains of her mother's rose garden, though. This spring wouldn't bring forth the rainbow of colored petals looking almost too beautiful to be real.

In the past, Jean had always helped Annemarie with the roses and seemed truly delighted to do so. The two women had tried to teach Marissa how to tend roses and she hadn't been interested. Now she cared. She would read, she thought. She would read everything she could find about raising and caring for roses and she would ask Jean to help her plant a new garden. The project would keep her busy and also make certain Jean didn't spend all her time sitting in that tiny house mourning Mitch. After they finished with the garden, she would take Jean out for dinner and a movie.

As Marissa looked out at the vacant dark night, musing over roses and her plans to help Jean get through a difficult year, she suddenly had the creeping feeling of being watched through the windows. The feeling was sharp, cold, malevolent, and so powerful she shuddered. Marissa lowered all the blinds and turned off all the lights except one. She didn't think she was letting her imagination run wild. At the same time, she was certain someone in the chill of the night watched through the thin blinds—not casually, like a neighbor standing in a yard looking around absently—but someone whose gaze purposely sought out Marissa Gray. For a moment, she thought of calling for Eric, but this wasn't the time to interrupt him.

Marissa pushed aside a blind and peeked out. When she saw a pair of golden eyes near ground level next to the locust tree, she recognized the neighbor's small black cat. Marissa was much more frightened and upset this week than she'd admitted, even to herself, if she'd let herself be spooked by a cat, she thought, trying to smile to herself.

But Marissa didn't feel relieved. She felt exactly the way she had before she'd realized just a cat had been watching her. Quickly she let go of the kitchen blind. Inexplicably shaken and uneasy, she didn't want anyone to see her, even a cat. In fact, she wished she could become invisible.

Marissa closed her eyes, tried to clear her head, and sat down at the counter, inspecting her nails to see if she needed a fresh manicure. Giving herself a manicure every few days had become a habit long ago when she and Gretchen had discovered nail polish. They used to joke that if her dream of being a concert pianist and Marissa's dream of being a world-renowned journalist failed, they could always get jobs as manicurists. Gretchen had loved painting Marissa's semi-long nails in fun colors. Gretchen's had to be short for the piano and Susan Montgomery had always been strict about Gretchen's nail polish, making sure she wore nothing darker than a shell pink. Pink. Just like her room, Marissa thought. Little-girl pink.

Marissa felt as if she'd sat in the kitchen for nearly an hour, but the clock showed she'd been at the counter only twenty minutes before Eric called for her. She hoped the envelope contained something helpful. At the same time, she dreaded what he might have found. She steeled herself mentally and walked into the living room, where Eric sat on the couch with papers spread around him.

She stood in front of him—not certain he wanted her to sit beside him—and tried to read his expression, which told her nothing. In a moment, he looked up and asked, "What do you know about tremors?"

"Tremors? Like shaking or vibrating?"

"Yes."

"Well, that's about all I know except that a lot of elderly people suffer from them. My father's mother did. They started when she was in her late seventies."

"That's what most people think about tremors. It's what I thought. I just found out differently." Eric fell silent and stared at a paper in his hand. "May I be completely decadent and ask for another drink?"

"You're not on duty tonight. You can get rip-roaring drunk if it will help."

A few minutes later, Marissa brought him a fresh drink. He thanked her and then patted a spot beside him on the couch.

"Gretchen copied some pages from a medical book and put them in here," he began, and went on in a cool, toneless voice. "They describe 'kinetic tremor' or 'essential tremor.' It's a tremor that usually begins in the arms and spreads to other parts of the body, even the head and voice. It can cause a person to have trouble thinking clearly, to have anxiety and depressive symptoms, and there's a risk of developing dementia. The tremors often start with people around sixty and less commonly around age forty, but they can start at any age. The shaking is usually seen in the hands and arms, even when the hands are at rest. The tremor gets worse when a person has to 'perform.' " Eric stopped scanning the pages and looked at Marissa. "She included results from medical tests. *Her* medical tests. She went to three doctors and her diagnosis was always the same. Gretchen had essential tremor."

Marissa stared at the medical test results, not understanding a lot of what she saw but not willing to accept what she did understand. "We're not doctors. We don't really know how to read these test results or what tests were run." She looked at him pleadingly. "Can Catherine look at them? She's not a medical doctor, but I'm sure she knows more about this condition than we do."

Eric nodded. "I'd like to get her opinion, if she wouldn't mind being disturbed."

Ten minutes later Catherine sat in the family room wearing a mint green kimono robe and delicate silver slippers. In spite of the shock of reading Gretchen's hidden papers, Marissa pictured herself the night of the wreck in her bulky white robe and big bunny slippers. Catherine had pulled back her hair with a beautiful clip at the neck so the line of every one of her perfect features showed. Mitch was right, Marissa thought. Catherine did look like Annemarie.

When Catherine glanced up, Marissa almost jumped, realizing she'd been analyzing Catherine's looks to divert herself from the deepening line between Catherine's eyebrows. Eric gently shook Marissa's hand. She'd been squeezing his hand as hard as she could and hadn't known it.

"If you want a really thorough explanation of essential tremor, you should talk to a neurologist," Catherine said. "It's a neurological disorder."

Eric shook his head. "I don't want to talk to a neurologist now. I—we—just want the basics tonight."

"Well, I believe the basics are fairly well described in these articles. Essential tremors affect the kinetic muscles. The condition can cause trembling and shaking. Physical activity or stress can make it worse. So can fatigue and cold and caffeine. It becomes more noticeable when sufferers try to do exact, precise tasks—"

"Like playing the piano," Eric said flatly.

Catherine nodded. "The tremors can even attack the voice—it becomes shaky and the singing voice can become vibrato. Essential tremor can also affect balance and the way the patient walks. It creates general unsteadiness." She hesitated. "Sometimes, mostly in older people, it can result in dementia."

"What causes it?" Marissa asked.

"It seems to be genetic. That's why it's sometimes called 'familial tremors.' It runs in families. Here we get into genetics and I'm out of my area of expertise. I do know it usually doesn't manifest itself until later in life, but it's sometimes seen in people in their twenties."

"Treatment?" Eric asked crisply.

"Some drugs have helped. Physical therapy. Even alcohol sometimes helps—it has a calming effect in moderation. But there really is no effective treatment right now." Eric looked straight ahead and Marissa looked at her sister. "Didn't your family know about Gretchen's condition?" Catherine asked Eric.

"No. She didn't tell us. She even kept those papers hidden. Marissa managed to get them."

"How—"

"I'll tell you later," Marissa said quickly.

"All right. Is there anything else you'd like to ask me?"

Eric shook his head again but didn't speak.

Marissa smiled at Catherine. "Thanks. I think we—especially Eric—just need some time to let this sink in."

"I understand." Catherine smiled at her in return. "I'll leave you two alone to talk. Don't hesitate to come upstairs and get me if there's anything else I can do."

Marissa looked over at Eric, and when she looked back Catherine had already disappeared up the stairs, silently and swiftly, not remaining to watch their reactions or hear their discussion. Such sensitivity was one of the reasons Catherine had excelled in her training, Marissa thought.

Marissa sat quietly, listening to Ivy's "Worry About You," until she couldn't stand it any longer. "Eric, was anything else in the envelope?"

He nodded, reached into the envelope lying beside him, and pulled out a color photograph. He glanced at it, then handed it to Marissa. She saw Catherine in a strapless lavender gown with a diaphanous tulle skirt. She'd pulled up her brown hair behind her right ear and fastened it with a silk gardenia while the other side waved to the top of her gown. She held a glass of champagne and laughed at something the woman beside her was saying. Will Addison stood on Catherine's other side, looking at her with something in his eyes beyond adoration.

"This was taken at the Carlisle wedding," Marissa said. "Catherine was a bridesmaid and I remember how beautiful she looked. That would have been . . ." She closed her eyes and thought. "Late April. Will and Gretchen were dating then."

"And afterward she cooled things with Addison, started hanging out with Dillon Archer, and in June she died."

Marissa tried to remember exactly how Gretchen had felt about Will. Cautious because of his good looks, his sophistication, his practiced charm, his reputation for never getting serious with a girl, Marissa had been stunned when Susan Montgomery let Gretchen have even one date with Will, but one had turned into many.

"Eric, Will Addison would have been one of the last people I'd have imagined your mother letting Gretchen date. Did she approve of him?"

Eric remained silent for a moment and Marissa felt as if he was struggling with truth versus loyalty. He took a deep breath. "My mother didn't approve of Will. You know she pretty much runs the ship at home, but for once my father crossed her and said Gretchen *could* date Will. They had had a ferocious argument in their room—they seemed to think no matter how loud their voices got, Gretchen and I couldn't hear if they had the door closed.

"My father said, 'Do you realize how much money the Addisons have?' Mom asked what that had to do with anything and Dad started shouting about how much Gretchen's piano, violin, voice lessons had cost, not to mention her years at Juilliard. She lived in an apartment with Mom's sister, whose husband charged substantial room and board. Dad said, 'Gretchen has just about drained us, Susan. I wouldn't change any of it—I'm so proud of her—but our financial position is precarious.'" Eric smiled bitterly. "*Precarious*. I'd never heard my dad use that word. He went on about how Wilfred Addison couldn't live forever, when he died his money would go to Evelyn, and Evelyn would deny Will nothing, especially if he was married to someone she considered not only a lady but talented and, no doubt, one day famous."

"Oh, I see." Marissa tried to make her voice completely neutral, although she was deeply disappointed in Eric's father. "Did Gretchen talk to you about Will?"

"*Me?* No way. If she was going to talk to anyone, it would have been you."

"She never said much about him. That was my tip-off that she really cared for him, even loved him. She always kept her most personal feelings to herself."

"Meanwhile, Will was in love with your sister."

"I do know he didn't break off the relationship. Gretchen told me she ended things," Marissa said. "She claimed she and Will were just too different. After that, though, she started acting even more distant than she had when she was dating him. She never wanted to do anything." Marissa paused. "She never wanted to play the piano. You had to almost force her."

"Now we know why she didn't want to play the piano, or the violin, or to sing. The tremors must have been getting noticeable."

"The first doctor's report is dated in early December."

"So she knew at her last Christmas," Eric said.

"The second doctor's report is dated February and the third April."

"She put that picture of Will and Catherine taken in April in the envelope because it was important to her. 'A picture is worth a thousand words.' I told you she loved Will, but when she saw this photo she had to realize how Will felt about Catherine. We've learned stress and emotional upheaval can make the condition worse." Marissa paused. "And I hate to say this, but if Gretchen knew how your father felt about all the money he'd spent on her, she would have thought she'd put the family in financial straits for nothing. She might be able to perform on the concert circuit that was to start in the fall but not afterward. She couldn't have a long career."

Suddenly Eric moaned and put his head in his hands. Marissa placed her hand on his back. He didn't breathe. After nearly ten seconds, he uttered a sob that seemed to rip from the depths of his being. His entire body shook, and without a thought Marissa pulled him to her and wrapped her arms around him, murmuring comforting phrases in his ear and pressing his face against her shoulder. At last, he raised his head. Marissa put a hand on each side of his head, lifted her lips, and tenderly kissed each of his eyelids. Then, again and again, she gently kissed his cheeks wet with both their tears and finally pressed her lips against his. They didn't share a passionate kiss. Their tongues did not touch. But Marissa felt as if that chaste kiss, gentle as the flutter of a butterfly's wing, bore all the love in the world.

Eric settled for a while, breathing evenly, staring into the fireplace, his fingers twining softly with hers. Marissa thought his inner storm might be abating until he asked in a tortured voice, "Why did this have to happen to Gretchen?"

"Why does something like this happen to anyone?"

"But she was so sweet, so good, so *young*. We all kept her wrapped up in a cocoon and when it was finally time for her to burst free—*this* hit her!"

"I know, Eric. It's awful. I could tell you God has a reason and we just don't know it, but I wouldn't be sincere. I don't think the universe is always rational. Bad things happen to good people and I *cannot* believe that's just the way it's supposed to be, no matter how hard I try. I think all we can do is endure it. There's no universal bad guy you can bring to justice for all the wrongs in the world. There's no bad guy you can bring to justice for Gretchen's illness."

"That's the hell of it, Marissa," Eric said with soft despair. "I always believed there *was* justice and someone had to be responsible for the *in*justice. It's why I wanted to become a cop—so I could help set right all that was unfair in the world." He sighed. "I was so damned naïve."

"No, you weren't. Justice does exist in the world—it just doesn't always win the day, or so it seems. And you have to remember that Gretchen's tremors *didn't* take her life. *They* didn't kill her."

"You don't think she meant to jump off that rail, but Dillon got her first?"

"Absolutely. Gretchen wouldn't give up that easily. She had an inner strength I don't believe her family saw. I'm sure she would have tried everything to cure her condition. She did *not* intend to kill herself, Eric. Dillon Archer killed Gretchen. I just don't know why."

18

1

After Eric left Marissa's, surprisingly unembarrassed by letting her see his emotional weakness, even his tears, he'd checked to see that the deputy was still wide-awake and watching the Gray house. Then Eric had gone back to his Spartan apartment, listened to his answering machine, on which Robbie Landers asked him to call her.

"Sorry I'm calling so late," he told her a few minutes later. "Jean invited me to visit Mitch. Before you even ask, I'll tell you that he's in terrible shape. I don't think he'll live out the week."

"Oh no." Eric heard Robbie take a deep breath. "Well, we all knew he didn't have much time. I'm glad you were able to see him. He thought a lot of you, sir."

"I've known him since I was a little boy. So, how did your canvass of the local motels go today?"

"I went to eight places, ranging from moderately nice to bad. I followed all of your directions plus added a few of my own touches—lots of bright orange lipstick, false eyelashes, hair in a ponytail with a pink ribbon, and I giggled until I'm exhausted."

"Sounds like you were quite the peacock today." Suddenly Eric was smiling, enjoying himself. "False eyelashes?"

"And metallic black eyeliner."

"I'm proud of you, Robbie."

"Thank you, sir. I spent an extra half hour getting myself turned out this morning. I went to the nice places first. In most of them, people at the registration desks just glanced at the newspaper picture, said they hadn't seen him, and then wanted to know what he'd done. I smiled at the females, giggled at the males, and said he hadn't done a thing—we just wanted to ask him something about an old case. We wanted to know about something he'd seen—it wasn't very important. The registration staff at a couple of motels recognized him. They wanted to know if he'd been found, what he'd done, *and* if he'd killed Buddy and Tonya. I tried to look like I didn't know what they were talking about and I think I did a pretty good job." She paused. "Maybe that look came a little too easily."

"I'm sure it didn't, Robbie. You'd just gotten in character as the day wore on."

"Well, that's nice to hear, but I'm not sure you're right. Not that I ever doubt you, sir."

"It's okay to doubt me sometimes, Robbie, just as long as you follow my orders."

"I will. Always." She paused and he could feel her revving up for something she considered important. "The last place I went to was a real dump called Fall Inn."

Eric surprised himself by laughing. "What a classy name. I'm sure people are always getting it mixed up with the Larke Inn."

"Not once they set eyes on it. Really, we should set the health department on the place. I can't imagine how many diseases you could pick up in there overnight, although the manager volunteered the information that they usually rented rooms by the hour."

"Ah, we have a vice raid in our future," Eric said.

"At the other places where they recognized Dillon, they said sort of offhand that they hadn't seen him for years," Robbie continued. "The manager of Fall Inn—a guy in his mid-thirties, I'd guess—glanced at the picture, then looked away really fast and said he'd never seen that guy in his *whole* life. Sir, I could have sworn I saw recognition in his eyes and I think he went overboard about never having seen Dillon. He got very nervous even though I was giggling and acting like a loon.

"When I walked back to the patrol car, I glanced at the few cars in the parking lot to see if anything looked like what I imagined Dillon Archer might drive. I didn't—everything looked pretty pathetic and I was disappointed—but then I thought he'd want to blend into the crowd. He wouldn't drive anything showy."

"Very good job, Robbie! And you're right—Dillon did love flashy cars, but if he's here, he wouldn't want to draw attention to himself." He paused. "I think we'll watch Fall Inn for at least twenty-four hours."

"Do you want me to do it?" Robbie asked, dread in her voice.

"No. You've done the legwork. We'll stick one of the guys with surveillance."

She let out her breath. "Oh, I'm so glad. That place gave me the creeps, which I suppose I shouldn't have told you."

"It was okay to tell me." Eric smiled. "It would probably have given me the creeps, too."

After hanging up, Eric sighed in relief. This was their first lead in the case. Tenuous? Extremely. But at least something, which he certainly needed after the awful evening he'd had seeing Mitch and then finding out about Gretchen's illness.

Eric looked at the envelope Marissa had found in his sister's room, the one he'd been holding all through Robbie's call. He tossed it aside, refusing to read the information again or see Will Addison looking adoringly at Catherine, and crawled into bed, where he'd tossed and turned most of the night. He would have dragged in the television to see if it could bore him into slumber, but Marissa was right—the screen was so little, hauling the machine into the bedroom wasn't worth the effort. He'd vowed that he'd invest in a larger-screen TV.

The next day he leaned back in his chair and looked at the clock. Twelve thirty-five. He felt like he'd worked all day. Eric usually brought a sandwich for lunch, eating in his office and drinking some of Robbie Landers' good coffee. Today he decided to eat out. He'd splurge and go to Wendy's for a double hamburger, a chocolate Frosty, *and* top it all off with a cup of Robbie's coffee. He was just rising from his chair when the phone call stopped him.

"Chief Deputy Montgomery," he said without enthusiasm, picturing someone else sinking their teeth into a fresh double hamburger. "What can I do for you?"

"I live on Holmby Street." The woman's voice sounded middle-aged and furtive, as if she were doing something sly by calling the police. "My friends have all told me to mind my own business or I might get myself into some kind of trouble, but I'm afraid I'll get in *real* trouble if I don't tell you."

Eric waited for her to continue. His stomach growled and he rolled his eyes, knowing he'd have to urge this woman to talk. "What's your name, ma'am?"

"Oh! Well . . . that's classified."

"Classified? Are you with a federal agency?" Eric asked seriously, although he was grinning.

"Not exactly. Well, not at all, really, but I want to keep my name out of it."

"I see. And what would *it* be?"

"Lights. At night." Oh God, Eric thought. She's going to report UFO activity. "I see lights in the old Archer house. It's been vacant for years, ever since old Isaac Archer died, and in all those years I never saw lights. But now I do. I live down the street."

Eric snapped to attention. "Have you ever seen anyone coming or going from the house?"

"I saw somebody go in all sneaky-like just a few minutes ago. That's why I called right now. But I can't talk anymore. You're probably tracing this call. You'd better check that house." She paused and then said darkly, "God knows *what* is going on in there!"

Eric usually brushed aside a call coming from a person who sounded like this woman did. Those calls, however, did not involve the Archer house, a place where Dillon might be staying if he really had come back to Aurora Falls. Eric had checked the house the day after Buddy's murder and found nothing, but maybe Dillon had simply been more careful a few days ago.

Eric strode into the main room at headquarters saying loudly, "I'm going out. Don't need anyone to go with me. Let me know if there's any trouble," and managed to get out the door without anyone asking where he was going. He got in the sheriff's car, fought downtown Christmas traffic until he'd left the business area, and headed north.

Sebastian Larke, the founder of Aurora Falls, had formed this street first and named it Holmby after his family estate in England. During his lifetime, people called it Holmby Road. Sometime after in the 1830s, citizens had renamed it Holmby Street. As Eric drove past its ramshackle houses with their peeling paint, broken front porch steps, and sagging roofs, he thought Sebastian would be saddened to see what had happened to the place he'd named after his family's beautiful estate—an estate he was never allowed to visit after his expedition to America. Sebastian probably would have been pleased with neighborhoods like the ones where Eric's parents lived or where the Grays lived. No, Sebastian would have been pleased by the mansions of Oak Lane before time and a flood had taken their toll, Eric mused. He'd seen old pictures. The houses had been large, elegant, graceful, and exquisitely maintained. Now they sat on a nearly vacant street. Now they sat on a street where someone had brutally stabbed to death an annoying but harmless little man named Buddy Pruitt.

Isaac Archer, Andrew and Dillon's father, founded Archer Auto Repair when he was young and built it into the best car repair business in the city, in spite of its tumbledown appearance. Eric's father had patronized the place, as had Dr. Gray and Mitch Farrell. Eric knew the business was lucrative, but sour-faced Isaac didn't indulge his family. When he married pretty Belle Benson, age eighteen at the time of the marriage, he'd stuck her in the old house on Holmby Street with his stern, sharp-tongued mother, who couldn't stand her daughter-in-law, who was cute, joyful, and not overly bright.

Eric pulled up in front of the small ranch-style house painted gray, with a rusted white wrought-iron railing around the front porch. Several roof shingles lay in the front yard and dead leaves clogged the gutters. Half-dead shrubbery surrounded the house, looking as if a fungus had ravaged it. No cars sat near the house.

Eric looked down the street and saw an extremely thin woman wearing a down coat and knit cap pretending to be checking her garbage cans, all the while throwing surreptitious glances toward Eric. Miss *Classified,* no doubt, Eric thought, and gave her a salute. She scuttled into her house and slammed the door.

He knocked on the front door of the Archer house and wasn't surprised when no one answered. The draperies across the big front window showed discolored, rotting lining. They'd probably been hung over forty years ago, when Isaac Senior built the house. Eric couldn't picture Isaac Junior or Senior spending any money on interior design.

Eric noticed the for sale sign that had stood in the front yard since Andrew and Dillon's father had died three years ago. Even if the real estate market was good, the house would be a hard sell, Eric thought. The maintenance needed on this beauty would cost as much as the house. He walked around to the back, climbed two steps to a tiny back porch, and knocked on the back door that, to his surprise, clicked and opened simply from the force of the light thud.

Eric stayed on the porch but leaned into a small, dingy kitchen and called, "Anyone home?" He didn't expect anyone to answer but decided to try one more time: "This is Chief Deputy Montgomery. Is anyone here?"

Andrew Archer walked into the kitchen looking thin, haggard, and dead eyed. "Well, Eric, I guess you found me."

2

"Are you living here?" Eric asked after Andrew had insisted he sit on a hard, faded plaid couch.

"I don't know," Andrew said vaguely. "I spend a lot of time here."

"Do you sleep here?"

"I did last night. I go back to my house, the house I shared with Tonya, but I can't make myself stay. We were so happy." He paused. "At least I thought we were happy."

Eric was careful not to seize on the statement. "Everyone talks about how well you and Tonya got along. What do you mean you *thought* you were happy?"

Andrew took a minute, as if sorting his thoughts. "*I* was happy. I'd had a crush on Tonya ever since we went on those boat rides with Dr. Gray. When I went away to college, I did everything I could to improve myself. When I came back here, I heard she was in love with Will Addison. She wasn't seeing him, but she loved him." He stared down at his hands. "When I was certain they weren't together, I asked her out. Things went so fast. I couldn't believe it when she told me she loved me. But I've always wondered if I was a consolation prize because she couldn't have who she really wanted."

"I remember those river outings. Tonya tried to talk to you, but you were so shy you'd hardly say a word." Eric smiled. "You didn't give her a chance, Andrew."

"I tried, but I just couldn't get out a word." Andrew's face tightened. "That sure wasn't the case with Dillon, though. All the girls loved Dillon."

"Did they? Back in those days I didn't notice them falling all over themselves around Dillon. They talked to him more because *he* talked to them."

Andrew went on as if he hadn't heard Eric: "Marissa looked at you all the time when she thought you weren't looking at her. She's loved you for years. But Tonya and Dillon—there was something between those two, Eric. I never saw them together. He never talked about her. But there was *something*."

"I think you're wrong, but we can't know now."

Finally Andrew seemed to come alive. "Why can't we know now? Tonya can't tell us, but Dillon . . ."

Eric felt the muscles of his whole body grow taut. "But Dillon what? Dillon will tell us?"

"Dillon might, if he feels like it."

Eric forced himself to let a few moments pass and then ask quietly, "Is Dillon alive and in this city, Andrew?"

Andrew rubbed his big hands together and closed his eyes. "Dad was so mean to him. He wasn't nice to me, and with Mom he was just . . . strange. He stared at her all the time. He never said her name. Belle. I never heard that name come out of his mouth. He didn't beat her, though. But he did Dillon. I don't know why, but he hated Dillon. I should have done something— I was the big brother—but I was too cowardly to cross Dad. I just watched Dad and cringed.

"So I lost my brother—emotionally, I mean. Dillon didn't have any love or respect for me and who could blame him? And now I've lost my wife because I wasn't a good husband, because I didn't try harder to find out what was bothering her so much the last few days of her life. She had to know I'd be thrilled about the baby—she couldn't have been worried about that. But one day someone mentioned something about Dillon and she went so white, I thought she was going to faint. If I hadn't caught her, I think she would have dropped to the floor. I asked her what it was about Dillon that scared her, but she said she just had a dizzy spell. It didn't have anything to do with Dillon."

Andrew looked up at Eric with pale eyes and swollen eyelids. "But it did. When she got that photograph of us decorating our first Christmas tree and it said: 'Hope you're enjoying your new life,' Tonya was so shook up about it, she brought it to the newspaper office and made me leave with her so she could show it to me. And all I did was brush it off, tell her it was a prank, anything to settle her down." Andrew paused. "That night, someone murdered her. *Someone?* No, not just someone. Dillon." He shook his head. "I just don't know why he'd do something so horrible."

Eric nodded and then spoke slowly: "Andrew, you were a wonderful husband, but Tonya was strong willed. If she didn't want to tell you something, she wasn't going to tell you. Period. You couldn't cajole Tonya Ward into doing anything or saying anything she wanted to keep secret." He waited a moment for those words to sink in. "But Andrew, you never answered my question. Is Dillon here in Aurora Falls?"

Andrew stared emptily at the floor and Eric didn't think he was going to answer. Finally, he said softly, "If Dillon is in this city, I don't know it. That photograph was addressed to Tonya, not me. I haven't heard a word from him since the day he hit Buddy and jumped out of the boat."

"You haven't *heard* a word from him. Has he sent you even a note, some indication that he's around?"

Andrew shook his head. "No. Absolutely nothing." Andrew lifted his gaze and said strongly, "But when I came to this house after Tonya's murder, I found some food and beer in the refrigerator, and a blanket and pillow in Dillon's bedroom."

"Why didn't you let me know immediately?" Eric demanded.

"From time to time, vagrants have holed up in here, especially during the winter. I've seen that kind of stuff in here before. I didn't think it had anything to do with Dillon. But just about an hour before you came, I found something . . . important. I was going to call as soon as I got my wits about me."

"What the hell did you find?"

Andrew swallowed. "In a drawer in his old dresser, I found a . . . a photograph. Not an old one—something taken in the last week or so, judging by the Christmas decorations and the fake fur coat and high-heeled boots. Eric, it's a picture of Marissa."

3

As dusky evening floated into night, Will Addison turned into the cemetery and drove slowly to the north end, closest to the waterfall. Some people had strung tinsel and some had tied metallic balloons to gravestones, as if the bodies lying under the ground were going to rise up and have a party. Will found the practice tacky and the resulting image of partying corpses repulsive. He hoped when he died no one would garnish his gravestone with what he considered trash.

Will pulled to one side of the road and stopped the car. Then he picked up a dozen white silk lilies, their stems wrapped in green paper like fresh flowers, and walked a few feet, weaving around grave markers, feeling the short, cold grass crunching under his shoes, until he came to a small, gray granite stone reading:

JOHN DAVID ROWE

BELOVED SON

The birth and death dates showed that John Rowe had been eight years old when he died. "Eight," Will said each year when he came to the grave at Christmas. "You never had a chance to make your life good or bad." Will laid the lilies on the grave, touched the stone, slowly got up, and walked laggardly back to his car, as if he were an old man. He felt old tonight. He felt like he'd lived a whole lifetime in his twenty-seven years.

He lingered in his parked car a few minutes, watching the black of night pushing a rim of purple down behind the hills. With his window open, he could hear the rush of water tumbling over the falls and hitting the river. Soon they'd shine with colored Christmas lights behind them. Will preferred the white lights used the rest of the year—white lights shining pure and luminous on the sparkling veil of water.

Will didn't want to go home. An entire evening at home nearly drove him crazy with his mother chattering while his father hid behind a tome on some war—Will thought certainly by now his father must be back to the times before Alexander the Great. Because of a trust fund left to him by his grandmother, Will had the money to live other places and had always taken advantage of that freedom.

Christmas was another matter, though. His parents insisted he be home at Christmas, and considering how little grief they'd given him over the years for his many scholastic and business failures, he thought a couple of weeks in Aurora Falls wouldn't kill him. Besides, except for last year, Catherine Gray always came home for Christmas, too.

And Will always decorated little John David's grave—the grave Will knew would be there for the rest of his life, haunting him, calling to him.

The memory of John's death seemed to fill the cold night as Will reluctantly started for home. God, if only he'd gone out that night with some of his friends everything would have been different, but he didn't have a lot of friends in Aurora Falls. He'd gone to private schools and hadn't associated a lot with "the guys" when he came home summers. He didn't fit in with "the guys." He'd usually gotten along better with girls.

Girls like Melody Simmons. She danced in his dreams, drunk and loud, just as she had that fatal night. Then the dancing and singing would stop. He would see her sick and scared. Then he would see nothing except her big brown eyes, full of hatred and accusation.

Thinking of her sent him back through the years and made him remember the night she'd come to his house around nine o'clock, her long, dark hair tousled, her brown eyes sparkling, her jeans and T-shirt looking painted on her fantastic eighteen-year-old body. She was thrilled and had dragged him outside to see the silver Corvette her father had given her. Will had walked around the car, making all the appropriate noises, oohing and aahing as he sat in the driver's seat, looking under the hood and thinking this 345-horsepower engine was too much car for Melody, who had trouble even parallel parking.

She'd wanted them to go to the Lonesome Me Tavern to celebrate. Will hadn't wanted to go—even under normal circumstances, Melody talked too loud, squealed, burst into song, and did just about anything she could think of to get people's attention. On the other hand, earlier in the day Will had run into Catherine Gray, already preparing to enter her senior year of college in the fall. She'd been shopping for a birthday present for her mother and he'd invented a female cousin and asked Catherine to help him pick out a present for her.

Catherine had been even more beautiful than he remembered, serene, composed, and funny in her understated, charming way. Also, whenever they met, she somehow made him feel as if he were the person she'd most like to be with at the moment, although she never flirted. She'd intimidated the hell out of him that day as always. Still, after they'd parted, he'd berated himself for not asking her out and decided that somehow he must get up the nerve to ask for a date. He'd been mulling over the problem for hours, and having his deep thoughts about Catherine interrupted by boisterous Melody had made him irritable.

His mother made him more irritable, though, and when Melody insisted they go to the Lonesome Me and that she would drive, he'd consented, thinking maybe by the time he got home his mother would have gone to bed.

The Lonesome Me Tavern had been crowded and the music loud, but Melody had still managed to be seen and heard. She'd danced, she'd sung, she'd bragged about her new car, surreptitiously doing shots of gin she'd brought in a flask while Will chastely sipped on a tonic and lime, thinking that an evening at home with his mother would have been better than this.

On his second tonic and lime, this one spiked with a shot of Melody's gin, Will had struck up a conversation with a woman in her mid-twenties sitting beside him. Her husband was playing pool while Melody had been whooping and occasionally managing an unsteady belly dance on the dance floor. Suddenly Melody had nearly flown to Will's side, cursed him, called the woman a bitch, and slapped her. Before the manager had time to do anything, Will had grabbed Melody and tried to drag her from the bar. She'd broken free, called him a few more colorful names, and vanished out the door. Will had made it outside just in time to see her spinning gravel as she soared from the parking lot. A few people, enjoying the entertainment, had followed them outside, clapping and yelling as Melody disappeared in her new car.

Will had gone back inside, apologized profusely to the woman whose cheek had reddened from Melody's slap. While she'd talked her husband out of suing that little bitch for assault, Will had finished his drink. Because Melody had let everyone know *she'd* brought Will in her new Corvette, people knew she'd left him stranded. Someone offered to take him home, but he said he'd just as soon walk off how mad he was at her. That had brought a laugh.

Home being less than a mile away, he'd begun walking north. Construction interfered with traffic on this stretch of road during the day, and even at eleven thirty p.m. few cars drove farther than to the Lonesome Me.

Will had been humming, calming down, hoping he never saw Melody Simmons again in his life, when he spotted her Corvette stopped on the side of the road. He'd picked up his pace, and when he'd finally reached the car he'd seen Melody bent over the wheel. She must have passed out, he'd thought, until she raised her head and said, "God, Will, I'm sick. I'm sick enough to die. I'm . . ." She'd begun heaving and Will quickly opened the door, looking away until she'd finally stopped vomiting and started to cough.

"I can't drive home, Will. I just *can't*," she wailed. "Oh, my daddy is gonna be so mad at me."

"He's not the only one who's mad at you," Will had nearly shouted. "You acted like you were crazy in the bar. You hit that woman! Her husband is talking about having you arrested!"

"She was flirtin' . . . flirtin' . . ."

Melody nearly fell out of the car and onto her head as the last of her stomach contents streamed out. "Oh, Will, if you just drive me back home . . ."

"If I drive you back home, what? Your dad won't know you're drunk?"

"He'll be in bed and I'll be okay in the morning. I just gotta get the car home. We don't live too far apart. You could leave the car at my house—"

"And walk *back* to mine." Will had looked at her in disgust. He'd wanted to say no, not just to teach her a lesson for embarrassing him but also because he was already hot and miserable. Still, she *would* wreck if she tried to drive home, he'd thought. He hadn't wanted *that* on his conscience. "Scoot the hell over."

He'd stepped around the vomit and gotten behind the wheel while Melody had clambered into the passenger's seat. "Oh, fank you," she'd slurred. "I never felt so tur'ble in my whole life. Fanks."

"You're welcome. Now shut up."

Melody remained quiet for two whole minutes as they passed the lane leading to Will's house. Her house was less than half a mile farther, he'd thought in relief. He was doing the right thing by getting her home safely. After he got her in the door of her house, though, he never wanted to see her again.

Melody had suddenly come to life. "I'll send that woman flow'rs."

"Forget it. You can't send flowers—you don't even know her name."

"But she was flirtin' with you! You're *my* boyfrien'. *Mine!* Ever'body knows that!"

"I am *not* your boyfriend, Melody! Now just be quiet."

She'd lunged at him so fast he hadn't even sensed momentum gathering in her. She clawed at his face, screaming. Will fought her, knowing he'd have to pull off the road—

Then he'd seen a blur, heard a thump, felt the front tires rising over something—something small, something soft. In spite of her hysteria, Melody had been aware of it, too. She'd looked at him with wide bloodshot brown eyes and passed out.

Will had pushed her back to the passenger's side and gotten out of the car, muttering, "Oh my God. Let it just be an animal. God, *please*—"

He went absolutely still when he saw the body of a little boy lying no more than two feet behind the car. One blue-jeaned leg lay straight, the other at an angle from a small body that didn't move. Will stared at the child, for a few moments almost uncomprehending. A little kid? At this hour? Then he stooped down and looked at the boy's face, its eyes closed, blood oozing from the mouth.

Will knew he should do something like CPR, but he didn't know CPR. The child wore a faded jacket—too light for this weather—zipped shut. Will had tentatively unzipped the jacket and put out his right hand toward the little boy's chest, determined to find out if he had a heartbeat, when headlights cut through the night, freezing Will's body, stealing his breath.

Will's thoughts had gone wild. What could he say? It *was* an accident. Will hadn't deliberately run down a kid. That had to count for something!

"Looks like you're having a bad night, Will."

Will had slowly looked up to see Dillon Archer standing with his hands in his coat pockets, his gaze moving between the boy and Will.

Will had barely known Dillon, but that night he'd launched into a detailed account of the evening, including Melody leaving the Lonesome Me without him, his finding her pulled off the road and sick, taking over the wheel, and Melody attacking him in the car. He'd caught only a flash of movement before he ran over the child, he'd almost wailed. He'd sounded as if he were defending himself to a judge instead of a teenage guy he barely knew.

Dillon had looked at him without emotion. "You've had a little trouble with the cops before about your speeding, haven't you?"

"A warning. Two tickets. That's all."

"Yeah. And you've been drinking, haven't you?"

"A little bit."

"Could you pass a Breathalyzer test?"

"Sure." Will had thought about his automatic response. "I don't know."

"So you're in a whole lot of trouble here, Wilfred Addison the Fourth."

"It was an *accident*!"

"Do you think the cops care about that? You're drunk, you were no doubt driving too fast *again*, and you hit a *kid*."

"What am I going to do?" Will had shouted, nearly crying.

Dillon had cocked his head for a moment. Then he'd said, "You're going to let me help you. You're going to do everything I say and you're going to be fast about it. Alright?"

"Al—alright."

Dillon had gone straight to the child and put his ear against the boy's chest. Then he'd felt his pulse. "I was afraid of this."

"Afraid of what?" Will quavered.

Dillon had gotten in the Corvette, started it, and calmly backed over the child. Later Will remembered screaming like a girl. Then Dillon had put the car into drive and run over the boy again. He got out of the car and walked back to the child, feeling for a pulse, listening for a heartbeat. "Guess we got it right this time," he said more to himself than to Will. "No chance in hell of a witness."

Dillon had gone back to the car, hauled the still-unconscious Melody onto the driver's seat, pulled a handkerchief from his pocket, and run it around the steering wheel and over the top of the gearshift. He'd put Melody's right hand on the gearshift and both of her hands—especially the fingers—on the steering wheel before letting them drop back into her lap. He shut the car door, looked at Will, and said, "I'll take you home."

"Take me home?" a shuddering Will had asked.

"Yeah. It looks like she was headed for her house. You had to walk to your house, which isn't this far north. You didn't know a damned thing about this *accident* because you didn't walk this far, did you?" Will stared at him. "Well, *did* you?"

"N-no."

"Okay. Get in my car and hurry. People will be leaving the Lonesome Me pretty soon. I have to get you home before anyone sees us."

Later, Will couldn't remember his thoughts as Dillon turned around his car and headed to the Addison house. He'd pulled into the circular driveway, stopped, and turned to Will. "You know what would have happened if the cops knew *you* were driving that car, don't you? Think about prison. Pretty boy like you in prison?" Dillon shook his head. "Not a good thought. I know you feel bad about that kid, but he never knew what hit him, literally."

"And Melody Simmons is a total bitch. If the positions were reversed, she'd have thrown you to the wolves and never thought another thing about it. I know right now you're all shaken up and feeling bad and guilty, but later, when all of this has had a chance to sink in, the first thing you'll think of is how grateful you are that I *saved* you. Maybe someday you can do the same for me. Maybe we've never been friends, but we've never been enemies, either. I've always thought you were an okay guy. I don't want to see your life go down the drain because of Melody Simmons. So you think of all that. And don't you dare act guilty. Don't act anything except surprised when you hear the news. She'll claim you were driving, but you've got all those people in the Lonesome Me who know she took off without you.

"Now get in the house and go to your bedroom. You look like hell. We don't want anyone to see you looking like this. Try to sleep. And Will—don't forget what I said. Maybe I'll call on you someday for help and you'll remember what I did for you tonight."

Will had climbed from Dillon's car on shaking legs, used his key to get into the house, gone straight to his bedroom and the adjoining bathroom and thrown up. He'd undressed, crawled into bed, and shivered all night. He'd been cold, so cold. He'd added another blanket to his bed, but it hadn't helped.

Still, wracked with chills under his expensive blankets, he'd realized he had to feel warmer than that poor kid he'd left lying on the road in the middle of a frozen December night.

For years afterward, Will had tried to block out the image of John David Rowe with women, with liquor, with changes of universities. Everyone thought Will had been on the verge of expulsion from three universities before he quit. Actually, his grades had been fine. He'd simply lost interest and decided to drop out of each school. He only came home when his parents absolutely demanded it, although they could really *make* him do anything. In his twenties, he'd begun to wonder what he was going to do with a life he knew would be far longer than he'd like.

Then one Christmas his mother had dragged him to a party where Gretchen Montgomery would be giving a concert. Will didn't care for classical music, but he'd found the pianist pretty in a demure, old-fashioned way. He'd struck up a conversation with her after the crowd had finished with their expected compliments, and Gretchen had charmed Will with her unassuming manner, her intelligence, and her sense of humor. When they started dating, she seemed happy. They had even made love and he hadn't been surprised that she was a virgin.

After four months, though, she had begun to drift away—at first emotionally and then physically. The lovemaking had stopped altogether. Although Will had enjoyed the sexual part of their relationship, she had never overwhelmed him with passion. Or love. When Catherine Gray had come home in the spring to attend the Carlisle wedding, Will realized what he felt for Gretchen was fondness and deep friendship, but not "until death do us part" love like he did for Catherine. Shortly afterward, Gretchen had begun making excuses not to go places with him, and when they were together she didn't have much to say. Then she had ended their romantic relationship but hollowly assured him they'd always be friends.

Will had been appalled when he learned she was dating Dillon Archer. He couldn't understand why her parents let her see him. They'd barely let her see Will. Deeper than his shock, though, had been his concern for her. Although Will knew she wasn't as innocent as she pretended to be, she certainly wasn't experienced, not someone who would always make the right choices for herself, in many ways as naïve as a fifteen-year-old.

Will had never given much thought to former girlfriends. He wished them well and he hoped they wouldn't want to reconcile. He hadn't taken advantage of any of them, but when a relationship was over he hadn't cared to remain friends with them. His connection with Gretchen had been different from anything he'd ever known. Beyond his pride at dating a musical prodigy who at twenty-one was already poised to become world-renowned, Will's pleasure in compliments he received on his girlfriend's dainty, china doll beauty, his delight in their long talks about everything except who was dating whom, he *cared* about her maybe more than anyone he had in his life.

And that is why one evening when his parents were gone he'd insisted she come to his house. He'd planned what he was going to say to discourage her from seeing Dillon Archer, yet he didn't want to reveal his or Dillon's part in the little boy's death. When she'd arrived, Will was so nervous, so fumbling, that Gretchen didn't understand him. He remembered having a drink, another, another, another. Then came the one that put him over the edge and the whole, horrible story of John David Rowe had spilled out of him, shortly before the contents of his stomach when he realized what he'd done.

Gretchen had looked at him with disbelief at first, then in an old, tired, knowing way he would never forget. Just forty-eight hours later, she had fallen from the balcony in the Gray's Island church—a fall Marissa Gray told police Dillon Archer had caused. The next day, Dillon Archer had vanished.

Now Will shuddered, feeling just as cold and nervous as he had that awful night he'd run down John Rowe. Maybe it was because he'd gone to the boy's grave. Will's hands jittered, probably because he hadn't consumed any alcohol since the two martinis at a late lunch. He'd accepted that he'd become an alcoholic since the death of little John David Rowe—accepted it and didn't intend to do anything about it. Liquor was the only thing that obliterated his thoughts of the little boy and of Gretchen, whom he was certain Dillon had murdered.

Will turned down the little lane that led to his parents' big house. For once, he was glad to see it—the gigantic Christmas tree in the front window, colored lights around the double front doors, reindeer bearing miniature white lights on the front lawn. He wanted a drink, but almost as badly he wanted to be around people tonight. He didn't care what his mother talked about—he just couldn't stand to be alone in a silent house.

He shut off the car, opened the door, and stepped out. As soon as he closed the door, a powerful force slammed him against it, knocking the wind out of him. A strong arm encased in black wrapped around his neck, jerking back his head as a body pushed him so hard against the car he couldn't move. His heart pounding, Will gasped, "Dillon?"

A deep-throated, eerie laugh sounded in his ear. "Poor Melody is in prison. I'm sure she dreams about you every night. Do you dream about her?"

"Please. I . . . I . . ."

The front door of the house opened and Evelyn Addison called out, "Will? Willie, is that you, honey?"

"Mama looking out for her baby," the awful voice said in his ear. "She has to because you're always too drunk to take care of yourself. I have a piece of advice, although it's coming too late for *you*—when you have a guilty conscience, never turn your back."

The arm around his throat loosened. Just as he started to yell for help, a knife slid fast and deep across his throat. Blood spurted, but Will Addison felt no pain. Time seemed suspended. He gazed up and saw the stars. He closed his eyes and he saw Catherine Gray's face. Then he saw Gretchen's old, tired, knowing look and he groaned softly. Evelyn called again just as his attacker let go of him and Will's dying body crumpled limply to the cold driveway.

19

1

Marissa doubted that the *Aurora Falls Gazette* had experienced so many large late-breaking news stories in one week for at least twenty years, and Pete Hagarty requested that the regular staff come in and help for a few hours, although it was a Saturday. After all, Evelyn Addison had found Wilfred Ames Addison IV, her son, the son of the mayor, with his throat slashed in the driveway of the Addison home the previous night.

Buddy Pruitt had also been found by his mother, but Marissa knew that even though Bea Pruitt had been hauled off to the psychiatric ward, Evelyn Addison would manage to create an even bigger splash. She had called a press conference this morning and the newspaper would be running the photo of her sobbing copiously into a handkerchief while her husband stood looking wide-eyed and stunned behind her. In the conference, she had declared Chief Deputy Eric Montgomery "inexperienced," "incompetent," and "lazy." Marissa knew that last comment would keep Evelyn on Eric's blacklist for the rest of her life.

When Marissa arrived ten minutes early for work, she saw Hank Landers already seated at his desk and looking tired. She felt as if she'd been deadweight in the newsroom this week, but she couldn't help her involvement in the investigation that seemed tied to the attempt on her own life. Marissa interrupted Hank for a minute to tell him she appreciated all the time his daughter Robbie had put in on her case. Hank had replied abruptly that it was simply Robbie's job, then turned back to his work. He couldn't help but resent her a bit, Marissa thought. He was overloaded with work because of her and he was worried about Robbie, whom he'd never wanted to become a police officer.

Now Marissa was starting another workday to which she could contribute nothing. When Eric had called in the middle of the night to tell her about Will, he'd told her the police were linking the investigation into Will's murder with that of Buddy Pruitt's, in which she was considered a person of interest. She could not be involved with any newspaper stories covering the murders of Buddy Pruitt *or* Will Addison.

Marissa had liked Will, but after Eric had told her about Will's murder she couldn't picture Will's face or remember the sound of his voice. She couldn't even feel sympathy. Some part of her had gone numb with shock. And guilt. She had no idea how Will's murder could be connected to her, but she knew it was. Somehow, she had triggered the recent murders. A psychiatrist would call her a narcissist, but she knew she was right. She wanted immediately to leave the city and she would have done so except she was certain it wouldn't help. Marissa believed it was too late for her to do anything to help because just by moving back home months ago, she had set in motion a chain of events that wouldn't end until the last person in someone's ghastly plan was dead.

When Marissa awakened Catherine and told her about Will, Catherine had wept almost as much as she had when their mother died. Marissa knew Catherine was not in love with Will but also knew of Catherine's deep affection and concern for Will. Lindsay had accompanied Marissa into Catherine's room with the news. When Marissa said she would go to give Catherine some privacy, Catherine had asked if Lindsay could stay with her. Marissa was so used to having the dog at her heels as she moved around the house, she wasn't certain Lindsay would leave her. But just as with Marissa's mother, Marissa told the dog to "stay" and Lindsay obeyed. Marissa couldn't help putting her ear up to the door and hearing Catherine ask the dog to jump up on the bed.

At one o'clock Pete had told the regular staff to go home. Most of them were glad to get back what was left of Saturday, but Hank Landers decided to stay. Marissa wasn't surprised. His zealousness was almost legendary and Marissa admired him tremendously. She, on the other hand, was exhausted after not falling asleep until nearly two in the morning, then being awakened at three by Eric's call.

A chilling wind whipped around her when she stepped outside the *Gazette* office. The temperature must be at least ten degrees lower than it had been when she came to work, she thought. She didn't know if the weather service predicted another blizzard. She certainly hoped not. Catherine and James were supposed to go to the movies, and Marissa knew Catherine desperately needed the diversion.

When Marissa reached home, she found a note from Catherine saying James had taken her out for a casual lunch. Marissa smiled. Things were going well in that direction. Thank goodness for James, Marissa thought. This would have been a horrible Christmas for Catherine without him.

Lindsay rushed to greet Marissa, the stuffed giraffe in her mouth. Marissa petted her, told her she'd been a good girl for comforting Catherine this morning, then went into the kitchen looking for something simple to eat for lunch. She settled on a grilled cheese sandwich and tomato soup made with milk instead of water. Afterward, she felt so sleepy she couldn't imagine doing anything enterprising.

"Feel like taking a nap, Lindsay?" The dog knew the word *nap* and began racing up the stairs, giraffe held tightly in her mouth. "That settles it," Marissa said aloud. "We'll make it a short nap."

They sat at a table with a beautiful view of the waterfall. Eric, looking especially handsome with his slightly long blond hair combed back and looking almost conservative, had asked for a special table arrangement—two apricot-colored roses and two white roses to go along with the graceful white candle. For once, the dining room of the Larke Inn wasn't crowded but had just enough diners to make the room feel intimate and enjoyable.

Marissa was so excited, she felt as if her cheeks must be glowing red. She and Eric had eaten here before on special occasions like a birthday, but they'd never been so dressed up; there had never been such electricity seeming to crackle between them. The waiter had taken their drink orders and given them tall, elegant menus with violet and black covers with the dinner offerings described in gold calligraphy on parchment paper. Eric lifted his menu. Marissa opened hers and stared at it just a moment before she smelled smoke. She looked across the table to see the corner of Eric's menu on fire, one flame shooting up so high she squealed, he yelped, and everyone in the dining room looked at them as Eric threw his menu on the floor and began stomping out the fire. Meanwhile, Marissa scooted lower in her chair and raised her open menu in front of her face so Eric couldn't see how close she was to uncontrollable giggles.

She woke up giggling. A dog's face hung over hers, dark eyes looking concerned. Marissa had no idea where she was. The dog licked her face, then moved slightly, and Marissa saw a shaft of dull light coming through a window, a print of Toulouse-Lautrec's *Le Moulin Rouge,* a bright yellow upholstered chair, and she knew she was in her bedroom, not the Larke Inn the night Eric proposed to her. What a shame, she thought, smiling. That had been *quite* a night.

And from the look of the light coming through her window, it was almost night again, she mused. This was supposed to be a *short* nap. She looked at her bedside clock. Five fifteen. She must have been even more tired than she'd realized.

Marissa heard voices coming from downstairs. She listened for a moment. Catherine and James. Marissa rolled out of bed, straightened her hair and makeup, and went down to find them sitting side by side on the couch looking at movie offerings in the newspaper.

"Well, hello, sleepyhead," Catherine said, sounding just like their mother.

"That was my idea of a brief nap. Three hours. Have you decided on a movie?"

"No," James said. "I want romantic comedy and she wants racing movies."

Catherine rolled her eyes. "I really don't care that much, except that I don't want something sad."

Marissa walked to the window and looked out at snow falling steadily against a pewter sky. "This doesn't look like a cheerful Christmas snow."

"I know," Catherine said. "It looks like last Saturday night, and I'm not even going to *think* about your wreck. You almost scared the life out of me, Marissa Gray, racing off to your party in that stupid convertible during a blizzard—"

"I believe you said you weren't going to think about it," Marissa reminded her.

"I didn't say I wasn't going to talk about it."

"Watch out, James." Marissa grinned. "She's sassy tonight."

"I am *not*—"

"Hey, the movies don't start for at least a couple of hours. Let's go get something to eat," James interrupted. "It's dark already."

"I hate daylight saving time," Marissa said, glancing outside again. The patrol car sat in front of their house, but between the snow and the darkness she couldn't see the patrolman inside. "It gets dark way too early."

"Would you like to get dinner with us?"

Always polite James, Marissa thought. She looked at Catherine and James, both smiling broadly at her, both no doubt hoping she'd say no.

"I'm not very hungry," she said. "I'm just really thirsty. Can I get you two anything?"

They both shook their heads and went back to perusing the newspaper. Thank goodness Catherine would be with James tonight, Marissa thought. He'd already lightened her spirits, which Marissa knew would have been impossible for her to do. The weight of Will's death had finally descended on her as she'd driven home from the *Gazette* office and her nap had done nothing to dispel it. She felt as if she could never really be happy or laugh again.

Marissa wandered into the kitchen, opened the refrigerator door, and after staring for a minute decided she wanted a simple glass of water. When she shut the refrigerator door, she realized she'd forgotten to turn on a kitchen light. As she stood in the near darkness, she looked at the wall of windows at the kitchen's end. Catherine had forgotten to close the blinds and the neighbor's dusk-to-dawn light formed a backlight for a bulky figure standing close to the windows and holding something long and thick above its shoulders. Before Marissa could make a sound, the windows smashed. Glass flew, Marissa screamed, and another blow smashed more windows, another blow, another blow . . .

And through the entrance she'd created stepped a shrieking woman swinging a baseball bat.

2

"Marissa Gray! I come to kill you, Marissa Gray! I come to kill you for murderin' my Buddy!"

Marissa, horrified, froze and looked at a frizzy-haired, swollen-eyed Bea Pruitt for a moment. Then Marissa turned to run and tripped over a chair leg. She went down hard on her knees but still managed to scramble away, screaming for help, cringing as Bea swung the bat and came closer.

"You *whore*! You murderin' *bitch*! They thought they could keep you safe from me, but they didn't know how smart I am. I can play their game. I can play tricks better than they can!"

James burst into the kitchen, momentarily diverting Bea. She squinted at him, then yelled, "You got yourself another one already? Be careful, boy. She's a killer!"

"Stop it!" James shouted, striding toward Bea until she swung the bat in his direction. "Why are you doing this?"

"Not so smart, are you?" Marissa glanced up and saw Bea's wild eyes, the tiny cuts all over her face, and bare hands dripping blood. "I'm Buddy Pruitt's mama!"

"Ms. Pruitt—"

Marissa heard Catherine screaming out the front door for the patrolman as Bea snarled, "Sure, I'm Ms. Pruitt, but you can't stop me by bein' polite, boy. You can't stop me from makin' her pay for killin' my Buddy." Bea started to cry, tears running through the blood on her face. She started toward Marissa again, swinging the bat. Marissa stayed on her knees, cursing herself for backing into a corner. "You oughta thank me, boy. If you'd only seen what she did to my Buddy, you'd run a mile. Instead, in less than a week she's got a new boyfriend—"

"I'm not her boyfriend, Ms. Pruitt." Every time James spoke, Bea stopped swinging the baseball bat and looked curiously at him. He'd obviously noticed and was stalling her. He lowered his voice: "I've known Marissa for a long time and I don't think she'd kill *anybody*."

"Then you don't know her at all." Bea squinted, blinked, and squinted again. "I know you."

"Oh?" James asked, his voice suddenly soft and threateningly curious. "Who am I?"

"You're . . . you're someone I saw at the funeral." She pointed her bat at Marissa. "Her mother's funeral. My Buddy said you're no good. He said you're a wolf in sheep's clothing."

James held her gaze. "And why is that?"

"Because you . . ." Bea's eyes looked empty before she blinked. "'Cause you can do just what you did to me! Make people forget what they're thinkin' and tryin' to say!"

Bea took another swing, missing Marissa's shoulder by only a few inches. "No wonder she's with you. You both trick people."

"You said you played tricks in the hospital." She stared at James, who took two smooth steps toward her. "Ms. Pruitt, what makes you think Marissa killed Buddy?"

"'Cause she smacked him one time. Then he made a little joke at the police headquarters about Marissa's Monster and she threw a fit and said she'd kill him! I heard all about it!"

James looked surprised for an instant. "From whom?" She stared at him. "Who told you Marissa threw a fit and said she'd kill him?"

"I'm not tellin' you nothin'. Don't you go thinkin' you can trick *me*." She swung at Marissa again, this time so close Marissa could almost feel the bat against her head. She crouched lower, trying to cover her head with her arms. "I'm no tattletale, Mr. Whoever-you-are."

Bea took another swing and James leaped at her, throwing the swing off balance but not the woman. James had gotten between Bea and Marissa when Randall Crane ran in and whipped behind Bea so fast she didn't seem to realize Randall had entered the room. Bea tried one more swing clearly meant for either James or Marissa when Randall closed his arms around Bea's waist and yanked her backward. The bat crashed into a wall and stuck just long enough for James to grab it, toss it aside, and help hold the plunging, screaming Bea.

Catherine rushed into the kitchen. "I called nine-one-one. Oh my God, Marissa! Are you hurt?"

"I'm not sure." Marissa tried to stand up and couldn't make it.

Catherine ran to her side. "Hold still until the paramedics get here. Did she hit you?"

"I don't think so."

"Bitch!" Bea shrieked. "Whore! Murderer! God will send you right into the flames where you belong, but you won't see me and Buddy because we'll be together in heaven."

"Yeah, okay," Marissa said weakly.

Bea struggled violently. My God, doesn't the woman get tired? Marissa wondered, her panic fading with the certainty that even without the bat, this woman could kill her if she could free herself. Bea was stout, but James was young and Randall was astonishingly strong. Still, they had trouble getting Bea under control. She writhed, thrashed, and wiggled like something slick and gooey in their arms.

After what seemed like hours, Marissa vaguely heard sounds in the front part of the house. Two other patrolmen dashed into the kitchen, followed by a couple of paramedics. The last face Marissa saw before she fainted was Eric's.

20

1

Marissa opened her eyes. The handsome face above her swirled and she quickly closed them again. "Hi, Eric."

"Hi your own self."

"Am I alive? I mean all the way alive?"

"I think you're asking if you're injured. No. The paramedics didn't even drag you off to the hospital."

"*Please* tell me they took Bea."

"First they sedated her. Then they took her and this time she won't be back." Eric shook his head. "Bea Pruitt is a better actress than anyone realized."

Marissa finally opened her eyes. They had laid her on the couch and covered her with her grandmother's hideous afghan. Eric sat beside her. Catherine and James leaned forward in their chairs as if inspecting her. "I feel like a bug under a microscope," Marissa said.

Catherine looked as if she was recovering from a crying binge. "We were so worried. You could have been *killed*."

"So this is last Saturday night all over again. Me on the couch wrapped up in this awful afghan and the three of you staring at me after my brush with death. I tell you, this is getting *old*."

They laughed, asked again if she was all right, then told her they were all going to stay and keep her company. Marissa hadn't thought she could feel much worse than she had on the kitchen floor, but her spirits dropped like rocks.

"You don't all have to stay," she protested. "I feel fine. Really. I just need a couple of aspirins for a headache. Bea might be a great actress, but she's not a master with the bat. She didn't manage to hit me. Catherine, James, you were going out to eat, then to the movies."

"Oh, we'd rather stay with you," Catherine said sincerely.

"Yes. We would." James's sincerity wavered.

I can be polite or I can say what I want, Marissa thought. Nobody can get mad at me for saying what I want after what I've been through. "Well, I'll tell you what I'd rather you do," Marissa said. "Catherine and James, I'd like for you to go to dinner and a movie. Or two movies." Suddenly she felt shy, but she plowed ahead: "Eric, I'd like for you to stay with me."

Catherine frowned, undecided. James and Eric looked as if they were trying not to whoop with joy.

"I say the girl who nearly lost her life tonight gets her way," Eric said, grinning. "Catherine, James, off with you. And don't hurry back. Marissa, I would be most pleased to stay here in your hour of need."

Half an hour later, Eric walked into the family room and announced, "Your very kind neighbors have straightened up the kitchen as much as they could and nailed plywood over the space Bea left in the windows. I'm sure there will be a few drafts and Monday is Christmas Day, so you can't even get a glazier to measure and order the new windows until Tuesday. I also have to warn you that they'll probably be expensive."

"Does home owner's insurance cover damage done to the house by homicidal maniacs?"

"You'll have to check with your insurance agent about that one. Even he may have to call the main office."

"What happened to my surveillance?"

"It was dark, snowing, and that big holly bush you have at the corner of the house partially blocked Randall's view of the house's back left side, where Bea made her grand entrance. Also, something hadn't felt right with the car. Randall had gotten out to look at the right rear tire, which had picked up a nail and was leaking. No foul play—just a foul nail. He was calling it in when

Bea attacked. She must have been watching for quite a while, waiting until Randall's full attention wasn't on the house."

"Well, great."

"I'll tell you what's great," Eric said. "That Bea didn't bash your head in with that bat."

"You put it so gently."

"That's exactly what she would have done." He shook his head. "All these years I've never heard of Bea Pruitt so much as saying an unkind word, even about that bastard of a father she had. But when it came to Buddy . . ."

"Buddy was her world, Eric. She would have suffered anything her father handed out as long as the Old Man kept his hands off Buddy."

"You seem to know a lot about her."

"My father told us about Bea. He'd lived here all his life, you know, and he'd known Bea when she was in school. She got a crush on him, followed him around, sent him barely intelligible love notes. He was a kid and terribly embarrassed. It wasn't long before they put her in the special education classes, and Dad said he'd heard she'd gotten another boyfriend within two weeks." She smiled. " 'She just threw me in the gutter,' Dad used to say.

"Years later some kind soul gave her a job in Walmart. My mother was shopping in the sewing goods department, ran into Bea, whom she only knew by sight, and Bea told her she was going to have a baby and was *thrilled* about it."

Eric frowned. "Did your father have any idea who Buddy's father was?"

"I never heard him even speculate." Marissa paused, thinking. "Things were rather hectic in the kitchen and I'm not certain I heard everything correctly, but did Bea say Buddy had made a joke about Marissa's Monster and that I threatened to kill Buddy? I didn't throw a fit or threaten him, but he did make a joke about Marissa's Monster. Who told her that stuff?"

"Buddy and Bea talked on the phone a lot. He was always calling her and I'd have to tell him to put the cell phone away. Then she'd just call the office. We had to deal with her three or four times a day. I figure he called her and told her the whole story, embellishing it by saying you'd threatened to kill him so he could get sympathy."

"Well, if he did," Marissa said, "he almost cost me my life."

2

"Are you feeling okay?"

Marissa looked over at Eric. He'd built a fire in the fireplace and fixed her a glass of wine. He'd called and said they wouldn't need more surveillance until around ten o'clock because he would be staying, getting statements, et cetera. He'd winked at Marissa while he was talking to someone at headquarters, meaning he knew he wasn't fooling anybody and he didn't care. He wasn't on duty, he informed her, so having a bourbon and Coke was all right. He sat beside her on the couch, sipping his drink, talking casually, and kindly paying attention to Lindsay, who held her zebra, her smallest teddy bear, and her stuffed mouse in her mouth.

"I'm impressed, Lindsay," Eric said, pulling gently at the teddy bear with no luck. "Three toys at once."

"Lindsay's goal in life is to cram as many things in her mouth at one time as possible." Marissa laughed. "And you have to admit, this has been an exciting evening. She's pumped full of adrenaline."

Eric looked into Marissa's eyes. "And love for her mistress."

Marissa had known Eric since she was a child. She'd loved him and lost him and occasionally thought she hated him. Still, at this moment she felt shy with him and slightly lowered her head. "I guess love doesn't mean you come to your mistress's aid when someone is trying to kill her."

Eric put his hand under her chin and lifted her head. He looked at her solemnly and said, "Love means cramming stuffed animals in your mouth when your mistress is threatened."

Marissa burst into laughter. "And here I thought love meant never having to say you're sorry."

"Erich Segal got it wrong in more ways than one."

Marissa reached for her wineglass, missed, and turned over the glass. Wine spread over the coffee table and Eric dashed into the kitchen for paper towels. As they began wiping the liquid, Eric started to laugh. "Do you remember that night we were in the Larke Inn dining room and I knocked over the flower arrangement? Who knew that dainty vase could hold so much water? It soaked the tablecloth, dripped on the floor, and I nearly knocked the plates off the table trying to sop it up before it got on your dress." They both rocked with laughter. "And then you said, 'Eric, will you *please* propose before you destroy this whole end of the dining room'?"

Marissa managed to catch her breath. "Well, you'd almost pulled the chair out from under me and set fire to your menu. I didn't know what to expect next!"

Eric sat down beside her on the couch, wiping the tears of laughter from under his eyes. "Oh God, I'd planned such a perfect evening and it turned into such a mess."

"No, it *was* perfect, because you turned it into what you thought was a mess. I thought the entire evening was magical."

"Even when I pulled out the chair too far and you almost landed on the floor?"

"Even then."

He paused, tilting his head slightly, amusement in his eyes. "You were expecting me to propose that night. Gretchen told you, didn't she?"

"No. I knew when you suggested we go to the Larke Inn for dinner and you tried to sound offhand when you told me to 'really get dressed up,' and when you kept tapping your suit pocket in the dining room to make sure you hadn't lost the ring."

"Lost it before I created another spectacle. You're lucky I didn't turn over the table on you or knock you out of one of the windows into the waterfall. Maybe that's why you said yes. You feared for your life."

Marissa looked at him, tenderness overwhelming her. "That is *not* why I said yes. I think I've loved you since I was that skinny nine-year-old with crooked teeth."

"The one with potential." Eric smiled. "You more than surpassed your potential. Since you were about fifteen, I've thought you were the most beautiful, smart, unbelievably charming girl I've ever known."

"Beautiful? Everyone thinks Catherine is the most beautiful."

"She is—in her way. But your way—the slightly upturned nose with a few freckles, that wavy hair, the spectacular blue eyes, those *very* straight teeth—is the way that appeals to me."

He reached out and ran a finger down the side of her face. "For a long time, I had a lot of tortured nights. My heart would start pounding and I'd feel like I was hanging just on the edge of an abyss. Then I'd have the sensation of feeling your face. I'd recall how it felt to rub my fingers over every warm curve from your forehead over your temples and your closed eyes, down your nose to your lips—lips that would pucker and barely kiss my finger. I'd feel warm all over and—"

He went silent when Marissa lightly kissed his finger, never taking her gaze from his. His hand moved from her lips, sliding under her hair and lifting it before his own lips touched the hot, sensitive skin of her neck. She knew she made a soft sound of pleasure before she wrapped her arms around his shoulders and sought his lips with her own. The kiss seemed to go on and on and Marissa felt as if she were warm and safe and soaring through an exquisite world she'd hadn't known since the last time Eric kissed her—a magical, loving world where she wanted to stay forever.

She could feel her own breath quickening, her heart beating in time with his. She buried her hands in his thick hair and then let them drift down his back, feeling the heat of his skin through his shirt. She pulled the shirt loose from his pants and slipped her hands upward again, this time rubbing his skin as their tongues touched lightly, then with more confidence, more passion. Eric broke off their kiss and moved his mouth to her ear.

"Is your bedroom in the same place?"

"Of course."

"Then I won't need directions."

Eric rolled onto his side and propped his head on his hand, looking down at her. "I'm not going to tell you that I've always loved you."

"How gallant of you."

"I'm not going to tell you that I've always loved you because you won't believe me, but it's true."

"You having broken off our engagement two months before the wedding does make it hard to believe, Eric."

"I thought I'd explained all of that to you. Would you like to consult Catherine?"

"I don't think she can be objective. She wanted to throw a brick through your windshield."

"Oh. I didn't know how clinical psychologists handled these matters."

"Well, she wasn't a clinical psychologist yet, so I'm going to accept your explanation." She lifted her head and kissed him lightly. "Okay?"

"*Very* okay."

Eric looked around the room. "The few times your parents weren't home and we sneaked up here, I seem to remember this room done in subdued shades of blue. Have you changed it?"

"Yes." A week after you broke off our engagement, she thought, but didn't want to bring up that subject again or tell him she couldn't let herself forget one of the happiest times of her life. "You now see cream-colored carpet, azure walls, a bright yellow chair and bedspread. Do the colors remind you of anything?"

Eric closed his eyes for less than a minute. "Let's see—the beach in Jamaica?"

"Right! I guess it could be a lot of beaches, but I pictured the one we sneaked off to the spring break of my junior year of college."

"And the print of Toulouse-Lautrec's *Moulin Rouge*?"

"The nightlife! Don't you remember?"

"Oh, of course. I don't see anyone in the print wearing low-rise jeans and holding a piña colada, though."

"You need glasses."

"I wish we were in Jamaica right now," Eric said, leaning over to give her a kiss.

Marissa smiled. "How could you possibly want to leave all the fun we're having right here in Aurora Falls?"

"It's not all bad, Marissa. I got you back."

Marissa went still, barely breathing. Eric rattled on for a couple of minutes before asking, "What's wrong?"

"You got me back?" she asked. "Is that what you think? You got me back?"

Eric pulled her close to him and turned her face so she'd have to gaze at him instead of the ceiling. "I didn't get you back? What just happened? A jump in the hay for old times' sake?"

"No. Not at all. But you can't wipe away over four years of hurt, disappointment, and humiliation in a week, Eric. And I know you think you've analyzed everything that was going on with you after Gretchen died, but you haven't. You've come to some conclusions. You're thinking straighter. That's great. But it doesn't make everything all right with you, or me, or us."

Eric looked at her for a moment, his expression stunned. Then he rolled onto his other side. "I thought you loved me, Marissa. I felt it. At least I thought I felt it."

"I do love you, Eric. My love is different than it was the first time around, though. I'm older. I've realized I have to be cautious, especially when it comes to us."

"So I haven't suffered enough."

Marissa sighed. She started to say something sweet and comforting, but she couldn't and be honest, too. "Dammit, you're acting like a spoiled little boy. You didn't want me, so you threw me away. Now you feel better and I still love you, so you believe everything is okay again. You're twenty-nine years old, Eric. Think like it!" He didn't answer. "Have you fallen into a pouting spell?"

"I was on the verge, but you've shamed me out of it."

"That's good."

"So I've done one thing right."

"You have done many things right and I do love you. I've never been in love with another man. Honestly, I don't want *ever* to be in love with another man. I just want things to be right, Eric. We really screwed up once. I don't want us to get married, have a child, and screw up things again. I don't think I could bear it. Do you love me enough to give us time? To not assume we're a couple ready to set a wedding date?"

"Do you want to see other men?" he asked.

"No. If we do things my way, will you want to see other women?"

"No. Absolutely not."

Eric's back was still turned to her. Marissa reached over him, pressed her body against his, and nibbled on his ear. "Then there's no reason we can't start fresh, Chief Deputy. After all, we already have the most important thing on our side."

"And what is that?"

"Love, you goof." She laughed, tickling him and overjoyed to hear his raucous laughter. "Love!"

21

1

Marissa lay peacefully in Eric's arms as they listened to a Bryan Ferry CD. "When are you expecting Catherine and James home?" Eric asked.

"Probably not until eleven at the earliest. I'm so glad James took her out. Will's death hit her hard. She might have been his only real friend. I was afraid she'd completely fall apart when she heard he'd been murdered."

"It would take a lot to make Catherine fall apart."

Marissa lifted her head and looked at Eric. "What do you mean? You know she's . . . well, not fragile, but—"

"Honey, you're doing the same thing to your sister that I did to Gretchen."

"No, I'm not. I know Catherine isn't a little china doll, but she's just not as tough as I've always been." Eric started laughing. "What's so funny? You know it's true."

"Your sister *is* as tough as you are, Marissa. She's just not as noisy about it."

"Noisy!"

"Yes. You think you're indestructible and you let everybody know it. One day I expect to see you thumping your chest and roaring at the world."

"How charming, you sweet talker."

"Catherine's strength is quiet," Eric went on, ignoring Marissa's sarcasm. "I saw it the night you came to the cemetery to see your mother's grave. You were the one who looked into the grave without really seeing. It was Catherine who held your hand, who told you to take a deep breath and focus, who took you in her arms. Neither one of you knew what was in that hole, but Catherine wasn't afraid to look. You were. I saw the fear in your eyes."

"Oh," Marissa said slowly. "I didn't realize . . . she just seems to worry so much and she hates taking risks and—"

"And here's what used to be our song," Eric interrupted as "Slave to Love" began to play. "Remember the night we played this song so many times at the Lonesome Me the manager told us we'd have to leave if we didn't stop hogging the jukebox."

Marissa laughed. "So we let other people make selections for ten minutes, then played Slave to Love again."

"And got thrown out."

"I think we were the only people not trying to start a fight who were ever thrown out of the place. I believe our picture is on the wall." Marissa smiled. "Your mother would be so proud."

Eric grinned. "At least there would no chance of her stopping in there for dinner and seeing it."

The phone rang. Eric groaned out of habit and Marissa said, "Relax. It's our house phone. Probably someone wanting to know if I can tell them any more about Will Addison's murder." She picked up the handset. "Hello?"

"Marissa! Is that you?"

The voice was so loud Marissa almost didn't recognize it. "Jean?"

"Yes. Oh, thank God you're home. Mitch is dying."

"Dying!" Marissa felt as if she'd just been dealt a blow. "You have to call the hospital!"

"*No.* He said he wanted to die here and I won't go against his wishes about something so important. I've tried to get hold of Eric at his apartment—"

"He's here."

"Oh, thank God! Will you please come? I can't go through this alone. Mitch would want to see the three of you." Marissa heard a gurgling moan in the background. "*Hurry!*"

Before she could hang up, Eric asked urgently, "Is Mitch dying?"

"How did you know?"

"Jean was so loud, I could hear part of what she said."

"She wants us to come and be with her. She said 'the three of you.' She assumes Catherine is here."

Eric was already climbing out of bed. "Don't call Catherine. Let her enjoy herself. She doesn't need to see Mitch die."

"I thought you said she was so strong, yet you don't want *her* to see him die? What about me?"

Eric looked at her solemnly. "Sweetheart, no one should be asked to see someone they love die."

2

Eric redressed in his uniform and out of habit even included his holster and gun. When Eric had insisted on carrying Marissa up the stairs to her bedroom, she'd glanced out the window and seen snow and wind blowing around small limbs on trees. She knew the weather had only worsened since they'd been in bed, so she slipped into jeans, a heavy sweater, and knee-high boots. She pulled her tousled hair back into a ponytail and didn't even glance at her makeup. Downstairs they each put on down jackets, and Marissa fished in her pockets until she found her gloves.

They stepped outside into a darkness of damp, thrusting wind. Eric took her arm and pulled her close to him as they hurried to the sheriff's car. Inside, they both brushed snow from their shoulders and Marissa wished she'd remembered to grab her knit stocking cap.

"I didn't realize it was so bad out here," she said. "The newsman didn't predict a blizzard." Then she smiled ruefully. "Which is exactly what I told Catherine the night of my wreck."

"She thinks you're safe and sound with me at home," Eric

said. "She won't be worried like last Saturday night. And I think you can count on James to take good care of her." Eric looked over at Marissa and winked. "Very good care."

"You sound like a dirty old man. This is only their third date."

"Third date's the charm." Eric sobered. "I called in to headquarters, got Robbie, and told her where we're going. She promised not to tell Catherine if she calls, but my people need to know we haven't disappeared."

"Good," Marissa answered. "I wasn't thinking of anyone except Catherine."

They fell into silence, reminding Marissa of their drive back from seeing Mitch on Thursday. He'd looked bad then, but could he have gone downhill so fast in two days? Apparently, he had. Once again, Marissa wished Jean weren't so insistent on carrying out Mitch's last wishes. After all, a man as sick as he was couldn't be thinking clearly. Certainly having him die in the hospital would be easier on Jean, Marissa thought. Mitch would have doctors and nurses around, someone besides Jean would call the funeral home, and his loving wife wouldn't have only Marissa and Eric for company when Mitch told Jean good-bye for the last time.

Eric turned a knob and the windshield wipers swiped back and forth faster. The streets were nearly deserted, and as they drove through the edge of the downtown section Marissa noticed a few restaurants that usually stayed open until midnight had already closed for the night. She glanced at her watch. Eleven ten. Marissa thought she probably should have left a note for Catherine, but then Catherine would be determined to come to the Farrell house, James would insist on driving her instead of letting her come by herself, and two more people would be in danger. No, it would be better for Catherine to wonder where her sister was while she remained in their warm, safe home.

When Marissa and Eric left town and started toward the Farrells' on Falls Way, she noticed her hands were cold even in her gloves and she dug them into her pockets. She looked around and it seemed as if darkness had drifted to the earth and clung tenaciously to every sign, tree limb, telephone wire, and especially the road. She was reminded of the night of her wreck and was surprised when she began to tremble. She knew the shakiness was from partly cold but also fear—reliving that awful night in her mind. The dark and the snow blocked her view of the Orenda River, but she couldn't forget that just a week ago she'd gone for one last trip in her car, a trip that could have ended in her death.

"It's going to be hell getting an ambulance out here and loading Mitch's body into it," Eric said in a businesslike voice. "Jean will want to ride with him, and she might be in such bad shape, you'll have to ride with her."

Marissa flinched at the thought. Surprise also trickled through her that Eric was talking logistics so coolly. Then she reminded herself that cool logic had always been his way of dodging tragedy or danger long enough to get his job done. When he'd gotten everything in order, he would give in to what he really felt. Marissa reached over and touched his arm. He looked at her and smiled. She tried to smile back, but the smile turned out crooked.

Finally, they reached the Farrell house. Marissa wanted to rush in and ask for a strong drink. That would be useless, because Jean had never liked to keep liquor in the house and now that Mitch was so sick Marissa doubted if anything stronger than coffee had made it into this house for months. She was so nervous she didn't know how to behave. What was she supposed to say when they entered the house? "Hi, Jean. Sorry your husband's dying. We're here to watch."

"*What?*"

Stunned, Marissa looked over at Eric. "My God, did I say that out loud?"

"About telling Jean we're here to watch her husband die? You certainly did!"

Marissa groaned. "Oh, I'm sorry. I'm *so* flustered and upset.

I don't know what to do or say. I hope you're more in control of yourself than I am."

"Apparently I am," Eric said dryly.

"Then I'll follow your lead."

Eric pulled the car past the front door and stopped beside the house. Marissa knew he was leaving room for the ambulance that would be coming soon. He told her to sit still, walked around the car, and helped her out into the snow that was already about three inches thick. He held on to her tightly as they climbed the porch steps. He knocked on the door, and almost immediately Jean pulled it open.

"Oh, thank the Lord you're finally here," she said. Her face looked ashen and ghastly, the sharp bone structure appearing as if it might slice right through the skin, her eyes wide and glassy. "Come in, come in."

Marissa went first, shaking the snow from her hair, batting it off her lashes so it didn't blur her vision as it melted. "Take your coat off, honey," Jean said.

"I think I'll leave it on a few minutes. I'm still cold."

Apparently Jean was cold, too. She wore a bulky dark wool sweater, badly knit and at least two sizes too big for her. She had buttoned it to the neck and buried her hands in the oversized pockets.

Marissa felt Eric walking close behind her and heard the front door close. "Hurry in to Mitch, Marissa," Jean said. "He's conscious right now."

Marissa still felt cold to her bones and shrugged deeper into her coat. Although Jean wanted her to hurry, her steps were slow. When she neared the dining room, she saw Mitch lying on his hospital bed, his skin white as the pillowcase, his eyes huge, and she felt as if she were looking at a death's-head. Jean stayed between Eric and Marissa. Then she said, "Oh, Eric, just a minute. I wanted to show you this."

Marissa was trying to work up a smile for Mitch, but he was looking past her, his huge eyes seeming to grow even wider. "Hi, Mitch," Marissa said when suddenly he croaked, "Eric, watch out!"

Marissa turned around and screamed as muzzle fire flashed and the deafening sound of a gunshot exploded in the small living room. The smell of gunpowder burning the inside of her nose, Marissa saw Jean holding a handgun as Eric crashed to the floor, blood pouring from his thigh.

22

1

Marissa lost moments in sheer disbelief. She seemed to be floating, watching the scene from a high, cool distance. Then Eric made a sound—part surprise, part agony—and Marissa jerked back to life, hearing Eric moaning, seeing Jean drop to her knees and jerk Eric's gun from its holster and grab his walkie-talkie and cell phone. Mitch lapsed into weak, gurgling sobs.

"Did you see that, Mitch?" Jean shouted. "Did you see the golden boy brought down so smoothly by the woman you've always thought was stupid, good for nothing except cooking and cleaning?"

Marissa dived at Jean, trying to push her away from Eric, but the woman held firm, raising her gun and pointing it at Marissa. "Don't make me use this—yet. I'm not ready."

"He's going to bleed to death!" Marissa shouted.

Jean's eyes narrowed. "When I first got married, I used to buy books for nurses and read them cover to cover so I'd know what to do if the children I thought I'd have got hurt. I know more than you think about the body. I don't believe I hit any major vessels, but you can wrap his belt around his thigh and make a tourniquet. You do know how to make a tourniquet, don't you?"

Jean kept the gun pointed at Marissa as she pulled loose Eric's belt and wrapped it tightly above the gunshot wound. To her surprise, Marissa didn't cry. She looked into Eric's pain-filled eyes and felt strangely numb and almost businesslike. Shock, Marissa thought. Shock she hoped would not wear off in a matter of minutes. She needed every ounce of composure she possessed to handle this unbelievable situation.

"J—Jean, no," Mitch gasped from the other room. "Don't . . ."

"I'll do as I please. After all, you did all these years." Jean put Eric's gun in the pocket of her heavy sweater and looked at Marissa. "Help me pull him nearer to Mitch. I want Mitch to see Eric bleeding."

Eric said nothing. Marissa could tell he was gritting his teeth as he nodded to her. *He doesn't want to make things worse,* Marissa thought. *She might shoot him again, this time fatally. Do what Jean says.*

The two women pulled Eric about ten feet closer to Mitch, leaving a trail of blood behind them. A beautiful Tiffany-style lamp burned on the table beside Mitch's bed—a different lamp than the one Marissa had seen Thursday night. Incredibly, when they reached Mitch's room Jean jerked a bed pillow from under Mitch's head and placed it under Eric's. "Comfortable?" she asked.

"Yes," Eric answered mildly. "Thank you."

Jean looked at Marissa. "Stop gawking. You look half-witted. Pull yourself together. I'm going to tell you a very interesting story. A story about Dillon *Archer.*"

"Jean, no," Mitch begged in a grating voice. "Please, no."

"Oh yes. I want everyone to know the truth about wonderful Sheriff Mitchell Farrell." Jean looked at Marissa. "You'd better have a seat." She pointed to a wooden rocker on the left of Mitch's bed. "You might want to faint somewhere along the line. You're weak, just like your mother."

Marissa opened her mouth, ready to retort to the insult, but she caught Eric's warning glance. She left his side and sat down in the chair she knew Jean had once used to rock her baby girl.

Jean, still holding her own gun, looked at all three of them; then she smiled slightly. "You all know my background. You know my father worked me half to death on the farm, furious that he didn't have a son, determined to make *me* work like a strapping boy at least three years older than I was. I was miserable, but the work made me strong—physically and emotionally. I'd resigned myself to the notion that I'd work that farm until Papa died when Mitch Farrell came along. He wasn't the sheriff yet, but he knew what he wanted and everyone knew he'd get it. Not to mention that he was handsome and he was *manly*, what today you'd call *macho*. Papa thought he was wonderful. He was flattered that Mitch had started to come and see *him* so often."

Jean stopped and laughed. "Papa nearly lost his dentures when Mitch asked him for my hand in marriage. Mitch Farrell wanted *me*? Papa couldn't believe it. Then Papa decided Mitch only wanted me because I'd be left all that fine land when he died. He hadn't planned to—he was going to leave it to a nephew. Nobody knew that except me, though. Anyway, Papa said getting Mitch Farrell for a son-in-law must be some kind of sign from God—it certainly couldn't be *my* charms—so he pretended to think it over and in a couple of weeks told Mitch he could have me. Then Papa changed the will, leaving all hundred acres of that land to me."

Marissa kept her gaze fixed on Jean, afraid if she was caught looking away, Jean might get furious. She was telling what she considered an epic story that deserved everyone's complete attention.

"Mitch was a good husband. Kind, affectionate, not insisting I work myself to death around here. In fact, he even helped move furniture when I was cleaning floors and carried heavy rocks for my flower gardens. I loved him *so* much anyway, and that gentleness and protection of me—well, I just felt like a queen. And I wanted to give him what he wanted more than anything in the world—a son. But the years went by and I never got pregnant. The doctor said there was nothing wrong with me. Mitch got elected sheriff and afterward he had to work late a lot. I missed him, but I knew he was determined to be the best sheriff this town ever had. I didn't resent all those nights he didn't get in until I was almost asleep—and he was too tired for . . . well, marital relations."

Here it comes, Marissa thought with a sinking heart. A kind but plain wife, no children, late nights at work. She wanted to jump up from the rocking chair and say, We don't need to hear any more! We're really sorry for you, Jean, but we have to get Eric to the hospital. Of course, Marissa simply sat still, afraid to move. Jean kept a firm grip on her gun.

"After a while, Mitch started mentioning the Archer family. He'd always taken his car to Archer Auto Repair, but he said more about what a 'cold fish' Isaac Archer was even to his wife, Belle, and their little baby, Andrew, she'd just had. Mitch said he wasn't the cutest baby in the world, but all babies were sweet. Of course that just made me feel worse about our situation, but I never let on to Mitch.

"I think I was at a church picnic a year or so later when someone told me Belle Archer was pregnant again. She didn't go to our church. I don't think she went to church at all, but they said Isaac must be in a hurry to have helpers at his business and that's why she was having babies so fast."

Eric moved slightly and Jean swiftly bent over him. "Think you're going somewhere? Think you're going to make a break for it, hero? Everyone thought you were a hero when you saved Marissa from dying in the river last week."

"I had help," Eric said, his voice rough with pain.

"But you got all the credit. Mitch always did, too."

Seeming satisfied that Eric had only been shifting a bit because he lay on the hard floor, Jean turned her attention back to Marissa. "Belle had another boy. Everyone laughed and said Isaac must be pleased that in a few years he'd have another helper for the business. But he didn't act pleased. Mitch told me he was more sour than ever. Nobody could understand it. Nobody really cared all that much.

"And finally, a miracle happened. I got in the family way. Mitch was over the moon with joy. I thanked God a thousand times for answering all my prayers. You know that baby was Betsy. I thought Mitch might be disappointed the baby wasn't a boy, but he didn't seem to care. Betsy was an angel—beautiful, good-natured, quick to learn. I'd never been so happy in my whole life." She looked at Marissa. "Your daddy was Mitch's cousin and Bernard and Annemarie had invited us over to dinner in the years before Betsy was born. I always felt shy around Annemarie and with her being so pretty and all, I felt downright ugly. After we had Betsy, though, I didn't mind going to dinner in their fine home. They had Catherine and we had Betsy. I couldn't have been more proud."

Jean smiled at the vacant air in which she apparently saw Betsy. Her silence lasted so long and her mind seemed so far away, Marissa thought of doing something. She didn't dare try to take Jean's gun, but there had to be a heavy ashtray, plate, potted plant, *something*, she could throw at Jean. But a surreptitious glance around the room showed Marissa nothing convenient. Even Mitch lay with his eyes closed, and she wondered if he was already dead.

"I have so many pictures of Betsy's third birthday party. Mitch had been working more at night again. The evenings didn't seem so long as they had before Betsy was born, and he was gone a lot at night. She was such a lively, happy child. At that party, I didn't believe anyone could be as blessed as I was.

"The Saturday after her birthday, I planned a big Sunday meal for us," Jean went on. "I went to work on it that night. I was peeling potatoes and I cut my hand fairly deep and I ran all over the kitchen looking for a towel to wrap around it. Then I realized I hadn't heard Betsy for a while and I went through the house and she was gone. Betsy had gotten open the front door because I'd forgotten to fasten the chain.

"I ran outside and screamed and screamed for her, but she didn't answer. Finally Mitch turned up. He called a couple of our neighbors down the road. He kept trying to make me stay inside, but I wouldn't. I'll never forget that black, wild December night." Tears streamed down Jean's face. Marissa glanced at Mitch and saw tears glistening on his cheeks, too. "Near dawn they brought out the dogs. They kept going from the front of our house, and across Falls Way to the river. They finally found her little teddy bear beside the river." Jean stopped and drew in a loud, wrenching breath. "Her body surfaced three days later. Her *body*! My little Betsy!"

"I'm so sorry, Jean," Marissa couldn't help saying. "It must have been terrible. I can't even imagine—"

"No, you can't, so don't sit there giving me your sugar-sweet false sympathy!" Jean yelled. "You-don't-know!"

Marissa subsided, feeling she'd only made things worse, wishing she could snatch back the words that had gone straight from her brain and out her mouth without a thought. She held her breath while Jean heaved with anger and grief, then turned around and began to pound her fist against Mitch—his legs, his abdomen—ignoring his moans of pain and fright.

"Jean, stop it!" Marissa burst out again. "Don't—"

Jean pointed her gun at Eric. "Don't what? Kill him? I can, you know. It would be so easy."

"No, Jean," Mitch begged weakly. "You don't want that on your soul."

Jean looked at him and asked, "It's a little late for you to be worrying about my soul, don't you think?"

"Oh God," Mitch mumbled.

"God's not listening," Jean snapped.

"He's not listening to you because you're a killer, Jean," Marissa said evenly. "You killed Buddy Pruitt and Tonya Archer and Will Addison. You put on that stupid costume and you tried to kill me."

Jean looked at Marissa, tilted her head, and said perkily, "Well now, miss, don't you just know everything!" Then she straightened her head and lowered her voice. "God didn't stop listening to me because I killed anyone. Oh, I did kill them, but I knew it didn't matter, because when Betsy died I knew there couldn't be such a thing as God. He's just make-believe, like Santa Claus."

"You sound very offhand about that, Jean."

"You get used to things by the time you're my age, Marissa. I shouldn't have to tell you that, but I've never thought you were quite as smart as you should be. Maybe you'll understand if you show me the courtesy of letting me continue."

"Please, go ahead," Marissa said flatly.

"When your mama got in the family way again, she was so happy. So was your . . . Bernard. Your mama asked Mitch and me to be your godparents. We don't have fancy things like that in the church where I go to like I still believe in God, but Mitch wanted to so much, so I agreed. I remember holding you and pretending you were my second baby. I told Annemarie that."

Eric shifted again and mumbled, "'Rissa. I . . . I need help."

"Oh, please, Jean," Marissa cried. "Let me call the paramedics."

"The paramedics!" Jean laughed. "And while they're working on him, we'll just go on with our chat? Maybe I hit the femur, but I don't think so. He's just weak from blood loss."

"People can *die* from blood loss!" Marissa shouted.

"Lower your voice, young lady. This is *my* house and we will do what *I* say. Eric is fine. The Eric Montgomerys of the world are *always* fine." Marissa swallowed her anguish as Jean drew a deep breath and went on calmly. "So, Annemarie kept telling me I'd have another baby and she even loaned me your christening gown for luck, she said. She never meant for me to keep it, but I couldn't bear to give it back because you looked so much like my Betsy."

"My dress . . ."

"Yes, your dress. And your mother never asked me to give it back. I guess she was too polite. Everybody was so nice to me after I nearly died when Betsy did. Even my prince of a husband never said a bad word about me not fastening the chain and losing Betsy like I did. He never acted like he blamed me. That helped. *Then*. I know better *now*.

"After a few years, Mitch started bringing the Archer boys around. They were nice, polite boys and Dillon was cute and such a charmer. I should have recognized that kind of charm. Mitch said he felt sorry for them because their father, Isaac, was so hard on them and their mother, Belle, didn't stand up to him. Do you know her name wasn't really Belle? She just called herself that. Her real name was Jezebel. Think about it."

Jean fell silent, going off into her private world again. Marissa listened to the wail of the wind around the house, through the trees and the snow spitting against the windows. The night was worse than the night of her wreck, she thought. At least last week she'd been active, her mind alive with thoughts of how to save herself. Tonight, she knew at least one person was going to die— probably more.

"Jezebel was Dillon's mother," Jean said. Marissa looked at the woman's worn, bleak face. "Mitchell Farrell is his father. Oh yes. All those nights he was working late and I was sitting here by myself, being understanding and wishing for a baby, he was with that whore. Isaac never came home until about eleven o'clock. Mitch had plenty of time with his girlfriend before he came home to me, and that girlfriend gave him a son."

Marissa sat in stunned silence for a moment, then asked, "Mitch?"

Nothing. Then Jean jabbed at Mitch's leg with her elbow. He moaned, then said weakly, "Yes, Marissa. It's true."

"Oh." Marissa could not think of one other word. "Oh."

"Yes. *Oh*," Jean mimicked. "And he dared to bring that boy here! To have him stay for supper! To show him his woodworking! And I was glad he seemed to enjoy the boys, especially Dillon. I was glad that kid could take away some of Mitch's pain over losing his only child. Only Mitch hadn't lost his only child!"

"M-Mitch, did you tell her this about Dillon?" Marissa jumped at the sound of Eric's voice coming from the floor. He sounded weak, his voice slow and almost sleepy.

"Yes, he told me," Jean snapped. "Almost two weeks ago. Give him just the right amount of morphine and he'll tell you anything you want to know. Hell, he'll tell you things you *didn't* want to know. When I heard about Dillon being his son, I sat up all night, just trying to take it in. I thought he'd just gone crazy on the drugs. I asked him over and over and his story never changed, though. Then I went over everything about those old days, and I knew it was true."

All Marissa could think about was the blood Eric was losing with each minute Jean talked. If only someone would come to the door, she thought. If only she had a weapon, no matter how crude, she could at least disable Jean and, she hoped, get one of the guns away from her. Instead, all she could do was talk.

"I know learning that Mitch had an affair must have hurt so deeply," Marissa said. "But it was a long time ago. Does it really matter *now* when Mitch is—"

"Dying?" Jean looked frighteningly furious. "Yes, it matters, because he didn't just have a fling with one of the town sluts that produced a kid—he didn't *do* anything for that kid except drag him out here once in a while! He knew Isaac was hard on Dillon—Isaac was no fool. He knew Dillon wasn't his. But Mitch couldn't have his reputation ruined by having people find out about him and Belle. No, not Mitch Farrell.

"Belle died when Dillon was nine, and she told him then who his real daddy was. I remember a day before she died when the boys were here and Dillon asked Mitch if he'd be his daddy and protect him from Isaac. Mitch said he was real sorry, but he couldn't do that. He said, 'Isaac *is* your father, you know.' I didn't suspect Mitch then, but I could tell Dillon didn't believe Isaac was his father. Children sense the truth and it was true, wasn't it, Mitch? *Wasn't* it?"

"Yes," Mitch croaked. "Yes, he was my boy."

Marissa's cell phone went off and she almost screamed. She still wore her jacket and she reached in the pocket and pulled out the phone, but before she could even look at the caller ID Jean shouted, "Shut it off!" It rang again before Marissa could turn it off. Please let that have been Catherine, she thought. Catherine, the worrier, might think something was wrong. But no matter how worried Catherine was, she could never guess what was wrong. Never.

"That's enough, Jean," Mitch said hopelessly. "Just kill me."

Jean didn't even look at Mitch. "You have to keep in mind that all these years I still thought I had the most wonderful husband in the world. I didn't know about Belle. I didn't know about . . . another one. And I was so thankful that Mitch didn't seem to blame me for Betsy, even though I blamed myself.

"But every night, I've taken Mitch to the point on the morphine where he talks and talks. He tells me everything because he gets this notion I'm God and I can forgive him before he dies. He's sorry for most of it, but even if there was a God, he wouldn't forgive Mitch. God will never forgive him for Dillon. You see, Dillon had been treated bad all his life. Then he found out the truth and he thought he was saved— his real daddy would take him and be good to him. But his real daddy wasn't one bit interested in taking him—just protecting himself and his own good name. I don't know if Dillon was born different or old Isaac made him different by beating him or if later Dillon's hatred for Mitch killed his conscience, but when he was about twelve or thirteen he started striking back. That's what Mitch said: 'He started striking back.'

"Dillon was smart and clever and sneaky, just like Mitch. The first thing he did that we know about is kill Buddy Pruitt's grandpa."

"No," Eric said in a thin voice. "Accident."

"Dillon told Buddy how to make it *look* like an accident. He pretended to be Buddy's friend, pretended to be helping him by getting that terror of an old man out of the way, but all he really wanted to do was make Buddy his slave." Jean paused. "Marissa doesn't believe me. I can tell by the look in her eyes. *You* tell her about Buddy, Mitch."

"It's true," Mitch managed miserably. "Dillon boasted to me. He got into a sort of . . . pattern. I wouldn't claim him, so he'd torture me." Mitch began that gurgling cough that sent chills down Marissa's spine. Please let him choke and die, she thought. But if he dies, then what?

"Buddy was scared silly of Dillon after that because Dillon could expose him as an accomplice to Old Man Pruitt's death," Jean explained. "So Buddy became Dillon's little lapdog. Did whatever Dillon told him to. Pathetic!"

Another cell phone went off. Jean cursed impressively and grabbed Eric's cell phone, which she'd kept near her along with his walkie-talkie. She turned it off and glared at Eric and Marissa. "You two are certainly the popular ones."

"People know where we are!" Marissa could have bitten off her tongue, particularly when Jean gave her that weird smile.

"Well maybe I should kill you before they come," she said in a soft, vicious voice.

I'm sorry, Eric, Marissa thought. I'm a fool and I'm so, so sorry.

"Let's see, I believe Tonya Ward came next. You remember that scandal when Edgar Blume literally got caught with his pants down when his wife and boy came back to town? Edgar was stone-cold dead and looked like he'd been having one hell of a party. He hadn't, although he was no pillar of virtue. It seems Tonya got tangled up with him and Dillon helped her out. He ended up killing Blume and"—Jean snapped her fingers—"just like that Dillon had someone else in his debt."

"Mitch, you said Dillon *bragged* to you as a form of torture. What makes you so sure Dillon was telling the truth?" Marissa asked.

"Knew too many details," Mitch croaked. "I headed investigations. It was always just like Dillon said it was. And sometimes, he'd take a little something to prove what he'd done. He told me to hide the stuff for him and I did. Had me under his finger, too, 'cause he knew I was ashamed of myself for not claiming him. I'd protect him from prosecution, though."

"For yourself, not out of love for him." Jean lifted her head and rubbed the muzzle of the gun under her chin, slowly, absently. Let it go off, Marissa thought furiously. Let the gun blow off her head.

"Oh yes, there's one more thing Eric will particularly enjoy," Jean continued in a disturbingly casual, chatty tone. "Maybe you recall when Melody Simmons got drunk out of her mind, went tearing away from the Lonesome Me Tavern, and ran over that little eight-year-old boy. Well, it seems she'd gotten mad at her date, Will Addison, and took off without him. Everyone thought he'd just walked home and she'd kept on driving. She didn't. She got sick and pulled to the side of the road. Will was walking when he came upon the car. Melody was so drunk, for once Sir Will decided to act like a gentleman and take her home. They were having a fight, and *Will* hit that child with the car!

"Melody passed out and Dillon happened along," Jean continued as if relishing the story. "I don't remember all the logistics, but Dillon made it look like Melody had hit the boy. Dillon told Mitch that the boy wasn't dead after Will hit him, so Dillon ran over him again just to make sure! Then Dillon took Will home and added another lackey to his collection. Melody, barely eighteen, was prosecuted as an adult and went to prison."

Although Marissa had been cringing throughout Jean's telling of the story, she'd tried to keep her face as calm as Jean's. "You said Eric would particularly enjoy that. Why?"

"Because later Gretchen dated Will. Then for some reason, she gave him the heave-ho and began seeing Dillon. People knew Will wasn't happy about losing her, particularly to Dillon. I think he pursued her in a way. After your little party at Gray's Island, Dillon told Mitch he should never have 'helped' Will because Will was a drunk and drunks talk. Somebody saw Will with Gretchen the afternoon before she died. Dillon said that night he got her drunk—she wasn't used to alcohol—and she started talking about knowing secrets and asking people if you ever *really* know someone else. He told Mitch after she'd say that, she'd look at him.

"Dillon was sure Will had told her about running over the little boy. Dillon said he had to do something to protect himself, and so he pushed her off that railing in the church. Did you hear that, Eric? Dillon *killed* your sister! He even took her ring and gave it to Mitch to hide for him.

"Tonya, another person who *owed* Dillon, said he'd tried to grab Gretchen and drag her off the rail and down to the balcony. Dillon said you'd seen exactly what happened and you told the police, Marissa. Dillon didn't know what to do about you. He was between a real rock and a hard place when it came to you."

"Why?" Marissa asked coldly.

Jean paused and then slowly smiled. "Because, honey, you are Dillon's sister."

2

Marissa felt turned to ice as Jean looked at her with a mixture of amusement and hatred. Finally, she asked, "What are you talking about?"

"I'm talking about what Dillon was talking about—the fact that Mitch is your father, too."

Marissa shook her head, harder and harder and harder.

"Your head is going to fly right off your neck if you don't stop that," Jean said in amused warning. "Isn't it clear once you think about it? Mitch was what they now call a player. He wasn't working the night Betsy drowned—he was paying one of his last visits to Belle and his little boy because he had something else new and more exciting in his life. He left me alone for *them* on that horrible night—" Jean groaned in pain, then pulled herself together.

"Your parents were nice to us, Marissa. Your mother just couldn't have been *sweeter*. I always knew Mitch thought Annemarie was beautiful, but I was a trusting fool. When he got tired of Belle, Mitch left her in Isaac's loving hands and went straight to your mother. I'm sure she thought he was as handsome as I did. I could tell it. And he could smooth-talk a woman into doing whatever he wanted. Mitch always had that effect on women and Annemarie Gray was no different." Jean paused. "She must have gotten pregnant with you almost right away, Marissa."

"My mother did *not* have an affair with Mitch," Marissa nearly screamed. "She loved my father!"

"Mitch loved me in a way. Did that stop *him*?"

"No! I do not believe you!" Marissa jumped up from the rocking chair, forgetting about Jean's gun. "Mitch, tell her!"

He gurgled, coughed, gurgled again, and finally said, "No affair with Anne. Never, Jean."

"And I am supposed to believe *you*?" Jean hissed.

The house phone began ringing, loud and insistent. Jean looked at the nearest one and shouted, "Shut up!" To Marissa, the phone seemed to ring at least twenty times, but she had time to draw a deep breath, to make her heart slow down, to cool her anger. You're arguing with Jean as if what she's saying might be true, Marissa thought. It isn't. You *know* it isn't. Don't for one second betray Mom by even wondering if it's true.

When the phone finally stopped ringing, Jean looked up at her. Marissa hadn't realized she was still standing. "What's the matter, dear, aren't you proud to have Dillon for a brother? Or half brother. Only a half brother."

"Who told him such a thing?" Marissa asked.

"I always said Dillon was smart. He listened to how Mitch's voice changed when he talked about Annemarie. He saw you several times with Mitch and he could tell how much Mitch loved you. Mitch loved Catherine, too, because she looked so much like Annemarie. I was hoping she could be here this evening, but it's not a great loss. You were the one Mitch especially loved." Jean paused. "And so did Dillon. He'll tell you when he comes back and he *will* come back when he hears his daddy is dead."

"The picture in my mother's grave. A picture of Dillon and me that said 'Together Forever' on the back. That was Dillon's."

"Yes, but Mitch kept it for him so Isaac wouldn't find it. You tell her, Mitch."

Marissa had been hearing Mitch's breathing grow raspier by the minute. She was afraid he could no longer talk. She looked at his face and saw the agonizing effort he made to say a few words. "Couldn't convince him . . . not sister. Made it all up in his head . . . because of the eyes."

"Eyes?"

"Oh really, Marissa, I know you aren't as smart as your sister, but I thought you were sharper than this. You and Dillon have exactly the same color eyes. Not just blue. Sapphire. So blue sometimes people thought you were wearing colored contacts. That is inherited. You both inherited those blue-blue eyes from Mitch."

It was hardly possible now to know how blue Mitch's eyes had been when he was young, but Marissa knew Mitch and her father had the same grandmother. She'd been married to Bernard's grandfather, and two years after his death she had married Mitch's grandfather, both blue-eyed men.

"Dillon and I inherited this eye color from Dad and Mitch's grandmother," Marissa said slowly. "We have a few color photographs of her and I know Mitch does, too. Look at them—look at her eyes. The same as mine. The same as Betsy's!"

"Don't you talk about Betsy in the same breath with your vile brother!"

"He's her brother, too."

Infuriated, Jean swung at her, but Marissa dodged. Attacked by two women in the same day, she thought, a breath away from bursting into hysteria. Bea and Jean—women everyone thought were kind and harmless. But they weren't. There was a difference, though—this one was cunning.

Terror rushed through Marissa. This woman was going to kill her. Then she looked at Eric. Even in the dim light, she could see his alarmingly pale face, the fluttering eyelids, the circle of blood under his leg—the circle growing larger and larger. He can't lose much more blood and live, she thought, feeling as if an icy rapier were piercing her heart. He's going to lie on this floor and die because I didn't do enough to help him, because I wasn't the fearless, ingenious Marissa Gray I've always believed I was.

No, *knew* I was, she thought suddenly, fiercely. Know I *am.* The real Marissa didn't die when Eric broke our engagement or when Mom died. The real Marissa has just been drifting, letting life take her where it will. I used to control where I went and I will again. Jean is cunning, but I can be cunning, too. It's time for that chest-pounding Eric mentioned just hours ago. I can be clever and I can be mean and I can be a surprise. If I just let go,

Jean won't see me coming and I can throw her so far off balance that maybe I can save both Eric and me. But especially Eric.

Marissa tried to calm her breathing, soften her voice. "So you knew nothing about all of this until Mitch got so bad you had to put him on morphine, and when he'd had a certain amount of morphine, he'd start babbling."

"I told you that," Jean said disdainfully.

"*Babbling,* Jean. He doesn't know what he's talking about half the time. But you were determined to believe anything bad he said about himself, to find out as much as you could about Mitch Farrell. That's why you didn't take him to the hospital. You wanted to keep him here all to yourself and torture him by withholding morphine, giving him half doses, asking him a hundred questions. Maybe you are right about Dillon being his son—he committed adultery. But what have *you* been doing? You've been *killing* people!"

"The people Dillon managed to get in his power, just like Satan does."

"You don't believe in God, but you believe in Satan?"

"Don't try to confuse me. I killed those people because they were as evil as Dillon. They did what he told them to do to protect *themselves.* If they hadn't been like him, they would have stood up to him. They wouldn't have injured and killed and let Dillon kill for them and kept their mouths shut. They would have told the police about what they'd done and about Dillon. Instead, there they all were, Dillon's minions, basking in their fine lives like they'd never done a wrong thing. It was up to *me* to punish them for their evil!"

"Let's talk about evil, Jean." Marissa made her eyes flash and turned her voice to acid. "Do you know what I think? You were shocked when Mitch married you. Then you gave him nothing except your fawning love and your plain face and your bony body—no daughter, no son. He started working late all the time. You *had* to suspect there might be another woman. Almost any woman would suspect her husband in those circumstances.

"I also think you've suspected for a long time that Dillon was Mitch's son. You're too smart, too observant, not to notice how Mitch acted around the boy when Dillon was here. I think you hated Mitch for having an affair and you hated him even more for not being here when Betsy died! He was with another woman when you were peeling potatoes instead of watching your child as closely as you should. You let her *die!*"

Jean screeched at her, launched, and missed again. She held up the gun and tried to cock it, but her hands trembled while Marissa went on relentlessly: "You killed people you'd decided were evil. *You* decided. Is that your job?"

Jean looked at her with flaring nostrils and eyes more blood-shot than usual. "I don't have to explain myself to you!"

"Then why have you been doing it all evening, Jean? Why have you been spinning out your sad tale about your horrible husband and your dead child? You want sympathy, and when you don't get it you get mad, and that's when you get dangerous."

"I was never dangerous before Mitch started telling me all the awful things he'd done!"

"I see. You were a paragon until less than two weeks ago when you decided to start messing with your dying husband's morphine dosages and got him talking. Then you became a killer, murdering people because they'd been involved with Dillon." Marissa made herself laugh softly. "It's ridiculous. People don't change that quickly, Jean. Maybe you did have a psychotic break—my sister would know more about that than I do—but it didn't come out of the blue. And if you'd had one, you wouldn't have been so . . . organized about your killings. You never left one trace. You perfectly executed your little scare tactics—my christening dress and the picture of Dillon and me in the grave, the postcard to me signed with 'D.A.', the picture of Tonya and Andrew decorating their Christmas tree, also signed 'D.A.' Laying a few things around the Archer house, including my picture, to make it seem like Dillon was staying there. And maybe worst of all, putting the ring I'd given

Gretchen, the ring Mitch had been keeping since her death, on her grave, all wrapped up like a present.

"Those were extremely clever acts. Sly. Not the work of a woman who'd just learned something horrible and went to pieces. I'm sure you started the rumor that Dillon had come home *before* you went on the vengeance spree you claim wasn't wrong. If it wasn't wrong, why did you intend to keep it a secret forever? You were never going to confess to your murders. You were never going to confess about calling poor Bea Pruitt, a woman who's never hurt anyone and telling her a lie about me threatening to kill Buddy, a lie that will probably result in her spending years in a mental institution.

"You have mental problems, Jean, much worse than Bea, and I don't mean problems caused solely by the loss of Betsy. You've probably had them since you were a girl working like a man on that farm of your father's and you've ended up destroying more lives than Dillon has."

Marissa went on, frantically reaching for anything she could say to enrage Jean. "I don't think Dillon started believing I was his sister because we have the same color eyes. I think you dropped hints and he decided that was the truth. You took verbal shots at Mitch and at my mother. You envied her beauty and her charm and the love she had from *her* husband—that's why you set fire to her rose garden. You'd helped plant it, but everyone thought of it as *Annemarie's* rose garden. Now you're trying to ruin her reputation and turn me into the result of an affair."

"You *are*!"

"You thought Mitch had replaced Betsy with me and that's why you tried to send me into the Orenda River in that wreck— because Betsy died in the Orenda River."

"Yes. If *my* daughter died in the river, Mitch's daughter would, too."

"So you thought I'd die because I'm Mitch's daughter, but it didn't work, Jean. I've loved Mitch all my life, but I will never believe I'm his daughter, because I'm *not!*"

"You *are* Mitch's daughter!"

"Then that would make me Betsy's sister and Dillon her *brother*!"

"No!" Jean shrieked. "No!"

"You can't have it all ways, Jean. You can't have Dillon and me as Mitch's children and *not* have us related to Betsy. It just isn't possible."

"You and Dillon are no relation to Betsy," Jean's guttural voice rolled.

"Jean, my morph ... please." Mitch's voice was so low and scratchy, Marissa could barely hear it. "Such pain. Please."

Jean didn't even look at him, but Marissa did and saw that his gaze was fixed on her as his left hand barely tapped the bed. Was it uncontrollable movement? Marissa wondered.

"Aren't you going to give him something for pain *now*, Jean? Haven't you made him watch enough?"

Jean's eyes narrowed. "No. Not quite."

Marissa's gaze flashed back to Mitch, whose left hand tapped harder on the bed. He was signaling her, she realized. But what did he want?

Jean stood on the right side of the bed, close to Eric, who wasn't moving, whose eyes had closed. She still held the gun, but her hands shook and her eyes looked wild and unfocused.

"What do you think is going to happen to you after all of this, Jean?" Slowly Marissa took a small sideways step from the foot of the bed, hoping to inch her way up to Mitch's tapping hand. "Do you think you're going to just run away?"

"Maybe."

"Do you have all of your papers in order? Birth certificate, driver's license, credit card? Oh, wait, you couldn't use any of those because they all have your name on them. Even your credit card. Have you been stockpiling cash?"

"Yes!" Jean answered triumphantly. "I have cash."

"You must have been saving it for quite some time." Marissa took another small step. "More than two weeks."

"I was saving it for a rainy day. Some time when Mitch and I might need money in a hurry. I was thinking of me *and* Mitch."

"Oh, I'm sure you were," Marissa said sarcastically. "And what about your father's land? Rather, your land. Everybody always wondered why you didn't sell it. Even a chunk of it would have given you *and* Mitch the money to lead a more comfortable life, take some trips, buy a bigger house and a boat like my dad's. Mitch loved going out on that boat."

"I didn't."

"No. And you weren't going to sell the land so you could buy some nice things because you were punishing him." Another step. "You've been punishing Mitch for years. Long before Betsy died. Was it because you thought he only married you for the land? You wanted to see if he'd stay with you if you didn't sell it? Or was it because you suspected he was with other women?"

"I was saving for our old age! I wanted us to be comfortable! To be able to live a nice life!"

One more step. "Comfortable doing what? Leaving Mitch to his woodworking while you tended your flower gardens? Oh, he'd probably be too old for the woodworking and you'd have arthritis in your knees and couldn't stoop down to dig in the dirt." She glanced down and saw the edge of something dark beneath a fold in the sheet. Mitch tapped at it once, then moved his hand. "I guess you two could have just stayed closed up in this house together. He wouldn't be the handsome sheriff anymore. You'd finally have him all to yourself, completely under your control."

"I never wanted to control him! I just wanted him to love me!"

"He did, Jean. Maybe not in that wild, passionate way we see in the movies, but he loved you, he cared about you, he stayed with you, he protected you. It's just that he couldn't make you his whole life. No man could."

"Yes! A real man of character could have loved me the way I should have been loved!"

In a panic, Marissa thought she'd run out of things to say. She was reaching the end of her endurance. Then she thought of the person who was the crux of the situation.

"Have you thought about what Dillon will do if you kill me?" Marissa asked, smirking. "He thinks I'm his sister and he loves me. He's probably convinced himself I love him, too, so if you murder me, he'll hunt you down. You know he will. You'll have *nowhere* to hide from *him*. He's smart and relentless and totally without a conscience. He's more clever than even you and he's younger than you. He'll run you to the ground and make you pay for killing me, Jean."

"He won't find me."

"Yes, he will," Marissa said with slow, quiet certainty as she touched the dark, hard corner under the sheet. She even moved it slightly. A gun. God, Mitch had a gun tucked under the sheets. For a moment, Marissa thought she might faint from surprise and relief; then she saw Jean looking intensely at her eyes. "He won't have any pity for you, no matter how many sad stories you tell him," Marissa said coldly. "He'll look at you and see only the ugly, possessive, conniving murderer of his sister!"

"No!" Jean screamed. "I'm not those things, you little bitch." She raised the gun and pointed it toward Marissa. "I'm a good woman with an evil husband who I've kept alive so he could see me kill the man he *wishes* was his son and the spawn of his and that whore who was your mother. He'll live to see it—"

Mitch rose in his bed and let out a bloodcurdling scream Marissa knew she'd remember until she died. She raised the gun, cocked it just like Mitch had shown her many years ago, and pointed it at Jean just as Jean pointed her gun at Marissa. They fired at the same time, the noise sounding as if the whole world were shattering. No one in the room moved. Then slowly, Jean toppled onto Eric, blood from her head spilling over his chest. Marissa stood still for a moment, then slowly looked around at the small hole in the wall a good foot to her left.

As soon as she realized she was still alive, she ran to Eric. She pushed Jean off him and took his face in her hands. It was white—even his lips. "Eric," she cried. "Eric!" But he didn't open his eyes; he didn't make a sound.

Then she heard the thin wails of police cars and ambulances as they turned into the slanting driveway of the Farrell house.

EPILOGUE

Marissa and Eric sat in the Grays' family room, watching the New Year's Eve festivities on television. Catherine and James had gone to a small New Year's Eve party at James's parents' home. "My sister is turning into a party girl," Marissa said. "I'm beginning to think I should worry."

Eric, his leg swathed in a cast that almost reached the trunk of his body, grinned at her. "I think your sister has finally gotten her mind off her studies long enough to have some fun."

"She has another semester of work to do before she gets her license."

"You know something? You sound like she's twelve and you're her mother. Relax, Marissa. Catherine knows what she's doing. I think she proved that last week."

Marissa frowned. "I'm glad I didn't leave her a note saying we were going to the Farrell house. She and James would have walked into that nightmare."

"And they wouldn't have been able to save us. Not to be selfish or anything."

"Oh, of course not, sweetie." Marissa went back to frowning. "But we were gone; there was no note; they couldn't reach me; no one could reach you. The cops couldn't even raise you on your walkie-talkie. Robbie knew where we were going and, bless her, harangued about there being trouble at Mitch's until everyone gave up and came on what they thought was probably a wild-goose chase."

"I was the hero last week. This week is Robbie's turn."

"Her father will be *so* proud of her, not that he isn't already."

Lindsay pranced into the living room wearing a party hat and holding a stuffed animal in her mouth. "I can't believe she's not fighting to remove that hat you brought her," Marissa said.

"She knows it's New Year's Eve and we're having our own private party. Besides, you and I are wearing them."

"And looking like complete fools. Anyway, thank you for her Christmas present, too. I think the one animal she didn't have was a stuffed panda. She loves it."

"Let's make certain she doesn't love it too much. I'd hate for you to take her for a walk and have her go in hot pursuit of what she thinks is her panda only to find out it's a skunk."

Marissa started laughing. "Given the luck we've had lately, it's bound to happen."

Eric tightened the arm he'd draped across her shoulders. "I don't think our luck has been so bad. We're . . . seeing each other again." Marissa noticed he was careful not to say they were "back together." "We've discovered what was wrong with Gretchen. We have her ring. Mom was so grateful to get it."

Marissa sighed. "Even though your parents have the ring again, I still feel guilty because we didn't tell them about Gretchen's essential tremor."

"We will soon, when they've gotten over the shock of everything that's happened."

"Such as you being alive. Eric, you were so close to death from blood loss."

"But you, my darling one, saved me. You stood up and talked so loud and so fast and said such awful things, you knocked Jean for a loop. Then you came up with a *gun*."

"Mitch always loved to put those little secret hiding places in the things he made, like that little table by his bed. I guess Jean didn't know he had a gun hidden in there, but he got it when she left the room to call and tell us he was dying. It must have been a tremendous effort for him."

"Jean must have forgotten both to search the table and that you're a good shot thanks to Mitch's lessons. You saved the day."

"I didn't save him."

"Nobody could save Mitch, Marissa. But he lived two more days, enough to know that you and I were all right. Enough to tell you a few things you still didn't know."

Marissa nodded, then made a decision. "He lived long enough to tell me that after Dillon killed Gretchen, he knew what he had to do. He told Dillon he'd get him out of the city, told him to go fishing with Buddy, hit him on the head, and Mitch would be waiting in a car in the woods on the other side of the Orenda. And he was. Then deep in the woods where they were far away from everyone, he killed Dillon." Eric looked at her in astonishment. "He killed his own son before Dillon could do any more harm. That was one secret Jean wasn't able to pry out of Mitch."

"My God, Marissa. All this time people thought Dillon was alive!"

Marissa shook her head. "Well, he wasn't. And although I know how horrible Dillon was, I still almost cry when I think of what Mitch had to do," Marissa said.

"That's because you know you were the only person in the world Dillon loved—his sister, or so he thought." Eric shook his head slowly. "I don't suppose Mitch told you where he buried Dillon?"

"No." Marissa gave Eric a slanting look. Mitch *hadn't* told her where he'd buried Dillon, but she knew, maybe by instinct, maybe because of the beautiful photograph of the Gray's Island church on the old desk in Mitch's room. She was certain Mitch had waited until night and taken his son's body to Gray's Island. Dillon lay buried there, probably near the church, and in less than a hundred years the entire island would be underwater.

Eric swallowed hard and asked almost warily, "Are you sure you're not Mitch's daughter?"

She smiled. "I'm sure. I've spent quite a bit of time in hospital rooms the last three years. Being a nosy journalist, I couldn't help taking a look at charts." Eric raised an eyebrow. "I have AB blood. My mother had A and my father had B. Mitch had O. I couldn't have type AB if there was an O in the mix." Marissa sighed. "I knew anyway. My parents had a true love story—the kind of thing Jean wanted with Mitch. It wasn't possible for them, Jean being Jean. Maybe Mitch wasn't capable of constancy, either. My parents were, though. They had the kind of love I want to have someday."

"Maybe you already have it." Before she could say a word, Eric glanced at his watch and boomed, "Enough of this depressing talk. It's three minutes until midnight!"

Marissa jumped up, ran into the kitchen, and took the champagne out of the refrigerator. She put it on a tray with a corkscrew, two champagne flutes, and a piece of beef jerky for Lindsay. When she rushed back in, Lindsay and Eric sat close together, both looking absurd in their party hats, both avidly watching television.

Marissa set the tray in front of Eric and he went to work on the champagne bottle as people on the television counted down. The champagne bubbled over when Eric pulled out the cork. He quickly poured two glasses and Marissa tossed the beef jerky on the floor, where Lindsay immediately went after it. Then Eric handed Marissa a glass.

"Four, three, two, one, Happy New Year!" the people on television shouted as the ball dropped in Times Square.

"Happy New Year," Marissa and Eric said together, looking into each other's eyes as they each took a sip of champagne.

"To sad endings and happy beginnings," Eric said.

"You'll jinx us talking like that."

He grinned. "I don't believe in jinxes. I believe in skinny little crooked-toothed girls who grow up to be strong, beautiful, magnificent women." Lindsay barked loudly. "Even the best dog in the world agrees with me, so I can't be wrong!"

"I was right. You really are a goof." Marissa laughed lovingly and pulled him to her for a very long New Year's kiss.

TO THE GRAVE

Catherine Gray has returned to her hometown of Aurora Falls. Her first love James has recently divorced, and they can finally build a life together. But then Catherine stumbles upon the murdered body of James's first wife Renée, who has been missing for the past three years.

Catherine starts to ask herself how well she really knows James. What secret destroyed his marriage – and who killed his wife?

When a mysterious fire destroys the crime scene, Catherine starts looking for answers. But when the next victim is revealed, it becomes terrifyingly clear that an obsessed killer is on the loose, and Catherine is next in line . . .

HODDER

YOU CAN RUN . . .

Penny Conley is still recovering from the untimely death of her husband. But she and her five-year-old daughter, Willow, seem to be thriving in their West Virginia suburb. Penny's boss, noted archaeologist Simon Van Etton, and his niece Diana have become like family to her.

Late one night Diana receives a phone call from a distraught Penny. Just as Diana arrives at her friend's house, it explodes, leaving Penny in a coma.

Diana and Simon vow to figure out what happened, but they are deeply shaken when new facts about Penny's dark past start to come to light. Determined to help her friend, Diana keeps digging for clues. But someone is following her every move, ready to act if she gets too close to the truth . . .

HODDER